THE AWAKENING OF GODS

MORGAN KIELISCH

SECOND CHILD PRESS

Copyright © 2024 by Morgan Kielisch

All rights reserved.

No part of this publication may be reproduced, distributed, or transmitted in any form or by any means, including pho-tocopying, recording, or other electronic or mechanical methods, without the prior written permission of the publisher, except as permitted by U.S. copyright law. For permission requests, contact Morgan Kielisch at mkielisch@gmail.com.

The story, all names, characters, and incidents portrayed in this production are fictitious. No identification with actual persons (living or deceased), places, buildings, and products is intended or should be inferred.

Book Cover and Illustrations by Laura Gang https://lauragang.com/

Proofread and Coached by Laura R. Samotin http://www.laurarsamotin.com/

Proofread by Katie Schott

The Continent of Astrellia

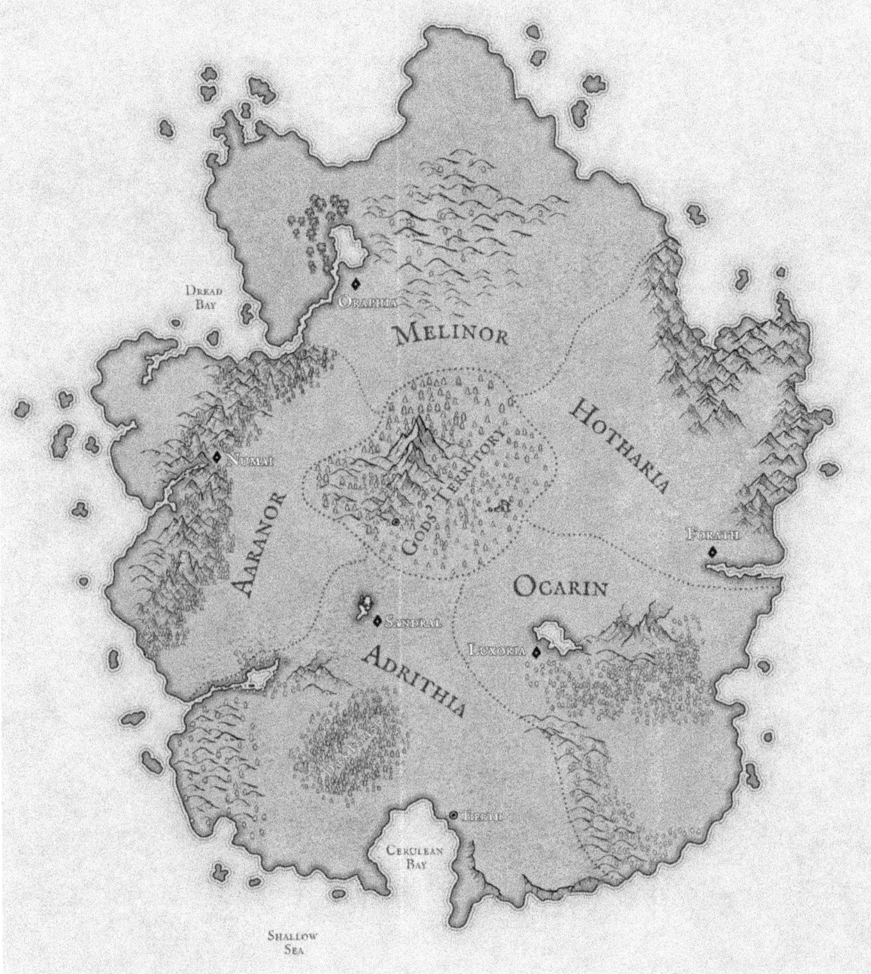

To everyone who has their own story to tell. I hope you get to tell it someday.

CHAPTER ONE

I stand in the middle of a dark, unnatural storm. Wind batters me as rain pelts my exposed skin. My nightdress clings to me, weighing me down and I stumble blindly. Lightning flashes, raising goosebumps on my arms, and the earth gives a rumbling shake. I scream, but the sound is ripped from my mouth. There's nowhere to go, no place to escape the pummeling elements. I sink to my knees and cover my head with my arms. I close my eyes, shutting out the terrifying nothingness around me. The noise is as deafening as it is disorientating. I can't hear anything beyond the roar of thunder building around me.

Goddess Avani help me, I think, but she's my father's patron, not mine. Besides, none of the Gods have ever helped me before.

The storm continues, and so does my terror.

"Elana, wake up," I hear, but I cannot move, cannot open my eyes to see. All I feel is fear, panic, and pain. Another flash of lightning burns my eyes through my lids. When will it end?

"Elana, wake up!" Hands shake my shoulders and I wrench my eyes open, gasping for breath. I'm in my bed, the blankets twisted around me. They're damp with sweat, even as a chill snakes its way up my spine.

My sister Aislinn stands over me, eyebrows pinched together, breathing quickly.

"You were screaming in your sleep," she says, sitting down on the plush bed next to me.

I sit up and catch my breath. "It was just a bad dream," I say, clenching my hands to keep them from shaking.

"Do you want to talk about it?" Aislinn asks.

I shake my head quickly, not trusting my voice to be steady in any verbal response.

She stares at me for a moment longer and then nods, letting it go. "Okay, then how about we sneak out and watch the sunrise?"

I give her a shaky smile. There's nothing more I'd rather do with her today.

"Get changed and meet me in the kitchen in five minutes," she says, and hurries out the door.

I throw off the covers and scramble out of bed, nightgown clinging to me like the remnants of my nightmare. I really need a bath, but there's no time. I race to my wardrobe and pull out a warm black dress, one that laces in the front across my curvy chest so I won't have to call my maid Senara to help me dress.

Most of my shoes are glorified slippers, but I find my oldest pair, the ones that don't squeak when I walk, and slip them on my feet. A guard isn't posted at my door this early, so I'm able to slip out of my room without trouble.

I carefully walk down the hallway, moving quickly but keeping my steps light. There weren't always guards patrolling this wing of the castle at night, but after the first time Ash and I got caught sneaking out, almost six years ago, they started doing random patrols. Still, we've only been caught a few times by the guards. Our mother's lectures the following mornings could have put a priestess of Goddess Avani's to shame. Apparently, princesses weren't permitted to leave the castle at night, even though one of the princesses was arguably the strongest warrior on all of Astrellia.

"You have doors that lock from the inside for a reason," Mother had said after our first botched foray out of the castle. She made us scrub pans for hours in the kitchens as punishment for our grave mistake. For the following two weeks there was a guard posted at each of our doors. Since then, we've had years to perfect the art of sneaking through the castle, and we haven't been caught for nearly two years.

This morning the broad hallway is mercifully clear as I head down the servant's stairs behind a statue of a phoenix and into the warm kitchen. Fires are roaring and breakfast prep is well underway. Several kitchen staff see me and roll their eyes. I smile at them, knowing they won't sound the alarm. We have a mutually beneficial relationship. Whenever I'm in the woods searching for medicinal plants for my healer's studies, I always make an effort to bring back as many herbs and edible plants as I can find. In return, they keep quiet about my sister's and my antics, and occasionally slip us extra desserts. It's never a bad thing to be in the good graces of the cooks.

Aislinn is already by the back door, holding a bundle of blankets and pillows. I walk up to her and she nods at the basket on the counter beside her. "Bring that and let's go."

I grab the basket and follow her outside. Even though it's the height of summer, the morning air is still crisp and cool. We walk past the expansive gardens on the eastern side of the castle and towards a line of tall maple trees. In fall, I spend my days staring at their fiery red leaves. The whole perimeter of the castle grounds, minus the large wooden gates, is lined with these trees, hiding the stone battlements.

Calling them battlements might be slightly exaggerating their grandeur, since they barely stand taller than my sister. They were built by one of my long-dead Sable ancestors who was blessed by the earth goddess, like my father. They used to tower over the trees, but when I was a child my father lowered them, sinking the ornately carved rock back into the ground. He claimed he wanted to see the capital city of Sandral, just down the hill. Besides, our Kingdom had been at peace for hundreds of years. The wall wasn't needed anymore.

Ash and I hustle to the wall, shooting glances behind us as we move swiftly through the grass. When Ash gets to one of the maple trees, she tosses the blankets and pillows over the wall and climbs up a low-hanging branch. She gracefully swings her legs onto the stone wall and lets go of the branch. I pass off the basket to her, and then follow her path with much less grace and a lot more struggling, thanks to being nearly a head shorter than my sister.

This is the easier side to scale. The return side has no trees, but we discovered a spot with some larger gaps between bricks, big enough to fit our fingers and feet into.

When we were younger, Aislinn helped me scale the wall, but I quickly learned that due to my height, momentum is key to pulling myself up and over it.

Past the wall is an expanse of open field where we hold occasional festivals and jousting tournaments for the noble families of Adrithia. The field has a long gradual slope that leads to Sandral, which partially sits in a valley surrounding a massive lake. Our view of the sunrise from here is unparalleled. I set the basket in the grass and help Aislinn spread out the blanket and arrange the two pillows. We lie on our backs and wait for the show to begin.

There's nothing better than watching the sun come up. I revel in the silence of mornings. Most creatures of the world are either just rousing or curling up to sleep in their nests and burrows. It's that in-between time, when the darkness fades and the light doesn't blind.

As we watch, the sky alights with color before the sun makes its appearance. Oranges, pinks and yellows contrast with the deep blue of the night sky.

I lie on the woven blanket next to Aislinn. She devours one of the pastries we stole from the kitchen while the head cook Gwyneth had her back turned. Although I'm not sure if it can be called stealing when she leaves an extra pan of pastries unattended whenever we happen to sneak through her domain.

"I think Gwen is blessed by the goddess of food," Aislinn moans as she takes another bite, and I'm surprised when I don't see drool dripping down her chin.

"Do you and that pastry need some alone time to frolic among the hills?" I tease. I'm rewarded with a smack to my shoulder.

"You're jealous that I took the only lemon-flavored one," she shoves the half-eaten delicacy in my face. I try to take a bite as she waves it in front of me, but she pulls it back lightning quick and shoves the rest into her mouth.

I make a noise of exaggerated disgust. "You're such a princess. The most modest of them all."

I grab one of the other pastries from the basket and take a bite. The sweetness of strawberries overwhelms my senses. It's peak time for midsummer berries in Adrithia. There are only twenty days until summer solstice.

It's also twenty days until I say goodbye to Aislinn. After the crowning ceremony today, she will prepare to leave on her quest to claim her birthright from the Gods.

I stare at her out of the corner of my eyes. How many more stolen days will we get to do this? Once she returns from the mountains and is imbued with new, incredible power, will she have time to spare? And with my own wedding looming next spring, I'll be busy preparing to leave the life I've always known.

"What're you thinking about, El?" Aislinn asks me, turning on her side. She's twenty-three years old, a year and a few days older than me. Her long, shiny blonde hair falls over her shoulder. Sometimes it's hard to believe we're sisters. She has the same golden hair and honeyed beige skin as our mother. Her hazel eyes and high cheekbones are also inherited from our mother. The only features we share are our small noses and the scattering of light freckles across our cheeks.

"Just thinking about how many more desserts I'll get to eat without you around to steal them from me," I tease her.

I don't even see the pillow coming. It smacks my face hard enough to knock the rest of the pastry out of my hand.

"Hey!" I shout at her, "that's a waste of a good breakfast."

I try to snatch the pillow away from her, but she's too quick, placing it back beneath her head and cackling to herself.

"You're going to miss me and you know it, if only for breakfast heists." She smiles up at the sky. It turns lighter, oranges and pinks fading as the sun crests the horizon, light blues rising to overtake the warmth.

I lie back down next to her and stare up, vision blurring. I blink away a few tears. "I am going to miss you, sister."

Aislinn grabs my hand and squeezes.

It's selfish of me, but I want to stay here in this moment forever. Over the past few years, the time Ash and I have gotten to spend together has been cut to mere hours every week, when we were hardly separated for hours per week when we were children.

Today, when my sister accepts her role as heir, she'll officially leave me behind. And I'll have my own duties to see to, I remind myself with a detached sort of resignation. It's all my mother talks about to me nowadays. How to be a good wife, a good mother, and a good supporter of the crown. Never mind what I want. Never mind that I haven't even met my betrothed, Lord Percival Lyons, and have only exchanged the dullest letters with him. The thought of marrying him makes my stomach knot and puts me off my breakfast.

We lie side-by-side on the grass for as long as we dare. If we don't leave soon, Aislinn's lady's maid will start running around the castle in a panic, alerting everyone that she's gone. No one will care I'm missing. I'm the spare. The contingency. The backup sister. Honestly, it's a position I rather enjoy. I'm allowed slightly several hours of freedom every day, whereas every minute of Aislinn's life is planned out for her.

Today is the most important day of our lives. Ash will be presented in front of our people and crowned the heir of Adrithia. It's a day that demands perfection. Not a single thing can be out of place.

"Your Highnesses," a deep male voice calls from the ridge towards the castle. Aislinn and I exchange looks, and she wiggles her eyebrows at me suggestively. He's the one person who knows where we disappear to these early mornings.

"Ugh, he found us," Aislinn whispers to me. I chuckle at her sarcasm.

"Nice of you to join us, Aric," I call to him. My guard has been protecting me for nearly a decade. His family moved here from a village on the outskirts of our kingdom to offer their services to the crown in exchange for a more comfortable life. Aric's story isn't unique, but its uncommon for an outsider to climb the ladder of Sandral's society so quickly.

Aric started as a stable boy when he was about ten years old. According to him, after seeing Aric defend himself from a group of older stable boys, the weapons master took him under his wing and trained him to become a royal guard. He quickly outpaced everyone his own age and was given the honor of being my personal guard when I turned thirteen. He's only a few years older than me, but possesses the fortitude of men twice his age.

At first, I hated him. He was like a shadow, following me everywhere and never giving me a moment alone. All I wanted was to sneak away from my lessons and spend my time with Aislinn, or alone in the woods. Aric constantly hauled me back to the castle, which made him an enemy in my eyes. It took years for us to warm up to each other. Now he's the best friend I have besides Aislinn. I trust him with my secrets, and he trusts me enough to allow me some hard-earned freedom.

He bows slightly as he approaches. From where he's standing, the rising sun shines in his face, illuminating the strong jawline and pale blond hair that grows nearly to his shoulders. I blush and look away. I've only recently begun to notice how handsome he is.

"The King and Queen are awake and searching the castle for Princess Aislinn." His one hand rests on his longsword, sitting on his hip. He prizes that sword more than any other possession. He polishes it every spare second, in between training and escorting me places, before and after meals. I bet he sleeps with it, too.

"Thank you for letting us know, Sir Aric," Aislinn says, using his formal title. Something she rarely does.

I sigh and pack up our remaining pastries, helping Ash shake out and fold the blanket. We hand Aric the pillows and let him lead the way back to the castle. He helps boost us over the wall, tosses us the pillows, then grabs the top of the wall and hauls himself over like it's barely an obstacle. His exceptionally tall, muscular frame helps with that. Gods, when did I start noticing his *frame*?

We walk back inside, heading into the kitchen and finishing off the last two pastries in the basket before stuffing the blankets and basket into a large cupboard near the door.

Aric walks behind us, a silent shadow as we make our way back upstairs and to our rooms, conveniently situated across the hall from each other. We pause at our doors, knowing when we emerge from them again, everything will change.

"See you soon," Ash says, a smile lighting up her face. She shuts the door gently behind her, and I'm left staring after her.

Hours later, I stand in front of my full-length mirror, wearing a long dark blue gown with glittering silver trim. I expect my parents and Aislinn will be wearing similar shades, as they're the Sable family colors. My lady's maid, Senara, is tightening the laces on the back of the dress, constricting my stomach so much I regret the third pastry from this morning. I'll never forgive whoever decided these corset contraptions were fashionable.

A knock sounds at my door and my mother breezes in like a cold wind. "Elana, I hope you're ready. We leave for the temple of the Gods soon."

"Yes, Mother, I'm ready," I say, sliding on my silver slippers and turning to see her. Senara bows low and excuses herself to the corner of the room.

As I'd thought, Mother wears a gown the same color as mine, the only difference is the flowing cape clasped around her shoulders. At least three feet of it trail behind her as she walks towards me. Her blonde hair is meticulously coiled on top of her head and stuck with shining silver pins. She forgoes her usual crown, as is customary today. At the crowning ceremony, only one person is allowed to wear a crown. And that's Aislinn, the firstborn child of the family and our next heir.

Mother's eyes narrow on my unbound hair. It's a cause of contention between us—we've had so many arguments over the proper way a princess' hair should be worn that I can't begin to recount them. She studies me with her sharp eyes, ensuring there's not a speck of mud or dirt on me. Queen Maris may be nearing her fifth decade, but she's still a force to be reckoned with.

"Paint your lips, tame your hair, and let's go." She picks up a boar bristle brush from my dusty vanity and hands it to me.

"Sir Aric will escort you and Aislinn to your carriage." She turns around, flicks her cape behind her, and storms out.

I let out a breath I didn't realize I'd been holding since she walked in and turn towards the mirror again, setting the brush down. I dab my finger in a pot of rouge and swipe my lips. It's a dark pinky peach color, one that goes best with my pale complexion.

I study my eyes, gray with a black ring around the iris. At least there aren't any dark bags underneath them like this morning. I stare at the charcoal pencil but decide to leave it be for today. The last thing I need is to sweat it off and end up with black streaks down my face.

My auburn hair is extra wavy today. I run my fingers through it, working through a few tangles towards the bottom.

Senara approaches me and grabs the hairbrush, "Shall I coil your hair like the Queen's, Princess?"

A knock at the door, and Aric enters. "Your Highness, it's time to leave," he says, hovering in the entranceway.

I smile and nod at him. "No need, Senara. Thank you." I head towards the door, and Aric extends his hand.

"You look beautiful, Princess," he says as I loop my elbow with his. Outside of my room, Aislinn leans on her door frame and steps up to take Aric's other arm. Her solid dark blue dress is made of velvet and cut low, with sleeves off her shoulders. It flows down to the floor and she, too, has a train behind her.

Her dress is simple, designed to show off the crown which will soon rest upon her head. Her golden hair is perfectly arranged and coiled like Mother's.

"Ash, you look stunning," I say, looking around Aric at her.

She smiles. "Thanks, sister, so do you."

Her gaze flicks to my hair. "Will you let me do your hair in the carriage?"

I roll my eyes. "No one's going to pay attention to my hair. They're going to be too busy staring at you."

"Well duh." She quirks a smile, but I can tell by her eyes flicking on my loose curls that she isn't fully convinced.

There's no time for her to argue as we reach the grand staircase and hoist up the bottom of our dresses so we don't trip.

The main double doors are thrown open for us, and I see our parents stepping into their elaborate blue and silver carriage, pulled by two stunning black horses.

Aislinn and I hurry to ours. As is customary, she gets in first and I follow. Aric closes the door with a soft smile and a quick nod. He will follow us on horseback to the center of Sandral.

Today will be relatively simple. Across the continent of Astrellia, the citizens of each of the five kingdoms will gather in their capital cities and bear witness to the Crowning Ceremony. It happens once every generation. The Gods' messenger will place a crown on the head of the King and Queen's eldest child. That's it. It's a formality, really.

The act symbolizes that the heir has been chosen by the Gods to lead the Kingdom. The chosen heir will then depart on the summer solstice and travel to the Land of the

Gods, a wild piece of the continent where few dare to venture. There's nothing there but the ruins of a once-great city, and the Gods' Peaks, an expansive mountain range with five summits. There, the Gods challenge the heirs and, if they're found worthy, imbue them with their elemental abilities. Once the heirs receive their gifts, they return to their home kingdoms, where they are formally recognized as the next-in-line ruler.

I don't know why the ceremony is such a big deal. From what I'm told, the people of the city will celebrate afterwards. Gwen told Aislinn and me that when Father was crowned, the party lasted for days following the crowning. Maybe if Aislinn has time, she and I can sneak out to the city to enjoy part of the celebrations. Although I won't hold my breath, as she's about to be busy preparing for the challenges.

"Aren't you excited to see the phoenix again?" Aislinn asks, and I realize we've been sitting in silence for the past few minutes. The phoenix is the chosen messenger of the Gods, an elusive creature caught in the eternal cycle of life and death and rebirth.

Once per week for the last five weeks, the phoenix arrived at the castle with a totem representing each of the Gods. The first week it was a stone, the second a feather, the third a branch on fire, the fourth was an arrowhead, and finally it arrived last week with snow gripped in its talons. After the last totem was delivered, the phoenix would return in seven days to crown the next heir. This was what our family has been waiting for since Aislinn's birth. The Gods have finally decided to host the trials for the next generation of rulers. Every kingdom will celebrate today.

"Of course." I smile widely. "We hardly got glimpses of it these past few weeks. I wish Father allowed us to get closer to it."

"It's a giant bird on fire, El. I think he was right to tell us to keep our distance. After all, no one in our family was gifted by the God Kai...yet." She gives me a conspiratorial wink.

"Do you really think you'll be chosen by the water god?"

"I'm not sure. I love the water, but I don't think I've got the right personality for it." Aislinn says, and I can't agree more. Those gifted with water have a way of going with the flow, and my sister has always carved her own path.

"Are you sure I can't do your hair?" she asks, noticeably changing the subject and flexing her fingers like she's ready to rip it all out instead of style it.

"Oh no, look at that, we're here already. Such a pity," I say, looking out the window of the carriage.

Ash makes a noise like she's about to contest, but our carriage jerks to a stop in front of the temple of the Gods. Aric opens the door and Ash stands up, smoothing her dark blue gown. There isn't a wrinkle on it, but perhaps she's actually nervous for once. She descends the two steps and cheers erupt from the waiting crowd.

I follow her out of the carriage, grabbing Aric's outstretched hand for balance. He walks us to the raised platform at the city center, one that I haven't seen before. Ash and I venture out to Sandral every fortnight under disguise, to escape our royal duties for a few hours. This platform must have been raised solely for this occasion. It's made of slate black stone, smooth and polished. It's no doubt our father's creation.

Flanking the dais are our family banners, towering over the heads of the crowd and waving slightly in the wind. Our crest has a solid navy background, with the outline of our castle walls in silver and a large two-headed gray bird underneath the castle walls. The shield is adorned with a silver and blue crown above it. Legend has it that all four of the kingdoms created their coat of arms after the first heirs were gifted with the Gods' powers. That was about eight hundred years ago.

Aric leaves us at the base of the platform's steps and stands at the bottom, scanning the crowd for any signs of trouble. Aislinn and I walk up the steps together, joining our parents in the center.

I shift on my feet. The midday sun scorches the back of my neck, the heat radiating up from the black stone beneath us, and not for the first time I wish my hair was the lighter color of Aislinn's so it wouldn't absorb so much heat. I wipe the sweat from my brow as casually as I can, hoping I don't catch the disapproving glare of my mother. Princesses aren't supposed to sweat.

Aislinn stands tall and proud on the dais, our father standing next to her. Mother and I are positioned slightly behind them, as is customary for the spares.

A screech pierces our ears and a large, radiant bird comes into view as it dips below the fluffy clouds. I suck in a breath. I've already seen it five times, but it's as magnificent now as it was the first time. The phoenix looks like fire itself was given form, with feathers of red, orange and gold. Long tail feathers trail out behind its body, and a few wisps of smoke follow behind it as the bird swoops lower, angling its body and circling above us. Its deadly talons grasp a shimmering golden crown. The chosen heir's crown. I glimpse a design of peaks rising to the center of the gold circlet, with white gems adorning it.

The messenger of the Gods has arrived.

Aislinn clasps her hands in front of her and rolls her shoulders back as she bows her golden blonde head, the perfect picture of grace as she prepares to receive the crown that will seal her fate as the future queen of Adrithia.

The phoenix flies mere feet over our heads, and I feel the heat radiating off it, warming the top of my head even more. A bead of sweat slowly moves from my temple down past my ears, tickling as it goes. I want nothing more than to swipe it away, but I don't risk the movement, afraid to draw the ire of the Gods.

I feel the whoosh of wings as it passes by me and hovers in front of my father and sister. We slowly drop to our knees, bowing our heads. In the crowd, I see thousands following suit, everyone bowing in deference to this magnificent creature and the ancient Gods it serves.

With a bowed head, I only risk raising my eyes slightly to watch the bird place the crown on Aislinn. Only, it doesn't place the crown on her head. It flaps its wings slowly, hovering with minimal effort, as it stares at my sister. It opens its beak and screeches, feathers flaring briefly with what looks like agitation. Then it swings its head towards me, and for a split second I meet its molten gaze before returning my eyes to the ground in front of me.

Wingbeats sound and hot air blows in my face. The phoenix hovers in front of me. I'm frozen with fear and shock. Did I do something wrong? Maybe I angered the bird by looking at it. Oh Gods, if I mess this up for Aislinn I'll never hear the end of it. A million questions run through my mind, but in one swift motion, the phoenix silences them as it places the crown on my head.

CHAPTER TWO

The crown is on my head, I think to myself. *Why is the crown on my head?*

Wings flap, and hot air blasts me as the bird flies backwards, screeching righteously. My eyes raise to the bird and I suppress an eyeroll. Showoff. I see my father and mother stand out of the edges of my vision so I, too, rise. The crown is heavier than I would have guessed, and all I can think about is how I should have let Aislinn do my hair.

A flash of light and heat, and the phoenix vanishes.

The uproar is instantaneous. People leap to their feet and start shouting. I want to cover my ears against the noise, but shock keeps me frozen.

My family stares at me. My father's open mouth portrays his shock. My mother's hands shake at her sides, and Aislinn's eyes are as wide as I've ever seen them.

Earth rumbles underneath my father's feet as he takes a step in front of me.

"What have you done?" He stands in front of me, blocking my view of the upset crowd, but to my surprise he's looking at my mother. His power shakes the surface of the ground, threatening my balance.

"I-I have no idea what happened," I say, meeting his eyes. They pinch together with a look I've never seen before. If I didn't know better, I'd think it's fear.

It's my mother who speaks. She grabs my father's arm gently and says, "it was the Gods who chose. Devon, we must address the people."

They turn their back on me and walk to the edge of the dais, where my father raises his arms. Aislinn steps back to me, her face no longer betrays her shock. She's been schooling her features into submission for years, but I know her well enough to see the pain she hides. On instinct I try to tear the crown from my head, but she grabs my hands in hers, firmly.

"You were chosen, sister," she flashes a fragile smile and glances up at the crown. "Do not remove it. Let them s-see."

It's the slight break in her voice which has me forcing my hands down. She drops one of mine, but keeps the other clasped in hers. She gives me a reassuring squeeze and then tugs me forward, to stand in line with our parents.

I feel itchy everywhere. The crowd has quieted, but they're looking up at us as though we owe them answers, an explanation, anything.

"Adrithian Citizens!" my father's voice booms. Any remaining talking dies instantly. I catch a glimpse of Aric at the foot of the temple's stairs. His face is full of disbelief and horror as he stares up at us.

"The Gods have spoken. They have chosen my youngest daughter, Princess Elana, as the heir to this kingdom." He turns towards me, and the anger I saw there moments ago is replaced by a mask of surprised delight. No wonder Aislinn is so good at it. She learned from the best. There are some grumblings in the crowd, but no one dares voice their unrest while the king stands in front of them.

"What a surprise for us all!" He barks a laugh that sounds so forced I wonder if anyone will believe it, "I have no doubt that Elana will bring honor to Adrithia." His hand lands on my shoulder in a move that's meant to look supportive.

"The Gods have plans for us all. No matter how small our roles, we will rise to meet them," he says, bringing his arms up. A large rock breaks free from the ground in front of the crowd, and pieces shave off it until our Sable family crest is all that remains.

Father raises his hands high above his head and the pedestal rises further into the air. "I look forward to the day when we reintroduce Princess Elana as blessed by one of the Gods." He drops his arms, spins around, and heads for his carriage.

Cheers break out among the crowd, and there are a few who shout, "Long live the King!" in his wake. The people of Adrithia have always respected strength above all else, I wonder what they think of me. Did they even know my name before today?

My mother quickly follows behind my father, and Aislinn tugs me along, which I'm eternally grateful for because my feet feel like bricks.

Our parents climb into their carriage, and Aislinn and I step up to our own. I hang back as I usually do, allowing Aislinn to enter first, but she stops and gently pushes me forward.

"You're the heir now," she says simply when I hesitate. I blow out a sharp breath and launch myself in, forever thankful I don't trip on my impractical skirts.

Once we're inside, Aislinn closes the plush curtains, sits next to me, and grabs my hands. My emotions and anxiety burst from me and warm tears trail down my face.

"Aislinn, I'm so sorry," I cry.

My sister holds tight. "Don't you apologize, Elana. Don't ever apologize."

"But this is your birthright. You've been training for this your entire life. I don't know what happened. Why did they choose me?" Even through my heaving sobs, Aislinn understands me.

"The Gods have plans for you. We must trust them," she drops one of my hands and wipes my tears away with her perfectly pressed glove. "As for my birthright, I don't care. You are my sister, and I will always love you."

I try to crack a smile, but it wobbles and more tears spill down my face. I suck in the snot that threatens to slip out of my nose. Gods, I'm a shitty princess. And now I'm going to have to learn how to be a queen.

My entire future has gone up in smoke with one bird's actions. My designation as a healer, my forced engagement to Lord Percival, everything I've accepted about my future has been flipped upside down. It's terrifying, and a little bit exciting.

"I love you too, Aislinn."

She smiles fiercely at me and sits back, leveling me with a look of sheer determination.

"Be strong, El. I'm sure our parents will have some insight," she says, leaning back on her plush seat.

Our carriage slows to a stop and Aislinn gestures for me to exit first. I take a deep breath and throw my shoulders back, the same move I've seen Aislinn make a thousand times. On her it looks natural, like regal is her natural state of being. On me it feels like a lie, like I'm faking confidence when all I want to do is break.

The idea of facing my parents and figuring out what to do next is almost as unnerving as being tossed to the wilderness with four strangers in twenty days.

I step out of the carriage and see Mother waiting for us. Aislinn follows me and stiffens as she takes in who waits for us. We both automatically correct our posture. Queen Maris has always put on a charismatic, warm act in front of her people, but she stands in front of us with a face like stone. I used to wonder if our father had hewn her out of stone to be his wife.

"Daughters, come with me," she leads the way—not inside the palace as I'd expected, but to one of the sprawling gardens. This garden is her favorite, and my least. All the plants here have thorns. I've lost count of the number of times I've pricked a finger, arm, or even leg on one of these spiteful shrubs.

We walk through the carefully manicured aisles and the queen finally stops by one of the large white stone statues near the center of the garden. She turns to us, and her brows are pulled together in a rare show of emotion.

"Aislinn, I have no idea why the Gods would forsake your claim." Her voice only a little louder than a whisper. "I'm so sorry."

She fidgets, actually *fidgets*, on her feet. The woman I've never seen make a misstep or move that wasn't calculated is rocking back and forth on her feet and wringing her hands. Aislinn doesn't respond, but her predatory focus is trained on our mother, no doubt taking notice of the same awkwardness I see.

"You've prepared for this your entire life, and it must feel like your path has been ripped from you." She stares at Aislinn with an emotion akin to sorrow.

My sister dips her head, her expression controlled, "I appreciate your concern, but I'm alright."

Mother nods her head at her eldest, smiling softly, "You will be. You're strong, Aislinn."

She turns to me, that soft smile turning into something sad, "Now you must teach Elana. She *must* survive the test of the mountains. Our future depends on it."

"I'll train her as hard as I can," Aislinn says. Our mother nods at her again, then addresses me.

"The Gods' challenges are designed to push you to your limits, if not break you. They will test your body and soul. A few heirs have perished during the quest. Promise me you won't give up," she says, face pinching into concern. "Promise me you'll fight until the end, and if the Gods deny you, you will come home despite them. Promise me you'll come back to us. Promise me, Elana."

Never, *never* have I heard her speak like this before. So open, so candid. I'm so taken aback I nod my head and stammer, "I-I promise, Mother."

"Good. That's good." She turns back towards the house, smoothing her skirts even though a crease would never dare show up on her dress. "Time to see the king."

We walk to the castle together. Mother's face has returned to its natural state, that carefully crafted mask.

Two guards swing the doors open for us. The breathtaking foyer was designed centuries ago and my father added his own stone embellishments after he came into his power. The same polished white stone of the statues is everywhere—the grand staircase which splits in two and curves up, the gleaming polished floor, the tall columns, the decorations on the side of the staircase.

We pass through the bright entrance, through one of our sitting rooms and head towards the king's private study. The doors are open wide, an uncommon sight. Father values his privacy.

He stands behind his large gleaming granite desk, facing the large glass windows. There's a slight rumble to the ground as we approach. I can't tell if it's anger or concern that moves the ground. He usually keeps his power on a tight leash, but every once in a while, when emotions run high, we feel the effects of it leaking through.

There's a giant sphere of white polished stone sitting on a pedestal next to his desk. It spins as if on its own axis. It takes a fraction of my father's power, hardly a thought for him. It's as much of an anxious tic as he'd ever allow anyone to see.

"The Gods have chosen. There's nothing we can do to change that," he says, turning to face us. His crown gleams gold atop his head. He wears it so naturally. My own head itches from the new weight upon it. It feels so much heavier than the delicate tiaras I wear for official occasions.

"If the other heirs see that you're anything but prepared for this, they'll strike you down. Weakness in the royal lines means weakness in the kingdom. They would have reason to attack us, try to overthrow our rule," he says, pacing back and forth. The ground starts shaking again, and I bend my knees slightly to absorb some of the shock. Glasses clatter slightly and papers shuffle on his desk.

"You will need to be trained, Elana. From sunup to sundown every single day. You will train with the weapons master," he says. "You will be taught how to defend yourself, how to survive the harsh conditions of the Gods' Peaks, and what to expect from the other heirs."

"Father," Aislinn says, waiting for him to nod at her before she continues. "I would like to train Elana in the weapons master's stead. As you know, I'm the best fighter in Adrithia. I would be a better instructor. I know her strengths and weaknesses."

It's not pride or vanity that fuels Aislinn's words, but honesty. Stark truth that she is the greatest warrior alive in our kingdom. She proved it last summer, when Father made her fight in the Solstice Tournament as part of her training. For fourteen days straight she fought against every top general in our army, every master of every weapon, and finally against the king himself. Thousands of people showed up to watch her conquest as she thrashed opponent after opponent, never killing them, only disarming or wounding them until they eventually surrendered. Some called her a warrior, some called her a goddess reborn, but most called her a queen.

That final day when she faced my father, he fought her with his mother's sword. He used no earth power, only brute strength as he attacked her again and again, each time he was driven back by her equal ferocity. The fight went on for a heart-pounding nine minutes. It was the longest any of her fights had lasted.

Finally, in a trick move I'd only seen her use one or two other times, she feinted one way, whirled back around, and caught his arm past his guard, causing him to drop the sword. The move would have been a killing one, if she wanted. Blood poured down his arm, but he'd never looked so proud.

Father nods his head. "Very well, Aislinn. You will teach her everything she needs to know to survive and best the challenges."

Aislinn and I exchange quick smiles. She's going to make my life miserable for the next twenty days, but I'd rather be battered and bruised by her than by the burly, boorish weapons master any day.

"We may never know why the Gods chose you, Elana, and I wish we had more time to prepare you for what's to come. We will do our best to ensure you're as ready as possible for the challenges ahead." He runs his hand through his light brown beard. "It won't be easy, child, but you just may surprise us all."

I nod my head. "I live to serve Adrithia, Father. I won't let this kingdom or our family down."

The rumbling of the earth finally stops. Father lets out a heavy sigh.

"I have faith in you. Now, go and begin your training," he says, nodding at the door. Ash and I bow our heads and quickly make a quick exit. Our mother remains behind. We close the study door behind us.

As soon as the door closes, I feel heavy. It's like the doors have closed on what I thought my life would be. Even though I was dreading marrying Lord Percival, it was a familiar path. As a married princess, I could have been free to pursue my healing skills or live a carefree life somewhere in the country. There would be no need to attend political meetings or hold court. I wouldn't have to worry about the health and happiness of the entire kingdom.

Everything I could have been was replaced in a moment and now this awful shiny gold crown sends pains down my neck. Before I can stop them, my shoulders start shaking, and tears well in my eyes. I inhale sharply and fight against overwhelming anxiety.

Aislinn throws her arms around my shoulders and pulls me in close to her. I turn my face to her shoulders and let the tears fall as I gasp in shuddering breaths.

"It'll be okay, El, I promise." She pulls back slightly and steers me towards the grand staircase. We sit on the steps together. She keeps her arms wrapped around me, holding me tightly. Gods, I don't deserve my sister. Here she is comforting me while her future goes up in flames.

"Ash, I'm so sorry. It should have been you. You're the eldest, and you've been preparing for this your whole life," I suck in a breath, "I can't do this."

Aislinn pushes me back a few inches to look me in the eyes. "Listen to me, Elana. You can do this. You will do this. You're stronger than you know. Don't let your fear and self-doubt stop you from meeting your destiny."

I sniffle and take a few breaths, focusing on blowing out the breath slowly. "Do you really not care that you were supposed to be heir?"

She takes a few moments to answer, "I can't say that I'm happy with how things turned out. I'm feeling a bit lost, not sure what's next for me. I know whatever it is, it'll be alright. For these next twenty days my sole purpose is to make sure you don't die on that mountain."

There it is. Her purpose. She's always thrived off knowing her purpose and working relentlessly towards it. It keeps her focused and content. Aislinn without a purpose is dangerous. She bores easily, and that spells trouble for the entire castle.

"You're going to kick my ass, aren't you?" I ask, wiping my tears on the sleeve of my gown.

Ash gives me a wicked grin. "Yes. Every single day."

I let out a hiccupping laugh. "Don't let Mother talk you into an arranged marriage."

"Oh, I'd like to see her try." She smirks in a way that leaves no doubt in my mind what would happen if she did try.

"Right," Aislinn stands up suddenly, holding out her hands for mine. I take them, and she pulls me to my feet. "We have work to do. There are only a few short weeks to turn you into an heir. *The* heir. But first, we need to ditch the dresses."

Aric meets us at the top of the stairs. Concern pinches his brows together. "Princesses, are you okay?"

I nod, though I can't seem to make words form.

"That was an unexpected turn of events," Ash says, speaking for us. "But we're going to make sure that Elana gets trained and is as ready as possible for the Gods' Peaks."

Aric startles, turning his too-intense gaze on me. "You can't mean to go through with it, Princess."

I sniffle, blowing out a long breath. "What choice is there?"

He hesitates at this, then addresses my sister. "Surely there's something that can be done? You could go in her place?"

"Elana was chosen, not me, Aric. If I show up there instead of her, the Gods will likely kill me, and everyone in Adrithia. You know in that thick skull of yours that she has to go."

He runs a hand through his hair, and Ash tugs me along, leaving him standing there in the hallway alone.

Chapter Three

A few hours later, Aislinn and I are on the sandy sparring field near the stables. She's dressed in soft brown leather training pants with a loose red tunic tucked in. Her leather shoes are laced up her ankles, and she twirls two wooden practice swords.

"Let's see how soft you are, sister," she tells me, tossing one of the swords to the sand in front of me.

We tried to find appropriate training clothes for me, but none of hers fit correctly, and I had only been allowed to wear dresses for most of my life. Not exactly fighting material. The pants were too long, and the shirts were too tight in the hips and chest. We had to send a message to our tailor and request new sets of clothes as quickly as possible. In the meantime, I made do with rolling up the legs on her pants and wearing one of my nightshirts with a solid black corset over it. Not glamorous, but it might keep me from tripping over myself.

I level a stare at her and cross my arms over my chest. "What do you mean by 'soft'?"

Aislinn rolls her eyes, "You haven't been training for this your entire life so it's natural that you have curves. We need to develop more muscle and endurance. I know you're not weak, and decent with a bow from our practice together, but mother kept you sequestered away for years, teaching you useless 'womanly arts' or whatever she calls them. We're starting from square one. I have to make sure you can hold your own in any kind of situation, whether it be a fight or outrunning an opponent. Only the Gods know what you'll face up in the mountains."

"Now," she continues, backing up a step, "pick up the sword and attack me."

I bend over and reach for the sword, and Aislinn swings at my arms, the blunt side of her wooden sword smacking my forearms.

"Shit, that hurt," I yell at her pulling my arms back.

She smiles. It's a wicked smile that fills me with dread. I'm about to be in a lot of pain. That look alone almost makes me wish for the crude shouting of the weapons master. I should've known…my sister doesn't show mercy.

A few hours later, Aislinn throws me to the ground for the fifteenth time. We began training with swords, but when I kept tripping over my feet, she decided it was best to practice sparring without weapons and footwork and work our way up to swordplay.

"Are you even trying?" she asks in frustration. This whole time we've been training she hasn't even broken a sweat.

I, on the other hand, hold my side and gasp for breath. "Are you even human?" I counter, taking the outstretched hand she offers, letting her pull me to my feet.

"I'm as human as you are," she rolls her eyes at me. "Let's take a break from physical exercise and talk about the types of challenges there have been in the past."

I throw myself onto the stone bench on the side of the sparring ring. Aislinn hands me a skin of water, and I drink from it greedily.

"Not too fast, Elana. You'll make yourself sick from drinking too quickly after training," she snatches the water away from me and if I had any breath left in me, I'd curse her. Knowing my sister though, she'd accept the insult and make me run around the castle five times.

"Okay, first thing you need to know about the challenges is that they're never the same as previous generations. The Gods always change it up. They're infinitely more powerful in their homeland, so the possibilities are endless. It could be a puzzle that tests your strategy, or a foot race against an avalanche, or a battle against giants. No one really knows what it'll be, so luckily all the heirs have the same disadvantage."

I nod my head, my breath slowly returning to its normal pace.

"Each God and Goddess looks for the heir that personifies the traits they're looking for. The Goddess Avani blessed Father with her Earth powers because he's strong, unyielding, and—"

"Generally stubborn," I suggest. She cracks a smile.

"I always wondered where we got it from," she says, her gaze turning serious once more. "We know from our grandmother that the fire goddess, Enya, prefers someone who is a fierce warrior, with a short temper, who's passionate about protecting their loved ones."

I think back, trying to remember our grandmother. I only remember her in glimpses now, her fiery red hair and freckles. She was loud. I remember her laugh, and I swear it was loud enough that the walls shook in her wake. Age never seemed to affect her much. She died from a terrible fever caused by the poison of a giant scorpion, a beast that roams in Adrithia's dark southern forest, when Aislinn and I were young. All her power could not save her. Our father and grandfather were stricken. She wasn't old—in fact she was one of the youngest monarchs to pass away on our continent in many generations. The ruling families from across Astrellia attended her funeral. Father was officially crowned king a few weeks after we laid her to rest. Our grandfather passed away less than a year later, heavy with grief at her sudden loss.

"It stands to reason that the water god, Kai, would seek someone level-headed but able to go with the flow, due to the vastly different forms water can take. I'd think being adaptable would be a sought-after trait for the god. On the other end of the spectrum, Father and I have always believed that the air god, Sepher, always chooses the most free-spirited of the heirs. And the last god, Tolliver, the metal god, would most likely choose someone who doesn't express emotion, someone who's pragmatic and reserved. Due to the nature of metals, they would have to thrive with change."

I nod my head, thinking of which traits suit me. I'd like to think I'm wild and untamable, but I also feel an affinity towards earth, having lived with my father. I've never had the opportunity to test my mental and physical abilities before, being subjected to our mother's lessons.

The "womanly arts" mostly consisted of how to be meek and pleasing to one's husband. How to maintain a household, which was simply how to hire staff to maintain a household, how to dance (at which I am terrible), how to sing (at which I'm average but occasionally pitchy), how to plan parties (which I don't care much to attend, let alone plan), and how to charm people from all walks of life (which I try to avoid as much as possible). My one joy in my so-called training has been my work as a healer, which my mother allowed me to receive special lessons in.

All of this effort was supposed to prepare me to be a prized "spare" daughter and marry someone who would help solidify Adrithia. My mother found that man in Lord Percival Lyons, the son of the Duke Aldrich Lyons. The Duke owns the largest metal mines in Adrithia. According to my mother, marrying his son would ensure our kingdom remained well-stocked with weapons and wealth. Lord Percival and I have yet to meet in person, and the few letters we've exchanged have been dull and impersonal. With me being chosen as heir, thus increasing my standing in society, I have no doubt that Mother will reevaluate the match and likely break the engagement entirely. Given his boredom with our communication thus far, I doubt Lord Percival will be too upset by the sudden change of plans.

A hand passes in front of my face. Aislinn looks at me with raised brows, "El, you there?"

I snap my focus back to her, wondering how long she was trying to get my attention. "Sorry, Ash, I'm here."

"What were you thinking about that could possibly be more important than training?"

"I'm thinking about how even though I'm possibly going to my death, I'm relieved that I won't be forced into marrying Duke Aldrich's son anytime soon," I say.

Aislinn looks down at her heavy leather gloves. "I'm sorry that it was almost a reality for you. I tried to stop it, I tried to convince Mother to wait until you were older, or to let you choose a suitor for yourself. But she was adamantly opposed to you receiving any training. There were so many times I wanted to barge into your lessons and drag you out here myself. I should have done it, to Hells with Mother's wishes."

"I would have loved to train with you. Too bad younger princesses are only good for marrying off," I roll my eyes, mocking our mother's tone.

"But," I start, "who knows, maybe one of the challenges will require singing or dancing."

"Great, then we really are doomed." Aislinn laughs, and I playfully smack her arm.

After another hour of training my balance and hand-to-hand combat, I'm shaking all over. A headache thrums steadily in my skull. The sun begins to set behind the tall pine trees. I'm utterly exhausted. I stopped sweating hours ago, and my limbs feel suspiciously boneless. Tomorrow I'm going to be in so much pain.

My stomach growls loudly, but before I can appease my starving body, I take a long hot bath. Aislinn gives me some of her oils and salts, saying the salt will ease some of the soreness. I thank her heartily before soaking long enough to turn my fingers into prunes.

I devour dinner, my sister encouraging me to take second helpings of meat to build muscle. Our parents are noticeably absent from dinner, which means there's no one around to watch Aislinn and I eat two slices of strawberry pie each.

"Tomorrow we'll continue to train in hand-to-hand and balance, and if you do well, we might add in some basic sword work," Aislinn says between large bites of pie.

"Wonderful," I sigh. My mind wanders. Tomorrow I'll have nineteen days left to train. Nineteen days before I'm thrust into the wilderness of literal mountains. Nineteen days until the Gods will test me against four other heirs and decide if I'm worthy to wield their power. My stomach roils and I lose my appetite, abandoning my second slice of pie.

"Aislinn," I almost whisper, afraid to raise my voice too much. I learned at a young age that this castle has ears everywhere. When I was ten years old I rode our giant mastiff, Rufus, around the castle like a horse after Ash dared me to. We inevitably crashed into the piano, causing the whole piece to collapse and creating one of the loudest noises I'd ever heard. Rufus took off down the hallway, passing a few of the servants who came to investigate the commotion, and I spent the next few hours hiding in my wardrobe. My mother found me and I had to scrub dishes in the kitchen for the next fortnight.

Aislinn stops eating and stares at me with her shining eyes reflecting the flickering lights of the candles on the table. Her brows pull together, sensing my fear the way only a sister could.

"What happens if no Gods find me worthy?"

Aislinn's eyes soften, "Put those thoughts out of your head, El. They will find you worthy."

"But what if they don't?"

She sighs and lays down her fork, "That has never happened in our history. Over eight hundred years' worth of reports, dating back to the first rulers chosen. The Gods wouldn't have given you a crown if they didn't think you deserved it. Remember, they've already chosen you."

The worry persists, but I nod my head. I don't want to rub salt into her wounds. I still can't believe this twist of fate. Ash is the first eldest child not chosen since the beginning.

"Are you doing okay?" I ask tentatively.

She scoops up another bite of pie with her fork and chews thoughtfully. "It's a bit of a relief, honestly. You're going to learn about the unimaginable pressure that comes from being next-in-line. It's constantly stressful. Even though I've been training for it since I can remember. It's not just the physical stuff, either. It's the emotional toll, knowing you'll live your whole life for your kingdom and all its people."

Aislinn's words form a knot in my throat, even though my heart lifts for her. She sounds relieved, more excited than I've heard her sound in a long time.

"I never had the freedom to pursue what I like, who I like," she says.

"Ash, do you have a crush on someone?" I gasp jokingly, wanting to hear more.

She laughs, and it's a warm, contagious sound. "You'd be the first to hear of it if I did."

She sounds so genuine and happy that I believe her.

"You deserve it," I say to her. "You deserve to have everything you could ever want. The Gods missed out on a great ruler, sister. You would be an amazing queen."

"You will be, too, El."

The door to our main dining room opens, and I half expect to see Mother or Father, so I'm pleasantly surprised to see Aric stomping towards us.

"Sir Aric," Aislinn calls out, waving him over. "Are you joining us for dessert? I'm afraid we've eaten most of the pie, but there's still a piece or two left."

"Unfortunately not, Your Highness," he says, one hand on his blade as he stands next to my chair, staring at me. His stricken and worried expression after the crowning ceremony is still burned into my mind. He looks composed now, his features betraying none of the earlier concern that was painted on his face.

"The King requested that I escort you to your chambers for the evening, Princess."

Aislinn and I exchange a confused look. It's not entirely strange that our parents didn't eat with us, but it is strange for our father to send Aric to escort me to bed.

"Is everything alright?" Aislinn asks, wiping pie filling from the corners of her lips as she stands.

"Yes, of course," Aric responds, albeit too quickly. He seems to realize his error and softens his features slightly. "Nothing to worry about, Highness."

Aislinn narrows her eyes to appraise him. "Very well. I think we're all done with the sweets tonight, anyway. I'll leave you both to it. Goodnight, El."

"Goodnight Ash."

She sweeps from the room, heading towards Father's study. Aric offers me his hand and I scoot back from the table and accept it. We walk arm in arm from the dining hall.

When we get to my door, I expect him to wish me goodnight and then retire to his own quarters. But he stays, glancing down the hallways, one hand on his sword hilt.

"Aren't you going to bed?" I ask.

"No, Princess," he says, "I'm standing guard tonight."

His words unsettle me, but I nod my head, unsure of what else to say. Aric is our best guard, but he has never guarded me during the night. It's never been needed before. I wonder what the precaution is for, but I know he won't answer me if I ask. His job is to protect me from everything, and sometimes that includes the truth.

Chapter Four

I wake in utter agony. My muscles burn with every movement, and I practically crawl out of bed. I'm halfway through turning myself into a rotten grape in the bathtub when Aislinn breezes in, holding a tray of fresh fruit, boiled eggs and bread.

"Morning, sunshine," she says, setting the tray down on the small desk outside the bathing room. "If you want breakfast, you'll have to meet me out here. Come, come, out of the tub."

I scoff and sink lower into the warm water, "I'm not a dog, Ash, I'm not going to be summoned to my meal."

She only lifts her eyebrows and sits down, cutting off a slice of the bread, still steaming, and slathering it with butter and a drizzle of honey. I groan as the smell of bread hits my nose and finally forces me from the tub.

"Shall I start calling you Rufus the Second, then?" She chuckles, handing me the knife to cut my own piece.

"Oh, you're in a mood this morning," I roll my eyes, cracking open a boiled egg.

"How're you feeling?" Ash asks innocently, as if she doesn't know that my whole body screams in pain with every little movement.

"Wonderful, thanks," I respond dryly.

She smiles wide. "I was going to make you spar with me all day, but instead I think I'll grant you a boon. I heard from my lady's maid that the festival is still going on in town. How would you like to see it this afternoon?"

My eyes shoot up at her, and my mouth gapes. "That sounds amazing."

"Good, then it's settled. We'll train until midday and then go to Sandral afterwards."

Hours later I'm panting on the ground, holding my stomach and trying to catch my breath. I wear one of my new training outfits, a near match to Aislinn's. The pants are soft and flexible, allowing for incredible movement. I don't trip over these like I did with the ones yesterday. The shirt has two straps that sit on my shoulders instead of sleeves, and it fits loosely, but not enough to get in my way. I asked Senara to help me wrap my breasts this morning, finding it easier to move with them firmly held in place.

Aislinn takes me through the same set of moves as yesterday, working on balance and hand-to-hand combat. This time I'm able to knock her down once, a considerable improvement, although she seems thoroughly distracted by the blacksmith's son hammering out some red-hot metal. Being a warm day, his shirt is soaked with sweat and clings to his bulging biceps. It seems my sister is already looking to pursue her other interests.

Aislinn taps my shoulder with her foot. "Come on, let's go inside and freshen up before we head into Sandral."

Senara helps me choose an outfit suitable for blending in with the townsfolk. It's a simple dark green dress. We don't want to stand out in the crowd with excessive jewelry or embellishments. Even though masks are typically worn at the celebration, we could still be targets for pickpockets.

Aislinn meets me outside my room with Aric. She's dressed in a black dress similar to mine. Her blonde hair is undone, spilling down her back in long golden tresses.

"He's coming to play our scary chaperone," Aislinn says brightly, stepping between us, grabbing our arms, and tugging us along.

We forego the carriage in a further attempt to blend in, instead opting to ride horses. This is another of the few useful skills I'm adept at. I've been riding with Ash since I could walk, first on ponies, then gradually on larger horses. My favorite horse is a stunning white mare painted with black spots. I've been riding Misty for more than five years now.

The short ride into town doesn't go by quickly enough. Every uneven step Misty takes jars my pained muscles.

We dismount our horses at the edge of town, leading them along until we find the stable where we usually leave them. The stable boy comes running out, a wide grin on his face. He recognizes his top customers and always takes immaculate care of our horses. Aislinn pays the stable boy handsomely to look after them, and he eagerly takes our three inside.

Aislinn grabs my hand, leading me through the throng of revelers. People around us are dressed in all kinds of garb. Some formal, some hardly there, some glittering, and some look like they just rolled out of a sewer. Masks of every size, shape, and color are all around us. Few shop owners and guards opt out of wearing them.

Ash tugs me to a booth lined with dozens of wooden masks and we each pick out our favorites. She chooses a full face covering painted pure silver, with swirling patterns of red trim. I select a green half mask to match my dress, with gold embellishments and large black feathers protruding from the top.

For Aric, since he refuses to choose for himself, I grab a simple light blue mask with gold swirls painted on it. He accepts it graciously but refuses to let Aislinn pay. He hands the coins to the booth attendant, and with that we move with the crowd through the busy streets.

Sandral isn't usually this crowded. The festival appears to be in full-swing, with street carts everywhere, and people eagerly jostling between them. On the occasions when Ash and I are able to slip out from the castle unnoticed, we've enjoyed the theater, the art halls, even a few of the well-known pubs. Ash has kept us clear of the seedier parts of the city, but here today there's no keeping us clear. People from all parts of the kingdom are celebrating together, high-class to low.

Over the past few decades, Father has passed and enforced laws to create a more equal society, but progress has been slow. While most of the capital city is thriving, areas remain where shady deals are done.

I inhale deeply, smelling all kinds of food. The three of us weave through the throng and stop at several of the busier food vendors. At the first booth we purchase some kind of smoked, seasoned fish on a stick. Aislinn and I share it, Aric shaking his head violently when we offered some to him. Fish aversion, he calls it. I call him a picky eater. Even as children, he kept the most basic diet. It's honestly a miracle his muscles developed as well as they did.

Next, we buy a small loaf of bread that smells of cinnamon, and sure enough we break it apart to find it has a rich center sprinkled with cinnamon sugar. Aric happily accepts a small piece of this when I offer.

The crowd grows steadily rowdier as people start pouring in and out of Sandral's pubs. We watch as a towering bald man, who must be part giant, throws another smaller man through the door of one of the taverns. Spectators back up to give them space. The man on the ground recovers quickly, jumping to his feet. He dances around the large man, raining blow after blow upon the giant man. A succession of quick kicks and punches has the large man hunched over, grunting in pain.

People start cheering for the men, money passed around as bets are taken. The smaller man levels a kick at the giant's head, but the giant catches it, and in a brutal move crashes his arm down upon the man's knee. An audible *crack* sounds, followed by a piercing shriek as the smaller man collapses onto the ground, trying to cradle his leg, which is bent in the wrong direction. Bile rises in my throat, and I look away. Aislinn scoffs in disgust and pulls me away, pushing through the spectators who are either groaning in frustration or cheering in victory. Aric follows behind me, keeping close.

We continue our way down the street, but I notice in the center of the worn cobblestone near the temple of the Gods is a small wooden plank stage. A single person dressed in an elaborate phoenix mask and long red robes walks to the center of it. Excited murmurs lift around us, and I pull on Aislinn's sleeve to redirect her towards the stage.

"Ladies and Gentlemen! It is my honor to present to you all our wonderful dancing troupe, The Phoenix Wings." He bows and cheers erupt. The man jogs off to the side of the stage as a group of lavishly clothed dancers fills the stage. Dancing women are dressed in skintight suits whose colors range between reds, oranges, and purples. Their hair is loose, blowing slightly in the breeze and with their movements. A few men on the stage help spot the women performing gymnastics. They wear long flowing robes of black with swirls of embellishments that match the women's outfits. Their hair is knotted at the top of their heads.

A slow tune begins playing, starting with a haunting flute. The dancers begin whirling around each other, grabbing arms and spinning in fluid movements. A lute joins in the song and the dancers spin faster, leaping and jumping around each other. It's addictive to watch. Their outfits look like fire, the way they move, rhythmic and passionate. The audience is nearly silent, watching it all unfold. As the music crescendos, one of the male dancers throws his female companion up in the air, her long sleeves whipping behind her and creating the appearance of wings. She lands effortlessly in his arms as the music stops. Loud claps and cheers erupt from the audience. I clap and cheer for the troupe, a wide smile plastered on my face.

The dancers bow and hurry off the stage, towards the curtains behind it. The leader of the troupe jogs to the center once again, clapping his hands together and bowing at the gathered crowd.

"Thank you, thank you for your love. Our troupe traveled here all the way from the Kingdom of Ocarin!" There are a few sporadic cheers in the audience, people who must have ties to Adrithia's neighboring kingdom.

"We had the immeasurable honor of attending the Crowning Ceremony yesterday by request of the King." He pauses for cheering, but only a few sound. My stomach drops, and I look at Aislinn. Underneath her mask, her mouth is set in a hard line.

"We've prepared a special presentation in honor of the event. I hope you all enjoy the show. Please drop a mark into the hat if you enjoy our performance, and we'll be back on this stage tomorrow at midday!" He flips his hat off his head, catches it, and then jumps off the front of the stage, walking through the rows and collecting coins.

Two women walk onto the stage, dressed in navy and silver gowns. I gasp as I realize they're playing Aislinn and me. My sister grabs my hand, and I know she realizes it too.

The actresses start talking about how wonderful the day will be. The blonde woman playing Ash talks about how excited she is to be crowned heir. The redheaded actress portraying myself agrees, but then "whispers" to the crowd that she plans on stealing the throne. The audience starts booing and heckling.

Then two more performers appear, playing the king and queen. They move to the center of the stage together, and the actor king announces it's time for the Crowning Ceremony. A small woman dressed in the same orange and red costume from the previous dance races onto the stage, only this time she wears a cape that makes her look like she truly has wings. She flits around, running in circles, showing off her stunning costume. In her hand she holds a crown made from white flowers. She flits up to the four in the center, and they all bow. Just as she's about to place the crown on the blonde actress' head, the redhead pushes her out of the way and steals the circlet from the phoenix actress' hands.

The audience gasps and more angry yelling ensues. The actress playing Aislinn starts crying, and the one playing me places the crown on her own head and skips away, cackling. The king and queen console the blonde actress. She stands up and delivers a few tear-filled lines about wanting to make Adrithia proud. They clearly paint me as the villain. She leaves in the arms of the actors playing the king and queen and exits the stage with a convincing sob.

Panic swells in my stomach, churning the rich food I'd eaten. They're talking about me. But if they were at the ceremony, they should know that's not what happened.

The fake me takes the stage again to the jeering of the crowd. I hear one woman nearby say, "the younger princess was always so power-hungry, but I can't believe she would doom us all by stealing the crown."

The man next to her shakes his head, "Princess Aislinn didn't deserve what that witch did to her. If I ever met Elana, I'd show her the only thing a younger princess is good for." He grabs his crotch for emphasis.

Nausea roils my stomach and my knees start to quake. If I don't leave this crowd, I'll be sick. I drop Aislinn's hand and turn sharply, pushing through the spectators. My breath comes in quick pants and there's a tightness in my chest that doesn't abate. I need to get this damned mask off my face.

I hear Aislinn and Aric shout after me. "Sister, wait!" Aislinn calls, wisely not using my name, but I'm already through the crowd and heading down a less busy street. I make a few more turns until I come to a nearly deserted alleyway, still damp with the last rain a few days ago and Gods only know what else. As soon as I'm alone I rip my mask off, sucking in a few greedy breaths.

Surely the people can't think I'm the villain. That I stole the crown from my own sister. But I was right there in that crowd, listening to them. They hate me. They don't know me at all and yet they hate me. The thought pains my chest.

I sniff, righting my body as I move through the near-deserted street. Some drunken revelers stumble out of a worn-down pub nearby and I turn away, moving further into the alleyway to hide my face.

Three long shadows catch my eye on the ground, and I turn. Three men dressed in ragged clothes approach me slowly. I attempt to put the mask back on, but in my rush to rip it off earlier I broke the straps.

"Well, well, well, gents. Look who we have here. I can't believe the thief princess herself decided to descend from on high and mingle with us commoners," the man in the center says. He has an eyepatch over his left eye and a scar that extends from his hairline to his jaw. He smiles a wicked grin at me, and I see he's missing more than a few teeth.

I take a step backwards. "I'm not the princess," I lie, "although it's a common misconception. I've been mistaken for her before."

The eyepatch man in the middle chuckles, "Oh, you're her alright, all prim and proper. I saw you, your sister, and that brute of a guard came down the road from the castle, and I saw you at the Crowning Ceremony only yesterday. I may have had my fair share of drinks, but I know a thief when I see one."

I back up to buy myself time to think. My mind twists and turns, trying to think how I can escape. He clearly knows who I am, so I won't be able to convince him otherwise. I don't have a weapon or money to bribe them. Ash carries all of that, and I've never had to worry about it until now. I don't even have pins in my hair to stab him with. I grip the single thing I have on me, the wooden mask. Maybe if I can outrun them to the main path I can lose them in the crowd.

I plant my back foot, lowering myself into a defensive stance. I grip the mask tight in my hand, ready to use it as a shield if needed.

"You see that? Little princess thinks she can take us on," eyepatch chuckles.

The three men slowly move towards me. When they're a few arms lengths away I throw the mask at them and use the distraction to dash forward, taking them by surprise. I spin and pivot my feet, whirling out of their reach and use my momentum to breeze past them. Or at least, I would have breezed past them, if my unpractical slippers didn't slide in the mud and cause me to nearly fall.

"Grab her!" Eyepatch growls, the wiry man closest to me snatches my arms, wrenching them painfully behind my back.

I gasp out, jolted by the sudden change in momentum.

"Gotcha!"

The man's breath reeks like smoke and alcohol. I gag. My already sore arms ache from where he holds them behind my back. I try to twist and wiggle my way out of his hold, but I only cause myself greater pain.

"Nobody wants you to be the heir, Princess." His face rubs against my own, and I stifle the urge to retch at his breath.

"Let me go!" I shout, closing my eyes and tugging against the man. The man with the eyepatch and scar slams his fist into my gut. I cry out sharply and pitch forward. I suck raspy breaths around the pain. Tears pool in my eyes and I swear I see stars. If not for the man restraining my arms, I would have sunk to the ground to cover my stomach.

"Just do it quickly, before we're noticed," the short man says, looking at the alleyway behind him, "You know what they'll do to us if we're caught."

"It's a shame we have to kill her, though," eyepatch says, drawing a long dagger out of the sheath on his belt. "She'd sell for a pretty price at the slave market. We could cut out her tongue so she doesn't tell anyone who she is."

He puts the flat end of the dagger to my face and traces a line from my temple to my throat. I breathe hard, painfully, against the sharp ache in my stomach. I steel myself for the blow, not sure if he intends to cut my throat or stab my heart.

If this is my end, I don't want to give them the satisfaction of seeing my fear.

A large shadow appears behind the eyepatch man with the dagger. There's a flash of steel, then a blade is ripping out of the devastating wound from his shoulder to the middle of his chest. Warm blood spatters my face, but I'm too shocked to flinch. Before his body can hit the ground, Aric's longsword whips out and skewers his short companion through the chest. The man lets out an "oomph" before he crumples at Aric's feet.

My eyes widen as I lock eyes with Aric. He's covered with blood, but I can't see any injuries. He looks me over from head to toe, as if he's checking me for them too.

The man behind me adjusts his grip on me, grabbing a fistful of my hair, tugging on my scalp to keep me close as and his other hand presses a dagger to my throat.

"Don't move, Princess, or else," he says. The blade bites into my neck. I feel a tickle as warm blood slowly trails down my throat. Every muscle in my body aches, but locks in place. I'm terrified to move, and my breath comes in shallow rasps.

Aric stills, his face set in a scowl of cold fury, "Release her, and I promise you a swift death."

The man behind me barks out a humorless laugh. "If I'm dead either way, I might as well just kill the bitch. Adrithia will be much better off without any heir."

Suddenly another shadow appears to my right and the man's blade drops away from my throat. He lets out a shrill scream, and I see his severed hand lying in the mud, the dagger next to it. He releases my hair and Aric surges towards me. He catches me before I stumble to the ground, holding me tight against his body.

"My hand!" the man shrieks, clutching his bloodied stump to his chest.

"Can you really call it your hand anymore? It looks like it belongs to the dirt now." Aislinn appears between the man and us, flicking the blood off her long thin sword. Gods, I didn't even realize she was carrying it. Knowing her she was concealing it somewhere under her dress.

The man stops his blood-curdling cry long enough to look wide-eyed at my sister, "P-Princess Aislinn," he cries, "we did this f-for you. You were robbed! It should be your crown."

Aislinn snarls, "silence, you insignificant shrew of a man. The Gods have chosen, and we honor that decision. I'm proud that my sister is the heir."

He simpers and seems to shrink back, his shoulders hunching over his injured arm.

"Please Your Highness, please spare me." He bows his head, weeping.

Aislinn wrinkles up her nose in disgust and raises her sword.

"Sister, wait!" I say from Aric's arms.

She turns to me, eyes narrowed with cold rage.

"Please don't kill him. We can lock him up, put him on trial," I plead, not wanting to watch another person die in this alleyway because of me.

Ash looks at me incredulously. "You can't be serious, Elana. This man tried to kill you. He held a *knife* to your *throat*."

I shake my head. "I know, but he deserves a trial. That's one of our governing laws, and one of the fundamental rights of Adrithians. Please, Ash."

The anger seems to war with Ash's logical side, because she slides her gaze back and forth between me and the man, who has relieved himself in his pants and cradles his stump of an arm. She settles back on me, and for a second I think I've convinced her, but then her eyes land on my neck, and the thin line of blood there. With one swift motion she spins, arcing her blade in a maneuver perfected over years of practice, and relieves the man of his head. It lands with a sickening *smush* face-down in the mud, and his body collapses in a heap behind it.

Chapter Five

A sh hikes her skirts and turns the man's face with her boot. She leans over and inspects his face, as if committing it to memory. The fear is still frozen on his face, and I turn away from Aric's arms to vomit the contents of my stomach into the muck. Aric pulls my hair behind my shoulders and traces reassuring circles on the middle of my back.

"I'm sorry I couldn't let him live, Elana." My sister's voice is quiet, as if she doesn't quite want to be heard. "Given the chance, he would have killed you in an instant. A man like that is too dangerous to be kept alive."

I don't respond because I'm still gagging on bile. Once I finish heaving, Aric hands me his waterskin. I rinse my mouth out and spit, then swallow a small sip. My stomach churns, so I hand it back to him, not sure I can keep anything down right now. I'm reeling at everything that transpired. The near-death experience, seeing people die before me, seeing Ash decapitate someone with the ease of cutting a slice of bread. This is a side of Aislinn she's always tried hard to shield me from. Now I know why. Her ruthlessness fills me with prickly dread.

Aric's strong hand lands on my shoulder, "Are you hurt, Your Highness?" he asks, his eyes narrowing on my neck. I can feel blood trickling—not a gush, which is good, but it'll still need attending to. If only I had a mirror on me to assess the damage, and some of my salves to take away the pain.

"I'm fine," I lie.

Aislinn glares at me, "Liar. Let me see." She approaches, staring at my neck. Aric rips a corner of his shirt off and hands it to her. She dabs the blood away with steady hands.

"Thank the Gods it's shallow. You'll want to clean it and use one of your antibiotic ointments on it, but it'll heal in a few days," she lets out a breath, then surprises me by pulling me tightly into a hug.

With that embrace, the ruthless warrior has been put back into her box, and my caring sister has returned.

"I was so scared, Elana." Her voice shakes, betraying her emotions. "Why did you leave us?"

"I'm sorry Ash," I release her, "I got so upset seeing that play, hearing the crowd. They really believe that I stole your crown. I needed to get some air; it was too much."

"I'm sorry you had to see that horrible performance. Did you see how the actress playing me sobbed? I would never..." She trails off, her attempt at humor falling short. "Listen, sister. None of those people know what the Hells they're talking about."

Ash suddenly shares a dark look with Aric over my shoulder, and then says "Now, we need to get out of here in case any of their buddies decide to come snooping."

She picks up my mask, although it's beyond repair, splattered with mud and blood. She tosses it back down, takes hers off, and hands it to me, "You wear mine, I'll wear Aric's, and he can show off his scowl to everyone."

We quickly exchange masks and head out of the alleyway, heading straight for the stables.

On our way back to the castle, Aric leads us, and Aislinn and I ride side-by-side on the path.

"I have to tell you something, sister," Ash says quietly. She's been uncharacteristically quiet since we left Sandral.

My eyes widen, and I lean in closer to her on instinct—not as easy as it would seem while on horseback, "What is it?"

She takes a deep breath, "Father knew there might be some unrest in the capital city. He asked me to take you to the festival and report back if we heard or saw anything that hinted at riots or rebellion."

I gape at her. She *knew* and she didn't say anything to me? "Why didn't you tell me? Why let me walk in there naive, when you knew the citizens hated me?"

"Because I didn't believe him. I never imagined people would be that upset by the Crowning Ceremony, or that they'd be bold enough to speak out against our family like that. I'm sorry, sister. If I'd known, I would have prepared you, armed you, protected you better," she says, her bright blue eyes pleading with me. She's protecting me, even though

I'll eventually be her queen and responsible for the entire kingdom, she will always try to protect me. The thought cools my temper slightly. I relax back into the saddle. Gods curse me, I can never stay mad at Aislinn. I shake my head at her.

"No more keeping secrets from me Ash. I know there were some things you couldn't tell me as the heir apparent growing up, but I hope you trust me enough to tell me everything from now on," I say.

She nods, smiling at me. "Of course, I promise."

My mind reels. I think of Aric escorting me from dinner and guarding my door last night. "Aric, did you know about the unrest too?"

He turns his head and regards me, "Yes. But I do not apologize for it. Everything I do is to keep you safe."

Fair enough, I guess. He is my guard.

Aislinn catches my gaze and rolls her eyes at him. While she and Aric are friendly towards each other now, it wasn't always that way between them. She's always hated the restrictions that come with having a personal guard. When she was fifteen years old she bested her guard in sword fighting, archery, knife-throwing, and running. After that she threw a fit, insisting that she would never train again unless our parents got rid of her shadow. She refused to leave her room for a week before they finally reassigned him. I was thirteen at the time and got it into my head that I could be just like Ash.

When I was first assigned Aric as a guard, I constantly fought him. Like Aislinn, I didn't think a guard was necessary, and I hated him out of principle. I wanted to be brave and strong like my older sister. Because I hated him, Ash did too. We were always a team that way.

It took weeks of Aric's constant presence before I finally felt bad enough to talk to him, and months before I actually *wanted* to talk to him. He wore down my harshness with kind words and by being a constant companion when Ash had to attend to her training. He kept me out of trouble as best as he could with my mother, and even convinced me to return to the castle a few times when I'd run away.

Over time, he wore Ash down too, much the same way he did me. She accepted that he was strong enough to protect me, especially since she didn't have time to protect me herself. Since the three of us never had much spare time to form many friendships, it's always been us. Thinking of our close bond brings a smile to my face as we ride up to the castle stables.

"Shit," Ash mutters under her breath, seeing Father stride towards us as we dismount. I try to swing my leg over my horse but suck in a quick, painful breath. I'm sorer than ever, and afraid I won't have the strength to dismount Misty safely. Aric sees my silent struggle and quickly helps me down. We hand our horses off to the attendants and look at each other. We're covered in varying amounts of blood, and I've got a wound on my neck. I'm suddenly anxious about how this conversation will go.

"Daughters," he calls, his voice pleasant—for now. "How was the festival?"

When we're less than a horse length away from him, his gaze swoops between us, eyebrows pulling together in concern, then anger as his eyes snap to my neck. "What happened? Are you alright?"

I nod my head, "Yes, Father, we're alright. Thanks to Aislinn and Aric."

The King looks to Ash and she nods, as if confirming something separately. "Sir Aric and I got separated from Elana, and three men cornered her in an alleyway. We found her and killed them. The wound on her neck is shallow, but I believe she needs to attend to it."

Father turns back to me, gently raising my chin so he can appraise my neck. "Yes, I agree. Go get yourself cleaned up and bandaged." He dismisses me and I turn to go, but the ground starts shaking as he faces Ash and Aric.

"How did this happen? What do you mean you got separated?" he snaps.

I whip back around, determined not to let them receive punishment for my mistake. "Father, it's not their fault. I got upset about something I'd seen and ran away from them. There were so many people there that I got lost in the crowd."

Rock roils under my feet, and I work my muscles to steady myself on the uneven ground. Father takes a deep breath, pinching the bridge of his nose. "Elana, you are Adrithia's future now. If something happened to you, it would have repercussions for us all."

Of course he's right. Whether or not I accept it, I have a destiny ahead of me. A future that doesn't belong only to me, but to everyone in this Kingdom. "I'm sorry, Father. It won't happen again."

The ground slowly stops shaking as the king regards me. I know he's still angry with me, and has every right to be angry with me, but he seems to accept my apology. He nods at the door. "Go tend to your wound, daughter. When you're done, you will not train your body any more today. You'll train your mind."

I dip my head and walk away swiftly, shocked that I escaped punishment. All I can do is hope that Aislinn and Aric escape the same.

Aislinn finds me in my room sometime later, lying on my bed. I have a bandage over my neck to keep my homemade ointment over the cut. Thankfully it's as shallow as Ash thought it was, so it'll heal in a few days. I'm more concerned about my bruised ribs, but there isn't anything I can do for them, other than continue to take long baths with soothing salts and take it easy on the training.

"Did you and Aric get in trouble because of me?" I ask, afraid of the answer.

Ash sighs and joins me on the bed, looking up at the ceiling. "We got yelled at for a while, but for good reason. We almost lost you. If we'd arrived a minute later, you could have died. Father has every right to be scared. Aric and I were too."

She groans and turns over, facing me. "Plus, he wanted to know more about the unrest we saw. I reported the dancing troupe, the one we saw at the square." I sit up, jarring my sore muscles and give her a sharp look. They weren't exactly kind to me, or painting me in a forgiving light, but still. I don't know what our father will do to them. He could easily make them disappear if he wanted to. "Oh, don't give me that look, El, I had to tell him. I don't think he'll throw them in the dungeons, but I think tonight will be their last night in Adrithia."

I breathe a heavy sigh at that and let it go.

"So what are you going to teach me this evening?" I wonder, seeing a notebook in her hands that she's been picking at since walking into my room.

"I thought we could go over what I know of the heirs. You'll need all the inside knowledge possible since you've only met them in passing moments," Aislinn sits up, opening her book.

It sounds like as good a place to start as any, so I roll off the bed and grab parchment, ink, and quill. I dip the tip of the quill into the ink and give my sister a nod.

"Right, so let's start with our neighbors. Ocarin is to our east, ruled by Queen Amira and King Edward Ashfall. Queen Amira possesses Enya blessed abilities, and she's an incredibly strong wielder. Their eldest son and heir is Prince Aidan. He's tall, built like a warrior, arrogant, and quick to anger, like his mother. Of all the heirs, he's the most dangerous. I'd advise you to stay away from him."

"Moving on to our northern neighbors, the kingdom of Aaranor," Aislinn continues. "Prince Rian is the heir."

She doesn't stop until she has gone over all the kingdoms of Astrellia, their current kings and queens, their heirs, their relationship with us, and their chief imports and exports. It's getting late by the time Aric knocks on my door and informs us that he is to escort us to dinner. I guess our parents aren't taking any more chances with me.

Once we get to the dining hall, Aric bows, whispers "good luck" to us, and then heads to the kitchen to snag his own dinner. Mother and Father sit at their respective ends of the table, the first course already set for us. Aislinn and I exchange a concerned look and take our seats in the center, facing each other.

We wait for Father to start eating before we slowly dig in.

"How is your neck, Elana?" Father asks, staring at the white bandage that wraps around my neck.

"It's slightly sore, but doesn't cause me any trouble," I say.

I notice Aislinn staring down at her food as if she's going to be sick all over it. My stomach drops, seeing her upset.

"Thank the Gods you're alright," Mother says, sounding genuinely concerned. My attention flickers to her, and I nod my head in acknowledgement. "How is training going?"

At that question the sadness leaves me, "It's going well. Aislinn is a great teacher."

"You're a good pupil, El," Ash smiles at me.

"Are you practicing with real weapons yet?" Father questions.

"We start with swords tomorrow," Ash responds directly to him, and he nods his head, seemingly satisfied.

The rest of dinner goes by slowly, with some more small talk and questions about what topics we've covered so far in the educational part of training.

Our parents seem satisfied with what we've covered since yesterday morning. I have a feeling these meals will be a common occurrence with only nineteen days left until I leave.

Chapter Six

"Your stance is all wrong, you're off-balance, and it's like I can hear the daydreams in your head," Aislinn snaps at me four days later. I'm huffing, hands on my knees, trying to catch my breath. She's been drilling me for days on basic parrying and attacking, and I'm still as uncoordinated as a child.

"We have fifteen days left to prepare you for the toughest challenge you might ever face in your life, and your head is in the clouds. You have to focus!"

"I'm trying, Ash," I wheeze, even though I'm well aware that my mind has been wandering. I keep thinking about the Gods, worrying what the challenges will be. I imagine having to fight the other heirs one-on-one, or facing a giant in battle. As for the difficulty of climbing a mountain itself, there's no way to prepare myself for that here. We don't have any comparable mountains in Adrithia to practice on. Our one peak is near the Dark Forest in the southern part of our kingdom, and we don't have time to travel seven days there and back to condition my body for the climb, especially when there are other survival skills I need to learn.

Father has been giving me basic mountain survival lessons instead. He mentioned that the air is more difficult to breathe the higher one climbs. But what would that feel like? I can't imagine air being difficult to breathe.

Ash picks up my fallen wooden sword, sighing heavily. She's been increasingly short with me these past few days. I think Father has been putting pressure on her to make sure I'm ready—a tall order.

"The other heirs are expecting to see someone who will pull their own weight and won't need any assistance on the journey. When they see you struggle to hold a sword upright, they might try to throw you off a cliff themselves."

"These longswords are too long for me. Don't we have anything shorter?" I grumble, as if that's my only problem.

"Father requested that you learn with a longsword. He doesn't want enemies to get close to you, which I understand."

I swing the wooden sword, feeling off-balance. "And what do you think I should be practicing with?"

Ash drops her offensive stance, relaxing for a moment. "I think you would be better suited to dual blades. Perhaps daggers or dual short swords. I'll talk to Father and see about switching your weapon."

"Thanks Ash," I say, beaming at her.

She narrows her eyes at my feet. "Plant your feet. Wider. Keep your knees bent. What if Aidan Ashfall decides to shove you off the mountain range? With a base like that he would barely have to touch you. You'd topple over with a strong wind."

I roll my eyes at her but correct my stance. "I think you're overreacting a bit. Do you really think the other heirs would risk the wrath of the Gods after they made their choice?"

Her only response is a grunt. Okay, so she *does* think they would risk it.

She's acting like I'm useless, even though there's one skill that will keep me alive. "You know I'm good with a bow. I don't see why I have to carry more than one weapon."

I'm more grateful than ever for all those stolen moments with her in the archery field. On my tenth birthday my mother gave me the choice of what I wanted to specialize in during my "womanly duties" training. My choices were stitching, playing an instrument, dancing, or healing. I chose the art of medicines. This was one topic she wasn't prepared enough to teach me, so she hired a tutor and purchased the best books from across the kingdom. During the one hour every day when I was supposed to be gathering medicinal herbs, I spent mere minutes gathering, then sneak away to learn archery from Aislinn.

She taught me the lessons she received from the weapons master hours before. It was the one thing we could practice without being caught on account of how far the practice field was away from the castle.

"What if you run out of arrows?" Aislinn asks as she crosses her arms over her chest. "What if your bow string breaks or you drop it or it's stolen?"

"I'll ration the arrows, bring an extra string, and keep it on my person at all times." I smile, silently pleading with her to take it easy on me.

She slams her wooden sword into the ground tip-first and crosses her arms at her chest. "Elana, you have to start taking this seriously. The Gods are going to throw everything they have at you. I know this isn't your choice, but we have to make the best of it."

Her words are a cold ice bath in the middle of summer. There's only so much of this I can take before I'm a trembling ball of nerves. Of course I didn't think I'd ever be chosen. It's unheard of for the younger sibling to be the heir. Unfortunately for us, the Gods are beholden to their own whims.

"I don't understand why they want me, when you're...you," I gesture at her, because everything about her screams heir of the Kingdom of Adrithia. The strong one, the brave one. The one that Adrithians would rally around, defend with their last breath.

"We don't command the Gods. You know that as well as I. I'm choosing to believe they have a plan for us both," she says, then squares off against me, "Okay, enough talking. Pick up your sword and come at me with everything you've got."

I do. Over and over and over again.

Until I can hold the sword without my arms shaking. Until I plant my feet and stack my hips subconsciously. Until I can lunge with my core and not my arms. Until the blisters on my hands start to build calluses instead of bleed. Only then does Aislinn move on from the sword to teaching daggers, with Father's permission.

Ten days in we take a break from physical and mental training. Today Father requested that Aislinn and I meet him in his study after we break our fast.

We're seated in front of his cold stone desk. He finishes a cup of tea as he scrawls his signature on a piece of parchment, rolls it up, then rings in his personal courtier, Sir Rigel Brand.

"This is the correspondence for Tierth, see that it's sent out via hawk today," He hands the parchment to his Rigel, who bows sharply and makes a swift exit. Our specialty trained hawks were bred over generations to be able to deliver messages across the continent. They're much swifter than carrier pigeons, although we also keep a healthy population of those, to deliver messages more discreetly.

"Trouble down south, Father?" Aislinn asks, narrowed gaze on him.

My brows pull together. I'm not aware of any conflicts we're involved in. No one has mentioned anything. Tierth is one of our larger southern-most cities. Located near the

Shallow Sea, and to the east of the dreaded Dark Forest, it's a port town. An important trade hub and a safe harbor for ships from other kingdoms making their way across the treacherous sea.

"I wouldn't call it *trouble*," he says, leaning back in his chair and leveling a gaze at us. "Some unrest has been popping up ever since the crowning ceremony. I wrote to the Duke of Tierth to get his people in line, or else he can expect a royal visit soon."

Aislinn nods her head, leaning back into her chair, striking a pose nearly identical to our father's. I briefly wonder what a royal visit would entail, and why the threat of it would be enough to staunch the unrest.

"Now, Elana, I'm sorry to take you away from your physical training, but I'd like to cover the challenges of my generation and what I remember my mother told me of her generation."

I nod my head and he sits forward, swiping a hand at his table, which instantly changes shape. The surface goes from smooth to rocky, resembling the maps I'd seen of the Gods' Peaks. He motions to it, and it reforms. It rumbles to a stop and I realize we're looking at a close-up of the first peak of the mountain range. Gods, earth power is something special to behold.

"My journey started off simple enough. We made the ascent up the first of the peaks with little interruption. We were three days into our journey when a shattering earthquake shook the mountain. We had been traveling through a great ravine with sheer rock on either side, rocks that couldn't be climbed, even by the best of us." The model shifts, showing the small crack of a ravine in the mountainside with walls rising higher than our castle on each side. A flick of his hand sends pieces of rock tumbling down into the ravine.

"The earthquake broke off chunks of the rocks and blocked our path. For hours we tried to figure out how to dig through to the other side, cutting our hands open on sharp edges and exhausting ourselves to move one boulder, but to no avail. The other four heirs wanted to turn back, to find another way up the mountain. But here is your first lesson, Elana: there is always only one way forward. Either you figure out a way forward or you die."

Chills run through my spine, keeping me rooted in my chair, eyes fixed on my father's depiction of his trial.

"That was the only way forward, so while the others took a break and tried to plan how far they'd need to backtrack out of the ravine, I found a large log and used it to lift boulders as tall as me." His model shifts and shows him using the leverage of the log to move boulders. "At last, I hit a critical weak point, and the whole pile of rocks tumbled down. Luckily, the Goddess Avani chose that moment to bless me with her powers and I was able to stop the rocks from crushing us all," he finishes, the table becoming smooth granite once again.

"What do you make of it?" he asks, staring at me. Testing, waiting.

"It was more a test of your intelligence than your strength or fighting prowess," I say hopefully. "The Goddess didn't expect you to physically move the rocks."

He nods at me, smiling slightly. "The Gods and Goddesses don't need the best fighters, because those gifted with their abilities won't be using metal weapons in battle anyway. Strength is, of course, helpful for surviving on the journey, and could be useful in case your powers are somehow nullified, but what they are really trying to figure out is who would make the best vessel for their power. I assume that Aislinn has already told you what traits each of the Gods possesses and looks for?"

"Yes, Father," I say, smiling at Ash.

"Good. And do you have one in mind that you think might suit you?" he asks, leaning back once again, resting his hand on his clean-shaven chin.

Again, I look at Ash, who looks like she's about to speak, but Father interrupts her. "No, don't look at your sister for this. I have no doubt she has a few in mind. I want to hear from you, Elana. Which god do you feel drawn to?"

I think back to all the traits Ash taught me. Definitely not fire, I'm not hot-headed enough for that. I don't think I'm a good fit for earth or metal, either.

"Maybe the god of water, Kai, or the air god, Sepher?" I don't feel a particularly strong pull towards any, but these two seem the most likely.

Father hums, staring at me, "Going into the journey I felt a pull towards two of them as well, and knew that the Goddess Avani was testing me when she sent that earthquake. I felt her presence the whole time, like a chill down my spine. It's not uncommon to feel unsure of which god will choose you. It's not a simple task to assess your own strengths and weaknesses.

"Oftentimes, the Gods seek out something inside of you that you don't even know exists. Being steadfast in the face of a monumental task was something that Goddess Avani appreciated. Once I was gifted with the power, I quickly realized that control over the power comes from willpower. It uses your energy and takes your creativity to wield."

To demonstrate this, the perfectly round globe near his desk lifts off its pedestal and reforms, shaping into a perfect cube.

"The limits of this power are only what your body and your imagination say they are."

I marvel at the display, wondering what the true limits I possess are. Even Ash sits forward in her chair, eyes on the cube as it shapes itself into a perfect replica of our mother's face, scowl and everything. Ash and I immediately burst out in laughter.

The king chuckles with us, waving his hand and smoothing the rock back into a ball, twirling slightly on its stand.

He tells us about the other challenges of his generation. The fire goddess Enya set an entire forest aflame. The flames were outmaneuvered by the queen of Ocarin, who kept everyone safe and earned the Goddess' blessing. The heir of Hotharia was gifted with the metal god Tolliver's ability after he was able to craft a key from a hairpin that opened a steel door to a cave. It was the queen of Aaranor who received the blessing of water from the God Kai after they all battled a sea-serpent that lived inside an ancient pool inside the cave, and she struck the final blow. And finally, the God Sepher granted his power to the king of Melinor after he was able to disrupt a tornado as part of a vicious storm.

Father's storytelling slowly starts to lift a stone from my gut. Only one of the challenges ended up being about fighting prowess. The rest could have been completed by nearly anyone. I have a chance.

"What will your strategy be to gain the trust of the other heirs and become invaluable?" Father asks, breaking me out of my reverie.

"Oh," I stammer, my brain working slowly as I struggle to think of what to say, "I think—well maybe I could...use archery, because I'm already decent at it..."

I trail off, entirely unsure of what the strategy will be. I glance over at Ash, and she has her gaze locked on the table, brows together and lips tightened. She's unsure too. Well, there goes the little bit of hope I was feeling.

Father sighs and stands up, putting his hands behind his back, and stares out of his window overlooking Sandral in the distance.

"Your mother was adamant about your training in the womanly ways to make us a prosperous match. If it were up to me, I'd have had you trained alongside Aislinn." He pauses, turning back around and looking at me in a way I almost think is sorrowful.

"I'm sorry. I should have insisted that at the very least you learn how to defend yourself." He leans against the brick frame of the window. "However, your mother's training did give you one advantage as far as I can see."

My eyes widen and I sit up straighter. "What's that?"

"Healing," he says. "You possess great knowledge in wound care and illnesses, and you know how to forage ingredients for your own salves and medicines."

He's right. I doubt the others will have much experience with this, as most castles employ their own healers. We haven't needed one in the castle in years because I've been here, treating most wounds and ailments of our residents and staff. There are a few skilled healers in Sandral that assist if there are any severe illnesses or injuries, but I'm perfectly capable of taking care of most ailments myself. The number of times I've stitched up Aislinn's injuries from training accidents, or just general accidents, should give me good reference for anything I'd see up on the mountain.

"That's a good plan," Ash says, nodding at me.

"The first few peaks will have ample resources, but the latter peaks are mostly barren. You'll have a hard time finding any healing ingredients the further you go. Plan to take most everything with you, preferably dried," Father says.

We plan what I will bring with me and what I can risk trying to gather on the mountain. I'll only bring the necessities to save on weight. After all, I'll be carrying everything needed with me for weeks.

Ash mentions adding strength training to our already arduous schedule. I groan, knowing I'll be crawling to my bed later tonight.

CHAPTER SEVEN

I stand on a cliff's edge, a straight drop before me and a sheer mountain at my back. I scream, but the sound is stolen by the wind. I can't hear anything but the roaring of the gale around me. How did I get here?

Rain assaults my eyes and I squeeze them shut against the torrent. I back myself up against the face of the mountain and sink to my knees, covering my head with my hands. The ledge I'm on is as wide as I am tall, but the amount of water rushing over it threatens to wash me away.

Rock bites into my hands and knees as I shuffle along the edge, stumbling along blindly. I have to keep going. I don't know how I know this, I just do. I see a cave ahead of me. I stagger to my feet and take slow, shaky steps towards it.

Lightning spears the side of the mountain and a horse-sized boulder breaks free, heading right for me. I have a split second to make a choice. Death by rock, or jump. I turn towards the ledge and throw myself into the dark abyss with a yell of frustration.

My muscles all spasm and I wake up bathed in cold sweat, gulping in breaths. It takes me a few moments to realize where I am, and that I'm not in any danger.

A knock sounds at the door to my rooms, and Aric enters. "Your Highness, are you alright?

Of course he heard me having a nightmare. He's hardly left my side these past few weeks. "Yes, Aric, I'm alright. It was only a bad dream."

I sit up and brush my damp auburn hair out of my face.

"Can I get you anything?" he asks, concern darkening his features.

"More time, perhaps?" I chuckle without humor. The past few days I've been sick with nerves, hardly eating, feeling nauseous all the time. I had a panic attack yesterday that Aislinn had to help me work through with deep breaths.

I leave tomorrow. One day. That short span of time is all that separates me from the mountains. I spent last night packing my belongings with Ash. More like, I packed, then she emptied my rucksack and repacked about half of what I thought I needed. That woman is ruthless.

Aric gives me a sad smile, "I wish I could," he says, moving into my room and shutting the door behind him. "There is something I *can* do, though."

My brows go up, and I get out of bed, throwing my dressing robe over my nightgown. "What is that?"

How did this muscled statue of a man figure out a way to help me with the challenges? Maybe the Gods spoke to him, or maybe he found a real-life seer, someone who can see the future.

The rare gift of sight was reportedly granted by the Gods in times of great need, and when the need was over, the power disappeared again for centuries. To my knowledge, there are less than a hundred accounts of a seer existing in the time since written history. The last account was over a century ago. I brace myself for whatever miracle my oldest friend is about to reveal.

"Run away with me," he says, closing the distance between us, an oddly frantic look on his face.

"W-what?" I sputter, not quite sure if I heard him correctly.

Aric grabs my arm, his grip firm, "Your Highness, I've already secured passage for us both to my homeland. You'll have sanctuary there and we can find you a job, perhaps as a healer. Please leave with me."

I go cold with shock. He wants me to *run away*? To his homeland? The unnamed village he never talks about, because he claims the memory of it fills him with shame for how poor and desolate its people are?

Leaving, running away, hiding. These are acts I did as a child, to get away from my mother, from the castle, and from the future I had no say in. It's never even crossed my mind to run away from the title of heir, and how could it when an entire kingdom's future rests on my shoulders?

I look into his pleading blue eyes, "If I leave, our kingdom will be at risk of war. How could I make a decision like that?"

He shakes his head, releasing my arm and running his hands through his hair. "I'd rather a thousand people die if it means you're safe by my side. I can't risk losing you, El."

He has only called me my nickname a handful of times. Each time it feels like a shock to my chest. More shocking, however, is Aric putting his hand behind my head and pressing his lips to mine.

His mouth moves against mine, and my thoughts eddy out of my mind. Oh Gods, Aric is kissing me. I start to open my lips to his, to say something or shout in shock, and he takes it as permission to angle his head and deepen the kiss, sliding his tongue between my teeth. I gasp from the intrusiveness of it and push back. He breaks off and steps back, eyes wide.

"I apologize. That was too sudden." He chuckles to himself, but I'm reeling on the inside. "I wanted to tell you this years ago. I love you, Elana. I want you as my wife."

My lips part, but I say nothing. I don't know what to say.

He loves me? He wants to marry me? He's telling me this now, when my life has been flipped on its head? As if things weren't confusing enough when the phoenix put the crown on my head, Aric goes and adds his feelings into the mix.

We kissed once before when I was nineteen because I'd never been kissed and I wanted to know what it felt like before being married off to Lord Percival for his father's ridiculously large metal mines. But we were both clear afterward that it meant nothing.

He plows forward, as if my lack of response opens up the floodgates for him to pour out his heart.

"We could have a life together. We could lead different lives, be different people. You won't have to worry about the dangers of being an heir. If you go to the mountains, you will die," he says, grabbing me by both shoulders and looking intently at my face.

This is Aric, my friend, who has always protected me. He cares for me and wants to marry me. I should be happy. But another part of me roars in defiance. He's underestimating everything about me. I focus on that, and a rush of anger rolls through me. "You don't know that. I'm stronger than you think."

"The other heirs will kill you. They'll see you as an unknown variable, a threat. You're not trained like they are. They've been working towards gaining their powers and leading their kingdoms their whole lives. You've had less than three weeks."

"Ash trained me well, Aric," I say, trying to wiggle my shoulders out of his grasp. "And there's no way of knowing what the other heirs will do. Ash was on good terms with them, and I doubt they'd risk retaliation by outright killing me."

Aric pulls back slightly, running a hand through his long blond hair. "I know one of them, and he will most certainly try."

He *knows* one of them? I twist my torso and rip my shoulder from the grasp of his other hand. "They would be crazy to want war. And how do you know one of them?"

"It doesn't matter how I know, that's part of my past. What matters is getting you out of here. I have spare horses and a wagon for us. We can leave right now." He straightens and nods his head to himself, as if everything is solved. He grabs my arm and starts to tug me along next to him towards the door, as if he'll put me on the back of a horse and ride away without a second thought.

"Aric stop," I rip my arm from him once more, narrowing my eyes at him. "I refuse your offer. I will not be leaving with you."

Aric startles. "Your Highness—"

"No," I tell him. "I may have been named heir as a surprise, but I will fulfill my duty to my kingdom. I won't let my family or my people down."

He meets my eyes with wide blue eyes. The eyes that once reminded me of the ocean, with their endless depths and calming waters. They seem frozen now.

I hate that I'm hurting him, but he needs to know this is my final decision. I soften my tone, "Please understand, Aric. The future of Adrithia lies with me. It may not be the future I always hoped for myself, but I can't turn away from it."

I grip his hand in mine, squeezing gently. "You're my best friend. I know you're worried about me. But you don't have to be. I'll survive, I promise. I will come back."

He looks down at our clasped hands and clears his throat. "Very well. You give me no choice but to believe in you. Just make sure you come back to me."

I smile up at him, "I will."

At that moment, the door to my suite bursts open and Aislinn struts through, wearing her training clothes.

"Rise and shine sister, it's time for—" She stops abruptly when she sees Aric standing there holding my hand and me in my robe, sleeping gown still on underneath. Her gaze holds mine, as if checking for any sign of danger before she breaks into a smirk.

"Well, well, well, I think someone forgot to invite me to—" she gestures at us, "—whatever awkward party this is."

My cheeks blaze with embarrassment as I pull my hands out of Aric's. "Ugh, Ash, nothing happened. Please go away."

Aric's gaze finally breaks and he straightens, clearing his throat. "Excuse me, Princesses. I'll return to my post."

Ash and I watch him go, my sister's eyes alight with devious interest, her brows raised.

"Spill it," she says as soon as he closes the door behind him.

I walk over to my wardrobe, throw open the doors, and take some steadying breaths.

"He asked me to run away with him," I say.

Ash starts and joins me in front of the wardrobe. "He did *what*?"

"He basically told me that I have no chance of surviving, because the heirs will kill me." I start biting my nails, staring at my sister. She looks at me with wide eyes and an open mouth.

"And then he told me he loved me and wanted me to be his wife. Oh, and then he kissed me." I turn back towards my wardrobe and pull out the first training outfit I set my fingers upon.

Ash slams the wardrobe closed and says with a lethal calmness, punctuating each word by drawing a hidden throwing dagger from her clothes. "He. Did. What."

I take in the three daggers and the cold glint in her eyes. "Shit, Ash, it's okay. I didn't *dislike* the kiss," I say, hoping to diffuse the situation.

She turns sharply towards me, eyes narrowed, holding her daggers in a grip that I haven't been able to perfect yet, but I know she has lethal precision with.

"It was weird, okay? But it wasn't bad. It's Aric. He's tall and gorgeous and has muscles for days. I'd be a fool to not...appreciate him," I say, throwing the training attire on my bed and plopping down next to it.

Ash sighs, stashing her daggers once more as she sits down on the bed next to me.

"He *is* attractive," she says, "and he's your closest friend. I'm sure he wants to protect you, like I do. What did you say when he asked you to run away with him?"

Her voice is carefully neutral, but I can hear the undercurrent of curiosity—and something else.

"I told him I'll be taking a hike. Up a mountain. In the Gods' Territory."

Ash smiles and her shoulders relax, as if she was worried I would want to leave with him. "When you come back, would he make you happy?"

I consider for a moment what a life with Aric would look like, but I can't picture it. I can't imagine walking arm-in-arm with him through the city or having dinners sitting across the table from him. Riding horses during our carefree afternoons. I can't picture any of it with him.

My head shakes before any words come out. "No. I don't think he would."

"I didn't think so, El. Don't settle. Find someone that fills your heart with so much joy you can't imagine life without them."

She picks up my outfit off the bed and shoves it at me. "Now get dressed. We have a lot to do today. You'll want to get some extra sleep tonight, too. The journey will be long, we'll have to leave right at dawn."

On horseback, it'll take almost two days to reach the Gods' Territory, that piece of land owned by no kingdom, but instead ruled over by the five Gods. Adrithia's capital is located relatively close to the neutral land, so I'll have a short trip compared to the other heirs.

"Wait, we?" I ask as I jump off the bed, heading behind my privacy screen by the wardrobe. "I thought no one was allowed to accompany me?"

"No one can be with you as you enter the Gods' Territory, but no one will know if I travel with you up until that point."

I pause, pulling up the soft leather leggings, "You're expecting more trouble on the road, aren't you?"

She doesn't answer me at first, and I worry that she's going to lie to me again. Until she blows out a long breath and says, "hopefully not, but I don't want to leave this to chance."

"I'm happy I don't have to make the journey to the Gods' Territory alone," I say, pulling back my hair into a swift knot at the base of my head. I step out from behind the screen. "However, if you're going to talk to me about anything else this morning, I need sustenance first."

"Good, you read my mind. That's what I came in here for anyway. We're having breakfast together. Our last breakfast together before the journey." Aislinn tugs my arm into hers, and we walk out the door together.

Aric, standing near the outside of my door, bows and follows us. He says nothing as we walk, and I exchange an uncomfortable glance with Ash.

At our dining table, a feast is prepared. Pastries, still-steaming bread, eggs, fruit, pork belly—there's more variety here than I've ever seen.

"Gwen and the kitchen staff wanted to send you off with this banquet tomorrow, but I informed them how uncomfortable it is to ride horses on a full stomach, so they decided to treat you today." Ash grins from ear to ear, watching me take in all the food with an open mouth.

Our parents are nowhere in sight, but I practically skip to my seat. We settle into our usual chairs and dig in. We're a few bites in when the doors open and our parents join us.

"I see you've already started. Couldn't wait for us?" Mother quips, sitting on her chair gracefully.

"Sorry, Mother," Ash says around a bite of buttered and honeyed bread. "I know how hard Gwen worked on this and didn't want any of it to get cold."

Mother smiles slightly, rolls her eyes, and scoops fruit onto her plate. Father is already tearing into a scone with abandon, scooping meat and boiled eggs onto his plate. He catches my eye and winks. I know where Ash and I get our love of food.

"How do you feel, Elana?" Mother asks, staring pointedly at me.

"I'm okay," I say. And for now, it's true. The nerves haven't set in yet for the day. I think the whole situation with Aric this morning threw my head out of whack.

"You should visit the Temple today to pray to the Gods before your journey," Mother says. As if any last-minute groveling from me will secure the gift—or pity—of the Gods.

I catch my sister's gaze, hesitant to commit until I consult with my schedule-keeper. She merely shrugs at me, as if saying the choice is mine.

Growing up we never sought out the Temple on our own. The Gods have always been part of our lives, due to Father having the earth goddess' powers, but as a family we rarely ever made an appearance at Temple. I recall Mother going a few times when our grandmother was stricken with her illness, and the few times when either Ash or I were injured or sick.

I once asked Father why he never visited the temple, to thank the Goddess Avani for her gift. He told me that he thanked her every day by using his abilities to help the people of the kingdom thrive and maintain the Astrellian peace that's persisted for hundreds of years. He built the Temple in Sandral to provide a safe place for all citizens to worship the Gods, no matter which elemental god they pray to.

There are the Gods of the underworlds as well, but luckily praying to them has fallen out of fashion. There are three realms of hell, each with its own ruling demon god. Not much is known about the Hells, and our citizens prefer to keep it that way. We know from ancient texts that the Hells were sealed off from our realm long before Astrellia was ever named. The idea of it is enough to scare children straight when threatened with the prospect of entering the demonic realms.

Regardless, I'm not keen on returning to Sandral anytime soon, and I don't think the Gods would appreciate a half-hearted prayer begging for a boon from someone who has never prayed to them before.

"I'll think about it," I say, cracking open a boiled egg. A noncommittal answer, but thankfully Mother doesn't pry further.

"What is on your schedule for today?" Father asks, studying me over his mouthful of pork belly.

"We're going to train this morning." Ash answers for me, "Nothing too intense, so you can ride your horse without discomfort tomorrow. Then this afternoon we can head into Sandral if you wish. If not, then you get the afternoon off. Either way, tonight we'll double check to make sure you packed everything you'll need."

I nod, thinking the plan sounds as good as any.

Father stands up and motions Rigel over. His courtier holds a small, wrapped bundle in his arms, which Father takes from him. "Good. That's good. Perhaps this morning you can practice with these, Elana."

I stop chewing and stare at the wrapped bundle he presents to me. I stand up, swallowing hard, trying not to choke on the bite of egg that feels like a rock in my throat.

The bundle is heavier than I expect from such a small size. I unwrap the thick cream-colored cotton and a glint of metal catches my eyes. Inside are two stunning twin daggers in black sheaths. I set aside the cloth and one dagger so I can unsheathe the other. There are no gems on the pommel, no intricate designs on the hilt, but it fits perfectly in my hand, slightly curved to fit my fingers. It has only a short, starkly plain cross-guard with a notch near the hilt, and the blade curves elegantly to a wicked point. The design is simple, polished, and lethal. The hilt seems to hum in my grasp. The whole dagger is about the length of my forearm.

"These daggers have been in our family for generations," Father says, nodding down at them. "They were forged long ago by one of our metal-gifted ancestors. The blades never dull or tarnish, and they always find their mark. Put your trust in these weapons, and they will serve you well."

I start, looking up at him. "You say that like they're alive."

Father gives me a sad smile. "Our ancestor, Hale Sable, made a great sacrifice for our family many years ago. He poured some of his life's essence into his weapons. They don't live and breathe as we do, but that doesn't mean they're not alive. The power they were imbued with lives on and serves our family well."

"Why, why would he do that?" I ask, staring at the pristine metal of the blade. It appears to wink back at me.

"No one knows why he did. We only know that he created a trove of weapons using his own soul to bind his power to them for all time. He gave his life to create these weapons, and they are called the Hale Trove in honor of his sacrifice. After he forged them, the trove was passed down to his heir, who passed it down to their heir, so on and so forth. Such as it will always be in our family."

"These weapons have a sibling," Father continues, looking at Ash, "Aislinn possesses Hale's sword. She won it from me during the last tournament."

Ash smiles, as if remembering the moment fondly.

"I thought that fight was to prove you didn't need a guard," I say, narrowing my eyes at her.

"It was," she says, shrugging. "I didn't know about the sword until after I won and Father presented it to me."

"As the best warrior in the Adrithia, you earned it. It will serve you far more than it will serve me anymore. I have my own power to utilize if needed," Father moves to sit, picking up his fork again.

I place the blades on the table next to me, about to continue eating when mother quips, "weapons off the table, please."

Ash catches my gaze and rolls her eyes. I stifle a laugh as I wrap up the blades and place them on my lap.

An hour later I'm in the lush green field with Aislinn, swinging around my new blades. The daggers feel at home in my hands. The metal sings when I slash through the air and slice through a straw dummy. Bits of straw scatter in the breeze around me. I smile at the sight of the dummy with a gaping cut through its middle. I'd never been able to cut that deep before, even with a steel sword.

"These daggers feel like they were made just for me," I say to Ash, almost reverently.

She smiles, moving closer as she appraises them. "I feel the same way about my sword."

She draws Hale's short sword out of its sheath. It, too, has a simple design. A sleek black grip with a gleaming diamond-shaped pommel, silver accents throughout and a simple curved guard. The warm weapons in my hand seem to hum in response, and as I step closer to my sister, I feel the humming get more intense.

"Do you feel that too?" I whisper.

"Yes," Ash responds, just as quiet. "These blades were forged with the very soul of our ancestor, I'm sure they recognize each other as kin."

It feels deeper than that. It's like what our father said—they feel alive, sentient. I turn back towards the dummy and swing the daggers, parrying and slicing at an invisible attacker.

"You're doing excellent with those," Ash says. "Let's see how you fare with them against a longer weapon. Come at me, sister."

I balk, turning sharply to face her. "Against your sword? Your actual sword? No, I think not."

"Oh, I think so," she says, advancing on me. "How else will you trust yourself with them in a real fight?"

"No, Aislinn, I can't," I say, backing up. "Use a training sword."

Ash's eyes darken and she raises her arm, aiming her blade at my heart, "No. You need to learn how to trust yourself with these weapons. Like Father said, if you put your trust in them, you won't be led astray."

She gives no warning before she swings her blade at my shoulders. I barely jump away in time. She lunges towards me, and I raise a dagger to deflect. With a quick parry she swipes it away and slashes out at my arm. I don't move out of the way quick enough, and a thin red line opens up on my forearm. It's shallow, and barely hurts, but it's enough to scare me.

"Ash, enough," I pant, launching myself into a forward roll to duck a cut aimed for my neck.

"Stop it!" I'm back on my feet, spinning around in time to block another move with both daggers that would have disemboweled me. I hold them in an X shape, keeping them there for a moment while I gasp for breath. Where the blades connect they seem to pulsate, and it suddenly feels wrong using these weapons against each other.

Ash's face pales as she, too, feels this. In one swift movement she jumps back, yanks her sword away from the hold of my daggers, and sheathes it. I almost sigh in relief, until I see her pull out her spare longsword on her right hip. This one's longer, thinner, and gives her a considerable advantage over my already shortened reach.

She charges, using both hands on the grip, bringing the sword down in a clean arc, and I dodge to the right, narrowly knocking a swift second attack away.

"Fight back, El!" Ash shouts at me as she goes in for another wide attack but leaves her right side open. I almost go for it, but stop myself, pulling my daggers back and tucking them close as I leap to the left, rolling in the grass to avoid her blade.

The sole of her boot connects with my rib cage as I stand. I'm sent flying backwards, losing my grip on my daggers as my back hits the ground. My breath leaves me in a whoosh and I roll over to my side to suck in a few quick breaths. The tip of Aislinn's sword hovers a hair's breadth above my chest. One glance at her expression and I see a simmering, shaking rage there. There's absolutely no way she would actually kill me, but I wouldn't put it past her to severely injure me to prove a point.

"You could have ended it, but you showed mercy. Look where your mercy has gotten you now, sister." Her voice is cold, so cold that I have to stop myself from quaking. I'm rattled, my mind careens, trying to make sense of this version of my sister in front of me. She's the same woman I saw in Sandral, who beheaded a cowering man.

I fight to steady my voice as I say, "I didn't want to hurt you."

At this, she has the nerve to laugh. Not a gleeful, joyful sound, but a sharp bitter noise that bursts from her. "You couldn't hurt me. I wouldn't let you."

I huff from my spot on the ground, still catching my breath.

"If you're out there, facing Gods-know-what, and you decide to show mercy, if you somehow survive the fight you'll be tossed from the mountain and left to rot. The other heirs have been trained to be lethal since they could stand. You must be just as brutal, or else you risk our entire kingdom."

I look down at where her sword is lightly pressed against my chest and feel the guilt creep up my neck. She's right, I know she is. I don't have the luxury of being naive anymore.

Ash pulls her sword away and backs up a step. "Again," she commands, and I listen, picking myself up from the ground. She sinks into a ready stance.

I don't know how to trust myself with these deadly weapons, with protecting Adrithia, and with the power of the Gods. But I do trust that there was a reason why I was chosen. There was a reason why my ancestor gave his life to forge these blades, and why I hold them today.

I take one slow, steady breath, sink into my toes, and launch myself at Aislinn. Her eyes widen slightly and then she moves, efficiently parrying my assaults. With the element of surprise, I'm able to get past her guard, in close where her sword isn't as useful. I feint right and slash left. She uses her steel bracer to knock my blade away and retreats a step, widening the distance between us and creating an opening for her to strike back.

We exchange blows and I start to notice her patterns. The way she puts her weight into her right foot before she lashes out. The way she readies one arm to block attacks after she swings. She's brilliant. The opening I saw before was fabricated for me, to give me the opportunity to strike her.

In our deadly dance, I somehow forget to think about what I'm doing. I simply move. I move with her, against her, in a constant push and pull, a dodge and parry and swipe. The daggers in my hand sing, they call out to me, encourage me, center my focus on this fight, this moment.

She fakes a lunge and spins to the side, aiming for my unprotected back. I flip the grip on one of my daggers and block her attack, slashing out with my second one. She knocks it away with her sword and kicks out, tripping me. I stumble but manage to stay on my feet. I find my balance in time to catch Aislinn's open palm to my left cheek. My head whips to the side and I cry out, dropping one dagger on instinct as I feel the spot on my face where her hand connected.

"Ash, what the Hells!" I shout, narrowing my eyes at her.

"Pick up your blade, Elana. We're not done yet," she says, nodding at it.

"Did you have to hit me so hard?" I ask, grabbing my dagger from the ground.

She actually has the nerve to shrug. I see red. I lunge at her with one dagger high, the other low and close to my body. Ash blocks my high attack with her wrist guard and kicks my stomach before my low attack can connect. I go flying into the dirt. My back hits hard, and my breath whooshes out of me. I lose grip on my daggers and they go flying.

I roll onto my side, taking a few steadying breaths. Ash stands over me, with her arm outstretched. A peace offering. I take her hand.

"Don't attack angry. It blinds you to your environment. Keep a level head and be aware of every possible advantage around you," Ash says as she pulls me to my feet.

I pick up my daggers once more. My grip on them tightens slightly as I ready myself to spar again. The hilts seem to thrum with energy as I take a few practice slices through the air, *Trust me, trust me, trust me,* they call. I let out a breath, surrendering to their pull.

Aislinn lifts her hand to strike, and I pivot on my back foot, dodging the attack and bringing my right blade down in a slashing motion. She uses her sword to parry my blade and I drop my weight into my back foot as I bring my other dagger to her side. She jumps back and we reset ourselves. She comes straight at me, sword arcing down, and I instinctively raise my hands to ward off the attack. A clanging metal sound, and her blade stops. I've caught it in between both of my own. I use my core and drive her sword back towards her side, I'm close enough now to be past her guard. I pull one of my blades away and aim it at her stomach. Her hands are tied up with her sword so she's unable to block. Her vibrant blue eyes snap to mine. My blade pauses against her lower rib cage.

We're both frozen until my hand starts shaking. I take a quick step back, dropping my eyes, sheathing my daggers. The intensity of the sparring match vanishes, and I feel exhausted.

When I look up, Aislinn smiles at me.

"Good work, sister," she says, sheathing her sword.

I shake my head, breath coming unevenly. "I could have hurt you."

She sighs. "Possibly. But you didn't. It was a well-placed strike. If we were on the battlefield, I wouldn't have survived a wound like that."

The way she says it is almost clinical, like she's analyzing the situation for any drawbacks.

"You didn't hesitate that time. You went right for the lethal strike. I'm proud of you for it."

My fists clench to stop them from quivering. "I didn't even think about what it would cost to wound you, Ash."

Ash grabs a skin of water on the stone bench near the sparring field and takes a few sips, handing it out to me.

I accept it with a nod of thanks and gulp down several mouthfuls.

"That's a good thing, El. In a real fight, if you hesitate, you die. If you pull your punches, you die. If you get in your head about the person who's trying to kill you, you die."

I sit down on the cool stone, staring down at my hands. "I don't think I can kill people."

Ash sits next to me, taking the water from me to drain it herself. She's silent for a few moments before she speaks, "It's not easy. I remember everyone I've killed. Of course, it hasn't been that many, but enough that it weighs on me."

I've never heard her talk about this before. She's always been the strong, confident one between us. She never second guesses herself, never shows any weakness.

"I would say it gets easier with time, but it doesn't. It becomes something you learn how to deal with better. Learn how to push those feelings aside and concentrate on who or what you're fighting for. I've found it's less complicated when I'm protecting someone."

I think back to our ordeal in Sandral, how she jumped in immediately to kill that man who threatened me with ease. Would I do the same? If I ever had to protect her, or our parents, or Aric, could I take someone's life without a second thought?

A cold feeling grips my gut, and I think I'll find out sooner than I'd like.

Chapter Eight

Ash and I are walking back to the castle in the late afternoon arm in arm, when Aric jogs over from the stables, falling into step with us on my left side. Ever since this morning I haven't been able to meet Aric's eyes. I felt his gaze on me during breakfast, and while we were walking here before he left to check on our horses for the long ride. I can feel his eyes on me now as I look at his broad chest, at the stables past him—basically anywhere but his face.

"Everything is prepared for your journey tomorrow. Your horses are in good shape, and the kitchen is packing a month's worth of food for each of you," he says.

My cheeks heat, and I feel warmer than usual in the humid summer heat.

"Thank you, Sir Aric," Ash says in a clipped tone. I glance up at her briefly. A muscle in her neck is so tense I'm worried it'll strain.

"Princess Elana, I was hoping I could speak with you for a moment," Aric says, brushing his hand across my arm like he's about to take hold of it. He looks at Ash and then puts his hand back by his side.

I exchange a look with my sister, who's clearly waiting for me to make up my mind. I nod at her and she rolls her eyes but walks into the castle.

"Very well, Aric, let's talk," I say, rounding on him and crossing my arms in front of my chest.

He takes a deep breath, smoothing out invisible wrinkles in his cotton shirt. "I'm sorry for what happened this morning. I didn't mean to kiss you like that. And I never intended to imply that you wouldn't survive the challenges."

I finally work up the nerve to glance at his face. His brow is creased, his eyes large, and his mouth downturned. I can't help but liken his expression to that of a scolded puppy. Seeing it sends a flicker of annoyance through me.

"Thank you for your apology, Aric." I'm unsure of what else there is to say. I haven't had time to think about what happened and how I feel about everything, the kiss and his complete lack of faith in me. But I also don't want to leave with bad blood between us.

"Let's forget it ever happened," I say, forcing a smile.

He lets out a breath and wraps me in a tight hug. "That sounds wonderful, thank you."

After a second or two too long he releases me slightly, only to bend down and plant a kiss on my forehead. My stomach flips and I pull back out of his embrace.

He flashes a sheepish smile and clears his throat, charging forward through the discomfort around us.

"Where are you off to now, Princess?" he asks, taking up his usual post at my left side.

I look at the castle for a few moments, taking in the towering white marble peaks, contrasting against the lush green of the forest and fields on either side of it. It's difficult to imagine leaving this place, the only home I've ever known and will ever know.

"My rooms," I say, fully intending to take the longest bath in Adrithia's history. After tonight, I don't know when I'll be able to bathe again properly. Possibly weeks, but if we get stuck for longer than normal on the mountain, it could be months. According to Aislinn and our ancestors' records, the full journey usually only takes a few weeks, but on occasion has stretched into more than a month.

"Would you like some company?" Aric interrupts my train of anxiety-producing thought with a whole different anxiety-producing thought.

"No, thank you," I blurt out quickly.

Aric stops walking for a beat. "Very well, Your Highness."

I realize how rude I must have sounded. "I would like some time alone to prepare for the challenges ahead," I amend.

He nods, flashing a half smile my way. "I understand, Elana. I can't imagine what must be going through your head."

"It's all very...overwhelming," I say slowly, struggling to articulate the way I feel.

Overwhelmed isn't exactly it, though. It's how everyone expects me to be, but a part of me is excited. In a way, this journey is freedom from a marriage to a stranger, from the wifely duties I was expected to perform. I never wanted to be a queen either, to have the entire kingdom's future rest on my shoulders, but at least I'll be able to make decisions for myself.

My mind wanders to Aislinn and what she'll do when I'm gone. Will she be forced to take my place in the engagement to Lord Percival? I almost laugh out loud. No. Absolutely not, she would never agree to that and no one would dare try to force her to do anything against her will. No, Aislinn will be fine without me. Maybe she'll convince Father to let her spy on a neighboring kingdom or train our armies in combat. The thought is intriguing. I'll have to ask her before we leave.

We reach my doors and Aric grabs my hand, holding it gently. "You know I'd go with you tomorrow if I could, right? I tried, really. Tried to tell your sister that I should be the one to accompany you."

My brows furrow. I hadn't heard that before. "Why did she say no?"

"She said three of us would attract too much attention on the road, and I'm too noticeable."

"Actually, I said you were a big brute who stands out like an oak tree in the middle of a wheat field," Ash says, walking up behind us, brushing between our shoulders and causing Aric to drop my hand.

He shuffles back and forth on his feet. Is he—uncomfortable? Gods, he's been my best friend for years and I've never noticed that he's actually afraid of my sister. I bark a sharp laugh.

"A big brute, Ash, really?" I laugh. "You're not much better, you know."

She playfully smacks my arm, smirking at me.

"We need to travel light and swiftly, El. I don't want anyone on the trip doting on you and letting you think it's okay to stop every few minutes to rest. I'm the best person to defend you if it comes to it and I know the path better than anyone."

Aric scoffs, but there's a playful gleam in his eye. "You know I'm as accomplished a fighter as you, Princess."

"I've put you on your ass before and I will do it again," Ash says, and while I'm not surprised by her skill, I'm surprised neither of them has told me this before.

"How do you know I didn't let you win?" Aric says, a dangerous smile playing on his lips.

"Oh, dear Aric, do you think I don't know how to tell when people are holding back? Unlike some, I know when people are *faking* it." She winks at him, grabs my arm in hers, and walks into my rooms with me, shutting the door firmly behind us.

It's all I can do to contain my giggles.

"Thought you could use a reprieve from the puppy-eyed giant," Ash says, flopping down on the plush green chaise near my fireplace.

"Thanks, Ash," I say, heading to my bathing room. Luckily there is already hot water in the giant tub, courtesy of Senara. Most days she prepares a hot bath for me in the early afternoon, anticipating my sore muscles after training with Ash. I make a mental note to myself to thank her profusely next time I see her.

What feels like hours later I finally pull myself from the tub, wrapping up in my favorite navy silk robe. Ash still lounges on my chaise, reading one of my healing books. It's a journal from one of my healing tutors, an accomplished and skilled woman named Clarisse. She is well known for curing poisons. I studied under her for nearly three years when I was in my late teens. During her stay in the castle, Clarisse doted on Ash and me, always bringing us small presents from her foraging outings.

She regularly traveled to the dark forests in the southern lands of Adrithia to capture rare venomous beasts. She would extract their venom and release them back into the wild when possible. Venom is an important ingredient for creating antidotes. Clarisse is younger than our parents by at least a decade, and if she had been around when our grandmother was poisoned, it's likely she would have survived the ordeal.

After a few years of me being her understudy, Clarisse and my mother got into a row. I remember hearing them scream at each other from outside the castle. I never knew what the fight was about, but my tutor said her tearful goodbyes to Ash and me a day later. We haven't seen her since, although we do occasionally write letters to each other.

"Did you know," Ash says as I come to sit next to her, "that our poison master Clarisse was in Sandral the day of the Crowning Ceremony?"

I startle, whipping my head at her, "She was there?"

"Yes, and apparently Mother ran her off." Ash closes the book, setting it on the table next to her.

"I don't believe it. How do you know?"

She sighs. "Gwen let it slip that Clarisse came to visit the morning of the ceremony. Apparently Clarisse was asking to speak to us, but Mother intercepted her before she could and had the guards throw her out."

I scoff, an ugly sound. "What reason would our mother have for throwing her out?"

"No idea, but I bet it has something to do with why she left in the first place. Mother still won't talk about it. I tried asking her about it the day after the ceremony. She damn near bit my head off for asking. Told me it was none of my business."

I can clearly picture our mother's reaction in my head. She gets the same look of cold fury that Aislinn gets when someone tells her no. Gods help the stubborn, vicious women in our family.

"Hopefully when I return I'll have more pull with our parents and will be able to bring Clarisse back to the castle," I say, considering how I could do it. I could ask our parents, or I could extend the invite first and ask forgiveness later.

Ash sits up quickly. "That's the first time you've spoken about life after the quest."

I look at her, startled as I realize she's right.

Pride and hope light up her face as she says, "you finally believe that you'll return?"

"I don't have much of a choice, Ash. It's either finding the strength to hope I'll return, or accepting that I'll die, and I really don't fancy the second option."

Ash smiles at me. "You're going to do great, Elena. There's no way in Hells you're going to die. You were, after all, trained by me."

I chuckle lightly, tensing my core muscles before I lunge out, shoving her off the chaise.

"I don't know how you get anything accomplished with that abnormally large head of yours," I joke.

A knock on my door has both of us standing up, I move to my bedroom and behind the dressing screen where I pull on a shirt and casual dress that ties in front.

Ash opens the door, and I hear our mother's voice from the foyer.

"Ah, should have known you'd be here." I hear the tightness in her voice that always seems to be present nowadays.

I'm lacing up my house shoes when I step back into my sitting area. Aislinn stands near our mother, who is staring at the fireplace.

"Are you ready for your journey Elana?" she asks, turning to face me.

I straighten under her appraising stare. "Yes, Mother. I have all the necessary food, clothes, weapons, and medical supplies."

She shakes her head and waves a dismissive hand. "I don't mean if your things are ready. I want to know if you, personally, are ready."

I start to give a canned response but pause. Could one ever be truly ready for this? I doubt it.

"I'm as ready as I could be," I say with a quick shrug.

"Good to hear," she says, turning to Aislinn. "And you're to escort her to the border?"

Aislinn dips her head. "Yes, Mother. The trip should take us two days as long as we don't have any...interruptions."

"What is the plan to avoid any potential...interruptions, as you call them?"

"We're leaving before first light, under cloaks, and without our family emblems. It's only the two of us, so we won't stand out with any unnecessary guards. To anyone passing us, we'll simply look like travelers."

Mother nods her head slowly, approving of Aislinn's explanation. I'm processing whether all of the anonymity is necessary when Mother makes a move that startles me, grabbing me into a crushing hug. We're the same height, so our heads rest next to each other on our shoulders.

I can't remember the last time she hugged me. Maybe it was when our grandmother died, or when Father left for a few months' long trip when I was nine, and he missed my winter birthday. In any case, the action is so rare I can count the number of times she's hugged me on one hand.

"I want you to know that I'm proud of you. Whatever happens at the Gods' Peaks, Elana, I'll always be so proud of you. And everything I did was to protect you."

My words leave me, it's all I can do to nod my head against her shoulder.

She releases me from the hug, clearing her throat, and I swear I see tears in her eyes. Aislinn looks just as stunned as I am, staring open-mouthed at our mother. Our mother who never shows emotion. Who never falters, never missteps. The woman who taught us from children that we must be perfect in everything we do.

"I know you hated your training in the womanly arts. I know you wanted to train with your sister. All I ever wanted for you was to live a safe life, Elana."

I take a few breaths, not sure I want to know the answer to my next question.

"What were you trying to keep me safe from?" I ask, wringing my hands together.

"The world," she says, turning her back on me and heading towards the door.

The world? What does that even mean? Why does she continue to treat me like a young child rather than trust me with honesty and real answers to my questions.

"Maybe if you had paid attention to what I wanted, not what you thought was best, I wouldn't have almost died in Sandral." My voice rises as I let more and more of my anger out. "I wouldn't feel like I'm walking into a giant scorpion's lair blindly. After all this time, you can't even give me a straight answer."

"I'm sorry, Elana. That's the only thing I can say right now." She walks out the door, oblivious to my anger.

Ash is at my side in a moment, holding my hand as we stare at the door she shut behind her.

"We can't change her, but you can prove her wrong, El. You're stronger and smarter than you know," she says.

"El, wake up," a voice calls to me, shaking me out of a restless sleep.

My eyelids squeeze tighter, and I try to roll back over to escape the sound threatening to pull me from the comfort of my mattress.

"It's time to go, get up," the voice says with more urgency. It's Aislinn.

I wrench my eyes open, and I see Ash holding a flickering candle in front of her face. Dread sinks into my stomach. Oh Gods, I'm not ready for this.

"That's it, come on. I've got some bread and eggs here for you," Ash shoves a plate of food at me while I wipe sleep from my eyes.

She walks over to my fire and stokes it, casting the room into brighter relief.

"Eat up, El. It's going to be a long day," she says, pulling my wardrobe open and grabbing the outfit we had picked out for the journey. She lays it over my dressing screen.

I eat slowly, my stomach not fully awake but already disagreeing with my anxiousness. A long day indeed.

Ash is already dressed for the journey, her hair braided, armed to the teeth under her thick cloak. I spot her longsword and Hale's sword slung around her hips.

I eat as much as I can tolerate and get ready, dressing quickly. Aislinn helps me braid my hair in two braids like hers, starting from the top of my scalp all the way to the nape of my neck. She doesn't finish the braid but allows some of the wavy ends to hang loose past the tie.

Neither of us say much as she works. Last night after our mother left, we sat by the fireplace and talked for hours. I unpacked and repacked my bag about five times, while Aislinn sharpened a set of throwing knives until they could cut parchment with no effort.

We're on our way out the door when our parents walk in. Father holds out his arms and I rush to embrace him for what I hope won't be the last time.

"In past generations, our family has held a small ceremony to send off the chosen heir, but since things are more...precarious this year, it's best you leave under cover of darkness," he says, releasing me from the hug, but holding onto my shoulders and pressing a kiss to my cheek.

"You will do great things, daughter," he says, smiling slightly down at me. "Go and see what the Gods have in store for you."

"I won't let you or Adrithia down, Father," I say with a practiced dip of my head.

"I know you won't, Elana," he says, releasing my shoulders and turning to Aislinn.

They look at each other and exchange a nonverbal command. "I'll see her safely to the border, Father. I swear it."

He nods his head. "Thank you, Aislinn. I trust you above all others with this task. I know you'll see it done."

Ash bows slightly to him. "It's my honor to do so."

Father sweeps his gaze to survey us both, as if he's trying to memorize our appearances. "I love you both and anxiously await your return."

Mother steps in front of him then, taking both of our hands in hers. Her usual mask of cold indifference is back in place after last night.

"Be safe girls, and return to us." She drops our hands and whisks out of the room. I watch her go and feel a mixture of sorrow and resignation.

"Come, Elana, we must leave," Ash breaks me out of my thoughts, handing me my pack and heading into her rooms to retrieve hers.

"Remember, Elana. The Gods chose you. You deserve to be there as much as any of the heirs. Don't let anyone tell you otherwise," Father says as he, too, turns around and walks down the hallway.

Ash returns with her pack.

"Time to go," she says.

The one other person I'm hoping to say goodbye to is missing. I feel his lack of presence like a hole in the ground. Maybe he's still upset that I rejected him? We haven't had much time to talk since then, and I don't want to leave with bad feelings.

Ash and I walk past the kitchens, where Gwen shoves a bundle of cured and dried foods in our hands, and extra water flasks. Her eyes swim as she hugs us and holds the hug on me for longer than I know what to do with.

Senara stands by the main doors, holding a handkerchief to her eyes. She curtsies and wishes me well through her tears, promising that my rooms will be kept pristine while

I'm gone. I want to reassure her it'll only be a few weeks, and that I'll be home before she knows it, but I'm not sure that'll be the case and I don't want to lie. I smile at her and pull her into a brief heartfelt hug, thanking her for all of her hard work.

Ash and I walk quickly to the stables. Misty is outside of her stall, already saddled with travel packs fixed to her saddle. Aric holds her reins. I smile and rush to him. He drops Misty's leads and crushes me into a hug that lifts me off the ground.

"I was worried I wouldn't get to say goodbye to you," I say, my words choking off slightly as I struggle to keep from crying.

"Princess," he whispers into my hair, "it's not too late to run away with me."

I suck in a breath. He still thinks I'll leave with him? That I'll abandon my duty to be with him? One moment is all it takes for my tears to dry up and frustration to course through me, warming my blood.

"You know I can't, Aric," I whisper back. He sets me down on the ground again but doesn't let me go.

"Can't blame me for trying," he says wryly and finally steps back, dropping his arms. He has the nerve to look embarrassed in the flickering torchlight outside the stables.

I roll my eyes at him and let go of my frustrations. I don't want to mar this goodbye with my anger. After more than a decade of friendship I can look past his protectiveness.

"Are you sure you don't want me to come with you?" he asks, tucking one of my braids behind my shoulder, cupping the back of my neck with his hand.

Ash appears over his shoulder, glaring. "Need I remind you that you stand out too much, you damn oaf?"

I let out a snort of laughter. "Ash, be nice," I chide her, but then lock eyes with Aric and give him a firm shake of my head.

"The two of us alone will travel quicker and are less likely to be seen," I say.

Something dark flashes in his eyes and he swallows hard, removing his hand from my neck. "As you wish, Your Highness."

His voice sounds strained, and I wonder if it's because of Aislinn's crabby presence or the lingering tension from our earlier conversations. I want to tell him how much he means to me as my closest friend and protector, but instead all I say is, "I'll miss you."

He smiles and kisses my forehead. "I'll miss you too. Be safe, Elana. And come back to me."

"Don't worry about me. I'll be back before you know it," I respond.

Ash clears her throat. "It's time to go, El."

I nod my head at her, placing my pack into the travel bags on Misty. She huffs once and shakes her mane, as anxious to be off as Ash apparently.

I pat her neck, and Aric kneels down and clasps his hands together to give me a leg up. I step onto his hands and he guides me to the saddle.

Ash gracefully mounts her chestnut-colored stallion named Hector and starts down the worn path away from the castle. I give one last look at Aric, waving. His mouth is set in a frown and his eyes have taken on the sad puppy look again, but he waves back.

As we trot down the road, the sun just starts to lighten the sky. The towering peaks of the castle, my home, are silhouetted against the oranges and pinks of the early morning.

When I return, I'll have one of the five powers and will officially step into my role as the heir. My breakfast protests in my stomach. I'll seal such thoughts away. For now.

Chapter Nine

Aislinn stands over me, frowning, as I retch my meager breakfast up in the grass next to the cobblestone path.

"If I'd known we'd stop four times this morning for you to be sick I would have planned for another day of travel," she says, handing me the waterskin as I wipe my mouth with the back of my hand.

"I'm sorry, Ash. Next time I'll try to give you three days' notice when I'm going to be ill so you can appropriately plan," I snap, already sick of this journey.

She chuckles, patting my back softly, which only irritates me further. It's not like I want to be sick, but between the uneven terrain, my nerves, and the breakfast that sits like lead, I've reached my limit.

"You'll feel better once you accept that you can do this, El. It's all in your head." She walks to my horse and rifles through my medicine satchel. She pulls out a few dried peppermint leaves and hands them to me. "Chew on these."

I lift my eyebrows at her, wondering how she knows. She rolls her eyes, sensing my question in the way only sisters can do. "I'm not an idiot. I paid attention all the times you've prepared tea for my various ailments."

I let out an impressed noise and crush the leaves in my palm, dropping them in my waterskin. I shake it gently and take a few tentative sips, washing away the gross taste in my mouth.

Ash helps me back onto Misty and we continue along. It's midday, and we're in the middle of a deciduous forest. According to Ash, we should make it to a small village tonight where we can take shelter at an inn and sleep in a real bed. It'll be my last time sleeping in a bed for weeks. The thought has me sipping more of my peppermint water.

"So, Ash," I say, eager to get my mind off the impending doom before me, "what do you plan on doing when you get back?"

She looks at me out of the corner of her eyes, "Well, first I'm going to take a nice long bath, and then I'll probably—"

"Ugh, spare me. You know what I mean," I interrupt before she goes through her boring daily routine with me.

She smirks, and then falls silent, "You know, I haven't really thought about it much. Father asked me to lead Adrithia's armies, which of course I'd be honored to do. But I think I'd like to travel too."

"Traveling sounds nice," I say, encouraging her to continue.

"Our whole lives were planned out for us. We never got to see much outside of our own walls. Sure, we had our occasional trips to Sandral, and Father took me along on a few of his diplomatic visits to nearby towns, and even to the other kingdoms, but I want to see all of Adrithia. I want to swim in the Shallow Sea, map out the Dark Forest, visit the inactive volcano that our grandmother raised decades ago. I want to see every village, meet our people, and learn about our culture. I want to go to the Gods' Territory and uncover the hidden temple that so many scholars speculate about. There's so much to do, so much to see before I commit my life to defending Adrithia."

Ash's face is bright with the prospect of her untethered future. All the possibilities of where she'll go and who she'll meet. I have no doubt that she will accomplish all of it.

"That sounds like an amazing life, Ash," I smile at her, and she returns it, bright and full of hope.

"What about you? Have you given any more thought to Aric's *proposal*?"

I want to sink down into the saddle and disappear. "No, I haven't exactly had much time to think about my marriage proposals. Besides, I think he only wanted to marry me if we ran away together."

"Hmm," Ash contemplates, "I wouldn't be so sure about that."

My eyes snap to her bright hazel ones. "What do you mean?"

She looks back towards the trail, steering her stallion away from a berry bush, "Aric is in love with you, sister."

Her words are ice-cold water in the bathtub when you expect warmth. "What?"

"It's no secret; in fact, it's the talk of the castle. Senara gossips more than anyone I've ever known," Ash says.

"Everyone in the castle knows?" Panic creeps in, and I have the sudden urge to jump off Misty and go vomit some more. Aric loves me? And everyone knows?

"Well, I suspect our parents are oblivious, or else Mother would have had him thrown out by now. She wouldn't have done anything to jeopardize your engagement to Lord Percival. Most of the castle staff talk about you two as if you've been a couple for years. I shut that talk down whenever I hear it, but still, people talk."

My face blazes and I duck my head so she doesn't see. How could I not realize it myself? He's been my only friend for years. And I left him there after rejecting him. I should have insisted he travel with us to the border, if only to ensure there were no bad feelings between us.

I could have grown to love him, I suppose. If given the chance to, I could have been happy with him. But I wouldn't want to put him in the situation where he has to earn my love. He deserves someone who will love him because there is no alternative, no other option. There's also no way I could live with myself if I'd left Adrithia without an heir. If I hadn't at least tried.

"He's better off without me," I say, staring straight ahead. "I can't give him what he wants. And I can't force myself to abandon everything I am just for him."

Ash doesn't say anything, but I swear I see a proud smile on her face out of the corner of my vision.

We ride in silence for some time. My stomach seems to have settled itself for the time being.

Time drags by and the landscape around us changes. We pass a few villages where the townsfolk are too busy to pay us much attention. Farmland, widespread forests, and rivers gradually give way to less inhabited land with sprawling meadows and rolling hills dotted with wildflowers and grasses as tall as I am.

As the sun starts to dip lower in the sky, Ash pushes us faster.

"If we want a room for the night, we'll have to hurry it up. There's only one inn in the village, and I don't want to sleep in the stables with Hector. He's gassy at night," she says, pushing an indignant Hector to a trot.

We urge our horses on quicker, and I inwardly cringe for Misty. She's not used to such long treks, and neither am I. I already feel the saddle bruising my backside. At least Ash and Hector have more experience with long trips, having crossed Adrithia multiple times with Father.

What seems like hours of hard riding later, the small village comes into sight. It's the smallest hamlet we've encountered so far. No more than a cluster of twenty buildings, a few barns, and a dilapidated temple.

Misty pants when we arrive at the small stables. An elderly man appears with a stool, but Ash jumps off her horse before he can make a move to help her. She unbuckles her longsword from Hector's saddle and removes her pack. I graciously accept the help of the man with the stool, hauling myself off Misty's back. Every movement sends a sharp ache up my spine. I wince and grab my weapons and pack from the saddle. Ash pays the man a gold coin and his eyes light up, thanking her profusely and promising our horses will be well tended. She flashes a charming smile and takes my arm, leading me to the inn.

We're blasted with noise and hot air as soon as we step inside. A fire roars on one wall, and it looks like the whole village is here enjoying a meal or enjoying various stages of drunkenness.

Ash tugs me towards the bar, where a woman past her prime stands behind the counter, pouring mugs of ale. She has a smattering of wrinkles near her eyes and a mane of gray hair piled on her head, but her eyes are sharp. They go wide when she sees us walk up.

"Ah, a pair of travelers if I've ever seen 'em!" she says, setting the mugs on the counter, where they're whisked away by a pretty brunette tavern maiden. "Welcome to Harold's Hill, misses. Named after my husband's grandfather. My name's Agatha. What can I do fer yeh?"

She speaks with a heavy accent, but I can't quite make out from where. It could be from one of the fishing villages along the coast?

"We'd like a room for the night, please, a bath, and two hot meals," Ash says, setting a few gold coins down on the counter.

The coins are snatched up in the blink of an eye. The woman moves quicker than I'd expected for her age.

"We 'ave a room with two beds, a fireplace, and a tub that I reckon would suit ye nicely. I can 'ave my daughter bring up some hot water and dinner, too," the woman replies, eyes crinkling into a genuine smile.

"That sounds wonderful, Agatha, thank you," Aislinn smiles at the woman and takes the worn bronze key Agatha hands her.

"Yer room is upstairs, all the way at the end. Reserved for my favorite folk. If there's anything I can do for ye to make yeh more comfortable, give a holler," Agatha says, before the tavern maiden calls out for more ales and she gets back to work filling mugs. I have a feeling her favorite folk is anyone who pays well, but I keep that thought to myself.

We haul our packs up the stairs and into our room at the end of the hall. There are two functional beds with extra blankets, a small bathing chamber, a fireplace and a small white clawfoot tub. Not glamorous, but at least it's clean. I honestly expected worse.

Ash claims the bed closest to the door and immediately stokes the fire. I all but collapse on my bed, soreness radiating from my thighs to my mid-back.

I must fall asleep because the next thing I know there's a knock on the door and Ash cracks it open with a dagger concealed behind her back.

"Good evening, ladies," a middle-aged woman says, carrying two steaming bowls and a small platter with bread. Ash opens the door wide and lets her in.

"That smells delicious," I say, inhaling deeply.

"Well, thank you. I made it myself, it's a veggie stew. Unfortunately, we don't have much meat here anymore, due to our livestock being killed by those monsters." The woman sets down the plates on the small wooden table near the burning fireplace.

Ash and I exchange wary glances. "What monsters?" my sister asks.

"Oh, you haven't heard?" The woman asks, and when we shake our heads she continues. "Well, I shouldn't be worrying you, but for months now Harold's Hill has been terrorized by beasts. Our local farmers have lost most of their flocks because of them."

Ash narrows her eyes. "What kind of beasts?"

"I don't know, miss. No one's ever seen them. But we hear them after nightfall," She shudders, pulling her woven shawl tighter across her chest. "We hear their shrieks, and then in the morning we find the half-eaten carcasses of our sheep and cattle. They come almost every night. A few of our townsfolk went looking for them right after we started finding dead livestock, but the group that went out never returned."

She stares at the door with a forlorn look, as if there was someone she was waiting for to return.

"Why haven't you written to the capital about this?" I ask. Surely our army would have taken care of these creatures if they knew about the problem.

The woman turns her gaze on me, looking sad and hopeless. "Sweet child, we learned long ago that those in the big city pay no mind to us commoners out here. Our past requests to the general were never answered. Way out here near the border we take care of our own problems."

Ash looks furious, but I know she's not angry with this woman. She catches my raised eyebrows and schools her features. She digs into her coin purse, tipping the woman generously.

"Thank you for the hot meal, ma'am," she says, smiling at her.

"Of course. I'll bring up some hot water shortly for the bath." She curtsies awkwardly and makes a swift exit, closing the door behind her.

"Ash, what's going on here? What creatures do you think those are?" I ask as we eat.

"I've heard rumors lately about our current army general being...selective about where he sends the army," Ash grumbles.

My spoon pauses halfway to my mouth as I gape at her. "What?"

"I thought they were nonsensical rumors, since I'd heard them from our soldiers who are lower in rank, so I brushed it off as discontent, but it seems like there's more to it than I thought. Worse than that, it's been happening for years under our noses." The fire reflects in her eyes, painting her face in angry contrast.

"I can't believe it," I say. "We've known General Calix our whole lives."

Ash scoffs. "Yes, but perhaps there's a reason he's maintained his post all these years, despite being past his prime."

"But what reason would he have to ignore requests from villages?" I wonder, unsure of the potential motive.

"I imagine it's the same reason he's maintained his power. Money," she says, stabbing a carrot in frustration. "He could be taking bribes from larger cities, while ignoring the smaller villages, perhaps because they can't—or refuse to—pay."

I gasp, disgusted. How could the general of our armies be corrupt? Another unsettling thought comes to my mind, but I'm almost afraid to voice it.

"Do you think Father knows?" The stew sits heavy in my stomach.

"No, there's no way." Ash shakes her head, but the tone of her voice says she won't rule it out. "In any case, I'll get to the bottom of it when I return home. There's no need to worry about it, El."

I nod, accepting that it's the most that can be done at this moment.

"As for the creatures, though, that troubles me more. There shouldn't be any beasts out here capable of killing livestock in that number, let alone armed civilians. I have no idea what they could be." Ash takes another bite of stew, chewing slowly as if she's turning the thought over in her mind like a puzzle.

"Could it be a golden bear?" I wonder. I've never seen one, but I've heard they can grow taller than a horse. There is a painting of one of our ancestors riding one into battle centuries ago.

Ash seems to contemplate that for a moment, "I don't think it would be a bear. They're tough, but not that difficult to kill. And she mentioned a shrieking noise and bears sound nothing like that. The only creatures I know to make noises like that live in the Dark Forest. Wyrms, blood bats, and of course, scorpions."

She rattles off the creatures of my worst nightmares like they were flavors of her favorite pies, unfazed by the untold horrors these beasts were responsible for.

"Isn't there anything we can do to help these people?" I ask her, already feeling a sense of responsibility for their livelihoods, since we've so clearly failed them before.

"No, Elana, we don't have time. When I return home, I'll inform Father, and offer to lead a battalion here to eviscerate these creatures."

I bite my cheek—surely these people can wait for help to arrive a bit longer, right? The thought doesn't sit well, but I accept it.

The woman appears at our door again with two large buckets of steaming water and dumps them into the tub. She tells us her name is Marie, the daughter of Agatha. She hands us thick but scratchy towels and tells us to holler if we need anything. She heads towards the door but pauses before opening it. "Make sure you bolt the window tonight. Townsfolk heard shrieking coming from the woods nearby."

Ash flashes her a grim smile and nods. Marie closes the door gently as she leaves, cutting out most of the boisterous tavern sounds below. It's hard to imagine that people could still be drinking and laughing when being stalked nightly by beasts, but maybe that's why they do it. For fear of it being the last time.

We bathe quickly before the water turns cold and sit by the fire talking until we're both too tired to keep any coherent train of thought.

This could be my last pleasant evening for weeks, even with the threat of the mysterious monsters hanging over our heads. I won't let thoughts of monsters stop me from enjoying these moments with my sister.

In the early morning we pack up and head to the tavern downstairs. Agatha waves us over to the bar and we sit on the worn wooden stools. There's a wiry, gray-haired man passed out on his stool at the far end of the bar, snoring slightly.

"Morning, ladies. How did ye sleep?" she asks, wiping down the wooden counter.

"Like a rock, thanks to your hospitality," Ash says, smiling at the aged woman.

"Oh dear, flattery will get ye everywhere here," Agatha chuckles. "Would ye like some breakfast before ye head out?"

My stomach chooses to let out a growl of anguish at that moment and I say, "breakfast, please."

Agatha nods, a smile crinkling her eyes, and goes into the kitchen. She returns moments later with two bowls of porridge topped with a few blueberries and some nuts. Ash and I dig in.

"Thank the Gods ye two arrived when ye did last night. A few of our dwindlin' cattle went missin', and I'm sure it's only time before those monsters turn their hunger to us townsfolk. You should be fine on the road. We 'aven't heard of any attacks along the path. Where are ye headed anyway?" Agatha asks, washing a pile of mugs that still smell like ale from the previous night.

I stay silent, expecting Ash to weave her lies that I've heard a few times on the trip, but she surprises me by saying, "we're heading to the border."

Agatha drops a half-cleaned mug back into the bucket of soapy water. "I knew it!" she exclaims. "Hey, Walter, ye owe me five bronze coins!" She throws her drying towel at the man snoring on the counter, who doesn't even stir, and looks back at us. "My husband bet me that yeh weren't the princesses, but I knew better. Yer too well spoken and dressed for these parts, and it's well-known that the chosen heirs always pass through Harold's Hill."

Walter stirs from his spot on the counter, and Agatha rolls her eyes at him. I burst out laughing. She finds out that we're princesses, and the first thing she does is try to collect her winnings from her husband. Oh, I really like her.

"So, that must make ye Princess Aislinn, because of the striking blonde hair, and ye," she turns to me, "Princess Elana, the Chosen heir." She bows her head to us.

"You are correct," Ash says, smiling slightly.

Agatha lifts her head and locks eyes with me. "We hear a lot of rumors 'ere, and some of them ain't too kind to ye," she says, and Ash and I stiffen. "But we never pay much mind to rumors. We prefer to see the truth fer ourselves."

She winks at me and I smile wide.

"Thank you, Agatha," I say, overcome with more emotion than I know how to handle in the moment.

Ash and I finish eating quickly and say our goodbyes to Agatha and Marie, who wish us well, promising to pray to the Gods for safe travels and luck during the trials. I promise to visit again, and Ash says she will stop back on her way home. Walter still snores on the bar when we head out the door to the stables.

Our horses are already saddled and ready to go by the time we get there, so we waste little time in packing and mounting up.

We're on the road again before the sun barely grazes the horizon. Ash is in front, riding swiftly, but I notice her head whipping around to scan the trees more than she did yesterday.

It seems like we've been riding for hours when a crack echoes through the forest.

"What was that?" I ask, leaning back and stopping Misty. Next to me, Hector pauses and Ash looks around. Harold's Hill is out of sight, and we haven't passed any settlements or signs of other life. A distinct clicking sound comes from the woods on our left.

Ash spins around on Hector and motions for us to turn around. She puts a finger to her lips, silencing any questions I'm about to ask. I urge Misty to follow her. She stops by a small group of trees right next to the path and hops off her horse, tying him to one of the trees. She motions for me to do the same. We tie Misty's reins to Hector's, and she holds her hand up for me to stay put. Her longsword is in her hands and she creeps forward on silent feet, a predator stalking her prey.

She's across the road heading to some tall trees and I take a few steps towards her, not wanting that much distance between us.

I jump as a massive deer races past Ash and our horses, bolting into the woods on the opposite side of the road. I chuckle, taking a few deep breaths to steady my nerves. Ash turns back towards me with an embarrassed laugh on her lips. Her gaze catches on something beyond me and the smile falls, her mouth dropping open in horror.

A skittering noise comes from behind me. I freeze on instinct and a chill runs up my spine as the clicking noises stop. I force myself to slowly turn around and stare straight into the beady eyes of a giant scorpion.

Chapter Ten

I stare at the beast as it stares down at me, legs quaking with anticipation. Its tail shakes back and forth menacingly. Our horses let out anxious snorts, and the scorpion turns its attention to them.

Several things happen all at once. I jump in front of the horses as the scorpion flicks its tail out to strike.

Ash screams, "get down," and I drop to the road in time to see her longsword sail past where I had been standing and slam into the scorpion's tail. The weight of the impact knocks its stinger off target and it slams into the ground next to me, impaled by the gleaming blade.

The creature shrieks, lashing back and forth, violently whipping its tail, its pincers snapping at the air. The creature almost steps on me, but I roll away from it at the last moment. I scramble to my feet, heading for Misty as the monster barrels towards my sister, pincers reaching for her. She leaps out of the way and unsheathes her heirloom sword.

Misty stomps her feet anxiously and blows her breath out in huffs when I reach her with shaky hands. I unhook my bow and a few arrows from the saddle and take cover behind a tall tree as I quickly nock an arrow, slamming the rest into the soft ground by the tree.

A quick peek from my hiding place and I see Ash block a strike from a pincer. I draw the string back to my anchor point and exhale, letting it go. The arrow strikes the scorpion through the underside of its tail. Not a great shot, but enough for it to turn its attention back to me. It throws its pincers up and scurries towards me.

"Shit, I did not think this through," I gasp and run the opposite way, dodging trees and leaping over brush. It follows, crashing through the forest debris.

"Bring it back this way!" I barely hear Aislinn's voice shout.

I turn in a wide arc, the scorpion gaining on me with every step. I push my legs harder, faster, discarding my bow and narrowing my focus on the branches on the ground, on the roots emerging from the earth, anything that could trip me.

A piercing shriek behind me startles me and causes me to stumble, but by the Gods' intervention, I don't lose my balance. Our horses are in view, but I don't see Ash. I run across the path towards where I last saw her. I'm almost across the worn dirt trail when I'm knocked off my feet by something hard. A pincer. The air leaves my lungs in a painful whoosh, and my shoulder takes the brunt of the impact on the worn dirt. I roll as soon as I hit the ground, pushing myself to a crouching position like Ash taught me.

I turn to face the scorpion and see it prowling towards me, no longer hurried. It knows its prey is exhausted, and it's readying for the kill. A dark blur in the trees above me catches my eye, and Aislinn launches herself from the branches of a nearby tree. She swings her sword as she drops, severing the beast's venomous tail in one fluid motion. Dark green ichor spurts from its nub of a tail. An agonized cry sounds from the scorpion and it thrashes its body, legs collapsing under it as it writhes.

Ash dodges the frantic swing of its pincers, jumps onto its back, and slams the blade of her short sword straight down behind its head. The scorpion shudders and then collapses, dead.

She rips her sword from the creature's back and leaps off it. Her nose wrinkles in disgust at the dark green blood now coating Hale's blade. She flicks it twice at the ground and the blade shines like new again. My eyes widen from my spot on the ground. I'm too shaky to move, so I watch my sister as she rips her longsword from the creature's severed tail and wipes it off on the damp morning grass.

"Are you alright, El?" Ash asks, wiping down her damp longsword.

I look down at my body, taking stock of my injuries. My shoulder is throbbing dully, but it's merely a bruise. I force my shaky fingers and toes to flex. I don't feel any blinding pain, so it's safe to stand. Once I'm on my feet I roll my shoulder and stretch it out.

"I'm okay," I finally respond to her. She nods and sheathes her blades.

"Isn't scorpion venom incredibly rare and useful in medicines and antidotes?" she asks, inspecting the stinger end of the tail.

"Yes, it's incredibly useful, and expensive should one need to purchase it."

Her eyebrows raise at me and she jerks her head towards the stinger. "Well, don't you want to collect some of it before it dries up?"

"Oh!" I start, shocked I didn't think of it. My blood races, but my mind is foggy and it's difficult to form coherent thoughts. "Yes, I should do that." I walk to Misty and rummage through my medical satchel for an empty glass vial.

Scorpion venom can burn the skin, even after the creature's death, so I'm careful not to allow any to drip on me as I hold the vial to the scorpion's stinger. Luckily the transparent light green liquid drips into the glass without much trouble. It's slightly viscous and almost shimmers in the rising sunlight. I put the stopper on the vial, wrap it with a spare bit of cloth, and store it with my other ingredients on Misty's saddle. I run a calming hand down her neck. She's restless but doesn't seem to sense any more danger.

Ash hands me my bow and a few arrows, which I forgot I'd discarded in the woods in my desperate bid to escape the scorpion. "I wonder what a baby scorpion was doing all the way up here," she says.

I startle and almost drop the bow. "That was a *baby*?"

"Yes, the fully matured ones are twice the size of a horse." She jabs her thumb in the direction of our horses, and my jaw drops. We could have been killed by a *baby* scorpion. I'd hate to see what the grown ones are capable of.

"That's a terrifying thought," I swallow hard and stash my weapons on Misty's saddle once more.

Ash nods her head in agreement. "It is. Now if you're done here, I'd like to get back on the trail before we meet its mommy."

"All done!" I say quickly, and use Ash's clasped hands to get back onto my horse.

We trot at a steady pace, leaving the area as quick as possible.

"Was that your first time fighting one?" I ask once we're further down the path.

My sister turns to me, a bleak expression on her face. "No, it wasn't. I fought one once with Father on our travels south. That one was full-grown and utterly horrible. Luckily, Father and I made quick work of it. It helps to have an ability that can basically trap anything in place. He had me deal the fatal blow, so I would know what it felt like."

"You never told me that before," I say, chewing on the inside of my lip. I don't know exactly when, but somehow the regular forest noises have started back up. Birds chirping, normal-sized insects buzzing, mammals scurrying through the brush.

"There was no need to tell you at the time. I didn't want to frighten you," she says, shrugging her shoulders.

I want to roll my eyes at that, but fighting this one has me understanding why she would keep it from me. I'm still shaking from our encounter with the adolescent scorpion.

We ride straight through the rest of the day, only stopping to see to our bodily needs. According to Ash, we're making good time and will reach the border by mid-afternoon.

The landscape doesn't change much—most of the land here is dominated by widespread prairie and scattered woods. It's teeming with wildlife, but luckily, we see no more terrifying creatures of the Dark Forest. Rabbits bound along the path, squirrels race between trees, deer graze, and birds sing and swoop around us.

Ash and I make small talk, swapping stories from our childhood. Stories about when we got into and out of trouble, like the time Ash, Aric and I built a castle out of snow, and then had a snowball fight trying to bring down the castle, which Aric was defending. The fun ended with a broken kitchen window, which sent Gwen into a fury the likes of which we haven't seen since. She banished us from the kitchen for a month after that, and we went without dessert for almost half a year.

Ash crests a gradual slope in front of me and drops Hector's reins. I wonder why she's stopped until I reach the top next to her.

Ahead of us, a stone gate arches over the pathway. We've reached the official entrance to the Gods' Territory. The arch is beautiful, with large chunks of stone framing the rounded top of the archway. It appears that over time the stone has been weathered and smoothed out, but it's no less impressive. Moss and vines nearly cover it and some branches bloom with light purple flowers.

The path beyond the gate is no longer compacted dirt and earth, but pieces of flattened rock with grass growing between. It looks perfectly maintained, even though it likely hasn't been touched in hundreds of years. It must be the lingering magic of the place.

Ash jumps down from Hector and moves to help me dismount Misty. I wave her off. I'm going to have to do this on my own from now on, so I can't rely on her this time. I jump down, miss the landing, and crash to my knees. I curse under my breath, but stand up, brushing the dirt off my pants.

"Smooth," Ash says, lifting her eyebrows. "You'll get better," she says with confidence.

I look to the gate and the path beyond. "So, this is it."

Ash joins me in staring at the wildlands before us. "Yes, it is."

She clears her throat and whips her head to stare at me. "Take that path straight to the foot of the first peak. Do not turn off anywhere, just continue to go straight. If you come across other paths, don't take them. Father always said the path you want is clear, so don't stray. It should take you about a day to reach the edge of the mountain. A few servants of the Gods live at the base of the first peak. I don't know who they are or what they're like, but Father said that's where you can leave Misty. Make sure you wear your daggers at all times. Sleep tonight on the side of the path but keep. Your. Daggers. On.

"The other heirs will be traveling there too. If you run into any of them and feel it's safe, then travel with them. There's safety in numbers. Play up your healer abilities. Make friends. Rayna and Rian are the best potential allies. Stay away from Calder, and do not cross Aidan. That man is more dangerous than ten fully grown scorpions." She takes a breath, having expelled more words in a moment than I have in a month.

I put my hand on her arm and squeeze.

"Ash," I say calmly, "I'll be okay."

I can't explain why, but I believe it. The moment I laid eyes on the gate I felt a sense of...rightness. Like this is where I'm meant to be. Some unseen force is coaxing me forward, and I know everything will be alright.

"Of course you will," Ash says, wrapping me in a tight hug. "You're going to do brilliantly."

"Not as brilliantly as you, but I'll try my hardest," I say, hugging her back.

We stay like that for a moment, neither of us ready to let go, but eventually I let my arms fall back to my sides. It's time. If I drag this on any longer, I'll lose my nerve.

Ash reluctantly releases me and steps back. Her eyes are shiny.

"Ugh, don't start crying Ash," I say, feeling my throat start to close. If the tears start now, I don't know I'll ever be able to stop them.

Ash wipes her eyes with her hand and smiles. "You're right. There's no room for tears here. This is a happy day. The day you start out on your quest to meet a god."

She leans forward and kisses my forehead. "I love you, Elana."

"I love you, too, Aislinn," I say, smiling up at her as I take Misty's reins and pull her along towards the gate.

We reach the precipice and I turn around, waving at my sister one last time. She waves back with a wide smile on her face. "Give those heirs hell for me!"

I laugh and turn back to the path ahead as I cross into the Gods' Territory.

CHAPTER ELEVEN

I don't look back. It's difficult not to, to see my sister one last time before she heads back home and I head towards an unknown future. I worry that if I turn around, my survival sense will kick in and I'll go running back towards her. But going this way feels…easier, somehow. Like a load has been lifted from my back and I can stand up straight for the first time in weeks.

I walk next to Misty for a while, until I'm long past the gate. Along the side of the trail I find a boulder, which is the perfect height to help me into the saddle. After I'm seated without too much struggle, we move along at a steady pace.

We pass a few small creatures I've never seen before: a solid white hare with a set of antlers like a stag's; some kind of large rodent with spotted fur, a long pointed nose, and equally long whiskers; and even a few birds with tail feathers almost as long as the phoenix's, but in brilliant shades of iridescent blues and greens.

The land feels alive here, teeming with life and energy. The lingering soreness in my back and shoulder dulls and Misty picks up her pace with no encouragement from me. I pat her neck as we ride and she snorts happily. She seems to feel as rejuvenated as I do.

As the sun starts to drop lower in the sky Misty finally begins to tire. I see a large tree right off the stepping stone pathway and I decide it's time to stop for the night. I swing my leg over and drop down, landing significantly better than last time. I lead Misty to the tree and tie her there while I unpack my sleeping roll, daggers, food, and waterskin. The rest I leave on her so I won't have much work to do in the morning.

I eat part of an apple, a handful of nuts, and aged cheese. Misty nudges my bruised shoulder until I give her the rest of the apple, which she happily gobbles up.

I wonder if Ash made it back to Harold's Hill and if she encountered any other scorpions along the way. Worry nudges into my thoughts, along with a sinking feeling that I won't see her again for weeks.

A chill breeze stirs and I unroll my pack to wrap myself in the thick material. I stare at the stars overhead and recite ingredients for common elixirs and teas to put myself to sleep. Slowly, ever so slowly, my eyelids droop closed.

I'm back on the dreaded mountain while the storm rages all around me. I've been here before, but this time I face a dark cave with a sheer drop to my back. Rocks crumble beneath my feet and I lunge into the inky blackness of the cave.

A torch lights up the darkness, hovering nearby. I reach for it, but before my fingers make contact it floats away from my outstretched fingers, dancing back towards the wall almost tauntingly.

"Damn!" I mumble, stumbling forward. I wrap my arms around myself and move closer to the back of the cavern. The entire cave is about twice as tall as I am, and at least twice as wide as my outstretched arms.

Suddenly the cave shakes, rocks trembling all around me. I hear a loud crack *and several large boulders crash down into the mouth of the cave, blocking my way out.*

I'm trapped, I realize with uneven breaths. Trapped in this cave with a floating torch.

I slowly approach the back of the cave to put some distance between myself and the cave-in, in case more rocks decide to rain down upon my head.

The eerie floating torch follows me, casting my distorted shadow against the rear wall, but something is off about the shape of it. As I watch, it ripples and shifts. A shining outline appears behind my shadow and I whip around, but there's nothing behind me. My focus turns back to the wall, where my shadow is now moving on its own. It grows larger, the blinding golden outline growing with it.

The shadow and halo reach the top of the cave and then voices—dozens of voices—scream at me from all angles. I shout and cover my ears, looking around frantically for the source of the noises, but nothing except shadow looms.

The cave gives another violent shake and a large chunk of rock breaks off above me, falling towards my head.

I bolt upright in my thick blanket, breathing hard. My hands go to my head, checking for blood or injury. Of course there's nothing to be found. It was a dream, and even as I try to remember what happened in it, the memories slip away and it feels like I'm grasping for smoke.

Unease ripples through me and I take stock of my surroundings. It's early morning, based on where the sun is in the sky. Nothing moves in the grassy forest and I don't hear any alarming sounds. I'm truly alone in the Gods' Territory. Misty chomps on some grass nearby. Not entirely alone, I guess.

I pack up my paltry belongings, eat a meager breakfast, and get back onto the path. I set Misty's pace at a slow trot, hoping to get to the foot of the mountains by early afternoon. Ash and I planned for me to be the first to arrive so I could have a slight upper hand, get to know the other heirs as they arrive rather than all at once. It's a good strategy, one I don't want to muck up with my tardiness.

As we pass hills, trees and streams, I think about the rest of my plan. How I can offer my services early on as a healer. Perhaps one of the heirs will trip and fall into a patch of fire bramble, which would require a poultice with a cooling ointment to stop the itchiness and the rash from spreading. Or maybe someone will eat some bad berries and need a stomach soothing charcoal tea.

I'm prepared to fully cure a variety of ailments, even more now with the scorpion venom. I'd still be hard-pressed to deal with any severely broken bones or some of the rare poisons from plants we don't have in Adrithia, but hopefully I won't come across anything that dire. If the other heirs are as skilled as Aislinn says they are, I shouldn't have anything to worry about.

Misty lets out a snort and stomps her hooves, jolting me from my thoughts.

"Misty, what is it?" I ask, gripping her reins with white knuckles.

Sticks crack in the woods to my right and Misty backs up a few paces, blowing out anxious breaths. I pat the daggers at my side and relief courses through me feeling their proximity. Suddenly I need to know what's out there, if only to reassure myself there's nothing to worry about. I take a deep breath and hop off Misty's back, landing hard, then leave her on the path while I investigate.

More shuffling comes from somewhere behind the cover of the forest. I unsheathe my daggers, creeping into the brush. I channel Aislinn's sneaking prowess as I dart between the trees, feeling the soothing coolness of my daggers' grips.

The trees thin, and I see a massive black horse eating grass on the side of a stepping stone path that looks identical to the one I left behind. The black horse snorts and paws the ground. Bags are slung across its back, but I see no rider.

A rustle comes from behind me and the sound of air moving too close to my back. I'm about to whirl around, daggers slashing, when an arm wraps around my neck and something sharp presses into my back, right behind my heart. Oh, this person's good. They hold me in a vice-like grip, not hard enough to choke but hard enough for me to understand how easily they could end my life. I don't try to fight it, knowing one wrong move will send that blade right into my hammering heart.

My breath hitches, nerves setting in. Anger courses through me in a flash. This is the second time I've been in a similar position in the past few weeks. Haven't I learned anything? Aislinn would be furious if she could see me right now.

"You have three seconds to tell me who you are and why you're here before I send you to meet the Gods," a deep male voice rasps in my ear.

Maybe he's some kind of servant of the Gods? Here to protect the land from anyone who doesn't belong. Although neither Ash nor Father ever mentioned such guards.

"Ironically enough, I'm here to see the Gods," I say through shallow breaths, careful not to move my body too much and push the dagger deeper in my back.

The hand across my neck releases me and I brace for the sharp pain of the knife, but it doesn't come. I slowly turn around, eyeing the sharp dagger in the man's hand, and study his movements for any sign of impending attack. He backs up a step and then stands perfectly still, in an unnatural way. He's tall, perhaps not quite as tall as Aric, but has more than a few inches on Aislinn.

His dark, wavy hair is pushed back away from his face and sits at the nape of his neck. He appraises me, his bright golden eyes dragging up and down my body. I shiver under his intense gaze.

"You're her?" He asks, sliding his dagger back into its sheath at his hip.

"I'm...who?" I ask, confused. Taking it as a good sign that he holsters his own blade, I relax my grip on my own daggers, but don't sheathe them.

He gives me a look that suggests annoyance. "Aislinn's sister. The one who was chosen and nearly caused a rebellion."

"Ah, yes, and you're some rude degenerate who goes around threatening people with daggers before ever asking their name," I huff, letting my anger get the better of me before I can cap it.

A corner of his mouth quirks up. "Definitely Aislinn's sister. The same cocky mouth."

My face heats and I feel redness creeping up my neck, "My name is *Elana,* not *Aislinn's sister.* And what do you know about my sister anyway?" I snap at him.

"Only that she has the same foul attitude as you, apparently. Must be a family trait. I bet dinners are real fun in that marble palace of yours." He turns from me and moves to a nearby tree, grabbing a travel pack off the ground and hoisting it onto his back.

"Excuse me!" I nearly shout, stomping after him. "You still have not introduced yourself or told me why you're here. Should I continue to call you degenerate or do you have a name?"

He pauses, turning back around at me, annoyance narrows his eyes. "My name is Prince Aidan Ashfall, but you, bunny, can call me Your Handsomeness, Your Regalness, or Your Exalted One, whichever you like. And as for what I'm doing here, well, I think you're smart enough to figure that one out."

My stomach lurches and I stop walking, nearly tripping over a large tree root sticking up out of the ground. Oh, spectacular. I've already picked a fight with the one heir Aislinn warned me about time and time again. In my defense, I didn't expect to meet him in the woods. And I also didn't expect him to be so infuriating.

"Don't call me bunny," I say, catching back up with him.

The prince doesn't say anything, he keeps walking towards his massive stallion. I realize now that it's not just any stallion, either, but one of Ocarin's specially trained warhorses.

He stands several feet taller than my mare and seems to be unhindered by the luggage he carries, which appears excessive. I see a bow and quiver full of arrows, a plush-looking bedroll, and lots of other supplies. I wonder if Aidan plans on carrying that all up the mountain. Seeing his substantially defined muscles, though, I wouldn't be surprised. Not that I'm staring at his substantial muscles, but his black shirt with the top three buttons undone across his wide chest leaves little to the imagination.

"See you at the mountain, bunny," he says, mounting the horse in one swift movement. He settles in his saddle, gives a light tap to the horse's side, and tears down the path.

An angry scream almost tears from my throat, but I hold it back, letting out a frustrated sigh instead as I watch him ride away. I see where his path and mine connect, bridging together towards the mountain, silhouetted in the distance.

I put my lips together and whistle loudly. An answering neigh sounds from Misty as she trots through the woods to me.

"Couldn't have warned me about him, could you?" I say to her, exasperated. I look around to find something to give me the added height to get into the saddle.

Once I'm situated, we canter off after Aidan. I doubt Misty will be able to catch up to the warhorse, so there's no chance I'll arrive first at the mountain. But with any luck, at least I won't be the last.

Aidan is infuriating. Aislinn warned me about his temper and his ability in battle, but she never mentioned anything about how frustrating he would be.

"Hold it together, Elana. You met one heir. *One.* You can't afford to get in your head about him when you have three others to worry about," I mutter out loud, if only to remind myself about the real challenge ahead.

In the distance, the shadow of the mountain grows. I can make out the five individual peaks, each higher than the last. The terrain around me grows hillier, with denser woods, leaving behind spots of tall grasses and prairie. I see larger creatures here. A stag with horns as black as soot. Wolves with coats of crystal, the varied shards catching in the sunlight and reflecting rainbows back at my eyes. Wildcats the size of Misty with long fur and large pointed ears.

One of these felines jumps out in front of my horse, startling her into rearing back. I grapple for the reins but lose my balance and topple backwards off Misty. My shoulders take the brunt of the impact and I wheeze in a breath as I roll away from Misty's frantic hooves. The pure-white feline lets out a loud roar and then bolts back into the trees. Misty takes off down the path, towards the Gods' Peaks. I'm left panting on the ground, cursing loudly.

I pick myself up off the stone road and whistle. There's no response.

"Fantastic," I say to the empty road. She has all my food, supplies, weapons, everything. The only items I carry are Hale's twin daggers.

"Misty!" I shout down the road where she disappeared and I whistle again. There's no hint she hears me.

A soft growl catches my attention, and a white blur darts between the trees on my left where the giant feline vanished. I unsheathe the daggers and stare at the white beast that prowls towards me. The metal in my hands hums, as if it's trying to tell me something. Its large ears bent forward, the cat stalks closer on large silent feet. Its long tail swishes behind it slowly, curling slightly towards the end.

I force myself not to back up as prey would, but instead stand as tall as possible, gripping my daggers tightly. The cat has bright blue eyes which roam up and down my body. Its whiskers twitch as it sniffs the air above my head. I don't know what this giant cat is doing, but I don't sense any predatory intent. A huff of warm breath on the back of my head makes the fine hairs on my arms stand up. I slowly turn my head and see an equally large black feline standing behind me. Its shining yellow eyes lock onto mine for a moment before I drop my gaze. It appears almost identical in size and shape to the white one in front of me.

Now I understand why no one comes to this land. Yes, it's beautiful, but if there are animals like this wandering around, I can't imagine tourism being very popular.

Something bumps the center of my back, and I startle, turning to see the black feline's head lower as it nudges me again. The white cat steps around me, standing next to the black one. They stand side by side, staring at me. Either they really like playing with their food before they eat, or these felines want me to continue down the road.

I turn my head again and the white cat's lips curl up from its teeth slightly as it lets out a low snarl. Okay, point taken. I sheathe my daggers, setting off down the path at a slow jog. A quick glance behind me sends a shiver up my spine. The felines are gone.

The sun is high overhead when the foot of the mountain comes into view. I run until my lungs ache and my throat feels scratchy. My feet hurt from the hard rocks of the path. I slow to a fast walk. I haven't seen any signs of Misty or the two cats, but I've been so focused on running that I didn't really have the energy to look for them either.

As I get closer, I see the end of the road. It leads to a large stone structure at the base of the mountain, with a path cutting a gradual ascent into the trees. Two other roads converge at this point as well, and I imagine that's the direction the other heirs will come from. Horses snort nearby, and I see stables off the road. I head there first.

Misty is unbridled and unsaddled in the first stall inside the door. I rush to her and she whinnies, happy to see me.

"You big baby, leaving me there all alone with those overgrown cats," I say, running my hand down her neck. My eyes catch on my pack, hanging up on a metal hook on the side of her stall. I race to it, ensuring all my supplies are still safely stored inside. Sure enough, everything is where it belongs. I breathe a sigh of relief.

"Excuse me, miss." I jump as a feminine voice calls out behind me.

I whip around and see a tall figure in a dark green robe, hood concealing their face. They pull an apple out of their long sleeve and present it to Misty.

"Smart horse, ran all the way here," the woman—yes, I'm convinced this person is a woman now—says. "Gave us quite a fright. And the heirs, too. They debated whether they should go after you."

I inwardly curse myself and look around. Four other horses are in these stables.

"Thank you for taking care of Misty for me," is all I say, hefting my pack onto my back. Already my muscles ache from the run, and now I add insult to injury.

The robed figure bows slightly, and then points towards the stone house. "They wait for you."

I bow back to her and with one last pat on Misty's side, I rush out of the stables.

As I enter the living area of the stone home, four sets of eyes train themselves on me and confirm my dreaded suspicion. I've arrived at the mountain dead last.

CHAPTER TWELVE

My eyes rake over the group, snagging on Aidan's. He smirks and turns to the man standing next to him with golden blond hair, elbowing him and presenting him with an open palm. I watch as the blonde man pulls a few gold coins out of his pocket and slams them into Aidan's hand with a glare. Aidan chuckles humorlessly. My blood cools and my cheeks heat. Were they betting on my survival?

"Welcome, Princess Elana. We've been waiting for you," the man closest to me says. He's tall and lean with muddy brown hair down to his shoulders, dimples on each tanned cheek, light brown eyes, and a half smile. He wears sturdy traveling clothes, much like me. "My name is Rian Yarrow of Aaranor."

I fight the urge to bow to him since we're all equals here. I quickly dredge up all I know about him from Aislinn's lessons. He's one of the nicest heirs, almost too nice, according to Aislinn. She was never positive if he was faking it for the sake of an alliance, or if he was genuinely kind. Either way, since he never showed any outright hostility towards anyone, it was moderately safe to trust him.

I offer a polite nod and small smile. "Hello, Rian. It's wonderful to meet you."

"You kept us waiting long enough," the golden blond-haired man next to Aidan snaps. He seems to be taking it well, losing his money. His hair is nearly to his shoulders and swept back from his face, which leaves his deep blue eyes and cocky attitude on display. His pale skin complements his features. I instantly know him as Calder Vernier, heir of Hotharia, without him having to introduce himself.

"Calder, thank you for your *patience*," I emphasize the word just to needle him. If I'm already breaking Aislinn's rules, I might as well do a thorough job. "I had...an encounter with some giant felines on the way," I explain, tensing my shoulder muscles to square off at him as I narrow my gray eyes on his.

The Hotharian heir bristles. "If we have to make any other *accommodations* for you, I guarantee you won't be making it back down the mountain."

I want to rage at the threat but take a deep breath instead, letting go of my building tide of anger. "I'm sure the Gods would be interested to know all about your guarantee to thwart one of their chosen heirs."

The mark hits home, and Calder seems to remember where we are as he scoffs and turns away. This is the land of the Gods, where their power is greatest. We're in their servants' home, at the foot of their mountain, which was raised from their strength. I don't know where this sudden sense of confidence comes from, but in this moment, I'd love to nudge him over the edge to see what kind of wrath the Gods would exact.

Rayna steps forward, pushing past Rian. As the only other female heir, it's easy to identify her. She stands a hand or so taller than me, with sharply beautiful features, smooth dark skin and deep brown eyes. Her shiny black hair is tightly braided on her scalp, and tied at the back of her head, the ends loose and falling in tight curls past her shoulders. Every bit of her looks like Melinor's famed warrior queens of old.

"I'm Rayna, heir of Melinor. It's good to finally meet you, Elana. I've had to endure these three men bickering for too long. I think it's past time they whip out a measuring stick and get it over with," she says, glaring at the three men, who all express various degrees of discontent at her words. Calder is the loudest, grousing about how disrespectful she is to a future king.

A laugh bursts out of me before I can temper it. Oh, I like her already. Rayna shoots me a savage smile and I flash one back. Aislinn said in a few of our lessons that of all the heirs, she got along best with Rayna, and I can see why. I hope the same will be true for me, too.

The green robed servant walks inside, arms folded in front of her robes. The other heirs and I go silent. She slowly pushes back her hood and reveals a bland face that's neither young nor touched by age, but somewhere in between. Creamy alabaster skin, a sign of too much time spent indoors, is framed by long, raven hair. Her bright green eyes are like jewels, unnatural in color. Her gaze roves over all of us.

"You may call me the Maiden. I dwell here with my brother, the Steward. We have served the Gods for generations," I notice Rian and Rayna exchange a doubtful look, and the Maiden catches it too. "Yes, children, I'm older than I appear."

Calder scoffs again, and I wonder if the only emotion he's capable of expressing is disgust. "We're not children."

The Maiden smiles without warmth at him, her green eyes seeming to flare. "When you've lived hundreds of years and seen dozens of generations go through the challenges to meet the Gods, you, too, would raise your expectation of adulthood."

Calder shuffles on his feet but doesn't offer a reply. I have the urge to give this woman a hug, but it quickly dies when she turns her focus on me and speaks. "You will all be tested. At times, the challenges may be brutal. But the Gods are not without reason. The best advice I can give you is to keep moving forward, always."

She finally turns her unnerving gaze on the others after almost echoing what my father told me in his study.

"Do you have any questions before you begin your journey?" The Maiden asks, giving us ample time to respond.

When no one speaks, she lowers her head. "Very well, then you may follow me. The Steward will lead you to the trail."

She whisks out the front door and I quickly follow, the heirs falling into line behind. Outside, I see the sun is past the zenith and beginning its downward descent.

The Maiden leads us away from the stables and towards the slope of the Gods' Peaks. A searing heat rushes past my shoulder and a piercing cry fills the silence hanging around us.

The phoenix—possibly the same phoenix from the crowning ceremony—flies low, feathers alight and trailing smoke behind it.

The bird swoops towards the ground, there's a flash of light and burst of heat, and then a man stands there in dark maroon robes.

"*Shapeshifter,*" Calder hisses behind me, like the word is a curse. "That's unnatural. What's a monster like that doing here?"

"Quiet, you dim-witted dolt," Rayna whispers back. "That's the Messenger."

Calder mutters something under his breath that I can't make out, and then wisely goes silent as the man walks towards us.

There is lore about shapeshifters. They appear occasionally in our ancient myths and legends, but not much is known about them, other than they're as rare as seers. According to the stories that father loved telling Aislinn and I, shifters can change into anything—or anyone—they choose, making them incredibly effective and dangerous spies.

Long ago, the rulers of the kingdoms decided to hunt them to extinction, with the hope that shapeshifters' powers could never be used against them. They offered bountiful rewards to anyone who brought forth a proven shifter. How did they prove it? According to legend, shifters have shimmering, iridescent blood.

Everyone thought they'd been wiped out centuries ago, but it appears a few escaped the hunts. I smile. I hated hearing how the shifters were hunted down and slaughtered by the so-called "heroes". Father always agreed with me whenever I expressed my unhappiness about the tale. He insisted it was an important one to pass on, so we don't repeat the same mistakes as our ancestors.

"Welcome, heirs." The man in the maroon robe bows. "I am the Steward. We have already met once. I was the phoenix who crowned you."

He glances at us in turn, gaze lingering on me. He has the same raven black hair as his sister with a face as startlingly plain. His eyes are a fiery orange color, uniquely his own. I swallow hard, preparing for him to realize he made a mistake and throw me out, but no hammer falls.

"My sister and I are two of the last shifters alive. The rest of our kin hide throughout Astrellia, but our numbers dwindle every decade. To ensure my sister's and my safety, there is a spell placed upon your tongues. Once you leave the Gods' Territory, you'll never be able to utter a word about us. The Gods have promised us safety in exchange for our servitude, and so we happily serve," the Steward says, smiling slightly at his sister.

"Are you ready to be tested?" he asks.

We all nod, silent.

"May the Gods watch over you and choose well," the Maiden says. She raises her hood and walks back towards the stone house without another word.

The Steward turns around and motions for us to follow. We walk for a minute or so before he stops and turns around, gesturing to the winding path beyond him.

"This is where you shall begin your journey. No one will force you to walk this path, but should you choose to continue, understand that no aid will be provided other than what the Gods will. If you choose to leave and not participate in these trials, do so now. No harm will come to you." He waits.

Calder elbows me, wagging his eyebrows like he expects me to take the offer. I glare at him and square my shoulders, staring at the phoenix, who watches me with fiery appraising eyes. When no one moves, he steps back out of the way of the path.

"I wish you luck on this journey, heirs of Astrellia." The Steward bows his head and walks away, leaving the five of us standing in front of the trail, waiting to meet our future.

CHAPTER THIRTEEN

Aidan takes the first step. He hefts his pack onto his shoulders and sets out up the hill. Rayna follows, then Calder, Rian, and finally me.

The path is hard packed dirt and easy to see as it winds around gigantic trees and large moss-covered boulders. Everything under the canopy of trees is lush dark greens and earthy browns. Multiple layers of trees grow, the tallest ones so large it would take all of us with our arms spread wide to wrap around the trunks. Pinecones the size of my head litter the trail. Calder makes a habit of kicking them whenever possible.

The sound of water bubbling nearby has us stopping after a little while to fill up our waterskins in a clear, fast-moving stream. I filter the water through a homemade contraption made of cloth and a metal ring on the outside to hold the cloth in place. It filters out most dirt and other organic matter. Rian takes an interest in the filter, so I explain the basics of it. He nods along with my explanation, then tears off a small corner of his shirt and fits it to his water skin to try to mimic me.

"Ah, so that's what non-gritty water feels like," he says and winks at me. I smile back and we fall back into line as the other heirs head out.

Luckily, this part of the trail isn't terribly difficult to tread. No roots stick up through the dirt, and the incline isn't too steep. This side of the mountain, from what I can see, has similar trees and creatures as the area around it. We won't have a difficult time finding game to hunt or fresh water to drink.

Silence fills the space around us for some time, each heir seeming to be in their own head, and it doesn't take long for me to start trailing behind. At first it's only a step or two, then the gap slowly widens as the afternoon wears on. My heavy pack weighs me down, and I mentally curse my lack of stamina. My legs ache from my earlier run, already worn down.

"Hey, crown stealer, you coming or what?" Calder calls from ahead, stopping his trek and staring back at me. I bristle and flip him a rude gesture, but quicken my pace, breathing heavily to catch up with the heirs.

Crown stealer. He called me a crown stealer, and no one corrected him. I wonder if they all believe that, or if no one cares enough to argue with him about it. Maybe they're waiting for me to show strength and stand up for myself. I really should say something. I open my mouth—

"What do you think the first challenge will be?" Rian asks, cutting off my retort before I even start to say it. My jaw snaps closed. The moment is gone now. I sigh. At least I can still answer Rian's question.

"Last generation the earth goddess went first, so I doubt it'll be anything with earth," I say between breaths. "It could be the opposite this time, air maybe? Perhaps a storm of some sort."

A flash of my recurring nightmare suddenly comes back to me. The storm, the intensity of it. I shiver despite the afternoon heat. I hope we don't encounter anything like that.

Calder kicks at some stray pebbles, sending them scattering down the gradual slope towards me. "It won't be a storm. That's dull and has been done way too often."

I wonder if this angry, entitled prince has ever been happy in his life. Surely not, if he's this argumentative about every little thing spoken aloud in his presence.

"What do you think it will be then, Calder?" Rayna asks.

"Don't know and don't care. All I care about is impressing Tolliver. Metal is the superior element, and I'm going to follow in my father's footsteps and claim that power for myself," he says, brushing past Aidan, who levels narrowed eyes at him. His look isn't something I'd want to be on the other side of. It sends chills down my spine.

We all stare. I've never heard anyone speak so disrespectfully about the Gods before, especially in their own land.

"Metal is fine for crafting weapons, but it means nothing if you can't even feed your people, Vernier," Aidan says with disdain dripping from his words.

"What the Hells did you say, Ashfall?" Calder bristles, drawing his spear from his back in one sweeping motion. Even though he stands slightly higher on the hill than Aidan, he still has to angle his head up to meet his gaze.

Rayna and Rian back away from the two, moving to stand near me off the side of the path. I realize they're giving the two space in case this turns into a fight. Neither heir seems overly concerned about the situation, so I gather this might be normal for the group.

"Put that weapon away, Vernier. We all know how well it ended for you the last time," Aidan's voice betrays his barely concealed fury. He takes a half step up, pushing his chest right against the lethal tip of Calder's spear. "Peacock for some other group, Prince. We're all in the same shit here. Unless you think you can take out the competition without any...consequences."

Some kind of recognition flares in Calder's eyes, and he huffs but lowers his spear. He spins on his heels and stalks off back up the path.

Rian lets out a low whistle and steps forward, following Calder. Rayna files in behind him, and I trail her. I pass Aidan, whose gaze snaps to mine.

"I'm following you, Magpie, so don't even think about falling behind again. I'd like to get home this century," he says, a smirk pulling up a corner of his lips. Like he didn't threaten another heir just moments ago.

"Magpie?" I ask as I walk, scowling.

"Ah, yes, I've decided you're too foul-tempered and noisy for a bunny," he says.

"My name is Elana. I suggest you start using it, or else you'll find out all about my foul temper," I snap, whipping around. I intend to flash him a glare I've seen Aislinn give those who disrespect her, except when I spin, I come face-to-chest with him. I stumble backwards, tripping over my feet. I start to fall backwards, and his hand shoots out, catching my arm effortlessly. I let out a gasp of surprise, and he firmly tugs me back until I find my balance.

His golden eyes pierce me as he leans closer and whispers above my ear. "That sounded a lot like a squawk."

Heat erupts from my neck to the top of my head as I yank my arm out of his grasp. He chuckles and lets me go, gesturing for me to move onwards. I do, spinning around and hoping my auburn braids whip him right in his stupidly attractive face. Gods spare me from Aidan Ashfall.

My lungs burn and legs shake. Every breath feels like someone is squeezing my chest. There's a cramp slowly pulsing in my side. This must be the Gods' cruel punishment.

The trail turned steep about an hour ago. The sun is starting to set, but the group wants to push on as far as possible. While we're strong, I guess. It makes sense, it really does, even though I hate this climb with a burning passion.

Gods, this is only the first day, and I'm already feeling exhausted. I wonder if the Gods grant us physical stamina in addition to elemental abilities.

The first peak is the smallest, I recall Aislinn teaching me. Animal life is abundant here, so we're to hunt what we find here and save our dried, cured food for the barren peaks later.

Lush forest surrounds us, towering coniferous and deciduous trees line the path upwards. Dying evening light streams through the branches of the trees, golden in color. Birds call out above us, and rodents and other mammals scatter through the thick brush near our feet.

This, at least, feels almost like home. Even if those birds are about three times the size of birds back home, and the rabbits here have antlers to rival the oldest stag. I swear I've even seen a flying white fox floating between the trees, flapping its gigantic fluffy ears. Although, that could have been due to the lack of oxygen making it to my brain with how quickly I'm breathing.

My pack slid down my shoulders sometime in the last few steps, so I hitch it up, pausing briefly to take a few deep breaths.

"Hey heirs, the weakling stopped to take a break again," Calder shoulders past me. So far everyone but me has taken their turn in the front. We've naturally shuffled our positions since setting out, and lucky me, I've had Calder on my ass since the last shuffle.

Rayna turns back and rolls her eyes at Calder. "Don't be a prick, Calder. She was chosen like the rest of us."

I flash a quick, tentative smile at her. She smiles back and turns back to the trail, catching up to Rian with a burst of speed I envy.

"We need to find a flat spot to rest before the sun goes down," Aidan calls out from his position behind me in the rear.

"I'll run ahead and see if I can find one," Rayna says, passing Rian and jogging up the trail. How does she do it? I glance at Rian and notice with a pang of guilty satisfaction that he, too, seems slightly out of breath.

We continue walking, but it's not long before Rayna jogs back, finally breathing hard. "The ground levels out not too far ahead. The path looks flat as far as I can see after that."

I sigh with relief, feeling newly motivated as we continue our upwards climb. The sky is darkening when we finally make it to the leveled-out part of the path. It looks like the trail ahead wraps towards the side of the mountain. Rayna's right, the incline is gentle.

The others waste no time in spreading out their bed rolls. They seem to be organizing themselves around a central area, where Rian currently strikes flint against his knife, attempting to light a fire.

I claim a spot near the rocky face of the mountain to lay my pack down, in between Rayna and Rian and as far away from Calder as I can get. Rayna appraises me for a moment, brown eyes narrowing when she sees me setting up my sleeping pack, and then motions me closer to her.

"You don't know if any rocks will fall during the night. I'd sleep a bit further away from the cliff if I were you," she says, pointing at the steep rock face which ends in a slight slope. She's right—if anything knocks loose, I'll be crushed. I should have realized that earlier. Death by rock doesn't seem like a good way to go.

"Oh, I didn't even think of that. Thank you, Rayna," I say, moving my thick blanket away from the wall.

She gives me a short nod and unrolls a thin blanket onto her sleeping mat. Across the circle I watch Aidan move to help Rian light the fire, who loudly curses the wood for being too damp.

"You're doing it wrong." Aidan takes the flint and steel away from Rian. He strikes it down towards the kindling a few times in quick succession. Glowing sparks land on the wood and Aidan leans over it, blowing gently on the sparks. They flicker and grow, catching more of the kindling. Aidan carefully arranges the sticks on top of the pile into a pyramid shape. Within a few moments the fire roars. Aidan tosses the flint and steel back at Rian.

"You can't force the fire, you feed it," Aidan says. He grabs his bow from near his pack and slings his quiver over his shoulder, then walks off without explanation.

My stomach gives an unhappy rumble. I look around the nearby foliage for anything edible. I've been gathering medicinal plants for years now. I know which roots are delicious and which ones are deadly. I can identify poisonous berries and mushrooms that make you see sound before shutting down vital organs.

"I'm going to find something for us to eat," I tell Rayna.

She smiles at me. "Want any help looking?"

"Are you good at foraging?" I ask, patting my hips to reassure myself that the twin daggers are still with me. It's not that I don't trust Rayna, I just don't want to be without weapons out here. The Gods could send a challenge to us at any time, so we have to be constantly vigilant.

"I'm not, but I can hunt," she picks up her sleek black bow. It's noticeably shorter than mine, with a thicker string. She wears a quiver on her hip. She wears tan pants and a dark orange tunic, with dark leather bracers and armor covering her chest, shoulders, and legs. She looks like one of the portraits of the warrior queens I've seen in history books. I wonder if she plans on wearing the armor the entire time we're here.

I nod at her, securing my pack once again before we head out. Ash warned me not to leave my possessions unguarded, and I have a feeling this is one warning of hers I should heed.

Rayna and I stalk through the woods. I keep my eyes on the ground and brush, scanning for any familiar plants. I spot a blackberry bush, plucking a handful of the juicy berries off, holding my hand out towards Rayna in offering.

"How do you know these aren't poisonous?" she asks skeptically, eyeing the berries offered to her with furrowed eyebrows.

"They're blackberries. They don't have any poisonous look-alikes," I say, popping one in my mouth to demonstrate their safety. I chew a few times and swallow, smiling at the taste that reminds me of Gwen's breakfast pastries.

Rayna considers, scanning my face for any ill effect before taking a few and chewing carefully at first, then swallowing quickly. "They're very sweet."

"Our cook, Gwen, makes the best pastries out of them," I say. I spot another blackberry bush up ahead and move towards it.

"We don't have many berries in Melinor," Rayna says, helping me pluck the ripe ones. "Actually, we don't have many sweet foods at all."

"What kinds of foods do you eat?" I ask, because Ash's intensive curriculum didn't cover the local cuisine of each kingdom.

Rayna considers, popping another blackberry into her mouth. "We eat a lot of fish closer to the coast, beef, and lamb. Rice and cassava are common, and we have the best sauces in all of Astrellia. You could eat the same meal with a different sauce for months and not tire of it."

"That sounds delicious," I say.

"You'll have to travel to Melinor one day to find out," Rayna replies with a slight smile on her face. I wonder if she's thinking of home. I know little of Melinor's geography, other than that most of the kingdom is covered by a large savanna. Grasses and sparse trees as far as you can see. Their main exports are tree nuts, nut oils, wheat, and potatoes. A lot of our clothing fibers come from Melinor, too. It's well-known that centuries ago, the Semere royal line, Rayna's family, fought off invaders from the north who came to conquer the continent of Astrellia. They lost their only two Gods-blessed elemental wielders at the time and suffered heavy losses before the armies from the rest of the kingdoms arrived to assist and beat back the invading forces. Melinor has always had incredibly gifted wielders and a well-trained army. Only the army of Ocarin is said to be stronger.

I take stock of the forest around me. The trees and terrain might be different, but it's the tranquil energy of the forest that reminds me of home. I spot some wild mushrooms growing around the base of a decaying tree and bend down to pick them. They're absolutely delicious when cooked in soups or stews.

"Is foraging like this normal for Adrithia?" Rayna asks, crouching next to me to inspect the mushrooms I pick.

"Not for people in town, but for smaller villages, yes. At the castle, we eat a lot of bread, cheese, soups, stews, beef, and potatoes. Our cook loves to make sweet desserts, though, so we often have pastries, cakes, and pies."

A rustle sounds in the brush nearby and Rayna draws her bow in an instant. She aims and fires at something I don't see. Her arrow flies too fast for me to glimpse, but I hear the dull impact.

"Got it," Rayna says and runs towards the sound. I follow her and finally see the large pheasant with the arrow protruding from it. She makes sure the bird isn't suffering before taking the arrow out and cleaning it on a spare bit of cloth. A pang of guilt hits my stomach. The bird is beautiful. But we need to eat meat or else risk weakness or starvation. The life of one bird is not more important than the lives of my entire kingdom.

"Nice shot," I tell Rayna, to get my mind off unpleasant feelings.

"Thanks," she replies. "Archery was the first skill taught to me as a child. You probably noticed that my bow is smaller, yes?"

"Yes, and it's curved more than mine too."

"These short bows are common in Melinor. They are specialized to our style of shooting while riding horses," she says. "Shorter bows are easier to maneuver on horseback."

"Oh, so Melinor has warhorses too?" I wonder, remembering Aidan's giant stallion.

Rayna makes a sound of disgust. "No, not like those hulking murderous beasts. Our horses are swift, nimble, and steady. They've been bred that way for generations."

I smile at her description. "I'd like to see those horses."

"And so you shall, when we get back down the mountain," Rayna says matter-of-factly.

"I hope so," I say, walking towards the sound of a river, hoping to find more mushrooms near the water.

"Elana," Rayna's voice, turned low and serious, stops me in my tracks and I look back at her, "I idolize Aislinn. She was years ahead of me in training, skill, intelligence, in every way that matters for an heir. I spent most of the last decade trying to catch up to her in every way. Out of respect for her, I will do what I can to help you."

"There are rumors that you stole the crown from Aislinn at the ceremony, but that's an insult to the Gods. There's no way the phoenix would have allowed that. It would have roasted you alive. Plus, you don't seem like you actually want to be here, unlike the rest of us. So there must be some reason you were chosen, and I'm curious what that reason is, since you were clearly so physically unprepared for the role."

I look up at her in shock, not sure what to say. What can be said after that? I feel a mixture of pride and offense at her words.

"I, um, thank you, Rayna," I say tentatively.

She smirks down at me, then nudges my shoulder. "I won't coddle you, but I'll do what I can to keep Calder and the others off your back. Rian is friendly and should be easy enough to persuade to join our little...alliance, if you can convince him you're competent."

"I'll convince him," I promise, turning to point at a group of skinny reed-like plants on the bank of the river. "That's wild onion, perfect for pheasant stew."

Rayna barks a quick laugh. "Ah yes, the quickest way to a man's heart is through his stomach."

CHAPTER FOURTEEN

We get back to the campsite as darkness truly sets in. I silently thank the Gods that Rayna has a better sense of direction than me, because she led us back effortlessly while I was truly lost. I can find my way in the daytime with no problems, but nighttime takes all the visual cues away. Rian sits on the ground near the crackling fire, alone.

"Ah, you're back." He lights up when he sees us, his eyes going right to Rayna and the plump pheasant in her hands. "And you've brought dinner?"

Rayna sets her bow down and pulls out a small knife, efficiently dressing the bird. I look away, stomach turning at the sight of it. She catches my sickly pallor and rolls her eyes.

"Where did you think your food came from?" she asks.

I busy myself with removing the wild onion, blackberries, and mushrooms from a pocket in my pack.

"I'm well aware of where I get my food, but that doesn't mean I want to stare into its cold, dead eyes," I break up the onions, removing the roots and brushing dirt from the stalks. The bitter but sweet smell of onions fills the air around us.

"Where are Aidan and Calder?" I ask Rian as I work, moving on to brush off the mushrooms and break them into pieces.

"They both went out hunting, I assume. They didn't exactly say," Rian replies, shrugging.

Rayna cleans her hands with water and pulls an iron cooking pot out of her pack. It's just large enough for the bird and half of the mushrooms and onions to boil in. How she carried that heavy pot around with her without complaining, I'll never know.

We watch the stew simmer for a while, listening to crickets chirp and our stomachs rumble. Brush rustles down the path and we all turn, Rian and Rayna already armed. I fumble with the twin daggers until I see Calder's blond hair reflecting the moonlight. Aidan's tall dark form appears behind him. Aidan carries a few antlered rabbits.

"What took you guys so long? Did you get lost?" Rian asks.

"Vernier scared away our dinner for the next week," Aidan grumbles, chucking the rabbits next to the fire.

"That's bullshit, Ashfall. You were never going to hit that stag," Calder snaps, sitting down on his sleeping roll.

"I would have, if you had only shut your Gods-damned mouth," Aidan says between clenched, bared teeth. He sets his longbow down on the other side of Rayna and makes quick work of preparing the rabbits to roast over the fire. I study the boiling pot while he does.

By the time we finally eat the rabbits and pheasant stew, I'm half asleep. Luckily Aislinn convinced me to bring a small fork and spoon, and a lightweight wooden bowl. I scoop the stew out, savoring the flavors. It's good. I glance around the fire. Rian eagerly finishes his second bowl, scooping out a third. Rayna lounges on her makeshift bed, popping blackberries into her mouth like they're a dessert sent from the heavens. Calder chews on a piece of rabbit. He refuses to eat any of the stew when he finds out I foraged some of the ingredients. I almost laugh at his absurdity.

I glance at Aidan last and find him watching me across the fire, the flames dancing in his golden eyes, reflecting off his dark hair. His bowl lays empty next to him.

"Any last takers before I finish it off?" Rian asks, looking around at us. I shake my head, Rayna and Aidan both say no, and Calder scoffs. Rian tips the last of the stew into his bowl.

"It's really good. How did you find the onions and mushrooms out here?" Rian asks me through a full mouth.

His eating habits remind me of Aislinn and I crack a smile. "Wild onions grow near water sources, so the river was a natural spot to look. And mushrooms feed on decaying matter, so old tree trunks or downed branches are the perfect place for them to grow."

"And you expect me to believe that you know the difference between poisonous mushrooms and safe ones?" Calder sneers at me. "You probably poisoned us all."

"I'm trained as a healer and have been gathering ingredients for medicines for almost ten years. I haven't poisoned anyone—yet," I say, staring Calder down. I sit taller as I finish my stew with an audible hum of pleasure as I chew the final bite.

He levels a murderous look at me and I smile back sweetly. I give my best impression of an Aislinn hair-flick, flipping my braid back behind my shoulder. It's a move she always used to piss off Aric, especially when she and I would get up to something reckless. It must infuriate all men, because Calder hisses something about "*bitch*" under his breath.

A light chuckle sounds from across the fire, and Aidan locks amused eyes on me. He raises his eyebrows at me and my stomach tightens. I turn away before he can see the shock register on my features.

"You know, it would be a lot easier to keep him off your back if you wouldn't antagonize him," Rayna mutters to me, throwing a blackberry at my face.

"Yes, but where's the fun in that?" I whisper back, brushing the dirt off the berry and popping it in my mouth.

Rayna gives me a wicked smirk. "Oh, you're definitely Aislinn's sister. This journey is going to be fun."

Rian offers to clean up the meal, since he was the one who stayed behind to watch the campsite. He takes the pot off towards the river. How he manages to see well enough not to trip merely by the light of the waxing moon is beyond me.

I arrange my cocoon, keeping my head towards Rayna, my first official ally. The ground is mercifully flat, with no large stones or roots poking me through the layers of my bedroll.

Exhaustion sweeps in moments after I close my eyes, like the adrenaline fueling me the whole day finally releases me from its tight grasp.

I'm back in the cave, staring at the wall, where my shadow and the halo behind it writhe on the wall. Unintelligible whispers surround me, and the sheer number of them screams in my ears. I reach my hands up to cover my ears against the barrage of noise.

"I can't understand you," I say, closing my eyes and trying to block out the voices screaming at me. "It's too loud. Please stop."

The torch behind me suddenly extinguishes, and the voices go silent. I open my eyes to darkness and take my hands away from my ears.

I exhale a shaky breath, alone in the pitch black of the cave. "Are you still there?"

The torch flickers to life in response.

"Okay then, can you try speaking again, maybe one at a time?"

My shadow on the wall stirs, and two feminine voices say softly, "we wait, we wait, we wait, we wait."

The voices fade out at the end, my shadow shrinking and slowly disappearing. I reach towards the wall, trying to grasp my shadow. "Where can I find you?"

I don't know why these voices in the cave are reaching out to me, but I feel a tug towards them, an invisible line connecting us and I need to know why.

"We wait, we wait, we wait," the voices continue to whisper, becoming inaudible, as the shadow vanishes.

A familiar rumbling starts up in the cave, and this time I don't look up at the rocks moments away from crushing me. I close my eyes and let out a final breath.

My muscles spasm as I abruptly sit up on my sleeping mat. Bright colors fill the sky, and birds twitter and sing in the trees around us. Rian snores softly to my left. The fire is a pile of smoking embers. It didn't get cold enough last night to need the fire, but it's a comforting presence nonetheless.

A dry mouth has me reaching for my water-skin, but it feels too light. Empty. I sigh as I remember draining it last night. On feet as silent as I can achieve, to not disturb anyone in their sleep, I leave camp and head towards the river.

Morning dew glistens on the grass as I wend my way through the trees and thick brush. I'm thankful for my waterproof boots so I don't have to deal with wet feet all day. I fill my waterskin, reveling in the coolness of the river. I splash my face a few times, rubbing off the residue of sweat that coated it yesterday.

It's peaceful here, and I sit on the sandy riverbank for a few moments, trying to remember what woke me so suddenly from sleep. There was a cave and darkness. I recall voices, but not what they said. I close my eyes and take myself back to the cave, the feeling of the complete darkness. It's fading fast. The longer I'm awake the further the dream slips away.

I sigh, knowing it's a futile fight, and stand back up, securing the water on a strap across my shoulder. I start to turn back towards the camp when I see a broad figure, backlit by the sun, stalking towards me, long spear in hand.

Light shines off his golden hair. Calder. I swallow hard, laying my hands on the hilts of my daggers.

"Morning, Calder," I say loudly over the sound of the river behind me. With any luck Rayna will hear, or notice we're both gone and come to investigate.

He moves closer, and I hear Aislinn's teachings in my brain. Don't let yourself get trapped in a corner, don't turn your back on your enemy, get to higher ground, and always leave an escape route. I move, casually putting the river to my left, making a show to not appear afraid as I head towards a bright red berry bush slightly uphill and back in the direction of camp. These aren't an edible variety, but Calder doesn't know that.

"Want some berries?" I offer, plucking them slowly and lowering a hand to one of the daggers at my hip. The cool hilt steadies me, giving me the clear head I need to strategize a way out of this.

"No, I don't want any fucking berries. What I want, crown stealer, is for you to turn around and go home," Calder's voice is laced with venom instead of his usual boisterous disdain. His tone is lower, words slower. He's been waiting for me to be alone, I realize. A cold snake of fear wends its way around my spine.

"And if I refuse?" I attempt to sound casual, but my voice shakes slightly, giving away my fear.

"Then you'll still be going home, but in a wooden box," he says and walks closer. His grip on the spear shifts and he twirls it around once, flipping it so the point aims at my chest. "Look, it's nothing personal, okay? I like Aislinn. I respect her. But you, you're nothing but a hindrance to us out here. You can't keep up with us on the trail, and you'll only bring us down in a fight. It would be a mercy to kill you quickly instead of letting the Gods punish you later."

My eyebrows pull together. I need to figure out a way to stall him until help arrives. *If* help arrives. He might intend to kill me when we're alone, but would he have the guts to do it with an audience?

"How do you know I'll bring you down in a fight? You've never seen me fight," I say, dropping the berries and withdrawing my daggers. Maybe I can intimidate him with the unknown of my skill. I am still Aislinn's sister.

"Oh, little princess," Calder says in perhaps the most condescending tone I've ever heard. "Stop pretending. I know you haven't had any relevant training until after the Crowning Ceremony. In fact, you were about to be married off to some preening rich lordling, weren't you?"

My breath hitches in my throat. How does he know that? Sure, the details of my engagement weren't exactly kept a secret, but I didn't think news would travel across the continent. And for him to know about the training? I shiver, thinking of who in our house would have betrayed us.

"Who's the spy?" I ask, gripping the hilts of my daggers tighter hard.

Calder laughs humorlessly. "As if I'd tell. Now, be a good little girl and try not to scream."

He lunges, closing the gap between us in a few quick steps. He's got the advantage of attacking from a distance and uses it as he jabs his spear towards my chest. I move on instinct, spinning away, but not quite quickly enough. A small, shallow cut opens on my bicep, the blow that was meant for my heart. I let out a hiss of pain but keep my eyes on Calder. He starts to circle, and I move to stand opposite of him, not allowing him access to my back.

A presence is suddenly behind me, and hot breath tickles the top of my head, sending a chill down my neck. Calder pauses, face paling. He moves into a defensive stance, planting his feet with a grip on his spear so hard his knuckles are white.

I don't dare move to see what's behind me until whiskers brush the side of my face. I startle and lock eyes with the giant black feline. It nudges my cheek with its massive head, turning my head towards camp. I don't dare move.

The brush to my left rustles and the twin white feline steps up to my other side, growling softly. It fixes narrowed eyes on Calder, lips curled back to expose long sharp teeth as it prowls forward. Calder's throat bobs as he gulps, taking a step back.

"Is this a trial?" Calder asks, gripping his spear as if he's prepared to stab the white feline in the chest.

I consider that for a moment, but one glance at the black cat next to me, the intelligence shining in its yellow eyes, and I know the answer.

"No," I say, although I don't owe him a response. He threatened to kill me only moments ago. I should leave him to become kitty chow.

The black feline nudges me again, and this time I don't hesitate. They're protecting me. I know it instinctually. So I walk towards camp, keeping my daggers in my hands, not turning my back to Calder and the giant cats. A shape moves towards me from the direction of camp, sword drawn. It's Aidan, assessing the scene, eyes flickering over me, the cats, and then Calder.

The two cats don't even turn to look at him. They face Calder, stalking towards him. He backs up another step, glancing up at Aidan with wide eyes.

"You wanna help me, Ashfall?"

Aidan chuckles darkly. "Not particularly. What the Hells did you do to piss them off, Vernier?"

"Nothing!" Calder says, at the same time I say, "he tried to kill me."

Aidan's gaze cuts to me, roving up and down my body. He spots the cut on my arm, and his eyes darken as he takes it in.

"He didn't get a chance to though. The cats showed up in time," I say, shrugging and angling my body so he can't stare at my wound anymore.

Aidan turns back to Calder. "Seems like a god is warning you. I would lower your spear, if I were you."

"Fuck that, these cats will kill me if I do!" Calder's voice raises an octave or two, making him sound almost squeaky.

"Lower your spear, you idiot." Rayna's voice comes from behind Aidan. She stands behind Aidan a few paces, Rian with her. They must have heard the commotion and come running.

Rayna catches my eyes, worry flashing through them, but I give her a tight smile. Letting her know I'm—for the most part—unharmed. She gives me a quick nod of acknowledgement.

Calder doesn't take his eyes off the cats, but I swear I see a flash of embarrassment on his face. "Fine," he mutters, slowly lowering the spear to the ground, setting it on the grass.

The closest feline to him, the white one with stunning blue eyes, lets out a hiss and leaps past him, disappearing into the woods behind him. The black one turns back and locks eyes with me.

"Thank you," I whisper, and watch as it bolts after the white one.

When there's no trace or sign of them left in the woods, I slowly turn my back on Calder and walk to camp. Rayna follows me, Rian at her side. Aidan trails behind us, not bothering to wait for Calder.

"You're alright?" Rayna asks when we reach the circle of sleeping rolls.

"Yes, Rayna, thank you," I say, letting out a few deep breaths and finally sheathing my daggers. A weight I didn't realize had been pressing down on me lifts off my chest and my shoulders droop. I turn my arm to inspect the stinging cut on my bicep. It's shallow, bleeding slowly. I take a piece of clean cotton from my pack and wrap it. It should heal just fine on its own in a few days.

I start to roll up my bedroll and blanket, preparing to leave. As long as I keep moving, I won't worry about what just transpired.

"Did he really try to kill you?" Rian whispers at me. He's packing up his blankets next to me, but his eyes are on me and my shaky hands. Worry pinches his brows together.

"Yes, but he didn't get a chance to attempt it. Those giant cats jumped in before he was able to do any serious harm."

I see them eyeing my arm, where the shallow wound is, but they don't mention it.

"You've seen them before," Aidan says, not a question. He's already put it together.

"Yes, those were the two I encountered on my way to the mountain. They spooked my horse, so I had to run the rest of the way," I say. The Steward mentioned we would receive no help unless the Gods decided to offer it. The felines must be some kind of messenger for whatever god wanted me here.

"Divine intervention," Aidan says, a hint of wonder in his tone. "One of the Gods must really want you here, Magpie."

I roll my eyes at the pet name. Rian lets out a chuckle, and I stare at him, ready to snap if he starts calling me Magpie too. "What's so funny?"

"Can you imagine how embarrassing it would be for him if we had to explain his death to his parents in Hotharia? Death by kitty cat," he says, not quietly, and lets out another snort and continues packing his things. A wide smile stretches across my face and I, too, release a little giggle. Rayna lets out a bark of laughter, and Aidan rolls his eyes, but they glitter with amusement as he chews on some leftover dried rabbit that smoked slowly overnight.

Rayna and I share some of yesterday's blackberries and I eat some of the bread I packed from Agatha's inn. The bread won't keep, so it's either eat it soon or throw it away later.

Calder rejoins us, glowering at us all. He tears into the rest of the rabbit strips silently as he packs.

I avoid locking eyes with him but can't help the occasional glance in his direction. From here on, I won't allow him the opportunity to get me alone, walk behind me, or handle my food or drink in any way. I should have done this from the beginning, I realize, but that was my mistake, wanting to trust everyone. I refuse to let him end me. I will survive this.

As we're about to set out, Aidan brushes the embers of the fire with his boot, covering the coals with dirt so they won't catch.

The morning flies by. There's a wonderful breeze behind us, pushing us along and providing much-needed respite from the damp heat of the morning. The sun shines overhead, and sweat trickles down my neck, soaking the collar of my tunic.

So far, the path is only a slight incline and as smooth as dirt can be. Calder leads us, on request from Rayna. Apparently, I'm not the only one who doesn't trust him at their back. He hasn't said much since we departed, still brooding from this morning.

"Elana, I'm wondering," Rian asks tentatively, as if he's not sure of whatever question he wants to ask.

"Yes?" I prompt, when he doesn't continue.

"What really happened at the Crowning Ceremony?"

I inhale sharply. I'm not sure why I'm surprised. Even Aislinn warned me that they'd ask this question early on. Luckily there's not much of a story to tell, so it should be easy to dispel any rumors.

The quiet conversation about bows that Rayna and Aidan were having comes to an abrupt halt, and they blatantly wait for my answer. Even Calder half-turns his head to listen in.

"Everything was going as planned. We were all standing in front of the temple when the phoenix arrived. We kneeled, and the bird went to Aislinn first, but then it flew right past her and put the crown on my head instead. There's not much to tell. I don't know why the Gods chose me instead of her," I say, keeping my head down as I walk.

"That's it?" Calder bursts out. "No fight between you, no phoenix dropping the crown on accident and you picking it up?"

I start, looking up at him and the first words he spoke since we set off this morning. "Yes, that's it. I didn't steal the crown. I would never do that to my sister."

Calder regards me with distrust, while the others look contemplative.

"If that's the case, then there's only one explanation," Calder says, a sneer on his face. "Aislinn must be a bastard."

"Excuse me?" I snap, my hand going to the hilt of my dagger.

"It's the only other logical explanation. Your mother must have taken a lover who wasn't your father."

Rage boils me from the inside. Who the Hells does he think he is? I'm about to snap when I hear the familiar noise of a bow string drawing back.

I whip my head and look behind me. Rayna has an arrow aimed at Calder's heart.

CHAPTER FIFTEEN

"**A**pologize," Rayna barely whispers, eyes like slits and focused solely on him. Her form is perfect, arrow resting at the anchor point near her chin, left arm slightly bent, legs planted hip width apart.

Calder recovers from his shock in time to reach for his spear, but Rayna's arrow soars, catching his sleeve and sinking into a tree behind him. He freezes as she nocks another arrow faster than I've ever seen.

"That was a warning shot, Calder," Rayna's voice is as steady as her arm. "Apologize to Elana."

I gape at Rayna, as shocked as everyone else appears to be. The respect and friendship Aislinn and Rayna have for each other must be deeper than I realized, more than Ash ever let on.

For the second time this morning, Calder stands humbled in front of everyone. He shifts on his feet, glancing between Rayna and me, as if weighing how serious the Melinorian heir really is.

Whatever he sees in her face has his jaw clenching, and he drops his hands to his sides. "Gods, you're touchy this morning, Semere. I was only saying what we were all thinking."

"Apologize, now," Rayna's voice is low, deadly. She doesn't relax her bow.

Calder doesn't take his eyes off Rayna as he says through gritted teeth, "Elana, I'm terribly sorry for offending you and your family."

"Thank you, Calder," I say, eager for this uncomfortable moment to be over.

A few tense moments pass before Rayna lowers her bow, stashing the arrow in her side quiver and clipping her bow back between her shoulder blades.

I let out a breath and Calder sharply turns away, stalking back up the trail with renewed vigor, no doubt fueled by embarrassment.

Rian, who looks at me with raised eyebrows, follows Calder. Aidan catches my attention behind Rayna and pushes past her, gazing down at me with an unreadable expression before he goes ahead. I walk slowly, giving Rayna space to walk next to me.

"You didn't need to do that," I keep my voice low. I'm aware the others can likely hear anyway, but I would like to keep some semblance of privacy. "But thank you for doing it."

Rayna doesn't smile like I expect her to. She merely nods.

"Someone needed to do something about him. The five of us are supposed to be a team, working together to conquer the trials, impress the Gods, and rule our kingdoms in peace and harmony. How are we supposed to accomplish that if we're at odds with each other?"

I watch the ground as we walk. It feels like my fault somehow. I didn't want to be chosen, but I could have asked Ash to come here instead of me. I wonder if the Gods would have noticed, if the heirs would have gotten along better without me.

"Maybe you all would be better off if I wasn't here. I don't live up to Aislinn, and I never will. Even if one of the Gods grants me their power," I say quietly, "maybe it would be better if I hadn't made it to the mountain."

Rayna grabs my arm suddenly—not painfully, but hard enough to give me pause. She speaks as quietly as me, "I need to tell you something."

Then, to the group, she raises her voice. "It's midday, perfect time for a short break. Elana and I will be right back."

Without waiting to see if they stop, Rayna tugs me away from the path into a grouping of conifer trees.

Rayna takes a deep breath before she starts. "A week after the Crowning Ceremony I received a letter from your sister."

My eyes widen at the thought that Ash would reach out to the heirs. "You did?"

She nods. "Yes. We correspond regularly through letters, so it wasn't out of the ordinary. But her message was anything but ordinary. She asked me to watch out for you."

I stop breathing. Ash really did that? She never mentioned anything about her close friendship with Rayna, nor any letter she sent. Did she keep it a secret to spare me the embarrassment of thinking I'm not good enough? Or did she know something that I didn't about Calder and his intentions?

"In her letter, she asked me to keep it secret, but I thought you should know. It shocked me, to read her words. They were clearly her words too, as blunt as ever. I couldn't believe she asked this of me. That she trusted me with this, with your safety. I won't let her down," Rayna swings her pack to her front and digs through it, pulling out a folded and wrinkled piece of parchment. The edges are worn, like it has been read over and over again. She hands me the note. "This is her letter. You can keep it. I've memorized it."

Unshed tears sting my eyes as they build up, threatening to spill over. I hold them back, refusing to shed them in front of Rayna. Aislinn is still protecting me, even way out here where she can't reach me.

The parchment feels warm in my hand as I take a deep breath and nod, putting the folded paper into an inner pocket of my pack. I want nothing more than to read it right here, right now, but if I do, I'm worried I'll break down, and who knows how long it'll take to put the pieces back together.

"Thank you for giving it to me, Rayna. This is a gift," I tell her with a wobbly smile.

She smiles back and reaches out her arm. "My pleasure. Now come, we should return to the others. I wasn't very discreet in dragging you away. I'm surprised Rian hasn't come snooping. He's as fascinated with gossip as an old spinster."

I chuckle, grateful for the respite from serious talk and take her elbow, locking it in mine, something Ash and I always did. We walk side by side back to the path where we abandoned the other heirs, and indeed Rian meets us halfway, claiming to be searching for water.

"The river is back that way," I point in the opposite direction, towards the sound of water rushing by.

"Ah, and so it is," Rian laughs a bit forcefully, turning on his heels. "I'd be lost without you two!"

I roll my eyes at Rayna and she covers her mouth with her hand to suppress a laugh.

"Rian, will you fill up mine too, please?" Rayna chucks a nearly empty waterskin at him. He fumbles but catches it after a moment of juggling.

"Of course." Rian plasters a grin on his face, dropping into a dramatic bow, his brown hair dropping over his eyes as he says with elaborate grace, "Happy to, my dear Rayna."

Rayna blows him a kiss and tugs me along back to the path. Aidan leans against a tree and raises his dark eyebrows at us as we approach, noting our locked arms and presumed alliance. He doesn't react, except for a brief nod.

Calder paces on the dirt trail. He briefly pauses his pacing to glare at Rayna. "You're really allying yourself with her?" He punctuates by jabbing an accusatory finger in my direction.

Rayna straightens, leveling her own stare at him. "Yes. Melinor fully backs Adrithia's *rightful* heir."

Heat blooms in my chest. I don't know what I did to earn her trust, what Aislinn wrote to her to convince her, but her support of me means everything in this moment. I only hope I live up to her expectations.

Calder pinches his nose in disgust, waving his hand towards both of us as if in dismissal. "You're making a huge mistake, Semere."

"The only mistake around here is the one your mother made when she married your father," Rayna mutters quietly. I cough to cover my laugh and catch Calder's narrowed gaze.

"I will remember this. When I'm king, you'll—" Calder cuts himself off, shaking his head and turning his back on us. He stalks up the trail on his own.

Aidan pushes off the tree and his gaze lands on mine, the corners of his mouth turning up in an amused half smile. "You sure have a way of making things interesting, Magpie."

A scent like cedar hits me as he brushes past and follows Calder on the trail, walking slowly like he doesn't have a care in the world. There's almost a swagger to his gait. What an insufferable, infuriating man.

Rian runs up to us, holding out Rayna's waterskin with another low bow. "Here you are my lady."

Rayna takes it, thanks him, and then follows Aidan. Rian and I exchange a look, and he glances back and forth between everyone—Calder's disappearing form, Rayna's tight shoulders, Aidan's amused steps.

"I've missed something terribly interesting, haven't I?"

I crack a smile at him. "I'll fill you in."

It's early evening when we stop again. The landscape is similar to the previous night's camp, so we arrange ourselves the same way. I check the bandage on my arm. A tinge of pink stains the top of it, but the cut underneath looks like it has stopped bleeding hours ago. I rub some antibiotic salve on it, which tingles slightly, and put another fresh piece of cloth on it. By tomorrow morning I expect to see scar tissue.

Aidan and Calder go off to hunt, and Rayna offers to stay behind and watch our things while Rian and I look for water. The stream that we walked next to most of the day turned away from us, so finding water will be vital tonight.

Rian jumps at the chance to go with me. Rayna stares at him with raised eyebrows, but gives me a shrug, putting my nerves at ease. He's given me no reason to be suspicious of him, but I still touch the daggers at my hips, if only out of habit.

"So Elana, is traipsing through the woods with us everything you thought it would be?" Rian asks, casually twirling his polearm around like it's weightless. Between his spinning movements I catch a better glimpse of the design. It's a similar length to Calder's spear, but the end doesn't have the same diamond shape. Instead, it has a curved blade attached to a simple, but clearly sturdy pole. The wood sings as he swings it. It's not an unpleasant sound.

I eye the sharp end warily as it cuts through the air and think about how easily it could cut through flesh. "Will you please put your giant pointy stick away? You're making me nervous, and I can't listen for water with all that whooshing."

"It's called a naginata, Elana," Rian says with a chuckle. "And you're perfectly safe. I've been training with this weapon for over fifteen years."

All heirs are well trained, but for some reason I expected Rian to be the least impressive of the bunch. Seeing him twirl the polearm around like it's an extension of himself once again makes me feel inferior.

"It's a beautiful weapon," I say, earning a wide grin from him. "I don't know exactly what I expected, but this mostly lives up to my expectations."

I strain my ears, hoping to pinpoint some water.

The swinging slows and finally stops. Rian puts the spear—no, the naginata—back into the straps between his shoulder blades. "I'm sorry you don't get to have the life you thought you were going to."

I startle. "You're the first person to apologize to me for it. People usually congratulate me, or think I stole the crown, so they assume it's an honor. Which, of course, it is. But you're right, this isn't the life I would have chosen for myself."

"It's not mine, either," Rian surprises me by saying.

I crack my neck spinning so fast to look at him. "It's not?"

His lips pull up into a sad smile. He faces straight ahead as he walks, not looking at me. "I know, it must be strange, since I've known my whole life that this is the only path for me."

There's no doubt that I should be thinking about this critically. He could be revealing this information to get me to lower my guard so he can dispatch me. That's what Aislinn would think, anyway. But there's something brutally honest in his expression, eyes looking at the ground rather than what's ahead of him, his brown hair falling in front of his face.

"What would you do if you weren't the heir of Aaranor?"

At this, he turns to face me with such sadness I feel a pang in my own heart. "It doesn't matter."

There's nothing I can say to that. He's right, it doesn't matter. We're all here now, with only one path forward, one future within our grasp. I take a deep breath and release it.

"Thank you for sharing that with me," I say, giving him an encouraging smile.

And then, because I'm feeling bold and slightly confused, I say, "I'm surprised you trust me enough to share."

Rian puts his hands up placatingly. "I know, it doesn't make any sense to me, either. My mother would drown me if she knew I shared a weakness without expecting anything in return. But I think that's part of why I'm telling you. I'm sick of being told not to trust people. And because I want you to know that you're not alone out here, that there's someone else who would rather be somewhere else. Someone that doesn't quite fit the mold of a perfect heir. Perhaps it's selfish of me to be glad I'm not alone. For the good of Aaranor, though, I'll do anything. Even risk death and Calder's dramatic moods on a mountain for weeks."

I chuckle. And maybe it's the exhaustion in my bones that makes me believe him, truly believe him. He seems desperate, but not for alliances like me. He seems to crave being understood.

"Well, Rian, in that case, let's be allies. You, me, and Rayna against Calder's dramatic moods," I say, throwing him a wink.

A childish grin brightens his features. "Oh, I do love the sound of that. I think the three of us should meet regularly to decide how best to annoy Calder."

We share a laugh and continue our search for water. Eventually, we come across a small spring, water bubbling up from the ground. Animal tracks are all around the pond, so we know it's a safe source of water.

I fill up my and Rayna's canteens and wait for Rian to fill his, Aidan's, and Calder's before we head back. Calder was loath to trust me, but he didn't see a threat from Rian. Aidan chucked his in our general direction before we set out, and Rian was the one to catch it.

"What's it like being Aislinn's sister?" Rian asks me on our way back to camp.

I answer quickly, "She's my best friend. So naturally it's both amazing and terrible to be her sister."

Rian's eyebrows raise, his request to continue clear in his expression.

"It's amazing because she's the strongest, smartest person I've ever known. Terrible for the same reasons. I'm often compared to her, and found lacking," I say, chewing on my bottom lip.

"She is incredibly strong and smart," Rian nods his head, "but so are you, from what I've seen. You stood up to Calder and found fresh food for us. I think it's impressive considering how little training you had before this."

I roll my eyes, chuckling humorlessly. "How does everyone know I haven't spent my whole life training for this like Aislinn?"

Rian cringes, looking apologetic as he says, "it was Aislinn herself who told us."

I stop walking, furrowing my brows. My brain whirls through the possibilities. "What do you mean? I thought...Calder mentioned spies...Ash would never...," I trail off, thinking of the letter she sent Rayna. Did she send one to Rian and the others as well?

"I'm not saying Aaranor doesn't have spies in your kingdom, but in this case, it was actually your sister who spilled the beans."

Rian sighs at my frustrated expression. "She didn't mean to, of course. No one expected you to be chosen as heir a few years later. The five of us were at a meeting to discuss trade routes with our parents. We were meant to shadow the proceedings and learn how to negotiate."

I remember that meeting, because I begged to go with, just to get away from my mother. It was held in the palace at Melinor's capital, Oraphia. Father said it was impossible for me to attend, and that they would only be gone one week. It ended up being more than two weeks, however, and while they were gone, I received some of the worst news of my life.

"Negotiations stalled after the first few days, when Hotharia refused to allow usage of their road south between Melinor and Ocarin without charging a tax. After the first week, Aislinn received a letter from Adrithia, from you."

My eyes drop to the forest floor. I vividly remember writing that letter. I'm surprised Aislinn could even read it, with how many tears fell onto the parchment while I wrote, smudging the ink. I sobbed all the way to the aviary, where our enchanted hawks resided. I sent it with my favorite dark brown bird, begging it to find Aislinn with swift wings.

"Aislinn flew into a rage after reading the letter. We were between meetings and everyone heard her arguing with your father in their rooms at Oraphia's palace. Rayna, Aidan, and I caught Aislinn when she stormed out of the suite. She explained that your mother secured a marriage for you. Some lord she deemed unworthy. She wanted to ride home immediately and force your mother to change her mind. We calmed her down and Calder found us in time to help convince her to stay at Oraphia until negotiations were over, that the wedding wouldn't happen immediately and she would have time to stop it after returning."

I had no idea she was that upset by the news. The letter she wrote back was soothing and reassured me that she would be home soon to talk to Mother about it. She wasn't able to break the engagement, but she helped me advocate for a few extra years before the wedding.

"We needed her at the summit, otherwise there would have been an uneven balance of power between the kingdoms. Once we calmed her down, she told us that you were too young to marry, that you were untrained in how to defend yourself, that your mother sheltered you and kept you from learning anything of value," Rian says. "Of course, this isn't uncommon for princesses. Most of our female siblings are untrained, with the exception of Rayna's two sisters, which we tried telling her. But she insisted upon her return she would train you herself and put a stop to the engagement."

I swallow hard, sniffling as I remember how helpless I felt for those years. Like my life wasn't my own and I had no autonomy whatsoever. I push those thoughts away and start walking back towards camp, "Unfortunately, she failed on both of those."

"I'm sorry I brought it up, Elana. I thought you should know. It wasn't spies that told us of your status. But Aislinn didn't mean any harm by it. She cares a great deal for you," Rian says, keeping pace by my side.

"It's fine, Rian, really," I lie. It comes out stiff, so I add earnestly. "I'm glad you told me."

We make our way back to camp in relative silence. I only spot one edible plant, wild asparagus. I hope Aidan has luck with hunting again.

He does. There's some kind of small animal roasting over a fire when we get back to camp. I don't even ask what it is, afraid it'll be one of the adorable flying squirrels I've seen scampering around the forest all day. It's fuel for all of us, only fuel. I ask Rayna for her cooking pot and add some water from my canteen. I set it on a large flat rock near the fire and toss in the asparagus.

My mind remains occupied with what Rian told me about Aislinn's fury, and how she almost left the summit early to come help me out of my engagement. The letter she wrote Rayna is currently burning a hole in the pocket of my pack. I need to read it, but not while the others are around.

The opportunity to make a brief escape from their prying eyes presents itself after we eat. Calder is the first to sleep, keeping his back to us all. A bold choice that proves he doesn't think we're threats. The others slowly drift off. I silently slip Aislinn's letter into the pocket of my trousers, take a lit branch from the fire, and quietly tiptoe into the night. I head down the path a little way, close enough I can still see the glow of the fire, but far enough that I can't hear Rian's snoring.

I hold the letter in one hand, the makeshift torch in my other. A few steadying breaths later I finally look down and start to read.

Dear Rayna,

I'm sure by now you've heard the news. My sister has been chosen as the heir. Do not fret over me, I'm quite content with the outcome for myself. I am, however, greatly concerned for Elana. She is wholly untrained and will be easily outmatched in matters of strength and endurance on the mountain. I'm begging you, Rayna, for the sake of any friendship we have, please help her. As much as you can, please watch out for her, guide her, and keep her safe. Especially from the other heirs. If harm befalls her, no force in all of Astrellia will stop me from seeking revenge tenfold.

She means everything to me, and I can't lose her.

Your friend,

Aislinn

Warmth trails down my cheeks. I brush away the tears and suck in a breath. I savor the scrawling handwriting, the anger and fear in her words, her signature. All pieces of my sister. Gods, I miss her so much. We've gone longer before without seeing each other, but this time feels different, being so far—

A twig snaps to my left. I grip the letter to my chest and swing the torch out in front of me at the approaching body. Aidan's golden eyes pierce mine. They glow almost unnaturally in the light of the fire.

I suck in a breath, wiping the back of my hand across my face to brush away the tears.

"Aidan, what're you doing out here?" I say, trying to sound confident through my shaky voice.

"You took the words right from my lips, Magpie," Aidan has one hand on the hilt of his sword.

I glance around to discern if he's alone. Nothing else moves or makes a sound around us. I let out a breath, even though I have no reason to feel relieved alone with this man. "I couldn't sleep, so I went for a walk. And my name's not Magpie, it's—"

"Elana, yes, I know." Even in the flickering golden light I can see Aidan's face pulled up into a smirk.

"Then why do you insist on calling me Magpie?" I fume, stashing the letter back in my pocket.

"Why do you get so angry when I do?" His eyebrows raise slightly, but there's a glimmer of amusement in his gaze.

I cross my arms in front of my chest. "Answering my question with a question is avoidance."

Aidan takes a step towards me until he's close enough for me to reach out and slap. I don't, of course. He could probably pick me up with one hand and toss me back down the mountain, and that's something I don't want to test. I barely come up to his shoulders in height, but I straighten my spine and channel all my ire into a glare.

"You avoided my question first, Magpie. I'm only playing by your rules. What brings you out here all by yourself?"

I debate shoving the torch in his eye, but surprisingly I don't sense any ill will from him, only curiosity.

"I wanted to be alone," I tell him, hoping he'll get the hint and go back to camp.

His eyes roam the length of my body before catching on my face again. "You shouldn't be alone and unarmed."

The blades at my hips seem to thrum in response, and I pat them gently. "I'm not unarmed, and I'm not afraid to be by myself."

Orange light from the torch reflects in his eyes and he tilts his head slightly, as if he's trying to puzzle something out.

"Now, if you'll excuse me, Prince Aidan, I'd like to bask in the little solitary time I have on this mountain," I say with a mocking curtsy, turning my back to him and readying to storm away.

"It's okay to be afraid, you know. It's what makes us human," he says, surprising me with the softness in his tone.

It's that tone that gives me pause. But it also ignites something in me. He's Aidan fucking Ashfall. I've heard the stories about him, even in Adrithia. He matches my sister in fighting skill and is the commander of his own regiment of Ocarin's army and has earned a fierce reputation as being completely ruthless to his enemies. There's no way he's ever been afraid in his life. I turn back around, raising my gaze to meet his eyes.

"Oh, and what would *you* know about being afraid?" I snap. "You have nothing to fear. A big powerful brute like you, strutting around like he was sent by the Gods themselves."

I expect anger or frustration at my words. My heart beats twice as I wait for his reaction, two quick dramatic beats—before Aidan laughs. A real laugh that crinkles his eyes and reveals a dimple on the right side of his face.

"A strutting brute, huh? I didn't realize you were paying attention to how I walk, Princess." Absolute glee lightens his eyes, making him appear younger than his twenty-six years, the oldest heir in our group.

My face warms, and I'm glad it's nighttime so he won't see the red now covering my face. He's handsome even when he's being moody and stoic, but Gods, when he laughs. The sight of his joy leeches all sensible thoughts from my head.

"I'm not paying attention, but it's hard to notice anything else when you walk in front of me for hours." I stammer and shift on my feet, finally lowering the torch.

"Well, if you're *so distracted* by me walking in front of you, by all means take the lead, and I'll have to suffer through all the distractions," he says, and then does the most absurd thing imaginable and winks at me.

I glare at him and swipe the torch in his direction. He jumps back, chuckling. He moves quicker and with more grace than I would expect of someone his height and build.

"The Magpie has talons," he teases, effortlessly swatting away my second swing.

I'm reminded by that nickname of his unanswered question. "You still haven't answered my question, Prince."

He runs his hand through his dark wavy hair before he speaks. "I think the name suits you."

I go through all I know about Magpies. Black and white birds, long tails, loud calls. That's about all I'm aware of, and I'm not sure I like the connotations of him calling me that, but I suppose it's better than "bunny".

A shuffling footstep has both of us whipping towards the sound. Rayna appears, backlit by the glow of the fire, but it's undoubtedly her.

"Elana, are you alright?" she asks. I see her bow and a few arrows in her hands.

I let out a breath, moving towards her. "Yes, I'm fine, thank you. I was just about to head back to camp."

I turn towards Aidan, who appraises me with raised eyebrows. He motions with his hand for me to go ahead of him and I shoot him a withering look before stomping to join Rayna.

I wake to a world cloaked in fog. Something feels wrong. The hair on my arms stands up and there's an uncomfortable pit in my stomach. I sit up and peer around the fire. Aidan is awake, watching the woods. He catches my eyes and puts a finger to his lips. My heart stutters as I realize he's gripping his sword with one hand.

There's no sound coming from the woods. It's unnerving. A whooshing noise comes from above us, and I pull myself up to a kneeling position, drawing my daggers. A ghost of a shadow passes over the treetops, flying up the mountain. It's too foggy to see what the shape is, but it's clearly massive. Another slow whoosh, quieter now, and the dark shape vanishes. The forest slowly comes alive again with the typical sounds. Birds caw, crickets chirp, frogs croak, Rian snores.

I let out a shaky breath, exchanging a relieved look with Aidan. His grip on his sword relaxes, and I slip my daggers back into their sheaths.

Calder stirs on his bedroll. "What're you doing, Ashfall?"

Aidan explains to him in hushed tones about the beast we witnessed, and I swear Calder's face turns even paler. We wake Rayna and Rian, urging them to silently pack up their things. It's time to move on, before we find out the hard way what that shadow belonged to.

We eat while we walk, devouring the dried meat from the night before and some raspberries that I spot along the trail. Not too long after we set out, Rian tries eating some yew berries off an evergreen shrub, but I smack them out of his hand before he can put them in his mouth. It's a close call that would have ended up with him in a lot of pain, and me using some of my rare medicinal ingredients to help him.

We're all on high alert and not talkative this morning. The path is steep again, rockier than we've dealt with before, with boulders taller than me blocking parts of the path. I breathe hard, focusing on putting one foot in front of the other. My unsteady breaths worsen the closer we get to midday.

Aidan, to my growing dismay, keeps his promise from last night, walking behind me all morning. I contemplate how it would feel to kick dirt in his face but decide against it—the effort wouldn't be worth the payoff.

The sun is at its peak when conversation picks back up between us. The fog has lightened slightly, but it still conceals the tops of the trees and reduces how far we can see in any direction.

"I think we're getting to the top," Calder says from the lead.

"Why do you think that?" Rayna asks.

"I have a feeling," he says, for once not sounding snarky. He seems hopeful. I guess despite his abrasive bravado, he's as eager as the rest of us to get off this mountain.

A whooshing noise cuts through the sounds of the forest. All the creatures fall silent again, like they did this morning. I pause, listening hard.

No one else stops to listen except Aidan, who stands at my side, looking up at the sky. Calder must have sensed that we've stopped, because he turns and sighs heavily. "Gods, Elana, keep up or give up!"

I start to respond when I hear the noise again. It's a slow sound, almost like...wings. I look to the sky as a massive shadow blocks out the little sunlight streaming through the fog.

"Dragon!" I scream.

CHAPTER SIXTEEN

The dragon is the largest creature I've ever seen. Taller than the towering trees around us, with a wingspan wide enough to cloak a large part of the mountain. Its scales are a deep red, accentuating the beast's burning yellow eyes.

I've only heard about dragons in stories. They used to dwell in mountain ranges across Astrellia but were said to be killed off centuries ago.

This dragon is very much real, however, and it appears to be taking our presence personally. The dragon roars and swoops low, wings beating, buffeting us with a blast of wind. I watch in shock as it banks tightly, whirls back around, and flies straight for us. Calder and Rayna are yelling something but I stand frozen, gaping at the creature. When the dragon is close enough for me to see its forked tongue lick its sword-like teeth, its mouth opens wide and I know the world is about to explode.

"Get down," Aidan yells from next to me. He yanks me down behind a nearby rock, covering my body with his own.

Fire assaults the rock around us and I scream at the sudden heat scorching the air around us. Aidan's arms hold fast. We're shielded here for now. From my spot on the ground, I'm staring up at him. He stares down at me, brows furrowed, lips pressed together. His dark hair is askew on his head and I have a mad urge to run my hands through it.

Oh Gods. What's wrong with me? We're in the middle of a dragon attack, and all I can think about is Aidan's perfectly silky black hair? For fucks sake, if Aislinn were here she'd feed me to the damn overgrown lizard.

"What're you thinking about, little Magpie?" He smirks as if he can sense the direction of my traitorous thoughts.

"Wouldn't you like to know?" I mutter. He chuckles and holds fast. One moment stretches into an endless inferno.

A guttural scream sounds from further up the trail. Rayna. I can't see her from where we're at, but I hope she's okay.

The intense heat cuts off. I peek out from around the rock, past the bits of red molten stone that drip from the boulder. Wings beat and I look past Aidan to where the dragon soars above the trees. It flies in a wide arc before circling back around.

"It's coming back," I whisper, but of course Aidan hears me. He nods and leaps up, drawing his bow from around his back and nocking an arrow.

"We have to attack it before it has a chance to breathe fire again. Let's see if we can get it on the ground," Aidan shouts to the group, "Use your bows. Once it lands, we strike from the ground."

I see Rian stand, helping Rayna to her feet. I see raw flesh on her shoulder peeking out of her torn—no, melted—shirt, and my stomach drops. Rian hands Rayna her bow and she takes a few quick breaths, brows pinched in pain, and draws it back. Rian draws his bow back next to her, his naginata discarded on the ground next to him. Calder didn't bring a bow, only his deadly-looking spear and a short sword, so he bends his knees and pulls back his spear for a throw. I draw my bow to my front and grab an arrow from my quiver.

I catch my breath in a few deep gulps, holding my inhale and releasing slowly to calm myself as I wait for the dragon to swoop close enough.

The moment arrives as it drops down between the trees, letting out an ear-piercing roar. I gag as I catch the scent of its horrid breath. I exhale slowly and let my arrow fly, aiming for its chest. The arrow hits its target but bounces off. I see two other arrows bounce off its body as well. Calder's spear goes flying, but the dragon banks hard and it sails harmlessly past.

The creature draws its wings back and plummets towards us. Aidan releases his arrow. It sinks into the dragon's left eye. Its piercing bellow has me covering my ears. The dragon pitches in flight and crashes towards the ground. The mountain shakes with the deafening impact and I'm almost tossed off my feet.

Aidan is already charging, bow discarded and longsword drawn. I shakily nock another arrow, aiming at the beast's head, but I can't get a clean shot with Aidan racing towards it. The dragon swipes its claw at its eye, dislodging the arrow, and whips its tail out, catching

Aidan in the chest and throwing him back. He lands with a groan in front of me and sucks in a sharp breath.

The dragon draws itself up, about to incinerate anything in its path—including Aidan.

"Aidan get down," I scream. I lunge for him as the dragon opens its maw and the world explodes once more in fire and blistering heat.

I'm going to die. I'm really going to die. Why would that damned soot chicken choose me instead of Ash? This is her birthright, something she's been training for her whole damned life. And now I'm going to die because one of the Gods decided it would be funny to watch me fail.

Fire blazes all around me. I squeeze my eyes shut and hold my breath so I don't burn my lungs. It's strange. I always thought burning to death would hurt. But I don't feel anything. Maybe my body is already gone, and it's taking my mind a minute to catch up.

As quickly as the blaze detonates, it dissipates. I open my eyes, coughing as I inhale ash and smoke. It catches in my throat, leaving behind an acrid taste that makes me gag. Smoke rises off burnt trees and scorched brush. Aidan stands panting in front of me, arms outstretched. His entire body heaves with exertion. But there's a hint of a smile on his face. Not the smirk I'm used to seeing on him, but a genuine smile. Even the dimple is back.

I slowly take in the scene. I notice some lingering flames on nearby trees at the same time as Aidan. He raises his hand, clenches his fist, and the flames gutter out.

I look at his hands, my mind racing to catch up. He stopped the fire. Golden eyes meet mine, and I smile.

"Goddess Enya blessed," I say, and he nods. He's the first of us granted a gift.

The dragon roars in anger, stomping towards us, stretching its neck out, probably hoping to eat us.

Aidan steps in front of me and a burst of fire explodes from his hands, catching the dragon in the face and pushing it back. It lets out a high-pitched screech and its wings flare, beating hard.

The dragon launches itself off the ground and then shoots straight into the sky. Aidan punches his fist out and a fireball shoots from his hand to the beast. It hits the dragon on its unprotected belly, and it lets out an angry roar before flipping around and barreling back towards us.

"Stay behind the rocks, everyone," Aidan says loudly enough for us all to hear. "I've got this."

I rush back to the boulder we sheltered behind before and watch in fascination and trepidation as Aidan walks off the path towards a clearing in the trees. He picks up his sword from where he dropped it earlier, holding it with both hands, knees slightly bent. The blade of the sword glows with an orange light in his grip, and I realize he's heating it with his power.

The dragon dives at a slight angle, mouth wide, exposing those deadly teeth, getting closer and closer to Aidan. I hold my breath. At the last moment the dragon pulls up—and Aidan jumps up, plunging the sword deep into the beast's underside.

It lets out a pained screech and its wings buckle. The dragon crashes into the ground, knocking over trees and sending dirt flying everywhere. The mountain shudders in response to the impact.

Aidan rushes it, not giving the dragon time to recover as he leaps onto its neck. With one wide swing of his glowing blade, he severs the dragon's head.

I let out the breath I've been holding, shakily forcing my legs to move towards Aidan and the dead dragon.

The others beat me to him, and I hear their gasps and congratulations. Well, most of them congratulate him.

"I always knew you were the hothead," Calder grumbles. He stalks off to retrieve his spear.

"That was incredible," Rayna says as she and Rian join us back on the path. I gasp as I see the damage to her arm. Blistering skin runs from the top of her shoulder to her elbow. She winces as she slings the bow over her opposite shoulder.

I drop my pack and sift through it. I grab the large silver tin from near the bottom and hand it to her. "Here, this will help with the pain and keep it from getting infected. You should bandage it loosely with a clean cloth for a few days until the blisters heal."

She takes the tin from me and nods. "Thank you, Elana." She uses her dagger to cut off the remains of her sleeve. I suck in a breath, seeing the full extent of the burn. Her dark amber skin is puckered with bright blisters that look like they could pop at any moment. I'm shocked she can move her arm, and even more shocked she can tolerate the pain without complaint.

Rayna struggles for a moment with the tin, her hand quivering uncontrollably.

"Here, let me," Rian says, holding his hands out for the tin.

Rayna hands it over with a nod of thanks and Rian helps her apply the salve with steady and gentle movements. Rayna sucks in a breath as he touches a particularly nasty blister, but she quickly sighs as the salve works its magic.

It's not actually magic, simply a combination of medicinal herbs and plants, some of them with numbing qualities. I read about the soothing and healing qualities of a spiky desert plant in my tome, *Healer's Guide to Salves and Tinctures,* which Clarisse drilled into me because it's the foundational book of all healing techniques.

Rayna pulls out a clean blue shirt from her bag and rips the bottom few inches off it. Rian ties it around her arm, and I watch as he's careful not to let the fabric stick to her skin too much. Rayna smiles at him when he's done and hands my tin back to me, but I shake her off.

"You should hold onto it, Rayna. You'll need to apply the salve at least twice per day," I say, hoisting my pack onto my back, sensing the others are anxious to move on.

We talk as we walk, the others quizzing Aidan about what it feels like to have the fire ability, and if he saw the Goddess.

"Yes, I saw her. It was only for a brief moment, right before the dragon tried to incinerate us," Aidan said, that smirk back on his face.

"Oh yeah, thanks for not letting that overgrown lizard fry us," I say to him.

He chuckles. "It was my pleasure. It would have been such a shame to see the Magpie burn before she could fly."

I roll my eyes at him. "Still calling me Magpie, Aidan?"

"Would you rather I call you something else?" he asks, staring down at me from his considerable height. "Sunshine, perhaps?"

My face heats, and I want anything but that right now. "No. But maybe you could use my name." I try to sound harsh, but it comes out more like a question. Gods, Aislinn would once again throw me off this mountain right now if she heard.

Aidan makes a show of considering it, leans in close, and whispers in my ear, "I don't think you actually want me to call you Elana."

His breath tickles my ear, and by the Gods, the way he says my name makes my toes curl in my boots.

I suck in a breath and I'm about to respond when Rian brushes past us.

"Pardon me, just slipping past," he says. He gives me a quick wink—letting me know he did, in fact, hear everything Aidan whispered to me.

Oh Gods, now I'm going to die of embarrassment. Too bad it's too late to throw myself into the dragon's teeth. At least that would have been a quick death.

Aidan lifts his eyebrows at me, then follows after Rian. He puts his hand up and a little flame burns there.

He plays with fire as he walks, changing its size, moving it at will, even changing its shape. He forms it into a prowling giant cat, like the ones that stopped Calder from trying to kill me. Then into a snake, making it slither through the air. He gives the snake wings and legs and turns it into a miniature dragon, the wings flapping realistically. Then he turns it into a bird and it flies around us heirs, weaving in and out between us until it circles around me a few times.

It's beautiful, with a long fiery tail. It's not large and majestic like the phoenix, but small and agile. It lands on my shoulder and I pull away from it, afraid of the burn, when I realize it's not hot.

Aidan chuckles and holds out his hand, making the fire bird land on it. I'm amazed at the level of control he demonstrates already. My father said it took him years to discover all the ways he could form and shape the earth, and that he still hasn't mastered everything.

I remember that Aidan's mother is also a fire wielder, and I wonder how much flame he's grown up around.

"How do you have such command over your fire already?" I blurt out before I can stop myself.

The little fire bird flaps its wings and turns back into a dragon, hovering by Aidan's shoulder.

"My mother is incredibly intuitive. I think she always knew I was destined for Enya's flames, so she taught me some basics of control. A lot of it is mental," he says. "Keeping emotions in check and working on breathing. So far it looks like her teachings have proven successful."

To prove his point, the dragon flies above all of us, growing larger and larger until it rivals the size of the beast Aidan slew. The flames writhe around its form, casting the foggy landscape around us in an eerie orange glow. The other heirs stop walking, their faces turned up to the fiery marvel above us.

As we watch, the dragon extends its wings wide, opens its mouth, and explodes in a burst of light and heat.

I look at Aidan, openmouthed. He hasn't even broken a sweat.

"Show-off," Calder growls and starts up the path again. Rian and Rayna follow him, but not before the latter gives Aidan an appreciative nod.

I'm struck with a feeling of awe for the first time since setting out on this journey. It's a marvel that I get to be here to witness these heirs coming into their power to strengthen our kingdoms and Astrellia as a whole.

Aidan starts walking again and I follow him. With as much control as he possesses, his mother, Queen Amira, must be capable of amazing feats.

"Will you tell me about your mother?" I ask, walking up next to him on the narrow path, forcing him to move over to allow me space.

He studies me for a moment, as if he's not sure he wants to respond. But he finally nods.

"She's an incredibly gifted wielder. Perhaps not as powerful as your grandmother, though. From what I hear, she was unbelievably blessed with power. Some scholars even consider her the most powerful of all rulers blessed by Enya."

I smile at that. Yes, she was a formidable woman. I'm proud to be her descendant, and prouder still that I have some memories left of her.

"But my mother still commands an impressive amount of fire, and I bet she would be a worthy opponent for your grandmother."

"Yes, I bet she would," I say, and truly mean it, especially with what little I've seen so far of Aidan's abilities.

Aidan scans my face, as if looking for the sarcasm, but upon seeing none, he flashes me a half-smile sans dimple and continues. "She's a great ruler for our people. She leads our armies herself, holds court for those who have grievances, regardless of their status, and she personally oversaw the training my brother and I received, even jumping into the sparring ring with us every fortnight."

"She sounds like a wonderful person. I hope to meet her someday," I tell him.

"Oh, you will. She was already dying to meet you after we heard what happened. The unknown heir."

I look down at the trail once more, stepping high over large rocks so I don't trip. "I bet she was upset like everyone else was when I was chosen."

"No, she wasn't upset. Intrigued, yes, but not upset," Aidan chuckles and gives me a sidelong glance. "She told me to be nice."

I snap my neck to look at him incredulously. "She told you...to be...nice?"

He holds his hands up, as if he, too, is confused. "My mother works in ways unknown to me. Maybe she received a letter from your father."

A wicked grin lifts my lips. "So, if your mother asked you to be nice, I wonder what she would say if I told her you held a knife to my back the first time we met."

Aidan raises his eyebrows at me, a gleam in his molten-gold eyes. "Are you threatening me? The only heir with a god's power at the moment?"

"No, of course not, degenerate Prince," I mock, giving him a quick curtsy for effect.

"If you were threatening me, I'd tell you to keep doing it. It's adorable." Aidan smirks.

Before I can come up with a response, Calder shouts from his position in the lead. "We're at the top of the peak!"

CHAPTER SEVENTEEN

We crest the steep slope to the top of the first peak. The fog is dense here, but we can see that the mountain slopes down in every direction. The summit isn't overly wide—perhaps the length of two horses, and it's overgrown with tall grass, a few short trees sprouting from the sides.

We all take a few moments to look off the side and stare into the fog. Reaching this milestone feels...underwhelming. I expected stunning views of the land around us, but all I see is gray.

"What a view," Rian says sarcastically. At least one other heir feels the same disappointment as me.

I sigh my agreement and walk to the opposite end of the summit, looking for our way to the next peak.

There's a trail leading down, which comes to a rickety wooden bridge that sways slowly over a deep chasm, like one of the Gods scooped out the space between the two peaks with a spade. I suck in a sharp breath, realizing that's the way we must travel to the next peak.

"I hope no one here is afraid of heights," I say, pointing down.

The others make their way to my side. One by one they groan when they behold the incredibly unstable-looking passage.

"There's got to be another way," Calder says, already walking around the perimeter.

I shake my head. "There's only one way to go, and that's forward. We have to cross."

"What would you know about it? You weren't even supposed to be here," Calder scoffs.

His petulance is starting to wear on me. I roll my eyes and say, "aren't you over it yet? You'd think there would be other things here to occupy your mind."

"Elana's right, there's only one way forward. My father told me that," Rayna says, coming to my aid.

"We should keep moving," Aidan says, pointing at the bridge. "We don't know if the weather will turn and I don't want to be on that thing when the winds pick up."

We head out quickly, leaving behind our first conquered summit.

It's a short, steep walk down. My muscles protest, used to exerting force on climbing, not descending.

We face the bridge. All five of us are at least united in our hatred for this bridge.

Calder curses. "There's no way in Hells it'll hold us," he grumbles.

"It'll hold," Rayna says, probably trying to encourage us, but she sounds unsure herself.

A wild idea overtakes me, reckless and asinine. Something that will show these heirs and maybe the Gods that I have what it takes to be here. An act of bravery, one that doesn't require a ton of muscles or endurance.

"I'll go first."

Everyone looks at me. Rayna's mouth drops open, concern lacing her dark eyes. Rian's raised eyebrows make him look surprised, and slightly impressed. Calder's lips pull up into smug satisfaction. Aidan appears thoughtful.

"If I make it across, you know it's at least somewhat safe," I say, shrugging.

"I should go first," Aidan interjects. "I'm the largest person here, and I have the best chance at surviving the fall with the power I've been granted."

"No. I'm going," I narrow my eyes up at him, and tilt my chin up in determination. "If I don't make it, at least Calder will shut the Hells up."

Aidan levels a look at me and rolls his eyes. "Oh yes, and then I'll have so much fun explaining to your sister how you died. I'm sure she would be very reasonable and understanding of how we all let you go first."

I think of my sister and her fearsome temper. The thought of that temper going against Aidan brings a gleeful smile to my face. "I'm going, so I guess you'll have to figure out how to deal with Aislinn on your own."

Without giving him another moment to argue I spin around and lightly step onto the bridge. Boards creak under my feet, and I feel the soft bend of wood that's ages past its prime. There's a rope on either side of me, but my arms are too short to reach both. I settle for taking the rope on my right. It's damp from the lingering moisture in the air. I blow out a shaky breath and take the next step. More creaking, but the board holds steady.

My focus is solely on my next steps as I make slow progress across the bridge. The boards are also slick from the fog, but the deep grooves in my boots grip tight. This isn't so bad as long as I keep my eyes forward and don't look at the horrendous drop below my feet. I hope I'm earning points with the Gods for bravery.

I'm almost halfway when a board beneath my left foot cracks and breaks. My leg falls, and my heart jumps to my throat, cutting off my scream. I drop into a crouch, the board my right foot is on taking my full weight. I grip the rope with both hands and in doing so, look down the chasm. My head spins as I try and fail to calculate how far the plummet is, and what would be left of my body if I were to fall. My vision starts to blur as my breathing turns erratic.

I glance behind quickly and see Rayna at the edge of the bridge, concern pinching her features. Aidan has a hand on her shoulder and it looks like he's saying something. Hopefully he's telling her that the bridge will only hold one, because if she tries to rush out here and help me, I'm fairly certain we'll both be making the drop.

It's that driving factor that pushes me past my fear. I suck in a few calming breaths and slowly stand up, putting my left leg on the board behind my right. This one, at least, is steady.

"Gods, if this isn't one of the trials, I'm going to be furious," I whisper under my breath and take a small leap to the next full board, using the rope to steady myself.

The wood beneath my feet bends and groans but holds steady. I continue across, stepping softer and trying to use the rope to keep weight off my feet.

A sudden wind gust picks up and I crouch down against the swaying of the bridge. The world rocks back and forth as the gale howls between the wooden planks. I squeeze my eyes closed to shut out the looming foggy chasm below.

Thankfully the wind dies down as quickly as it started and I stand up tentatively. I continue my slow crossing. There are five wooden boards left before the other side, now four, three, two, one. I collapse onto the hard-packed dirt, shaking all over.

No god comes to me, nothing happens to make me believe this was one of the challenges. Wherever the Gods are, they're probably watching and enjoying our plight.

With the little strength adrenaline has left me with, I stand up and turn back towards the other side. I barely make out the four other shapes of the heirs.

"I made it!" I shout, waving my arms. My voice is swallowed up by the fog, but they must get the idea, because the one I believe to be Rayna starts to cross.

She walks slowly, and I envy her ability to hold on to both ropes. When she makes it to the center, I can clearly make out her features. Her eyebrows are furrowed with concentration. She delicately leaps over the board that broke when I crossed. Once she passes that point, she picks up her tempo. Nearing the three quarters mark I hear the sharp *crack* of a board shattering.

I gasp as she flings herself forward, using her panic-fueled momentum to drive her to safety, abandoning all caution for the sake of speed.

She crosses over the threshold to safety, breathing hard. I put my hand on her shoulder, attempting to reassure her, and she winces in pain. I remember her burns and quickly remove my hand.

"Oh Gods, I'm so sorry," I say.

She waves my apology off with a brisk motion of her hand, bending over at the waist. She sucks in a few short breaths to steady herself.

"I hope I never have to do that again," she says between breaths. She waves back across the canyon for whoever is next to cross.

"It was awful, wasn't it?" I say, looking at the other side.

It's Calder crossing now. I see the setting sun glint off his blonde hair. He doesn't use the ropes until a breeze kicks up and sends the bridge swaying like a pendulum. I see his form wobble, arms flapping in the air. He finally captures the swinging ropes in his hands and steadies himself. Once the wind dies down, he continues again.

He's only halfway to the middle when the first board breaks under him. I hear his curse and have to fight the smile that quirks my lips up. He jumps forward a few planks, staying low. He slowly starts to move again, crossing the middle, making slow but steady progress.

There's another snapping and his leg drops into the empty air beneath the bridge. He's close enough that I see his beet-red face, rigid with concentration.

To my internal dismay, he pulls his leg free and makes it across. As soon as he crosses the threshold he collapses onto his knees, gripping the grass with meaty hands.

"You made it," I say encouragingly, hoping to garner a semblance of peace between us.

"Fuck off," he responds.

I roll my eyes and catch Rayna's gaze. She raises her eyebrows and mouths "baby," and I choke back a laugh. We wave to Rian and Aidan.

The three of us watch in stunned silence as Rian practically floats across the bridge with light surefootedness. A howling breeze kicks up when he's halfway across, but it doesn't even phase him. He continues practically hopping from plank to plank. The wind ruffles his curly brown hair, but he doesn't balk.

He makes it across in half the time it took any of us. My mouth hangs open.

"That was impressive, Rian," Rayna remarks.

He gives her a toothy grin. "Why thank you, Rayna dear."

"Seriously, how did you go that fast?" I ask.

Rian turns to me and shrugs with a sheepish smile. "I've never been bothered by heights. The palace in Aaranor is incredibly tall, and we have a lot of bridges between the towers."

I have the sudden, overwhelming urge to never set foot inside that castle. A shiver runs down my spine as I imagine many bridges, all like this one.

The world plummets into shadow as the sun dips below the second peak.

"Oh no," I whisper. "How is Aidan going to see anything in the dark?"

Aidan, of course, has no trouble. I should've known. A large flame lights his way, illuminating the bridge and clearing some of the fog. I grumble as I think how nice it would have been of him to get rid of the fog a bit earlier.

He doesn't cross as quickly as Rian, but he moves as confidently. The glow of the flame gets brighter and brighter until he stands directly in front of us.

"That went well," he says with a smirk.

I almost expect Calder to attack. But the Hotharian heir only scoffs and moves away from the cliff. He sets up his sleeping pack without another word.

"Well, indeed," I say with raised eyebrows as I set up my own sleeping spot between my usual buffers, Rayna and Rian.

We go to sleep with no fresh food, instead munching on our provisions. Aidan keeps a fire going in the center of our little circle all night. How he keeps it burning with no fuel and through sleep is a marvel, one that I try to remember to ask him about in the morning.

We're sluggish to wake at dawn. The fog has finally lifted, and we get our first clear view of the bridge we crossed yesterday. The chasm we crossed is deeper than I ever imagined it would be. I sincerely hope we won't be traveling back this way on the return journey.

I realize I never asked Father about the way back. He never offered any advice on it, never mentioned saving food or water once we reach the final summit. It makes me wonder if there's perhaps a shortcut to the base of the mountain.

Rayna applies another coat of the burn salve. The wound looks much worse today. The blisters weep as she wipes the ointment over them. She hisses, her shoulders taut and one fist clenched. After a few moments, she expels a breath and her muscles relax as the numbing takes effect.

"How's your arm doing today?" I ask her. I know it can't feel good, but I want to make sure it doesn't get infected. We aren't exactly the picture of cleanliness out here.

"It's alright," she says with a shrug. She packs the salve away and then rolls up her sleeping mat.

I simply stare at her, waiting for the truth. She noticeably avoids my gaze until I clear my throat, raising my eyebrows at her.

She sighs, rolls her eyes to the sky, mutters something about a *mother hen*, and then replies. "As painful as yesterday, if not more. My whole arm feels stiff, but I can still move it."

Rayna clenches her fist and extends her arm, bending it every way as if to show me she still has mobility.

"It's a natural part of the healing process for burns. Unfortunately, they hurt more before they heal. Let me know if your skin starts to get warm or puffy around the blisters."

She nods her thanks at me, hiking her pack onto her back, avoiding contact with the burns. Without further conversation, she heads up the path. I rush to follow her, my pack bouncing slightly on my lower back. The others fall into line behind us.

I get the distinct feeling that she doesn't want anyone to know she's in pain, although it makes sense she would be feeling it. I bite my tongue on any further questions.

Now that the sun is fully risen, I get a better look at the landscape around us. There are the same towering evergreen trees here, but they're sparser. The air is also significantly cooler, although it's still comfortable. Small creatures dart across the path in front of us and scamper up trees as we pass. Looks like we won't have much trouble finding dinner again this evening. My stomach drops at the thought of seeing one of these adorable furry critters roasting on a stick over the fire.

We only stop around mid-day, when Rian's protesting stomach becomes too loud for the rest of us to bear.

"I'm sorry, I can't help my stomach," he says with a shrug after Aidan threatens to toss him into the chasm.

Rian and I head off the trail to hunt down something edible. There's not much to forage, only a handful of hazelnuts and some blackberries. What I manage to pluck won't sustain us for long. Rian and I eat ours as we make our way back to the others.

The afternoon drags on. Our collective mood sours as our stomachs run emptier and emptier. Soon it's not only Rian's stomach that rumbles unhappily. We decide it's best to stop and gather food for an early dinner.

I want nothing to do with the hunting party, so once again I set out to forage. Rayna joins Calder and Aidan to search for game, while Rian stays back at camp.

My pockets are stuffed with nuts, berries, and wild carrots when I return to Rian. He eyes the carrots with disdain, but happily takes some nuts and berries.

The others return and present a few small forest animals, which Aidan roasts over his fire.

It's a clear, calm evening that lulls us all into an exhausted sleep.

"Please, Rian, for the love of the Gods, shut the Hells up!" Rayna kicks dirt in the direction of the Aaranor heir, who has been humming jovial tunes since we left our camp this several hours ago.

Two days later we're still climbing up the second peak. There's a river that once again follows along the trail, coursing down the mountain. The further we climb, the more intense the flow gets.

"Sorry, Rayna, I didn't realize you hated music." Rian looks affronted, going so far as to put his hand on his chest in mock horror.

"I don't hate music," Rayna grinds out through clenched teeth. "What you're butchering isn't music. Have you even heard of pitch?"

Rian flashes me a conspiratorial grin. "Well, if you think you know music better, then by all means, please honor us with your great gift of song."

I roll my eyes but admit I'm also curious. When Aislinn told me about Rayna, she included that she was a powerful warrior, her voice honed as finely as her blades. In fact, I'd heard that she once performed for the rulers at one of their meetings. Her songs nearly brought father to tears, Ash told me.

Rayna shakes her head and says sweetly, "perhaps if you're lucky, I'll sing at your funeral after I throw you off this cliff."

Rian mimics getting shot with an arrow in his heart, bending backwards with the blow. I chuckle, but also deflate slightly. I was hoping to hear her famed voice.

It's mid-morning when the lovely stream running next to us turns into a torrential beast, rapids spitting water up from the bank, and white cap waves crashing against rocks.

"I have a bad feeling," I whisper, but the roar of the rushing water whisks away my words. I look up the path, where the river inches closer and closer to our trail.

A few moments later, all five of us stand on the bank of the flowing river, trying to find a way to cross. The trail on the other side picks up on the opposite bank of the river, taunting us. There's a waterfall on the side of the cliff to our left. In any other circumstances, it would be a beautiful sight. Too bad it's paired with a river from the Hells.

"Maybe we can find some rocks to hop," Rayna suggests, walking up and down the bank trying to find something.

"Can you all swim?" Calder asks, staring at the water with determination.

I gape at him. "You can't be serious. We'll drown. If we do manage to stay afloat, the water will sweep us down the river and we'll be crushed on the rocks."

"So, you don't know how to swim." Calder smirks at me, cocky. I'm tempted to shove him into the river.

"Hey, there's a cave over here!" Rian shouts. We all turn, heading towards where he points to the waterfall—no, behind the waterfall.

"The question is, does it go where we need it to?" Aidan asks as we get close enough to see the large dark opening in the rock face of the cliff that was concealed by the jaw-dropping falls and the mist that rises around it.

Calder steps forward into the mouth of the cave, cautious of the damp, slick-looking rocks behind the falls. He peers inside, pausing for a moment, before he turns to us.

"I'm going in. You all can either follow or find your own way across the river." Without waiting for us to decide, he marches forward.

Rian is the first to fall in line behind Calder, then Aidan. Rayna and I exchange a withering look, but with no other viable option, we follow him into the darkness, with nothing but Aidan's flames lighting our way.

CHAPTER EIGHTEEN

A damp coolness sinks into my skin as we trudge through the rocky cave. Pointed stalactites line the ceiling, making me nervous whenever we pass underneath a particularly prominent one. The floor of the cave is solid rock, mostly dry except for a few puddles that we either splash through or jump over.

The cave is wide—large enough for Rian, Rayna, and I to walk next to each other. And it's at least double my height, although in some areas the stalactites are so large that Rian and Aidan have to duck around them.

A memory surfaces briefly in my mind, flashes of my forgotten dream. A torch. Shadows and whispering. I try to think harder about it, to recall anything else from that unconscious state of mind, but there's nothing.

"Does anyone else see that creepy blue light?" Rian whispers loudly next to me. He releases his naginata from the holder on his back and holds it in a defensive position. I palm my daggers and feel the reassuring weight in my grasp.

There's a faint pale blue glow in front of us, past a sharp bend in the path. We ready ourselves, armed with our chosen weapons. Aidan brushes past Calder to take the lead. If we're about to face another creature, it makes sense to send our strongest first.

As a group we rush around the corner and come face-to-face with—glowing goo.

The walls of the cave, as far ahead as we can see, are lined with a glimmering substance. It looks like plant matter, with a similar shape and growing style to lichen, but squishier and emitting cerulean light.

Aidan extinguishes his fire. The glow from the plants is enough to light our way.

"Wow, this is amazing," I say to no one in particular. The sight is unlike anything I've ever seen. The glow is serene, putting my tense muscles at ease. The sheer number of plants everywhere makes the cave look like another realm, like the night sky, illuminated by countless shining stars.

Rayna says from my side, "it's like something out of a fairytale."

I walk up to one of the walls and brush my fingers against one of the plants. The light fades where I touch it, but winks back to life a few moments later.

"Do you really think you should be touching that?" I startle at Aidan's voice right next to me, low and teasing. A slight shiver runs down my back. Gods, I could listen to him talk all day with that tone. If only he weren't so rude, grating, and foul-tempered. I clear my throat and mind of wild, ridiculous thoughts.

"I don't think whatever is causing the glow is toxic. I think it's a survival technique of this fungus, or whatever it is," I tell him as an idea strikes me. I twist my pack around and grab a small, shallow glass dish. If these plants exist in a cave with no sunlight and little nutrition, perhaps we could grow them. Once I'm home I'll enlist Aislinn's help in finding someone to study this plant.

Aidan watches as I scrape some of the plant matter off into the dish with the blade of my dagger. "What're you going to do with glowing fungus?"

I fill the glass as much as I can and then shove it into my pack. "I wonder if this stuff could replace candles and torches, if we can figure out how to recreate the growing conditions and food source."

He lets out a low hum, inspecting the wall closely. "If all goes well, you might have a fungus named after you someday, Magpie."

The temptation is strong, but I somehow resist the urge to shove his face in said fungus.

"Let's keep moving. We don't know how far this cave goes," Rayna suggests, and we all start off again.

The further we walk, the more I allow the glow to lull me into a sense of security. This place is pure magic. The Gods must have created this cave to give us a little respite from the harsh reality of the journey. To remind us that peace can be found in the midst of chaos.

It's not long before I start to hear noises from up ahead. I squint my eyes, because the tunnel appears brighter too.

"Is that water?" I ask, straining my ears to hear the familiar light trickling sounds.

"It must be. An underground spring maybe?" Calder responds. I'm caught off guard at the first non-insult he's said to me and snap my eyes to him, trying to catch a glimpse of the mockery or cruel words he's no doubt about to hurl my way. But he seems entirely focused on what's ahead. He moves like he's in a trance, walking quickly towards the sound.

The cerulean light gets brighter and brighter until at last we round a bend, the cave opening into a massive underground oasis. A glimmering pond reflects the blue light from above, casting the entire place in shimmering light. There's a low, gentle waterfall cascading into a round pool off to one side, mist rising around it. Its water feeds into the pond, but I can't see where the water flows out. A bare but luminescent pearl-white tree grows out of an island in the center of the oasis. It bears no leaves, but its gnarled branches seem to pulsate with life.

"Okay, now the Gods are just showing off," Rian remarks. I can't help but agree with him. This place is a marvel.

My eye catches on the pool with the waterfall, the mist rising from it. I walk over and realize the mist isn't mist at all. It's steam. I take a chance and dip a finger in the water and remove it quickly. It's warm but doesn't burn or scorch my skin. I plunge my whole hand in the water and sigh heavily.

Rayna joins me and sticks her hand in. She lets out a breathy moan that makes me giggle.

"Who would think that mere water could elicit a response like this from us," I say breathily.

We've all been starved of our normal comforts, and I want nothing more than to jump in and indulge myself in a bath. It's been days—no, a week, more even—since I was last clean. My skin has been getting itchy, and it feels like my body is covered with a layer of muck.

Rayna's dark eyes catch on mine. They reflect the blue lights around us like two dark mirrors. "I know what you're thinking, and no. This definitely feels like a trap the Gods have set for us."

She's right. I know she is, but at the moment, I don't care.

"Maybe the next challenge is being brave enough to get into the water." Rian joins us and puts his hand in the warm water.

Aidan and Calder meander over, both staring at the pool with longing. Aidan is the first to toss his pack and weapons on the ground, kick off each black boot, and start unbuttoning his dark shirt. I try not to stare at his impressively toned and tanned chest, with one major scar running across it. My eyes dart lower to his well-defined abdomen before my cheeks burst aflame and I look away.

"Excuse you, hothead, what do you think you're doing?" Rayna nearly shouts, her voice going high-pitched and echoing off the cave walls around us.

He finishes unbuttoning his shirt and tosses it aside. "What does it look like I'm doing? I'm getting in."

Rayna looks like she's about to protest but Aidan is already standing on the edge of the pool. He winks at her and dives into the steaming water, splashing the rest of us with his wake.

"Well, since I'm already wet." Rian shrugs, following Aidan in shucking off his boots, shirt, and stashing his pack and weapons where they're safe from the water. Calder is right behind him, and in a few moments, they jump into the pool.

I tip my head at Rayna, giving her an apologetic look. "I'm sorry, Rayna, but I reek. I don't think I could survive without this bath."

She sighs in defeat. "You melodramatic fool. How am I supposed to keep you safe from outside the water?"

"I guess you'll have to join us," I say, slipping my pack's straps off my shoulders and unhooking my bow and quiver from my back. I unlace my boots and set them aside. I remove my outer corset, but leave on my loose under shirt and pants.

It's with great reluctance that I remove my twin daggers from their sheaths, gently setting them inside my pack and folding some clothes around them. I feel stark naked without them and take a deep breath to calm my nerves.

Rayna finally gives in with a groan of frustration and neatly stacks her boots, weapons, and pack next to mine. We climb up to the edge of the pool together. I slowly lower myself into the warmth, feeling instant relief for my tired, aching muscles. It's shallow enough near the edge to stand, but I notice towards the center of the pool it gets deeper. Next to me, Rayna lets out a long sigh.

"Okay, I'll admit it. Even if this is a trap, it's worth it." She tilts her head back into the water, soaking her raven-colored braids and curly ends.

I smile in response, beyond words. Gods, this water feels like the heavens. Rian and Calder are across the pool from us, engaging in some kind of water duel, each trying to push the other's head under the surface. I'd be concerned they were attempting to drown each other if they weren't both laughing.

It's another shock, seeing Calder laugh like that. With real joy, not malice. Rian's antics seem to have that effect on everyone.

I glance around for Aidan and catch him leaning back on the smooth rock edge of the pool. His head is upturned, eyes closed. His dark hair is plastered to his head, dripping little droplets down his face, his angular jaw, his neck, and disappearing into the pool at the top of his chest.

His head tilts down as if sensing my gaze, and golden eyes capture mine, glinting with something like amusement? Encouragement?

I take a long slow breath and dip below the surface of the water, spinning around. My hair feels tight against my scalp, so I remove the bands securing the braids and use my fingers to untangle the tresses. My auburn hair floats freely around me, and I break through the surface to catch my breath.

Aidan's eyes are still burning into me, so I spin around with all the grace of a walrus and swim in the opposite direction towards the waterfall.

The steaming water flows gently through a wide crack in the wall. Because it's near the edge of the pool, I can stand and the water only reaches my chest. I cup my hands and put them under the falls, then splash my face with the water. I take a deep breath and a step forward so I'm surrounded by the falls.

It's surreal and incredible. A shiver snakes up my spine as I relax into the flow of the water, feeling my nerves tingle where the droplets hit my skin and clothes. I run my hands through my hair, scrubbing at my scalp and hoping the water washes away some of the dirt and oil built up there.

Being in this water reminds me of Aislinn, who taught me how to swim when I was young. Before I started my womanly duties training and Ash started her daily heir training, we used to visit a small, secluded lake a short walk from the castle. The lake wasn't deep, but when we first started going, I was terrified of the water. Ash was unsurprisingly a natural at swimming. She's a natural at everything. Gradually she taught me the basics of how to paddle, how to float, and eventually how to hold my breath and dive underwater. We spent a few summers by that lake until reality caught up to us and we started our respective trainings. I think I'd like to visit that lake again with Ash, when all of this is over.

Smiling at the memories, I scrub until I feel adequately cleaned and completely relaxed. I step out from under the waterfall and look around for the others. Rayna stands in chest-deep water, running her hands gently through the pool. Out of everyone, she seems the least comfortable in the water.

Calder floats on his back, eyes closed, the picture of relaxation. I glance towards Aidan, who still lounges on the side, a playful smirk on his lips and light dancing in his eyes as he talks to Rian, who's treading water near him. Aidan's dazzling smirk turns on me and it makes me want to pull him under the water and hold him there for a few seconds. I start swimming in his direction with the intention of doing exactly that.

Suddenly the cave walls shake. I stop swimming and start treading water, looking above us, waiting for the inevitable cave-in. Rayna was right. She was *so* right about this being a trap.

Ripples cascade through the pool, heading to the center where Calder startles and stares down at the depths of the water beneath him. One by one, the glowing moss-like plants wink out, plunging us into inky darkness. Aidan quickly sends a few fireballs out, floating around us. Fiery oranges and reds reflect off the ripples, casting us in an eerie setting.

A splashing noise comes from ahead of me. Aidan is on the edge of the water, staring at the center of the pool with horror in his expression.

"Out of the pool, now!" he yells.

There's a sucking feeling beneath me, like a river's strong current. I'm in an area of the pool where I can't stand and the realization hits me like a block of ice. It's a whirlpool.

I pump my arms and kick my legs ferociously, building as much speed as I can. I slowly inch towards the edge of the pool, where Aidan crouches, reaching his hands for Rian and me.

"A little further. You can do it. Keep kicking," he encourages us, but his wide eyes tell a different story.

I hear a scream and a splash. To my horror, Rayna's dark head disappears under the water and her hands flail above her wildly before being sucked under as well. Guilt slams into my gut as I realize I'm in no position to help her, unless I can get out of this pool. I look around for Calder, who struggles to keep his head above water in the center of the whirlpool.

Rian is a few paces ahead of me, so close to the edge, but his long limbs splash awkwardly and ineffectively in the current. All I think about is the boy who let his dream die to be here, to be an heir, only to end up drowning in this pool. Even though I might never know what that dream was, I think to myself *what a sad thing, a wasted dream.*

If there's hope for one of us, to have the opportunity to continue dreaming, continue living, let it be this boy who grew up and abandoned his dream, but somehow still has laughter in his heart, who spreads joy with his words.

With all my remaining strength, I use my momentum to dive down into the water, then kick straight up from the bottom, launching myself at Rian, shoving his feet hard. It's enough to propel him to the edge, where Aidan catches his hands and helps haul him out of the whirlpool. He's safe. Rian's safe.

The force I exerted with that shove sent me backwards in the pool. And now the ferocious current grips me in its talons. I kick feebly a few more times and see Aidan, face taut, bending over the edge of the water, hand outstretched towards me.

"Come on, Magpie, swim to me." He grunts with exertion, desperately clinging to the edge above the water. There's fear, real fear, in his liquid gold eyes as they meet mine.

I reach for him, but the motion splashes water into my mouth and I cough wetly. Three things happen at once: my strength leaves me, the current wraps around my legs and tugs down, and I tilt my head back and suck in one last gasp of life before I'm completely submerged.

CHAPTER NINETEEN

The water is dark and vicious as it presses against me. My body spirals and I momentarily lose my bearings. All I am aware of is my rapid sinking until a glowing hand submerges above me, reaching. I extend my own, stretching my muscles, my fingers aching with the effort.

The current yanks me down and bubbles of my life-saving air escape me. The hand slips away from my grasp. I distantly hear a panicked voice shout my name. Not Magpie, but Elana.

I shut my eyes against the spinning. My limbs are as limp as the ragdolls Ash and I used to play with as children. I'm pulled this way and that, my hair hitting my face one moment, then getting pulled behind me the next.

A small part of me hopes the water god Kai will appear to save me from this torrent, but it's a foolish thing to hope for. No one's coming. I sink lower and my ears pop painfully.

My feet still do not touch the bottom. I hadn't realized this pool was so deep before. It feels endless now, like I'll keep sinking forever. The last of my held breath punches from my lungs as they spasm. Water rushes in, invading my body. I cough to try and expel the water, but it only brings more in. It's painful, like my chest is tearing. I'm scared, but I refuse to let fear be my last thought. My eyes close and I call up a memory. In it, Ash laughs at something I said, her whole body shaking from the effort of her wheezing.

Peace washes over me. Everything slowly fades to blackness.

There's a figure of light and a shadow in front of me, whispering, screaming. It pierces my ears, and yet it's too quiet to hear. Darkness closes in around me, wrapping me in a gentle embrace. I'm struck by how peaceful it is to surrender myself to the water.

I vaguely feel my weightless body rising. My ears pop once more, and then my skin is set aflame with pain.

"Elana, can you hear me? Come on, open your eyes," a voice, low and panicked, calls to me from the blackness.

Something slams my chest, and then coughing overtakes me. It's a reflex I can't stop. I gag and spit a mouthful of water up. My lungs ache as they take in a gulp of raspy, wet air. Gods, it hurts to breathe. I peel my eyes open but everything's blurry. I blink against bright blue lights.

There's a face near mine, backlit by cerulean light. Concerned golden eyes hold my attention. I shut my eyes again, drawing in painful breath.

A calloused hand brushes down my cheek. Another hand gently rubs circles on my back. I'm cradled against a warm body. The urge to curl up on my side and nestle closer to the warmth is overwhelming, but my body hurts too much to move. I let the heat soothe the aching in my chest, where the pain of the water throbs.

"Magpie, come back to us," Aidan's voice whispers in my ear, his breath tickling my face. His words stir me out of my stupor.

I wrench open my eyes and look around frantically, trying to make sense of my surroundings. My gaze lands on Aidan and sharpens, my vision focusing on his pinched expression. It's his body I'm leaning against, keeping me warm.

"There you are, Princess," he says, a soft smile spreading across his face.

"Hi," my voice croaks and that one word sends me into another wet coughing fit.

Aidan helps me sit up, where I have a better view of the scene around me.

Rian crouches next to Aidan and me. His shining eyes are full of emotion. He reaches out and pulls me into a hug. "You saved my life, Elana. Thank you, thank you, thank you."

His squeeze triggers another wet rasp from my throat, followed by a healthy dose of sputtering. Rian lets me go quickly, shooting me an apologetic smile. Aidan rubs my back again with a warm hand, and I'm grateful for the soothing feel of it.

"I was just trying to push you out of my way," I wheeze out, attempting a wobbly smile at him.

He shakes his head. He looks startlingly serious for once. "I'll never forget this. I owe you a life debt."

He clenches a fist and taps his chest, right above his heart. The action is an Astrellian symbol of those indebted, or those honoring someone. I shiver at the intensity of the gesture, the meaning and power behind it.

"Yours is a life worth saving, Rian," I nod at him.

A hacking cough followed by a gag turns my attention to where Calder helps Rayna to a sitting position. She sounds as terrible as I feel. Her dark braids are plastered to her head, her eyes wild until they find me.

"No. More. Swimming," she says, each word punctuated by a gasping wheeze.

I can't help the laugh that bubbles up, bursting out, and then catches in my throat as another round of coughing starts. I don't know why it's funny, but all the panic, all the adrenaline-fueled exertion need a release.

Another thought strikes me, and the question burns in my mind. I'm afraid I already know the answer, but I need to hear it. I clear my throat.

"What happened to the whirlpool?"

Rian and Aidan turn to Calder. He's paler than usual, his blonde hair dripping down his face and neck.

"I stopped it," he says, not in a gloating tone for once, but very matter-of-factly. "The god Kai appeared to me while I was underwater. He gifted me with his abilities, and then I stopped the whirlpool."

"Well, thank you, for not leaving us in there to drown," Rayna says in a raspy voice. Her throat is probably as sore as mine.

Calder nods and turns away, making towards his discarded clothes and pack. "We should keep moving."

I stare at the pool. It has returned to its serene state and looks warm and inviting again. I shudder, feeling the water again fill my chest, choking my scream. Even the glowing wall fungus is shining again, like nothing ever happened. Like half of us didn't nearly die to please a god.

"Can you stand, Magpie?" Aidan's voice is in my ear again. His lips are so close to me his breath tickles my cheek. Thank goodness the blue light masks how red my face is right now.

"Yes," I whisper, standing up slowly, tentatively. My legs wobble slightly, part of me still feels the current beneath my feet, the dragging sensation and the twists and turns my body took while in the water.

Aidan rests a steadying hand on my back. I flash him a grateful half smile and head towards my pack. My clothes stick to me, uncomfortably wet and cold. The only thing on my mind is getting into something dry. I rifle through the pack, pulling out my spare set of clothing.

I catch Rayna's eyes as she, too, holds a bundle of dry clothes in her hands. We look around for somewhere with privacy. She finally points at the large white tree near the center of the oasis. I nod my head. It's the only thing large enough to conceal a whole person.

"Elana and I are going to change. If anyone tries to sneak a peek, I have an arrow with your name on it," Rayna warns. The three men instantly find the opposite wall very interesting and turn to inspect the glowing fungus there.

"How're you feeling?" I ask from behind the tree as I shuck off my dripping shirt.

Rayna wrings out her hair as she responds, "All right. Although I'm not too keen on getting back into water anytime soon. I thought I was going to die."

I nod my head, tugging on my dry pants. "I know what you mean. If Calder had waited any longer to stop the whirlpool, we would have drowned."

"I don't like the idea of owing him," Rayna says with a scowl.

"Neither do I, but what can be done about it?"

Rayna sighs and shakes her head, buttoning up her shirt. By her silence, I think we're stuck in his debt.

"How're the burns healing up?" I change the subject. It's only been a few days since she got burned, and she's hardly mentioned them at all. Either Rayna has an incredibly high pain tolerance, or they're healing more quickly than I expected.

She rolls her shoulder, tapping it lightly. "They're much better. Not painful anymore, and they've scabbed over nicely. Although this morning they started itching terribly."

I scrunch my brows. They shouldn't be scabbed over yet, and they should still be hurting.

"Do you mind if I take a look?"

She shrugs and slips her arm out of her shirt. Sure enough, the burns look several weeks old, not several days. I doubt my healing salve did this. It's never worked that quickly in the past. I gave some to our cook, Gwen, after she suffered a nasty burn from a kitchen accident, but it still took her weeks to fully heal. I wonder if it's the latent magic lingering in this land. Perhaps the Gods are speeding the process.

"Itching is a normal part of healing. Of course, try not to scratch if possible."

She gives me a look that makes me feel like an overbearing mother. I chuckle and hold my hands up placatingly. She tucks her arm back into her shirt, rolling her eyes. I quickly braid my hair. It's messy, and wet strands tug out of the braid, but at least it's functional. We grab our wet clothes and head back to the others.

Calder does us all a favor by siphoning the water out of our soaked clothing and packs. He gives me a cocky grin as he lets the water splash into the pool, as if reminding me that he can do something I can't. I hold his gaze, refusing to be intimidated.

We're all itching to leave this beautiful, terrible place, but there's no exit in sight.

"I don't suppose Kai told you how to get out of this cave?" Rian wonders as we search for a different passage from the one we walked in from.

"No," Calder's tone is clipped. He searches with the rest of us, using his newly granted abilities to search behind the waterfall in the pool. The opening is much too small for any of us to squeeze our way through.

After a frustrating stretch of time searching the walls for another way out, we decide the only way to go is back. By the time we reach the roaring waterfall at the mouth of the cave, the sun is already setting, the sky awash with orange, pink, and purple.

Aidan and Calder head into the woods to find food. I catch Rian staring at the clouds, tracing the shape of the fluffy colorful puffs with his index finger while he lounges on his sleeping mat.

I finish setting up my own mat and head to the river to fill my waterskin. I secure it and head back to camp as dusk begins to darken, but a flickering light downstream gives me pause. Without much thought, I head towards it.

As I draw closer, I realize it's Aidan's light, glinting in a clearing. I hear his low voice—it sounds angry. My curiosity overtakes me, and I need to know what he's saying. There's a large dense shrub that I take cover behind, allowing me limited view of the clearing, but the spot is excellent for hearing.

"It's done, Vernier," Aidan says sharply. "You will not hurt her."

Calder scoffs, his eyes two disbelieving orbs. "Seriously Ashfall? Just like that? You hardly even know her, and suddenly our entire alliance goes out the window? What are you thinking?"

Oh Gods, they're talking about me. I don't know how I know, but it's an instinctual feeling. My breath leaves me in short bursts. I will my breathing to be silent.

"I will remind you that I never agreed to your stupid little scheme, and if you make one move against her, you're dead. If you touch her, your life is forfeit," Aidan's voice is deadly low. I shiver down to my toes.

"And I will remind you that your father, *the king*, is the one who agreed to this," Calder says.

Aidan crosses his hands over his chest, the picture of unmoving stone. "My father does not make decisions for Ocarin, as much as he wishes otherwise. My mother, *the queen*, never agreed to this. *I* never agreed to this. This so-called 'alliance' is a farce. I don't understand why her presence here threatens you anyway. It's not as if she threatens your claim to Hotharia's throne."

I wait with bated breath for Calder's response. I've been wondering about this, too. Why is he so hostile towards me? I don't have to wait long for his answer.

"She threatens all of us. She's too weak to keep up, she almost drowned today, she brings nothing of value to the table. Aislinn is a warrior and was raised to be heir. Elana most likely stole the crown from her. If we remove her from the equation, Aislinn will be gifted her ability and all will be well again. If we allow Elana to continue, she could throw our whole system out of balance. What if other younger siblings think they can steal the crown in the future? What then? It'll be chaos," Calder takes a breath. "Besides, what if the Gods are waiting for us to end her? I bet it's a test."

He still believes I stole the crown from my sister. I haven't convinced him of anything. I knew he'd be difficult to win over, but I never imagined he would oppose my presence here this vehemently.

Aidan shakes his head, a humorless laugh falling from his mouth. "You're insane, Vernier."

Even in the light of Aidan's flame, I can see Calder's face turn red with rage. "What the fuck did you just say, Ashfall?"

"You. Are. Insane." Aidan enunciates every syllable. "This conspiracy bullshit is beneath you, yet here you are, jumping in headfirst. What happened to you? You used to be so level-headed."

Calder throws his hands up and growls. "You know what? I'm done trying to reason with you. I don't need this alliance. I don't need any of you. Hotharia is the strongest kingdom of Astrellia, and we will only continue to grow our strength. I don't need your help to end that pathetic excuse for an heir—"

His words are cut off by a bright flash of red and orange. There's an arrow made of flame aimed right at Calder's heart. A small wave of water appears at Calder's feet, but the arrow pushes closer, cutting off any chance Calder has to protect himself.

Holy Gods I think, *Aidan's going to kill him.*

"You're not going to like what happens if you finish that sentence," Aidan snarls, controlling the arrow with one finger. He moves it closer, ready to pierce straight through Calder's chest.

Calder slowly raises his hands in surrender, but his narrowed eyes suggest it's by choice. I give him credit, he's calmer than I could ever be in this situation.

"Do you really want me, want Hotharia, as an enemy? Because of *her*?" The venom in Calder's voice chills me to the bone.

"If you try to harm her, you'll find out," Aidan responds, staying perfectly poised to release him or run his arrow through Calder. My breath catches in my throat, my heart beating erratically.

Calder stares at the tip of the arrow, hissing as it singes the front of his shirt. Finally, after the longest standoff I've ever witnessed, he looks away from Aidan. "Fine, Ashfall. Have it your way. I won't hurt her. Now remove that arrow."

"Swear it, Vernier," Aidan hisses.

Another breath releases from me in a shocked inhale. A promise made on the soil of the Gods' Territory is binding. Something about the latent magical energy that lives here creates binding contracts. Anyone who breaks a promise made here dies a horrible death not long after.

"Gods, you're insufferable. I swear by the Gods I will not attempt to harm Elana Sable during this trial," Calder says.

Aidan drops his hand to his side and the flaming arrow vanishes into a puff of smoke. Calder promptly takes a step backwards and then turns around, boldly putting his back to Aidan, stomping off towards camp.

Aidan stands in the clearing, taking slow, deep breaths, his head tilting up to the sky as if he's seeking answers in the stars winking to life. My thoughts race. What was the agreement his father made with Hotharia? And why does he not make any decisions for Ocarin? Why did Aidan not accept the alliance? Why side with me, with Adrithia?

Before my common sense can catch up, I bolt from my hiding spot into the clearing.

"You were plotting to kill me?" I pull out one of my twin daggers and aim it at his chest.

From a hands-length away I can see Aidan's eyes snap open, tilting his head down to look at me with barely disguised annoyance.

"Magpie, of course you were eavesdropping. You can't help yourself, can you?" There's a glimmer of bitter amusement on his features.

"Answer me," I say, trying to sound ruthless, channeling a look I've seen on Aislinn's face dozens of times before.

A smirk dances across his lips as his shoulders relax. "You have nothing to fear from me, Princess."

"Why? Why would you deny the alliance offered by Hotharia? Their weapon-making skills are unparalleled."

Aidan steps forward, a gleam of fire in his eyes. He pauses at the very tip of my dagger. My arm shakes with the effort of keeping it steady. It would be too easy to apply a little more pressure and whoops, stab Ocarin's heir.

"Because, Magpie, you are...unexpected," Aidan's intense gaze threatens to melt my icy distrust.

I shift on my feet as I think of how it felt when he held me in the cave. The warmth and comfort I felt in his arms. I lower the dagger, but don't sheathe it. "What the Hells does that mean?"

"You healed Rayna. You saved Rian's life, risking yours in the process. You weren't prepared for this journey at all, but somehow, you're the most adaptable person here. You're smart, protective of those you care about, and so, so frustrating," he says. I'm too shocked to do anything but stand there with my mouth open, staring up at him. He takes the opportunity to move closer until he stands mere inches from me. He towers over me, but I don't feel threatened by his proximity.

Gods, I hardly breathe as he leans down, tucking a stray hair from my braid behind my ear. "You deserve a chance. To rule."

I gasp in a small breath, and his eyes are alight with mischievous delight as he rocks himself back, turning to camp. "So don't die, Magpie. I want to see you soar."

CHAPTER TWENTY

I want to see you soar. The words reverberate through me. I feel the heat of his gaze, his words, long after he leaves me in the clearing. It's utterly unnerving how quickly he switches from furious to teasing. It's even more unnerving how I find myself wanting more from him. I try to squash that from my mind as I find my way back to camp under the light of a full, shining moon.

Errant thoughts dance while I lie by the fire, keeping me from sleep. My eyes are closed, but the feeling of crushing water remains, haunting me. The fear as the last of my breath left me tastes acrid in my mouth, bringing up bile that I swallow down. I shiver and roll over, tucking myself deeper into my woven blanket.

I'm completely exhausted, yet sleep evades me. My teeth start to chatter and I clench my jaw to stop the nervous tick. A sigh and a shuffle sounds nearby and I wrench my heavy eyelids open as a warm weight settles on top of me. A thick wool blanket. I look up at Aidan's retreating form as he lays back down on his sleeping mat. He rests his head on top of his arms, staring up at the sky.

"You need that more than I do," he whispers, barely audible over the crackling of the fire. "Lest your chattering teeth wake everyone up. You know how melodramatic Rian is when he's woken before dawn."

I wrap Aidan's blanket tightly around myself. The smell of cedar hits me and I inhale deeply, taking comfort in his scent as it envelops me.

"Thank you," I whisper back at him. I don't know if he's already asleep, but he makes no reply.

Finally warm enough, my eyelids drift closed of their own accord.

A hand shakes my shoulder. I gasp awake, sitting abruptly, blinking the blurriness out of my eyes. My hands go to my dagger, gripping the hilt before I recognize Rayna standing before me, hand drawn back like she touched a frightened animal.

"It's almost time to head out," she says, her wide, dark eyes roving over the blanket that still smells like cedar and is definitely not mine. She discreetly glances at Aidan and then her eyes return to me, brows high, a questioning look that I don't answer.

I stretch slowly before standing and take in the surroundings of our camp. Rian and Calder are missing, their packs propped up on the ground near where they slept. Aidan is rolling his sleeping mat up, and I take this as my cue to return his blanket.

"Thank you for letting me use this," I say, handing it back to him, neatly rolled and ready to be stored.

"Don't mention it, Magpie. You can repay me by staying alive." A smirk pulls his lips up. Our fingers touch as he takes the blanket from my hands. *Warm hands, stroking my cheek, my back as I curl into him.* I jolt at the memory from the cave and clumsily step back, tripping over my feet towards the fire.

Aidan's hand shoots out, catching my elbow, righting me. A sudden irritation flashes across his expression. He drops my arm like a hot coal and growls at me, "you could at least try not to die."

Embarrassment burns through me, my face awash with it. I carefully step around the fire, packing up the rest of my sleeping gear. I push thoughts of my discomfort aside and refocus on the challenges. The mountain.

Rian waltzes back to camp with a full waterskin.

"Calder is by the river, splashing around, playing with his new powers. I think he intends to part the water so we can cross back to the path," he says, humor apparent in his tone.

Calder, however, does intend to do exactly that.

The five of us stand on the bank of the roaring river. Spray from the nearby rapids splashes our feet. Calder picks this place as the best crossing, claiming the river is shallow and narrow here. He raises his hands, sucking in a sharp breath. With a groan of determination, he uses his power to halt the upstream water. Waves slam against an invisible barrier as a muddy path opens up in front of us.

"Hurry," he says, voice straining with effort, hands shaking.

The way he wields his power seems fundamentally different from Aidan, who doesn't appear to require much physical movement to assist with wielding. I think back to one of my lessons with my father, where he told me that when an heir is first blessed with power, they often rely on their body to direct the power. Eventually using the ability becomes so second-nature that the movements are rendered unnecessary, but by then it's often a habit for the heirs. Some choose to continue using them.

We rush across the riverbed, slopping in the mud, slipping on algae-covered rocks. Calder is panting by the time we reach the other bank. The moment we cross onto the grass, his arms fall to his sides and he sinks to his knees.

The water, angry at being temporarily dammed, explodes back onto its path in a ferocious wave, extending past its banks. The sheer amount of water Calder managed to hold back is staggering.

I'm momentarily impressed with his skill, until he turns a bitter smirk on me, breathing hard, "Do you see, Sable, how mighty a true heir is?"

I narrow my eyes on him but don't respond other than to roll my eyes. His encounter with the god Kai didn't humble him in the slightest like I had hoped it might. For fuck's sake, it might have even made him *less* tolerable. I can't wait to prove him wrong. There are still three Gods left to bestow their gifts.

Sepher the wind god, Tolliver the metal god, and Avani the earth goddess are the three that have yet to make their appearance. Perhaps I'll meet Avani like my father, or Sepher. I've never felt a strong connection to metal, so I doubt I'll be chosen by Tolliver.

I remain lost in my thoughts for much of the day. It's another grueling hike nearly straight up. We all drain our water quickly, and the river is far beneath us. Calder deigns to help us, if only to shut up Rian's incessant whining. He summons a wave in midair and fills our canteens with all the precision of a toddler who has discovered paint.

We trudge along through late afternoon, when the sun turns golden and the shadows elongate. There appears to be a ledge in front of us, past the steep ridge we climb.

"We should make camp here," Rayna announces from the front of our group. "This appears to be the only flat spot for quite a while."

I take the final steep step to the ledge and look around. It's a large plateau, covered with long swaying grass, shining a golden green color that glints in the sun. Wildflowers grow in patches through the grass. The far side of the plateau is lined with bright orange rocks shaped like arches. The arches don't seem to connect to anything, but they are stark in their beauty.

The view from the top is nothing short of spectacular. I see the slope of the mountain behind us, the sharp angles and gradual hills of the landscape at the bottom. It looks so minuscule from up here. I can see far off into the distance, but the rest of the world appears...tiny. Tall trees are reduced to mottled green, lakes are specks of blue, and rivers are threads of string.

We're clearly at the top of the second peak. A feeling of relief and pride hits me. One step closer. One step closer to meeting whatever god brought me here. One step closer to finally figuring out why I was chosen and putting to rest all the rumors and speculations about me—and, apparently, about Aislinn as well.

Rayna walks towards the arches while the rest of us head to the center of the plateau to set up camp. Since we no longer need firewood due to Aidan's power, it takes much less time.

"I think this is the way down," Rayna calls, waving us over.

We stand next to her, looking down at the sheer drop in front of us. A rickety wood and rope ladder clacks against the rock face, swaying slightly in the breeze. The drop is nauseating, perhaps the height of Sandral's castle walls.

"Oh Gods," Calder groans. "Not again."

I glance at him. His face is blanched of color and his blue eyes are wide. I guess his encounter with the rope bridge didn't quell his fear of heights.

Feeling a similar paleness on my face, I back away from the edge. I will not borrow tomorrow's problems. My heart hammers in my chest, but I take slow even breaths to force it back into its regular cadence.

I head back to camp, searching for any edible plants along the way. Other than some dandelions and chamomile, I see nothing. Food might be more difficult to find here, with the steep slopes and lack of obvious animal life.

We eat conservatively out of our rations. I finish off the cheese I had stashed and eat a strip of dried meat. Through a quick visual check, I estimate that I have about seven days' worth of food remaining. Hopefully there will be more fresh food in the days approaching, so we don't have to worry about rationing.

I brush the worn-down letter Rayna gave me and think about Aislinn. What is she doing right now? Is she training with our army? Is she at our castle fighting off marriage proposals conveyed by our mother? Is she slaying more giant scorpions and saving small villages? I bet she's doing none of that. It's dinner time back home, too. She's probably gorging herself on my portion of dessert. I chuckle as I imagine her stealing sweets when Mother's back is turned.

"What're you thinking about?" Rayna gives me a curious look. I glance across the fire, where the men are engaged in a conversation about their weaponry, debating the positives and negatives of their favorites.

"I was thinking about Aislinn, and what she's doing right now," I say with a soft smile.

Rayna's eyebrows raise, but she doesn't speak, giving me time to continue if I wish.

"Considering the time, I think she's probably on her second course of dessert."

A bubbling chuckle escapes from Rayna. "Do you know that she once put me on my ass because she thought I stole a pastry from her?"

I choke out an unexpected laugh. "What? When?"

"We were attending a summit about six or seven years ago in Hotharia and we had to rush through breakfast. Aislinn took a few extra pastries and stashed them in her room. I caught her in the act of hiding them as I was sent to bring her to the meeting, and she swore me to secrecy. Later that day she returned to her room and must have found one pastry missing, because she started banging on my door demanding I return her stolen property."

I laugh, because it sounds exactly like my sister.

"When I told her I didn't take anything from her, she challenged me to a sparring match. I thought if I could win it would prove my innocence, but when we fought that evening, she had me on the ground and disarmed in moments." Rayna smirks, her eyes glittering, as if getting walloped by Ash is a fond memory.

"That sounds like Ash," I chuckle, a burning question in my mind. "Did she ever find out who stole her pastry?"

She opens her mouth to speak, but Rian cuts in with a wide-toothed grin. I'm startled to realize the others have been listening to our conversation.

"It was me. I was around the corner when I saw Aislinn go into her room with an armful of sweets and come out with nothing. After seeing Rayna get annihilated by her in the sparring ring, I was afraid to fess up. So I let her take the blame."

He shrugs nonchalantly, unbothered by the warrior princess staring him down across the fire with a lethal smile on her face.

"You little devil," Rayna says, but I don't miss the hint of affection in her voice. "I always knew you were a slippery snake."

Rian flashes her a full smile. "She must have forgiven you for the pastry mishap, because you two were inseparable at the last summit."

Rayna looks away from him, clears her throat, and takes a swig of water, looking past Aidan towards the rope ladder. I stare at her, surprised by her reaction. If I didn't know better, I'd say she was embarrassed.

"Aislinn could put any of you here to shame in hand-to-hand combat," Aidan muses, changing the subject, perhaps to throw Rayna a bone. "Although, after we all come into our power, that won't be the case. Strange how the mighty can be dethroned so quickly."

I eye him, confused. He both complimented and insulted Aislinn in the same breath.

"Yes, yes, she would have made a spectacular queen," Calder snaps brusquely as his focus lands on me. "It's a shame that Adrithia will be stuck with you as its ruler now."

My eyes narrow at him. "What exactly is your problem with me? If you think I'm going to make such a terrible ruler, doesn't that only serve to improve your standing?"

Calder levels a disgusted stare at me. For a moment I don't think he'll answer, until he finally takes a breath. "There is a natural order to our continent, *Elana*. Firstborn rulers have been chosen for centuries. You disrupt that pattern by being here. By showing younger siblings across the five kingdoms that it *could* be different."

The hatred rolling off him is palpable. I brush the hilts of my daggers.

"It's funny," I say humorlessly. "You don't seem like you really care about the natural order, Calder."

"You have no idea what you're talking about," he responds harshly. "I have three younger siblings, each with less common sense than the last. None of them are fit to rule Hotharia. Now that this precedent has been set, what's to stop them from killing me in my sleep and becoming heir in my place?"

I pause, thrown off by the possibility of the tenuous control these heirs have over their thrones. "Would your siblings really try to kill you for the crown?"

Calder makes a disgusted sound in his throat. "Of course they would, and you're naive to doubt it. Not everyone here has a loving, happy family."

I glance around the fire at the heirs. Aidan's gaze is trained on Calder, hands crossed over his chest. Rayna and Rian both avoid my eyes, the latter even staring down at his feet as he gently kicks the dirt. Surprise and shame creep up my neck. The thought never crossed my mind that the other heirs may have difficult relationships with their families.

"I'm sorry," I say to no one in particular. They may not want pity, but I hope I can give them my understanding.

I wake in the early hours of dawn, when the sky is still a luscious golden color that pangs my heart, golden like the color of Aislinn's hair. Gods, I miss her.

The morning is cool, even with the comforting heat of the fire. I rub my feet together to bring some warmth into them. I sit up and stretch my arms up over my head, stretching the sleeping soreness out of my limbs.

Aidan's bedroll is empty. I glance around the summit for him and see a flickering fire by the large arches on the far side of the plateau.

I wipe the sleep from my eyes as I walk towards the streams of fire dancing around Aidan's hands. He throws his arm out and a fire ball crashes into the stone, charring the orange surface.

"Like a moth to a flame. Or perhaps a Magpie to a roost." Aidan's voice catches me by surprise. His back is to me, but he must have heard me coming.

"What are you doing?" I ask, eyeing the scorch marks on the rock wall.

He turns to face me, his face is flushed, his breathing labored. He must've been at this for a while.

"I'm practicing," he says, and with a flick of his wrist he sends another impressive fireball smashing into the stone.

My eyebrows scrunch together. "Do you always push yourself this hard?"

He wipes his forehead with the back of his hand. A memory of that hand gently holding my body a few days ago flashes in my mind and I look away from him, feeling my cheeks heat. "Only when I have thoughts I can't escape."

"Oh?" I wonder, curiosity winding its way through my words. "And what thoughts can't you escape?"

Aidan sighs, staring down at me. "You, Magpie. I can't get you out of my head."

A breath leaves me and I shiver. "And what are you going to do about it?"

Devious golden eyes meet mine. "What do you want me to do about it?"

I gulp. I know exactly what I want him to do. It's the same thing I've been thinking about for the past week and replaying in my mind since the cave. I want those strong arms around me again. I want them touching me—everywhere.

His eyes trail down the length of my body slowly, savoring it. A crooked grin tugs up one corner of his mouth as he takes two steps towards me, closing the distance between us.

"What do you want, Elana?" My name on his lips is a whisper, a promise, one I desperately want to taste.

"You," I breathe out, my voice barely audible. But Aidan hears.

His arms slide around my waist, pressing me to him. I wrap my arms around his shoulders. Our lips meet, and it isn't like any of the kisses I've experienced before. It's pure heat. His tongue traces my lips and I open for him. He tastes me, drinks me in. I gasp and pull back to catch my breath.

He kisses my cheek, then down the column of my throat, biting gently on the soft skin there. A sound escapes me from the back of my throat, almost a whine, and I finally run my fingers through his hair. It's softer than I imagined it to be. I grip his hair hard and pull his head back from my neck, reclaiming his lips with my own.

He groans his approval. With a wicked chuckle he picks me up, spinning us and walking back to the rock wall, where he pins my body with his own. The wall is cool on my burning skin.

I startle and sit up in my bedroll, breathing heavily. My hand shoots to my lips, the phantom kiss lingering. My blankets are in a bundle by my feet, and the coolness of the morning nips at me, even though I'm flushed. A quick glance around the fire and I see everyone asleep on their own beds.

It's early dawn, as it was in the dream. Oh Gods, that dream. My skin is boiling. I stand up, eager for the breeze to cool me, but it's not quick enough. I take a sip of my water and savor the coolness in my mouth.

Someone stirs awake, and I don't look down, afraid it'll be Aidan, and somehow, he'll know about my dream. He'll see my red cheeks and he'll know.

"Is it morning already?" Rian grumbles, and his grumpiness brings so much relief to me I almost laugh.

"Yes, unfortunately it is," I say, busying myself with folding my blanket so he doesn't see my embarrassment.

The golden light of the morning is suddenly dampened, as if covered by a thick blanket. I look across the horizon and see dark, angry clouds slowly pushing towards us.

"Fuck," I whisper. Then I raise my voice. "Everyone up, a storm's moving in."

The other heirs wake in various stages of annoyance and we pack up our camp in record time. The looming threat of the storm hangs over our heads as we work. We need to climb down that daunting rope ladder before the rain starts.

We stand on the edge of the cliff, staring down at the ladder like it's the last thing on Astrellia we want to see.

"I'm going first," Aidan announces with a pointed look at me. I open my mouth, for once about to agree with him, but he cuts me off. "There's no arguing."

I wasn't about to, but I hold my hands up anyway and gesture to the ladder. It's all his.

A rolling rumble sounds a little closer than I expect. The dark mass of clouds stretches across the horizon like an impenetrable wall. Our view of the landscape disappears under the haze of rain.

"Better hurry, that storm's moving quickly," Rian says, his gaze locked on the clouds moving in.

Aidan lines up with the ladder and spins around to face us. He descends the first few steps slowly. His face is set in concentration, perhaps listening for any cracks in the wood or splitting fibers of the rope.

He makes steady progress down until we have to crane our necks over the edge to see him. Eventually he gets to a point where we can't see him at all.

After a few tense minutes he calls up to us. "It's safe."

We breathe a collective sigh of relief.

Rayna gently taps my shoulder. "You should go next, Elana."

I glance at Rian and Calder. Rian nods at me, taking a step back. Calder rolls his eyes, but doesn't say anything.

"All right," I reply, taking my turn at the top of the ladder. I don't allow myself to spare a glance at the steep drop, instead focusing on adjusting my pack tighter to my body.

I face Rayna as I take the first step onto the rickety ladder, who gives me an encouraging dip of her head.

The wood doesn't creak or bend under my feet this time, and I feel slightly reassured. I grip the rope tightly with my hands and take a step down. The ladder holds steady. I descend at a slow pace, pausing only briefly when a gust of wind sends me rocking. A few deep breaths later and the wind dies down, allowing me to continue.

Time seems to stretch like nights during the middle of winter as I focus. My confidence in my steps grows and I take them quicker. Another gust whips by and now that I'm well down the bottom half, the whole ladder jerks and sways.

The ladder starts to spin and I cling onto it with a white-knuckled grip. The whipping motion crashes my hand into the rock wall and I scream in pain, feeling the back of my hand split open. I don't realize that I've let go of the ladder. That realization hits me as I'm already falling. I reach for the rope, but it slips out of my fingers. I plummet towards the earth.

Something solid, but not rock, breaks my fall with a curse. My breath whooshes out of me as I look up into Aidan's golden eyes. His arms are under my knees and behind my back. How he managed to catch me is beyond me, but I'm grateful he did.

"I thought Magpies were supposed to fly, not drop like rocks," Aidan huffs.

"You caught me," I say, because it's the only thing that comes to my mind. My heartbeat flutters wildly in my chest. I look up at the ladder. I was only about a dozen rungs up, so I don't think the fall would have been fatal, but it would have hurt like Hells and possibly broken something.

"Did you really think I'd let you fall?" His voice is close to my face, a crooked half-smile on his lips.

I swallow with some difficulty and try not to stare into his eyes. This, too, brings back memories of that Gods-damned dream I had last night. I desperately shove those images away. I can't be attracted to this dangerous, hot-headed degenerate. The one heir that Aislinn told me to watch out for, the one who even she would think twice about messing with—and that was before he had his powers.

I clear my throat. "Thank you, Aidan."

I try to wiggle free of his arms, but hiss in pain as I brush my injured hand against my leg. Blood smears my pants. Aidan gently sets me down on my feet but stares at my wounded hand, inspecting it with concern.

"Are you alright?" Rayna yells from on top of the cliff.

I tilt my head back and shout back at her that I'm fine. Then I see her line up with the ladder and begin the descent.

"Your hand," Aidan says, reaching for it.

"I'll be fine," I say, pulling back slightly, not wanting to show my weakness. "Keep an eye on Rayna. The wind's picking up."

He stares at me, eyes hard for a moment, before going to spot Rayna.

I plop onto a nearby boulder, set my pack down, and dig through it with my good hand until I find the roll of clean bandages and some healing ointment.

I need to wash the wound first. I unstopper my water skin and take a deep breath, then pour some water. Pain hits me in a wave. I bite my lip against the whimper I feel in my throat. Tears sting my eyes and my hand shakes, but at least it's clean.

My hand throbs, as I thoroughly inspect the mangled flesh. The skin is torn off from my knuckles to my wrist. I slowly open and close my hand, hissing with the pain the small motion brings. None of the bones feel broken, which is good—but they're probably bruised, which accounts for the immediate swelling. This could take weeks to fully heal. I sigh. Not good, seeing that we're still in the middle of the challenges and who knows what they'll bring.

I glance up to check on Rayna's progress. She's already halfway down the ladder, moving with steady, confident steps.

My hand continues to shake as I dab some healing salve on it, breathing through the stinging pain. I take the strip of clean cloth to wrap it but find the task impossible with one hand. I sigh with frustration.

Aidan kneels down in front of me. "May I?" He holds his hand out for the bandage. I look up the ladder for Rayna, needing to know she's safe first. She's only a few rungs away from the bottom, so I glance up at Aidan and nod, giving him the cloth.

His calloused hands are surprisingly gentle as he wraps my injury, tying the fabric into a neat little bow.

"That isn't too tight, is it?" he asks, securing the knot.

"No, it's perfect," I whisper.

His hands linger on mine for a moment, his fingers tracing soft circles on the palm of my hand. I stare down at our entwined hands, wanting this moment to stretch on forever, but Rayna's feet hit the ground close by and he pulls away.

I let out a long breath and test my mobility and grip. It's abysmal, but at least the numbing qualities of the healing salve start working.

"Are you alright?" Rayna appears before me, staring down at my hand, concerned.

"It's a little scratch, I'll be fine."

Her eyebrows raise. "You know, you and your sister have one thing in common. You're both terrible liars."

A smile tugs the corner of my mouth up. "I scraped my hand on the rock when the ladder flipped. No broken bones, but it's pretty sore."

She nods. "I hope it heals quickly. Can you still hold your weapons?"

I wince as I try to grasp the handle of a dagger. "With my dominant hand, yes, but not so much with this one."

Rayna bites her bottom lip. "All right, it'll be okay. Hopefully we won't be fighting anything anytime soon. Try to keep it hidden from Calder."

I nod my head in agreement and we both look up to see him descending the ladder.

The wind, unfortunately, holds off while he climbs. A few fat droplets of water splash my face as he jumps down the last few steps.

He yells to Rian that he's clear, who wastes no time in mounting the ladder and climbing down. As he was on the bridge, he's the swiftest among us, moving with surety as he takes one step after another.

But even he cannot outrun the fury of the encroaching storm. Several large droplets splash the rocks around us and Rayna and I exchange looks.

Rian pauses and stares up at the sky.

"Come on, Rian," I whisper, willing him to keep moving.

"He needs to *move*," Aidan says under his breath, sounding uncharacteristically anxious.

Rian starts to move again, with a renewed fervor.

"That's it, Rian, keep it up," Rayna shouts up at him.

A jagged, broken bolt of lightning flashes in the sky above us followed by a peal of thunder that cracks over the rocks, echoing off the mountain.

We all look up at the sky as the writhing clouds above us open up to unleash a downpour. Calder instantly raises a water shield around us, blocking the rain, but Rian grips the ladder, caught in the torrent. He takes a few slow steps down, but there's a squeak as his boot slips and he falls several rungs before catching himself, cursing loud enough for us all to hear.

"Calder, can't you help him?" I dare to ask.

If I was the one on the ladder, I have no doubt that his answer would be a resounding no. But it's not me. It's Rian. And it's most likely that reason that has Calder gritting his teeth and raising his arms, extending his shield to encompass Aaranor's heir.

Rian takes advantage of the help offered and quickly makes his way to the bottom. His feet hit the dry ground, sheltered by Calder's shield. He blows out a long breath, bent over his knees.

"Thank you, Calder," he says, standing back up to his full height.

"Don't mention it," Calder replies, already turning his back on us to move ahead.

I watch Rian wince and shake out his hands. He catches my eye and smiles, hiding them in his pockets.

Rayna and Aidan fall into line behind Calder, but I snag Rian's arm, forcing him to walk besides me. "Let me see your hands."

He sighs and shows the perfectly pristine backs of his hands to me. I roll my eyes and grab his wrists gently, careful not to upset my own bandaged hand. I flip them over so his palms face me. Bright red blisters and angry skin greet me.

"Rian," I whisper, in empathy and scorn. "You can't hide an injury like this."

"It's not a big deal, they hardly hurt," he tries telling me, but the wince when I gently poke his hand says otherwise.

While we walk, I dig through my pack, pulling out the healing salve and handing it over.

"We'll need to share this, I'm afraid," I flash my injury at him. "Apply twice per day, keep them covered, and whatever you do, do *not* pop those blisters."

He gives me a grateful grin. A flash and a shuddering boom behind us makes us jump and turn. The ladder to the second peak is incinerated, and charred pieces of it fall to the ground.

"I'm glad that wasn't me," Rian's golden brown skin turns ashen. I nod silently in agreement and we both hurry to catch up to the others.

I look through Calder's rain barrier and hope the storm moves by quickly.

Chapter Twenty-One

As luck would have it, the rain doesn't pass quickly.

My boot slips in the endless tide of mud at my feet, but I manage to maintain my balance.

It's been raining for the last three days. Calder has used his power to keep a shield of water around us to block the rain, and Aidan has been keeping us warm, but the landscape remains dreary and sloppy.

My one solace is that the wound on my hand doesn't constantly ache anymore and Rian's blisters have scabbed over nicely. I'm sure of it now, something is accelerating our healing. Perhaps the Gods are taking pity on us or want us at our best for whatever trials are coming our way.

Our physical health may be perfect, but our moods are as sour as the weather.

"Can't you stop the rain, oh mighty water-gifted heir?" Rian mockingly asks Calder, who scowls and opens the water shield where he stands.

Rian snarls, shaking out his wet hair and drawing his naginata in front of himself. "Do that again and you'll be sorry."

I'm surprised by Rian's outburst. His playful, cheery exterior has been washed away to reveal an ornery old man. He's been at everyone's throats since he woke up.

Calder's shield dissipates over all of us except himself and the rain soaks us through in a matter of moments as the Hotharian heir stomps up the path by himself.

I throw my hands up and whirl on Rian. "Great, thanks for pissing off Calder. Now we all get wet."

Rian has the courtesy to look sheepish at me as he wipes rain out of his eyes. "Sorry. I'm sick of this rain."

My irritation flares, but I let out a long breath and hold back my retort. I tap my daggers for comfort. A hissing sound comes from next to me. I glance over and see steam billowing off Aidan's head. The sight takes me off guard, and I can't help the laugh that bubbles out of me. Aidan's eyebrows raise at me, and more vapor puffs over his head.

"Did you know there's steam," I point at his head and shoulders, "coming off of you?"

Aidan doesn't miss a beat, his mouth quirks up into a smirk. "It's because I'm so damn hot."

I roll my eyes at him, playfully shoving his arm, and open my mouth to say something, but I'm cut off by a rumbling beneath our feet.

"Thunder?" Rian asks, looking at the sky.

No, this is a feeling I recognize from living with my father. A constant roaring sound like this only comes from moving earth.

"Run!" a voice shouts. We all look up the path and see Calder tearing towards us, his face a mask of terror. "Run!" he yells again, briefly gesturing behind him.

Closing in behind him, a writhing mass of mud and rocks tumble down the mountain, heading right for us at breakneck speed.

"Oh fuck," Rayna breathes out. "Go!"

She pushes me ahead of her as the shaking ground seems to crescendo. My feet have never moved so swiftly. We race down the slope, desperately trying to beat the wave of death that threatens to catch us.

Aidan briefly halts to raise a wall of fire. Heat scorches our backs, but only for a few moments. The combined might of the rainwater and the falling mountain snuff out his fire with nothing more than a hiss.

A loud snapping noise comes from behind us, but I don't stop to see the cause. I sloppily wipe water from my eyes in attempt to clear my blurry vision. A large slab of rock, easily twice my height, breaks free from the side of the mountain and slams into the path before us, digging into the soft path and splashing mud all over us. The momentary pause in our flight has given the mudslide a chance to catch up. It laps at our ankles.

"Get on the other side," Rayna once again shoves me, pushing me behind the rock. We all huddle behind the piece of the mountain right as the full force of the mudslide slams into it. The sound is unlike anything I've ever heard. Like a volcano erupting, the noise builds. The rock skids and slides down, forcing us to move with it. On both sides of the boulder, rock and mud stream past.

A large conifer tree clatters into the rock as it floats by us in the deluge, and I realize the cracking I heard earlier was it snapping like a matchstick. The rock groans, sliding further and further down, until the top of it begins to tip towards us. If it falls, we're dead. If it gets caught up in the rockslide, we're dead. Our chances of survival dwindle by the second.

"Calder, can you wield any of the water that's in the mud? Maybe dry it out, or change its direction?" Aidan asks, arms balled into fists at his sides.

"No, I can't," Calder says with a curt shake of his head. "I've been trying, but it's like there's too much earth mixed in or something."

We're trapped, our options wearing thin. I look around for a nearby tree, another rock, anything, but there's nothing around except for this boulder and the sludge surrounding us. Rayna, in a last-ditch effort, pushes her body against the rock, digging her feet into the sloppy ground and shoving with all her weight. The sight of her desperation spurs me forward. I dig my heels in next to her and press my shoulder into the rock, my healing hand protesting against the exertion. After a moment, the others follow suit, but our pushing throws the boulder off balance, and as the bottom slides up the hill, the top tumbles towards us.

I gasp as warm, calloused hands wrap around my waist, tugging me down, shielding me. By the warmth and the cedar scent enveloping me, I know it's Aidan.

All I can hope is that this end will be quicker than drowning. I squeeze my eyes shut and wait for it. Two loud crashing noises have me tensing, but when no pain comes, I glance up past Aidan and see the boulder halt. It's knocked back into its standing position by two columns of stone.

Aidan unfolds his body from over me. A gentle tug as he pulls me to my feet next to him. My eyes meet his, and there's exhausted relief painted over his features as he stares at Rayna.

"She did it," he breathes.

She pushes her arms out and the two stone pillars grow taller, reinforcing the boulder we hide behind. When the boulder stands steady, she takes a deep breath and a third pillar raises her up as she surveys the raging mudslide. With one wide swooping motion, she slashes her hands down and the mountain gives another violent shudder.

Slowly, the mud surrounding us subsides, the tide settling before finally crawling to a stop. Rayna leaps back onto the third stone pillar as it sinks back into the earth.

"It should be safe now," she says, breathing hard.

I stare at her for a moment, letting my shock thaw. The Goddess Avani chose wisely. Rayna is the perfect embodiment of strength and resilience.

I smile broadly and splash up to her, pulling her into a fierce hug. "You are incredible."

She startles at first, but then softens and hugs me back with a chuckle.

"Oh, stop," she says, a bit out of breath as she breaks our hug. "I did what any of you would do."

"Thank you for saving our asses," Rian says, wrapping his arms around her and spinning her in a jubilant hug.

"As if I'd let you be crushed. Can you imagine the mess?" Rayna jokes as Rian gently sets her back onto her feet.

"Congratulations," Aidan says to her with a half-smile. She beams at us, pride and relief making her dark skin glow despite the rain.

Calder gives her a brief, acknowledging nod. I'm not surprised at his lack of enthusiasm for anyone but himself.

He waves his hand above us and the shield blocking out the rain forms once more.

We step out from around the rock. I gasp at the extent of destruction across the landscape. Rayna didn't just stop the mudslide, she carved deep gouges into the mountainside to reroute the flow. Two deep crevasses are before us. The tide of mud slowly slides down them and harmlessly away from us.

"Holy Gods," Rian whispers, mouth agape.

"It wasn't the perfect solution." Rayna shrugs. "But it was quick. And effective."

She raises both hands and squeezes her fists. The remaining mud along the path hardens, becoming solid, uneven stone.

"Rayna, you saved our lives. I don't think we're in a position to judge," I say, nudging her with my shoulder.

She chuckles and bumps me back. "I suppose."

It's still pouring when we stop for the night. Rayna is apparently tired of sleeping under Calder's rain shield, so she carves us a cave in the wall of the mountain. It's simple in design, but deep enough to protect us from the weather. Aidan's fire glows in the middle of the cave, warming us nicely and allowing us to set out our damp clothes to dry.

We eat cooked fish that Calder caught from a small lake. He says he was able to sense their movement in the water and catch them in a bubble, bringing them to the surface where our hungry hands waited.

This cave brings back flashes of my dream in the dark cavern with the torch, the shadows, and the whispers. Only fragments of it remain in my mind and I struggle to put the pieces together into anything coherent. An unsettled feeling washes over me and lingers long after the others fall asleep.

I listen to their steady breathing and Rian's light snoring for what feels like hours before admitting to myself I won't find sleep while chasing it. The thought drives me to my feet. The steady patter of the rain soothes my racing mind. I sit at the mouth of the cave with my hands hugging my knees and watch the droplets splatter the ground.

Absentmindedly, I cradle my injured hand, rubbing my fingers gently over the bandage. I changed the cloth earlier and was shocked to see the scabs had nearly healed over. The mottled purple bruises have reached their peak color and I anticipate they'll fade in a day or two.

A shuffling noise from behind startles me out of my reverie. One of my daggers is halfway out of its sheath when a warm blanket is thrown over my shoulders. I startle, but the scent of cedar hits me and I relax, slipping my blade back.

"Can't sleep, Magpie?"

Out of the corner of my eye I see Aidan sit down next to me, leaning against the cave wall. I don't answer him because it should be obvious. He nods to my hand.

"How's that hand?"

"How do you think?" I sigh and kick a pebble away. It splashes into a small puddle outside the cave.

He smirks and holds his hand out, palm up. I stare at him, scanning for any potential ill intentions, but come up empty. I place my hand in his and he gently tests the movement of each of my fingers, stopping when I flinch at a sore spot. "Will you be able to wield your weapons?"

I clench my fist and pain shoots up my arm. I wince. "Not with this hand, for a few more days at least."

I have no idea why I'm revealing this information to him. He knows I'm even more defenseless now and could use that knowledge to hurt me. But no, I truly don't think he would do that. Why would he give me his blanket if he wanted to harm me? Why would he have shielded my body against the boulder?

"At least it isn't your dominant hand," he says, as if that will make me feel better.

We fall into silence and he continues to stroke my palm with gentle caresses.

Light fills the space around us as a dozen little flames dance to life around our bodies. They chase away the lingering chill in my extremities.

After a few moments of watching the flames in awe and appreciation, I ask something I've wondered since the Goddess granted him his powers.

"Did you always know you were going to be chosen by Enya?"

Aidan is quiet for a few moments, long enough that I'm sure he won't respond.

"I thought I would be, and hoped for it," he says at last. "Looking back on it now, there were...signs that I was meant for the flames."

I turn my head to meet his gaze, interest piqued. "What signs?"

He flicks a finger out, and the same songbird from days ago bursts from his finger, flying around us gracefully.

"When I was a child, I fell into a fire pit and by the time my mother doused the flames, she was sure I'd be horribly injured. Instead, I was miraculously unscathed. Then in my teen years, I survived an assassination attempt. The assassins lured me into an abandoned home, locked me inside, and set the place on fire."

I suck in my breath in surprise and horror. "Did the Goddess save you?"

Aidan smiles. "No, my brother did. At some point in my attempt to escape I passed out, probably from the smoke. When I woke, my brother, Alek, was dragging me out of the rubble. Half of the wooden house had collapsed by the time he found me. But I lived. I still have a scar from where a piece of rubble landed on me, but no burn marks."

He unbuttons the top three buttons of his shirt, revealing a well-defined chest and a long, jagged, thin scar from the top of his right shoulder to the middle of his chest. It is the same mark I couldn't stop staring at in the cave pool.

A wound like that could have easily become infected and killed any other person. He's lucky to be alive, in more ways than merely surviving the fire.

"I can't believe you survived an assassination attempt. Actually, I'm more surprised that you had an attempt on your life at all. I thought everyone loved the heirs," I say.

Aidan chuckles softly. "Oh, Princess, surely you survived a few yourself? I know Aislinn had at least six of them."

That startles me. "What?"

He looks at me, brow furrowed and nose scrunched slightly. "We used to keep a running tally and would tell the stories during the summits. Didn't she tell you?"

I gape. No, she never mentioned any attempted assassinations to me. Why? Did she think I couldn't handle it? All these secrets keep piling up, making me wonder how much I truly know those closest to me.

"Damn, princess. Exactly how much did your family keep from you?" Of course Aidan can read my expression. I'm clearly not as skilled at hiding vital information as the rest of my family.

"It doesn't matter," I lie, shoving that knowledge down until I can process it later. "Besides all these signs of an affinity for fire, did Enya ever speak to you?"

Aidan sucks on his teeth. "Speak to me how?"

"Like in a dream or anything?" I press.

"No, never anything like that," he says. "Why do you ask?"

I stare at the floating fiery bird, choosing my words carefully. "I've had a few dreams ever since the Crowning Ceremony that feel like messages. Like maybe a god is trying to talk to me."

Aidan stares at me while I watch the bird.

"That must sound crazy. It's probably my imagination," I say, suddenly feeling self-conscious. I don't know why I'm trusting him with this. We only met a few weeks ago, and now I'm spilling my secrets to him. Perhaps that makes me a fool, but Aidan has helped and protected me multiple times already. There's no reason to suggest he would betray me.

"It's not crazy," Aidan says. He leans towards me and I glance away, surprised by his closeness. His hand gently, so gently, cups my chin and directs my face to look up into his molten eyes. "The Gods operate in their own unique ways, Elana. If one was trying to speak with me, I'd do my best to listen. Really, truly listen."

Oh Gods, my name on his lips sends a shiver down my spine, but it's his rough thumb on my chin that nearly undoes me. I take in a shaky breath and Aidan's mouth quirks up, as if he knows I'm not shivering from the cold.

"Would you like to tell me anything about these dreams?"

"I don't remember much," I say. He says nothing, but his eyebrow raises, as if urging me to continue. I sigh and gesture broadly to the cave. "What little I do remember is that I'm in a cave, and a terrible storm rages outside. Then there's whispering, from multiple voices, all at once. I remember it being loud."

I close my eyes and try to remember what the voices said. "They spoke in a riddle, I think. Something about waiting. And the fall."

Flashes come to me of the flame flickering over my shoulder, the shadowy figures on the wall dancing and writhing. I had to cover my ears, the voices were so loud. The dream always seemed to end with my death, under a pile of rocks, or by jumping off a cliff. That familiar unease settles into my stomach like a lead weight.

A hand caresses my cheek and my eyes snap open, finding Aidan's gaze immediately.

"It does sound like something a god would do. Perhaps the closer you get to meeting them, the more the dreams will make sense. I have a feeling the Gods are waiting to give us a show with your power. After choosing you with no precedent, they're building anticipation." He flashes me a sly smile, dimple on display.

I hadn't thought of it that way before. Maybe the Gods do have a plan for me. I could have a purpose other than being a wife and a healer. That feeling warms me and I smile broadly at him.

"Thank you, Aidan. For believing I can do this," I say. I take a few slow breaths and a weight I wasn't aware I was carrying lifts off my shoulders. My eyelids start to droop unbidden and my exhaustion hits me all at once. I tilt to the side and Aidan's arms gently catch me, folding around my waist.

"Sleep, Magpie," he whispers, and I swear I feel the faintest pressure on the top of my head, like a feather soft kiss.

As my heavy lids fully close and blackness washes over me, I hear his low voice once more, but I can't have heard it right, because there's no way he would say such a thing.

"Gods, you're stunning when you smile."

Chapter Twenty-Two

Something bright pierces my eyelids and I see red before they even open. I'm vaguely aware of a warm weight on me, and the scent of cedar. A body lies next to me.

My eyelids wrench open. Bright yellow morning light shines directly into my eyes. It's the first time I've seen the sun in days. I squint and raise my hand to block out the rays, pushing aside the weight on me. My arm brushes warm skin. I lift my head and see Aidan's arm draped over me. I'm still wrapped in his blanket, and his presence surrounds me.

I don't feel uncomfortable or stifled in the slightest. I feel safe in his arms.

There's a sound like a throat clearing and I sit up abruptly. My cheeks burn. Rayna stands over us, hands on her hips, eyes narrowed.

"Go away, mother hen," Aidan rumbles, covering his eyes with his balled up fist, flipping his middle finger up at her.

I stand quickly, embarrassed, and throw Aidan's blanket over him. He opens his eyes just enough to raise his eyebrows at me, then rolls onto his side and apparently falls back asleep.

Rayna jerks her head to indicate I should follow her outside the cave. I do, keeping a step behind her.

Rayna walks some distance from the cave, far enough so our conversation won't be overheard. Her black hair reflects the golden light of the morning. She stops, crosses her arms over her chest, and faces me.

"Elana, what are you doing with Aidan?" she asks, her voice hard but tinged with concern.

My face is still heated and I immediately feel like a child again, chastised by my mother for skipping my womanly arts lessons.

"I-I don't know, I couldn't sleep."

Rayna cuts me off. "I promised to protect you, and you're making it incredibly difficult right now. Being alone with Aidan is dangerous. We don't know where his loyalty lies."

"I'm sorry, I'll try to—" I pause, realizing I jumped straight to placating, like I used to do with my mother. It feels wrong. I'm a different person now. I fought a dragon, survived a whirlpool, and outran a mudslide. I deserve to be here, and I deserve to prove to everyone, including myself, that I'm strong.

"Look, Rayna, I appreciate all you've done for me, all you're still doing for me, but I'm a grown woman and I will make my own choices."

I take a deep breath and the knot in my chest loosens slightly.

"I trust him. He has shown me time and time again that he doesn't wish me harm. That might not be the choice you or Aislinn would make, but it's my decision."

Rayna stares at me, dark eyes still narrowed, before she cracks a grin. "You're right. You deserve to make your own choices. I'm only asking you to be careful because I don't want you getting hurt. He's always felt like the most secretive one among us."

I sigh. "We all have secrets, Rayna. I trust that his aren't going to hurt me."

"I suppose I can accept that."

A quirk of a smile lifts the corner of my mouth up. "Gods, you sound like Aislinn."

"Oh, you wish!" Rayna barks a laugh, then sobers, glancing at me. She shakes her head and chuckles. "You know, that was the first time I've heard you talk like one of us. Like a future ruler."

Her words sink in, and I let them settle in my head for a moment. Less than two weeks with the heirs and I'm already speaking like one? Hopefully that bodes well for when I return home...*if* I return home. I want to survive up here, to show the people of Adrithia that I'm as capable of ruling as Aislinn.

"Keep it up, Elana. I like this version of you."

I think I like this version of me, too.

To my growing surprise, my hand and Rian's palms heal quickly over the next few days. I'm more convinced than ever that the Gods' magic is at work helping us. I can delicately hold my dagger in my non-dominant hand now, although a grip tight enough to inflict any damage on opponents is still too painful.

We travel significantly faster thanks to Rayna. She figured out she could lift us up on a slab of stone and carry us up the mountain. At first, she could only go a few hours without tiring—abilities are taxing on one's energy. Similar to a muscle though, the more a power is used, the more the body becomes accustomed to it and the easier it is to wield.

Two days later she's able to carry us from dawn until nearly dusk. We end the day at the top of the third peak.

Rayna, who has hardly broken a sweat this entire journey, is panting from exertion.

"You're doing great, Rayna. Thank you for giving us a break from walking." I smile at her.

She waves me off in response, probably so she doesn't have to expend the energy to speak.

The evening is crisp. We huddle close together around Aidan's roaring fire. We haven't found anything fresh to eat since Calder caught fish days ago, so we've been eating sparingly out of our provisions. Luckily, he's been providing us with water, or else we'd be on the verge of death, since we also haven't seen any fresh water in days.

Across the fire, I feel Aidan's stare on me. We haven't had a moment alone to talk after the morning I woke up in his arms, and the weight of the things I want to say to him is nearly suffocating me.

I fall asleep quickly that night, letting another day of tense silence go between us.

The next morning Rayna, fully refreshed, creates a rock bridge for us across a chasm to the fourth mountain. There's nothing quite like the feeling of safety when crossing a canyon. Having solid earth under our feet the entire time is a relief like none other.

Rayna moves us quickly up the side of the fourth peak. We're all getting antsy and eager to find food. Our hopes are dashed slowly throughout the day when we realize the peak is mostly barren. No vegetation other than occasional grasses grows here, and we don't see any streams. There's nothing up here that would support animal life.

The air grows steadily colder, too. My long sleeves become necessary and I shiver when we stop for the night. Rayna creates another rock shelter for us, and Aidan's fire is extra warm. Still, we all move in a little closer.

The cave. I stand in the cave again, voices whispering all around me, echoing off the walls. The sound is agonizing. I cover my ears with shaking hands and sink to the ground. The coolness of the rock grounds me.

Aidan's voice comes to me. "If one was trying to speak with me, I'd do my best to listen. Really, truly listen." I take a few calming breaths and slowly lower my hands from my head. The noise batters me and I cringe against it, but do not cover my ears again.

"Please tell me. I'm here. I'm listening."

The voices slowly quiet and dampen until two distinct tones speak in tandem.

"Elana, make the journey, make the climb. Only you can fix what's broken in time.

We wait at the end of it all, when hope has gone and all will fall.

Stay true to your heart, for balance will bring peace. In yourself a forgotten power you will release.

You are the final fated piece."

I'm cast into a sudden darkness so complete and encompassing I can't even see my hands in front of my own face, or feel the oxygen filling my lungs or the heart beating in my chest.

I jolt awake, gasping for air before remembering where I am. I stifle the noise, breathing quieter and run my hands over my face. Gods, that felt so horrifically real.

I glance outside the cavern, at the midnight sky dotted with shining stars. On the other side of the glowing, roaring fire, Aidan sits up, brushing his unkempt black hair away from his face. He takes one assessing look at me and stands up silently, bringing his blanket with him. He holds out his hand and I get up, leaving my makeshift bed behind but wrapping myself in my blanket.

There's no hesitation in my mind as I grab his hand, so warm in mine, and let him lead me out of the cave and away from the others. Aidan stops when we're far enough away from the cave and on a relatively flat patch of rock.

"Another dream?" he asks quietly as he lays his blanket down on the ground and creates a large fire ring around us.

I nod my head and then smile in appreciation of both the warmth and privacy the fire provides. "Nice touch."

"That's what all the ladies say," Aidan says with a smirk, throwing himself down on the blanket and patting the spot next to him.

"Oh really, will you tell me about all of your lady friends?" I ask jokingly, but if I'm being honest with myself, I'm curious too. I fold myself down next to him.

Aidan huffs a laugh. "Are you asking so you don't have to tell me about your dream?"

I gasp in fake horror. "Of course not. I would never." Then, slightly more seriously, I say, "I'm still figuring out what it means."

His golden gaze slides over my face, from my eyes to my downturned lips. "All my 'lady friends,' if you must know, would give me incredibly high marks, I'm sure."

"High marks?" I squeak out, utterly shocked he rose to the teasing.

He gives a low rumbling laugh. "Oh yes, the highest. I'm sure they would cite my lips, fingers, and...stamina...as my assets."

I nearly choke on my tongue as the suggestion of what he almost said lingers in the air around us. Gods, this man has no decency.

"So it turns out I was right," I say, giving him a withering look.

His eyebrows raise. "About what, Magpie?"

"I was right when I called you a degenerate."

Aidan barks a contagious laugh that I'm worried will wake the others, but even from here I can hear Rian's snoring blocking out anything else. His dimple is back, and I relish the sight.

His laughter fades to a half-smile and he stands back up, reaching a hand down for me. "So, princess, if you don't want to talk about your dream, and I don't want to talk about my past lady friends or else risk being called a degenerate again, how about we spar?"

I wasn't expecting that.

He notices my confused look and draws his dagger from his side. "I've always found that training helps ease an overactive mind. If you're focused on something else you can't spiral into your own thoughts."

I consider for a brief moment before I flash him a decisive nod. I draw my daggers out as I stand, testing my grip strength on my mostly healed hand. It's sore, and if I squeeze too hard there's a dull ache that warns me to be careful.

It's been a little while since I've done more than just grip their hilts for comfort. I haven't actually needed them since Calder tried to kill me on the first peak, which strangely feels like months ago. The blades seem to sing as I slash them through the air in a few practice swings. By that whining sound alone I think they missed me as much as I missed them.

Aidan's at a disadvantage with only one weapon, but I know better than to underestimate him. Excluding Aislinn, he's quite possibly the most talented weapons wielder on Astrellia. He gives me a small smile and jerks his fingers at me in permission to strike. I don't give him time to ready himself, instead I launch myself at him.

He moves like lightning as he grips my wrist with his open hand and tugs me close to him. I gasp as his blade touches the soft spot under my chin. He gently lifts the dagger, tilting my head up so I have no choice but to look him in the eye.

"Is that the best you can do, Magpie?" he asks with a smirk.

My heart races and it's not all because of the adrenaline. I want to feel that smirk against my skin. My cheeks flush and I stare back at him with a slow swallow.

There's another burning desire that's beginning to wake. It's not one I've felt before, so it takes me a moment to recognize it. A desire to *win*.

I surrender my consciousness to the daggers, to the power and foresight of Hale Sable, who sacrificed his life so that his line could wield weapons capable of protecting Adrithia. Maybe he knew that such weapons would be required for unpracticed hands, because my attacks feel guided, as if someone moves my body for me, nudges me in the correct direction to dodge, then pushes me forward to strike. The moves are foreign even after Aislinn's training, more suited to close combat and dual wielding than the drills she took me through with a short sword.

Aidan flashes me a wicked smile as he dodges my attacks, moving swiftly through his own set of moves. Neither one of us manages a hit against the other, although I suspect he's holding back. We whirl around each other in a dance of blades.

Soon I'm breathing heavily through my exhaustion. My blades swipe by Aidan's shoulder in another lunge. He twists his torso, grabs my wrist firmly, and kicks his leg out behind me, tripping me backwards. Together we fall onto the ground with a huff, my daggers clattering to the dirt.

"Aidan," I whisper through quick breaths, "you're on top of me."

Gods, *what* am I saying? He's going to think I'm an idiot.

Except, he doesn't. He chuckles softly. "Is there somewhere else you wish me to be, Magpie?"

The redness on my cheeks has nothing to do with our previous exercise.

"No," I barely whisper.

His lips spread into a wide smirk, eyes aglow with feral hunger. Aidan brings that smirk down to my neck, grazing the soft spot where minutes ago he held his knife.

"Then tell me, Elana, what do you wish from me?"

His breath against my neck, those lips tantalizingly close—it's all too much, and not enough at the same time. I want more. Before I second-guess myself, I reach up, fist my fingers through his hair—soft, just like in my dream—and tug his head to mine.

Our mouths crash together in a frenzy. The kiss is not slow or gentle. One of his arms wraps around my waist, tugging me closer. A low groan rips from him as he angles his head to deepen the kiss. I open my mouth to him and he sweeps his tongue in. I gasp and he swallows the sound, drinking it in. We taste each other like we're the only two people on this mountain, on all of Astrellia.

Aidan's lips pause against mine and he pulls back slightly with a pained groan. He presses his lips to my forehead. "Gods, I hate that I have to stop this."

"Stop this?" I ask, my mind completely gone. I hardly get the words out. "Why?"

"Because we're about to have the most unpleasant audience." Aidan's voice is a husky snarl.

"Oh please, don't flatter yourselves. I've seen better." Calder's bitter tone shocks me out of my brain fog.

I gasp and sit up, forcing Aidan to a kneeling position in front of me.

"Because I'm feeling generous, I'm going to give you three seconds to remove your ass from our proximity before I light you on fire," Aidan growls, standing slowly.

Calder laughs humorlessly. "You wouldn't."

Aidan's eyebrow quirks up. "I'd barbeque a rat over your corpse." A ball of flame lights in his hand and grows larger with each second he counts down.

"One." Calder shifts uncomfortably.

"Two." He looks back and forth between Aidan and me.

"Thr—"

Calder jumps back, holding his hands at shoulder height. "Fine, fine, I'm going. I happen to think it's interesting that you found another lover so quickly after swearing off love mere months ago. Shame your betrothed isn't around to see how far you've fallen. At least she was actually attractive."

There's a roaring in my ears. Calder insulted me, but all I can think about is the word *betrothed*. Aidan is betrothed?

I slowly realize the roaring isn't in my ears, it's coming from Aidan's hand. The fire there burns so hot it turns white, flickering an eerie shade of blue.

He growls at Calder, who must see the stark rage on Aidan's face, because he backs up a few steps and puts up a shield of water. "I'll boil you alive."

This is escalating too quickly. I stand and put my arm on Aidan's bicep, but quickly yank it away with a hiss of pain. His skin—his whole body—is scalding. Instantly, the fire coating his hand gutters out.

"Are you okay?" he asks, whipping around, staring at my hand with something like devastation. I shake it out in front of me.

I inspect my slightly red hand, flexing the fingers. No blisters or extreme discoloration of the skin. A minor surface burn. "I'm fine, Aidan. I didn't realize your skin could get that hot."

His eyebrows remain pinched, his concern evident. "I'm so sorry, Elana. I lost control."

"Hey," I say, staring intently into his eyes so he listens. "I'm alright. There's nothing to apologize for. It's not even burned, look." I show him my palm.

He inspects it for a moment, then nods. I glance around for Calder, but as I guessed, he's already gone.

"He's not worth the trouble," Aidan says in a voice that promises violence, but when he turns to me, his features soften. "Gods, Elana, I didn't mean to hurt you. I'm so sorry."

"Don't apologize," I say, firmly. "You don't need to hide any part of yourself from me."

He gives me a soft smile, then runs his hand through his hair and blows out a long breath, as if centering himself.

"So," I say, making a poor attempt at a casual tone, "you're betrothed?"

Aidan stiffens, glancing away from me in a way that shatters my budding heart into a million pieces.

"I *was* betrothed," he says.

I wait, hoping he will go on, and when he doesn't, I ask, "what happened?"

He lets out a long sigh, stuffing his hands in his pockets. I've never seen him look so vulnerable.

"Her name was Nadia." There's so much pain in his voice and in the way he avoids my eyes. "And I don't want to talk about her right now."

The tone of his voice leaves little to argue with, and the past tense implies some tragic circumstance, so I don't ask. He turns away from me, picking up his blanket from the ground and extinguishing his fire as he wordlessly walks back into the cave.

I shiver in the noticeable absence of Aidan's fire. Despite being warm from training and...other things only moments ago, I feel colder now than ever. I can't help the leaden weight in my gut as I slowly follow him to the cavern. Is he keeping some dark secret? Or is Nadia's story that traumatic?

The thoughts chase me back into a fitful sleep.

CHAPTER TWENTY-THREE

Two days later we're still hungry and I'm starting to worry about our food situation. We set up camp early on a flat plateau that seems to jut from the side of the mountain, not having enough energy to travel until dusk.

Rayna's forehead is dripping sweat as she sucks in quick breaths. She moved us noticeably slower today, and I fear she's pushing herself too hard. If she keeps using this amount of energy without replenishing her body, she could quickly become malnourished.

"It's the air up here," Rian says, patting her back gently as she sucks in a few greedy breaths. "It's thinner, so you have to breathe more to feel comfortable."

A memory comes back to me of my father telling me that air becomes more difficult to breathe the further we climb. We're exerting more to keep our bodies functioning. Rayna needs to be more careful.

Aidan and Calder wander off to search for food, although we all know none will be found up here. Awkwardness sits heavily between Aidan and me. He has hardly spoken to me—or anyone—since Calder threw Nadia's name at him. I desperately want to know about her, but even more so I don't want to risk whatever fragile bond we've built. I think about our kiss for the hundredth time and my face flushes unprompted. I wonder if he's thought about it too, or if I'm merely a distraction up here.

Rian and I have a sort of mutual understanding of how terrible it feels being the last two heirs without an ability. The other three practice their elements nightly while Rian and I work to maintain hope. Air and metal are the last remaining elements. I feel no affinity with metal, so I doubt the god Tolliver will grant me his power. And if I'm being honest with myself, Rian is more suited to air than I am.

What the Hells will I do if no god chooses me and I end up having to make the journey home and reveal to everyone what a failure I am? No, I won't think that way. I deserve to be here, I know it. There is a god waiting for me.

"Hey, I found food!" Calder shouts from behind a boulder.

We all drop what we're doing and rush to him. There's a small tree, only a little taller than Rian, near the edge of the plateau. Its roots dip over the edge and the sad, spindly tree looks as if a strong wind gust could send it tumbling down the mountainside.

Five clusters of leaves bear fruit. Too easy. This is too easy. Calder plucks a fruit from the tree. It's about the size of his palm.

"Look who's the forager now, Elana." He shoves the fruit in my face, and in the sunlight, I get a good look at it. My stomach drops and I gasp. Its bright blue exterior is smooth like an apple, and I know from my studies the interior is a soft pink color. A beautiful fruit that hides an incredibly potent and deadly poison. Clarisse once took me to the only mountain in Adrithia and showed me this very fruit. She warned that only several rare ingredients could cure someone of its toxins.

"Wait, don't eat that," I warn. "It's highly poisonous."

Everyone's attention snaps to me, their hunger replaced by devastation, confusion—and in Calder's case, outright suspicion.

"Are you sure?" Rayna's voice sounds like she hopes it's not true. I wish I wasn't.

I nod at her. "My healing teacher taught me about them. It contains the deadliest poison ever discovered. One bite of the fruit is enough to put someone in a coma. Two bites are deadly. It's called the afterlife fruit."

I shut out the gnawing hunger in my stomach.

"Come on, Elana. We haven't had fresh food for days, the Gods grant us this gift, and you can't even accept it?"

"It's not a gift, Calder, it's a trap! Look at the tree. One for each of us. A little too convenient, don't you think?"

He scoffs, brushing off my observations and dragging a leering gaze along my body. "You probably only want us to think these are poisonous so you can eat them all yourself later. You're not exactly built like the rest of us."

I see red. It's the hunger talking, I know it is. But damn if I don't want to stick my daggers in his eyes anyway. Before I get the chance, a slap rings out around us so loud it echoes across the plateau and bounces off the side of the mountain back towards us. I glance at Rayna's hand, then at Calder's cheek. Sure enough, there's a perfect red imprint of her hand slowly brightening on his skin.

"You do not speak to any woman like that, ever." Her voice is low and deadly sharp.

Calder narrows his eyes at her and clenches his fist at his side. Ice coats it.

Fuck. This could all go very wrong, very quickly. Is it wrong that a part of me wants him to eat it? My rage simmers—it would be so easy to let him take a bite and succumb to the poison. There's no doubt if roles were reversed, he would let me eat it. But I think back to my healing lessons, and how devastated Clarisse would be if she knew I let someone die when I could prevent it. It goes against everything I promised to do when she first taught me.

When I first chose to study healing, I thought it would provide me the most freedom since it's one skill my mother doesn't possess. But from Clarisse, I learned to love helping people, making their lives easier and pain-free. Curing illnesses, healing injuries, and assisting others when they're vulnerable—*these* are the reasons why I continued my training long after my mother required it of me. And that's why I'll save Calder's life.

"Calder, hate me all you want, but do yourself a favor and do not eat it. Why else do you think it's called the afterlife fruit?"

A bitter laugh rips from his mouth. "Gods, are you hearing yourself? Afterlife fruit? There's no such thing. You're making this all up, and I'm sick of listening to you."

He lifts the bright blue fruit to his mouth.

"No!" I lunge for him, but I'm frozen—*literally* frozen—to the spot. I look down quickly to see the ice covering my boots and spreading out on the ground.

I look back up just in time to see him take a big bite, chew and swallow.

There's nothing I can do but stare at him, horrified. "You idiot."

He laughs and shakes his head at me, taking another bite, chewing it thoughtfully. Pink juice runs down his chin and he swipes it away.

My healer brain whirls as I start to mentally assemble the antidote. Thank the Gods that Ash and I encountered the giant scorpion on the way to the Gods' Territory, because its venom is the one thing that'll save him now.

"See? It's perfectly fine. Come on, Ashfall, Semere, Yarrow, try one." He plucks another one from the tree, holding it out towards Rian.

Rian glances back and forth between me and Calder. He doesn't take the fruit.

Calder clears his throat, adjusting the collar of his shirt.

"Is it getting hard to breathe yet?" I ask in a flat tone, observing him for the deadly symptoms. His fingers twitch on the fruit. "How are your fingers? Are they numb or merely tingly?"

"It's pretty good. A bit too sweet for me, but I can't complai—" He doubles over, clutching his stomach. He drops the fruit and collapses to his knees. His breath comes in raggedy rasps.

"Fuck," I say. I need to get to my pack. "Calder, release me from the ice. I can save you!"

He glances up, eyes bloodshot, veins popping in his temple. For a second, I see him without his hardened exterior. Underneath it all, he's afraid. That look steels my resolve.

He waves his hand at me and the ice melts away. I spin on my heels and race back towards camp. "I need my medicine!" I shout as I run. "Rayna, can you bring him to camp?"

I don't wait to see if she's honored my request. Aidan runs behind me and Rian behind him.

"What's the plan, Elana?" Aidan asks, keeping pace by my side.

"I need to put together an antidote," I say between breaths. "I hope we have time."

I'm panting and light-headed thanks to the altitude by the time I make it back to camp. As I reach for my pack, a sound like massive wings hits my ears. A shadow falls over me and I'm suddenly thrown to the ground.

I roll over onto my back and draw my twin daggers. Aidan stands above me and a wall of fire erupts above us. Rian is yelling, pointing up.

The largest vultures I've ever seen descend around us. They swoop down to our camp so quickly we don't have time to react before they flap wildly and fly away.

In their metal-tipped talons are all of our packs.

"No!" I shriek. "The antidote is in my pack. Calder won't last an hour without it."

Aidan's gaze whips to the group of birds. He drops his shield of fire and picks up his discarded bow from where it lies on the ground. His arrows are nowhere to be found, but he draws the string back anyway. An arrow made of fire burns to life on the string. He lets it loose and I watch as it strikes the closest bird in the center of its back, right between its wings.

The vulture lets out a piercing cry and plummets to the ground, crashing in a flurry of broken wings and flying feathers. The impact drops my stomach. If the glass vial of venom broke, Calder's dead. Rian rushes towards the downed beast, grabs my pack, and runs back.

He hands it to me and I frantically dig through it, hoping the little vial remained intact. I spot a familiar bundle near the bottom and grab it. Relief courses through me as I discover the vial unbroken.

Rayna arrives with Calder lying prone on a slab of stone.

"Where did those vultures come from?" She gently lowers the piece of earth with Calder onto the ground near me. I rush over to him.

"Don't know, but the damn birds took our packs," Aidan growls, staring at the two vultures that used our distraction to fly further up the mountain.

There's no time for me to worry about the vultures. I trust the others can take care of those overgrown chickens. Everything outside of healing has been switched off in my mind. I check on Calder. His skin is covered in sweat and his bloodshot eyes stare unseeing at the sky. He moans and his fists clench and unclench at his sides. I kneel down by his side and check his pulse. It's erratic and quick.

"He doesn't have much time," I say to no one in particular, moving back to my bag to pull out a second vial full of clear liquid—alcohol distilled with medicinal plants. The venom needs to bind to something in order to counteract the poison. It will make him vomit up the fruit and will hopefully stop the poison from reaching vital organs. I pour the clear liquid into the vial with the venom and swish it around. I need to keep the mixture moving until it fully combines.

Once he empties his stomach, I'll need to feed him charcoal to soak up any residual poison in his system and nullify it.

"Aidan, I need pure charcoal. Now," I demand of him.

He doesn't balk. He races out of sight and then reappears moments later holding a large branch from the fruit tree. He lights it, quickly incinerating it, leaving behind several long brittle pieces of charcoal.

I nod my thanks to him.

"We need to go after those vultures," Rian says, grabbing his naginata off his back holster.

Rayna moves to pick up her bow, but I snag her arm with my still-healing hand and wince. "I need someone to stay with me. I need help and protection in case those birds come back."

Rayna doesn't even bat an eye. "Okay, I'll stay."

Out of the corner of my eye, I see Aidan and Rian take off at a sprint up the steep side of the mountain. Aidan's fire stays lit nearby. The flames help comfort me.

"Rayna, can you crush the charcoal into a fine powder?" I ask, still swishing. She makes quick work of it with several rocks moving at breakneck speed.

Calder makes a sudden choking noise and I look down to see whitish foam seeping from his lips, expelling along with a weak cough. His throat is closing, and he's out of time. I inspect the swirling liquid in the vial. The venom has diluted, but still maintains a mossy green color. It's ready.

"What's next?" she asks nervously, looking from Calder to me.

"Help me hold him down? This won't taste pleasant, and I don't want him spitting it up if he regains consciousness."

Rayna nods her head. She straddles Calder's chest, pressing his shoulders down firmly. I gently open his jaw with one hand. I take a deep breath and pour the antidote down his throat slowly. He sputters, and I push his jaw closed and cover his mouth in case he tries to cough it up. His throat bobs as he swallows the mixture.

I breathe a sigh of relief, although there's no cause to celebrate yet.

"You can let him go now," I say to Rayna and put my fingers back on his wrist. His pulse thrums rapidly beneath my touch.

"What now?" Rayna asks, and I shush her, closing my eyes and keeping track of the heartbeats. They still race.

His eyes are closed now, and he's so still. Anxiety flutters in my gut. Was I too late? I glance up at Rayna, worry leaking into my expression. She grabs my free hand and we wait together.

The next hour or so is critical to his recovery. Clarisse explained what would happen if I ever needed to use venom to cure a poisoning, so I'm prepared for the unpleasant things that are about to happen.

The first is that Calder begins vomiting violently. Rayna and I turn him onto his side as he vomits green-tinged pieces of fruit. Rayna gags and I almost do, too.

Once the contents of his stomach are emptied, Calder breaks out in a sweat and starts shivering, a fever to burn out the corruption started by the poison. The red handprint on his cheek stands out even more on his pale face.

I pour the charcoal powder into his canteen, tipping the water into his mouth then forcing it closed. This time he swallows quickly. The charcoal mixture should soak up any remaining toxins in his system.

I don't move or speak for what feels like hours. Slowly, so slowly, his pulse returns to a normal pace. His breathing settles, and his veins no longer appear like they're going to burst free from his skin. I let out a breath I didn't realize I was holding. My whole body deflates and I slump into a sitting position.

"He's going to be okay," I whisper, to reassure Rayna as well as myself. "The antidote is working. I imagine he'll need to rest for a while, but he'll live."

"Holy Gods, Elana. You saved him." Rayna says softly, like she can't think of anything else to say.

I stare down at the empty vial in the dirt by my legs. The venom, which Aislinn slayed a giant scorpion to get, was used to save someone who would most likely kill me if he got the chance. And yet I don't feel guilty for using it. It was used to save a life. A life that has an opportunity to keep the peace in Hotharia and help us bring prosperity to Astrellia.

The fever gradually fades, although it could take him a few hours to wake up. The exhaustion will not let go of his body easily. When I'm certain his recovery is progressing and there's nothing more that can be done for him, Rayna and I stand watch at the edge of the plateau. We intently look where Aidan and Rian disappeared.

"Thank you," I tell her, and she looks at me with brows furrowed in confusion. "For defending me from Calder earlier."

Her hand rests gently on my arm. "He should have never said that. If you didn't just spend your time and resources saving his life, I swear I'd kill him for it."

I chuckle at her malice, but it makes me feel better. "I've never been built like my sister. I've always had generous curves. It doesn't usually bother me, but sometimes...,"

She nods her head, bumping me gently with her shoulder. "We all have insecurities, you know. But don't give his opinion another thought. Your body is beautiful, and it's exactly the size it needs to be to protect that brilliant mind and personality."

"Oh, stop," I blush and cover it with another little laugh. It's easy to see why Aislinn is so close to Rayna.

"I'm serious," Rayna says, smiling. "You're one of the most compassionate and intelligent people I know. The way you didn't hesitate to save Calder's life? You're the best of us, Elana."

I'm about to wave her off when two dark figures appear in the sky, moving towards us. The closer they get, the less they look like birds. Finally, my eyes recognize their two distinct shapes—both tall, one lean, the other muscular. They look like they have wings.

"Oh Gods, are they flying?!" Rayna gasps.

Chapter Twenty-Four

In the distance, I see large wings across Aidan and Rian's backs. I squint and shield my eyes from the sun. It looks like they're carrying a vulture.

Their flying is not smooth. They dip and rise, the movements jerky and inconsistent. Rian has a huge smile plastered on his face while Aidan's pinched expression betrays his extreme discomfort.

Rayna lets out a laugh. "Looks like the air god Sepher chose Rian."

Then, she seems to realize at the same time as me that it leaves only Tolliver, the metal god, remaining. And with a pitying, concerned look at me, she also realizes how unlikely my chances are considering I'm, well, me.

It's quickly forgotten when Rian and Aidan approach us at an alarming speed.

"Rian, slow us down!" Aidan shouts, his voice echoing around us.

Rayna and I share a look, jumping out of the way barely in time as Rian, Aidan, and the dead vulture on their back slam into the plateau where we had been standing. A cloud of feathers and dirt explodes from the ground.

I rush over to them. Rayna's already there, hauling the massive dead bird off them.

Rian and Aidan lay underneath. Aidan groans and sits up. He and Rian are both wearing two packs each. He pushes back his dark hair and glowers at Rian, who's sitting up next to him, laughing. There must be something wrong with his head, because he's *laughing*.

"That was fun," he says when he takes a breath between laughs.

"Fun? You call that fun?" Aidan shoves Rian without any real hostility. He topples over, still cackling.

Rayna stands back, glancing between the bird and the two heirs. "What the Hells happened?"

Aidan gives Rian an exasperated look and answers. "We found the vultures' nest. There were quite a few of them, actually, and we dispatched them quickly. All but this one."

He gestures to the dead bird by his feet.

"It was smarter than the others." Rian picks up the story, eyes watering from his laughter. "It flew away rather than try to fight us. It had my and Rayna's packs, so I jumped on its back as it flew away. Apparently, they're not meant to carry riders, because we plummeted down the mountain."

Rayna and I stare at him open mouthed.

"That's when the god Sepher showed up and granted me his element. At that point, the choices were fly or die, and I chose the former. Aidan didn't think I was strong enough to carry us both on the wind, so I had to prove him wrong." He finishes with a gleeful smile.

"I wouldn't call what you did flying," Aidan grumbles, standing. He brushes dirt off his chest.

His flying may not have been graceful, but I'm impressed by his abilities nonetheless. He managed to do what so many other air-wielders failed to do throughout our history. The fact that he's able to fly is amazing, but the fact that he's already strong enough in his power to have carried both Aidan and the vulture is downright unbelievable.

"Congratulations Rian, I'm happy for you," I say with a wide grin that he returns unabashedly.

He looks at Calder's prone form on the ground by my pack. "How's Calder?"

"He's alive," I say.

"He's lucky to be," Rayna mutters. I throw her a side-eyed look. She shrugs and walks to Rian, grabbing her pack from him.

"What's the bird for?" I ask, my attention again turning to the giant dead vulture laying on the ground.

"Dinner," Aidan smirks.

I blanch. "You're not serious." I hope, I really, really hope he's jesting.

"It's either that or starve before we make it to the final peak," he shrugs and flashes me a smirk.

Eyeing the dark bird with its oily feathers and metallic talons has me considering starvation.

"Oh come on, Elana, it'll taste just like chicken," Rian says cheerily.

It doesn't taste like chicken. Oddly enough, it tastes like bitter, drier turkey. But it's warm, and we haven't had a good meal in days. I scarf it down so fast I burn my mouth. The others don't fare much better.

We contemplate moving on, carrying Calder with us on a rock, but I'm worried about his recovery if we go much higher in elevation. We decide it's best to wait for him to awaken.

He wakes the following afternoon, groaning and clutching his stomach.

"Easy, Calder. Take it slow," I say, rushing to his side with his water canteen, after we rinse the charcoal out of it.

"Get away from me you bitch," he snarls, pushing my arm away and turning onto his side.

I've had it with him. I shove his canteen onto his chest, holding it there. "This bitch saved your life, so if I were you, I'd show a little respect."

I release my grip on the water and stalk off. My anger burns through me, and I have an overwhelming urge to march back to Calder and smack his other cheek. At least he would have a matching set then.

I walk until I'm standing in front of the fruit tree. Would anyone know if I squeezed a few drops of the juice into Calder's waterskin?

"He's a piece of work," Aidan says from behind me, jolting me from my intrusive thoughts. Of course he followed me when I wanted to be alone.

"That's the understatement of the century," I say with a humorless chuckle. "I don't know what I was thinking, that he would be grateful to me for saving him? That he would graciously apologize for his cruelty and we could become friends? I'm so stupid."

Aidan's arms wrap around my shoulders and I feel his chest against my head. He puts his chin on top of my head and I relax back into him.

"You're not stupid, Magpie. He's an exceptional asshole."

I sigh, sinking further into the hard planes of his body. "A part of me pities him. He only sees what his narrow view of the world tells him to see. The other part of me wants to slip some afterlife fruit juice into his water."

His voice practically purrs from above me. "Finally, the Magpie shows her talons. Do what you will, Elana. None of us will stop you."

The thought is so tempting, but I can't bring myself to move towards the fruit tree. The war it would cause with Hotharia would put my people in danger, and I refuse to allow others to die for a personal vendetta.

"He can keep his pathetic life. I hope he does something better with it when this is all over," My resolve is surprisingly determined.

"You're too good for us." Aidan releases my shoulders but spins me around to look at him. There's a satisfied grin on his face. "If you ever change your mind, I will be there to help in whatever capacity you need."

A devious smile creeps up my own lips. "In whatever way?"

He nods. "If you need me to clean the blood off your boots, I'd happily find you a chair to sit in while I scrub."

"What if I need help in...other ways?"

His eyebrows quirk up as he smirks, running his gaze along my body. "What might those ways be, Elana?"

I feel heat creeping up my neck and face. Ignoring it, I push myself closer to him, running my hands across his muscular chest. "You could start by finishing what you started before the exceptional asshole interrupted us."

He looks down at me with feral intent before capturing my mouth with his. His hands move from my shoulders down my body until he reaches my thighs. He picks me up and I wrap my legs around him. He groans against my lips then breaks away, kissing my chin and down the length of my neck.

Gods, his hands. One squeezes the back of my thigh, holding me to him, and the other cups my breast through my shirt. I gasp in a ragged breath and he catches my bottom lip between his teeth, biting gently.

A flash of need shoots down my core. I feel his hard length pressing against me and I angle my hips to be closer. I want to know what he feels like.

The sound of footsteps approaching halts our movements. We release each other, breathing hard.

"Elana, are you over here? I'm sorry Calder's such a dimwit," Rayna says from the other side of the boulder.

Aidan reluctantly takes a small step back, but his eyes remain on my lips. I straighten my clothes, flashing him an apologetic smile.

He leans over and whispers in my ear, "someday, we will actually finish this."

I chuckle and whisper back, "I'll hold you to that."

I squeeze his hand as I pass by him, then I raise my voice and call out to Rayna. "I'm here."

On the other side of the boulder, I almost smack into her. "Whoa, hey. Are you alright? Your face looks red. You weren't crying, were you? I swear, I'll slap him again."

A bark of a laugh escapes me before I have a chance to stop it. "Oh, please slap him any time you want."

She smiles at me, putting her arm around my shoulder. "You promise you're alright?"

"I promise, Rayna. Thank you for checking on me."

We walk back to camp together. Aidan is somehow already sitting there, next to his fire.

Calder ignores me as we approach, instead tearing into the last pieces of dried vulture we saved for him. He's lucky we saved him anything.

Rayna clears her throat and everyone's attention turns to her. "Now that Calder is awake and clearly doing fine, I say we get moving. We know there's no more fresh food here, unless we get attacked by another flock of vultures, and the only way to go is forward. We need to move on."

"I agree. We've lost enough time," Aidan says, standing.

Calder doesn't dare disagree when the rest of us pack up our belongings. He glares at each one of us in turn while we studiously ignore him.

He moves slowly—clearly, his body hasn't recovered from the effects of the poison and antidote yet. Once again luckily for him, Rayna moves us on her rock platform.

The landscape remains vastly unchanged. Large boulders dot the mountainside and a few sparse trees grow in groups, clinging to the mountain. And then it starts to snow.

We reach the fourth peak that evening and find it covered in a foot of fresh powder. It's a small area, barely large enough for us to set up camp. Rayna once again creates a rock cave. Aidan lights fires all around us, Calder provides fresh, warm water, and Rian is able to distribute the warm air in our cave evenly, keeping the frigid wind out of the cave.

Everyone has a task except me. I sit on my bedroll anxiously, trying not to feel useless.

"So...I have a question," Rian says in an uncharacteristically unsure tone.

We all stare at him, eyebrows raised.

"Yes?" Rayna asks, narrowing her eyes expectantly.

Rian swallows and looks down. "What did the Gods look like for you?"

Calder snorts. "What kind of question is that? They're Gods. They look like people."

Aidan and Rayna's attention snaps to Calder.

"Avani is a giant leopard," Rayna says. "She had a golden halo around her head and was twice the size of a normal leopard."

I turn to her, shocked.

Aidan speaks next. "Enya is born of flame. She is fire itself and has no physical body. She appeared to have a woman's shape and long hair but was entirely made of flames."

"What?" Calder shoots a bewildered glance back and forth. "Kai looks like a man. With long golden hair. He carried a trident."

They all exchange looks, as if trying to puzzle out the vast differences in the Gods' appearances.

"What did Sepher look like?" I ask Rian, who has been noticeably silent.

He takes a deep breath. "He appeared to me as a great, many-winged bird, with a dozen eyes and metal talons like spearheads. It was terrifying."

The other heirs seem confused. It appears none of them found their experience with the Gods frightening.

I think back to what my father has told me about Avani, but I don't remember him mentioning her appearance at all.

The idea is unsettling, that the Gods could take on a horrifying shape. I wonder if I'll see something completely different from all the others—if I ever meet a god, that is.

Chapter Twenty-Five

Two days later at breakfast, I share the last of my provisions with Rian. He and Calder ran out the evening before. Aidan reluctantly shares his final bites with Calder while Rayna finishes her handful of nuts slowly, relishing each one.

"We have to be close," I say hopefully, but I'm so tired and hungry my statement sounds more like a question. Looking around at the others, our desperation is on full display.

"If we aren't, I can try to fly back down the mountains and bring up some food," Rian says hopefully.

Aidan shakes his head, throwing a stick into his fire. "You'd never find us again. We're small dots on a mountain range half the size of your kingdom."

Rian pauses for a moment to think. "You could build a fire signal?" At the look Aidan gives him, he deflates slightly. "You could build a really big fire signal?"

A half smile quirks my mouth up.

"We have to hope that we're almost there, and that Tolliver has prepared a feast for us when he bestows your gift, Elana," Rayna says, flashing me a smile.

She means well, but a wave of unease settles in me. Tolliver the metal god. The one I've felt the least affinity to. Would he really grant me powers? The thought doesn't sit well. Doubt creeps into my mind. Now that I'm this close, and fully committed to proving myself, it all feels like everything is about to crumble down around me. Why would Tolliver choose me when literally any other heir here has more experience with weaponry and metals?

Anxiety coils around my gut for most of the day. Rayna pushes herself harder, making our trip up the mountain go quicker.

It's late morning when a cold mist rolls in, blocking out much of our view of the mountain. I shiver, my long sleeves not doing enough to keep the chill from my bones. Aidan summons a fire near the back of the rock slab, but it does little to warm us or lift our spirits.

Before long, we come to a large flat area. Rayna lets her stone platform come to a stop, breathing hard.

"I need a little break," she says, wiping beads of sweat from her forehead.

"Take all the time you need, Rayna," I tell her.

"Any idea where the path is?" Aidan asks, looking around at the misty landscape.

We look around the plateau for the path, but the fog and mist that coat the air make it nearly impossible.

"Hold on," Rian says, throwing his arms out wide and blowing a gust of wind in every direction. The fog dissipates, and even some of the mist is held back by the strength of the air he commands.

"Nice work, Rian," Rayna says, giving him an encouraging smile as our landscape sharpens around us.

My stomach drops and my knees shake when it clears enough for me to see. We're standing on a large flat area, but in all directions, it slopes downwards. There's nothing higher than this point. I forget the coldness of my skin, the chill in my bones, and the ache in my lungs that makes me feel like I can never catch my breath. All I feel is numb. Disbelieving numbness.

"We made it, it's the final peak," Calder says, motioning around.

The rest of the mountain range comes into view behind us. Sure enough, as far as we can see, several peaks jut out into the sky and the mountain slopes down towards the horizon.

"No," Rayna says. "It can't be. Elana still hasn't gotten her power yet."

A pit churns in my stomach. I let Adrithia down. Aislinn, my parents, Aric, they're all going to be in danger because of me. Because I wasn't strong enough to impress any of the Gods. My vision blurs, and I realize tears are welling up.

Calder scoffs, rounding on Rayna. "Don't you get it? That's the point. She's not going to get any power, because she was never supposed to be here! She either stole the crown from Aislinn, or the phoenix made a mistake. We should have killed her when we had the chance!"

He spins towards me, a whip of water lashing out for my neck. I let out a startled noise and put my hands up to block the attack. The water meets a burning wall of fire and sizzles into steam.

"What the Hells do you think you're doing, Vernier?" Aidan snarls, stepping in front of me.

"I'm righting a wrong, fixing an injustice," Calder snaps.

"She saved your pathetic excuse of a life, and this is how you repay that debt?" Aidan snarls.

"No, she tricked me into eating that fruit," Calder sneers. "That's what I'll tell everyone back home after I kill her. Who do you think they'll believe? A crown stealer, or an heir who actually deserves their power?"

"No one is going to believe you!" Rayna shouts at him.

I shake my head. How did he get so delusional? Does he really think that the other heirs will go along with his lies? Unless he's not trying to convince everyone else. If he's only trying to rally his own people...but for what purpose?

It also doesn't change the fact that he is right. This is the final peak, and I haven't met a god yet. None of them found me worthy. I'll have to go home and tell my whole family that I failed them. It's suddenly a fight to keep my tears in check as I suck in breath after breath.

"Getting rid of her is clearly the last test," Calder gestures at me. "I'm doing exactly what the rest of you are too *weak* to do."

Aidan moves closer to him, exuding confidence. He moves slowly, arrogantly, like he's already won this fight. He looks every bit a terrifying warrior I wouldn't want to face.

"Get your head out of your Gods-damned ass. She's supposed to be here. The Gods called her here the same as they did you and I. Get over it."

Calder matches Aidan step for step, moving closer. "If you don't stand down, Ashfall, I'll kill you, too."

Aidan's answering chuckle is humorless. "Go ahead and try, bubble boy."

"Hey, guys," Rian's loud voice cuts in, and I spin to look at him, blinking the blurriness from my eyes. "I think you should hold off trying to kill each other for a moment and take a look at what's about to kill us."

He's pointing off the edge of the peak, where shadowed forms rise from the ridge. They crest the edge slowly, moving in jerky, unnatural movements. From this distance, they appear to be nearly twice my height. The shadows ripple like dark cloaks. I can't see their faces—they're hidden under hoods.

"What the Hells are they?" Rayna asks, exchanging a worried glance with me.

"I don't know," I whisper, drawing my bow from my back and pulling an arrow from my quiver.

The figures—about a dozen in total—spread out and approach us, their forms shifting into grotesque, misshapen creatures. Long, sharp claws extend from their sleeves and some of them sprout dark, leathery wings.

The creatures pause a distance away, hovering like an ominous raincloud.

"They outnumber us, but we've got power on our side," Calder says, raising his hands, preparing for an attack.

"Wait," I whisper, lowering my bow. "They're not attacking us. Should we really go after them first?"

Calder responds by sending a wave of water towards them. The mountain shakes with its ferocity. The winged beings take flight while the others are simply washed off the cliff. The flying creatures screech in unison. The noise sends goosebumps up my arms as I cover my ears against the onslaught of piercing noise.

Rayna sends a rock barreling towards one of the flying shadows, which dodges and streaks towards us with unparalleled speed. She barely puts up a barrier in time.

Rian targets a wind gust at the shadow, sending it somersaulting back into the sky. It lets out an inhuman screech as it rolls in midair.

Heat singes the air as Aidan sends fireball after fireball at approaching shadow creatures. I grip my bow with white knuckles, loosing arrows at the ones that avoid the fire, but the arrows pass right through them.

"How are we supposed to fight shadows?" I shout, nocking another arrow and letting it fly. It sails directly through one of the winged creatures. Only Aidan's intense flames keep it from descending on me.

"No idea," Aidan shouts and launches another burst of flame at one that gets close to us. The shadow shrinks back from the fire.

I take note of the others as I loose arrow after arrow at the creatures to no effect. Wind and fire seem to be our best defenses. They shy away from Aidan's fire, and Rian's air attacks have enough force to blow them back. Rock and water only slow them down momentarily. Calder tries freezing a few, but the monsters pass right through the ice.

Rayna tries to use her bow, but quickly realizes it's useless. She provides ground support, literally moving the ground beneath our feet to erect walls between us and our attackers.

We slowly lose ground. The five of us have our backs to the edge of the mountain. I discard my bow after firing my last arrow and withdraw my daggers. They thrum in my grip, feeling more alive than ever. They visibly vibrate in my hands. I bring one up to inspect the blade and catch a glint of sunlight in the reflection of the polished metal. I squint and stare at it for a moment. My wrist suddenly twists, not of my own volition, and a shriek draws my attention in front of me, where the reflection from the sun on my blade burns a hole through a shadow creature. It thrashes its body and shrinks back until it's out of the light's reach.

A short, disbelieving laugh punches from me. "You brilliant blades," I say, and the metal pulses again in my grip before my wrist turns again and the reflection points at Aidan. I drag my eyes to his fire, full of fiery oranges and reds, and I understand.

"Aidan!" I shout to get his attention, then frantically point up at the sky. "They're weakened by the sun. Make your fire as bright as possible."

He looks from me to the sky and over to the approaching throng of shadow creatures, giving me a quick nod. With a flick of his wrist a large golden wall of flame erupts between the monsters and us. The creatures shriek, clawing at where their eyes should be.

It's enough to hold them back while we come up with a plan.

"Nice thinking, Magpie." Aidan smiles at me. "Any chance you have any other bright ideas in that beautiful brain of yours?"

I huff a quick laugh and look around at the others. "Rian, can you get rid of the clouds? Like, all of them? We need the sunlight to weaken the shadows."

Rian nods. "On it." He raises his hands and a vicious wind whips up around us, forming a tornado, blasting into the sky and dispersing the clouds. He slowly widens the cyclone until the hole in the clouds is nearly twice as wide as the mountain peak. Harsh midday sun shines down on us, and screeches come from the other side of the fire. Good. Hopefully the phantoms shrivel up into nothing.

"Got any other ideas?" Rayna asks, pointing at the wall of fire. "Because I think we only made them mad."

Sure enough, a dark spot grows in Aidan's flame wall, and three shadow creatures break through, charging us.

"I don't know, weapons don't seem to be effective," I say as Rian blows them back with a fierce gust of wind. Calder freezes the ground, his ice sending them sliding back through the flames back through the flames. Aidan reinforces his fire with another bright burst.

"Tolliver hasn't appeared to you yet?" Rayna asks, and I catch the glimmer of hope in her eyes.

I shake my head, and she gives me a pitying look. "It's okay. He'll probably intervene soon. In the meantime, we'll hold them off."

She breaks away from me, creating a slope in front of us that Calder freezes over, leading right back to Aidan's fire. A few more shadows make it through but find little purchase on the ice.

The flying ones, however, present a bigger challenge. Rian blasts them away with gust after gust, but they keep up their assault. Aidan sends a few streams of white-hot fire their way, but they expertly dodge, shrinking from the flames.

I'm all out of ideas, and everything has gone to shit. From the moment that damn fire chicken put the stupid crown on my unworthy head, everything has gone wrong. And now, if we fail, Astrellia will turn on itself. An entire generation of rulers will be wiped out, and who knows what chaos will descend on Adrithia.

There must be something we can do.

Aislinn would know what to do. She *always* knows what to do. She's the strong one, the smart one, the brave one. She should be here, not me. She'd know exactly what to do to beat these shadows. Panic seeps through me, and my breath hitches. I'll never see them again. My parents. Aislinn. What will she do? I wonder briefly as I look around at the heirs, struggling as they fling all their power at the shadows, to no effect. These monsters can't be beaten. Every attack against them is ineffective.

My eyes lock onto motion in front of me as a shadow creature claws its way up the ice, barreling towards me with determination. My daggers vibrate in my hands, as if they're once again trying to tell me something. I try not to think of the potential consequences of my decision as I rush the creature.

I take two steps when I'm pulled to the ground by my daggers. My breath *whooshes* out of me as my knees make contact with rock. Suddenly the blades weigh more than a boulder. They refuse to move.

"What the Hells?" I mumble to myself, tugging on them with all my strength. They don't budge, and they don't respond to my frustrated panic, remaining firmly planted in place. "No, no, no. Come on daggers! Help me!"

They remain lifeless and immovable. I want to scream and cry in my anger.

The powers the heirs were given mean nothing against these creatures. Why would the Gods grant these abilities only to kill us all? This doesn't make sense. There must be a reason.

Clawed hands find purchase in front of me as the shadow crests ice hill. It looms above me, cocking its dark head to the side. This close, I can see its form is made of solid darkness. There's no skin, no meat to it, it's just a writing mass of darkness.

My limbs shake as I close my eyes, waiting for the fatal strike. *Gods, let it be quick,* I think. My skin prickles, and my muscles tense subconsciously, but still I wait, struggling to calm my racing heart. Why isn't it attacking me? Why prolong my death? At last, when I can't take the anticipation any longer, I open my eyes. Slowly, the creature shrinks back, becoming shorter and shorter until it disappears entirely, as if absorbed back into the mountain itself.

What. The. Fuck. I take a shaky breath and stand up. I try to wrap my brain around what happened. I was sure it was about to kill me, but then it disappeared. I gasp. It disappeared when I stopped attacking it.

This is what the Gods are trying to tell us. For everything in life, there's balance. The heirs can have all the power in the world, but there's still a check for their abilities. It's each other. It's the Gods. No one element is stronger than the others. No one ruler is stronger than the others. By accepting our own weakness, that we're not all-powerful beings like the Gods, we can maintain true peace across all kingdoms.

"Stop," I shout, abandoning my daggers and rushing towards Aidan. I grab his arm. "Stop fighting them!"

Aidan looks down at me, eyes molten, brows knitted together. He's confused, but his flames instantly gutter out. Even the flame wall sizzles to nothing. The other three heirs look at me like I knocked my head too hard and continue to fight.

"It's balance. We're not supposed to win against these shadows," I say to Aidan, stepping before him, in front of the shadow monsters he had been attacking.

Aidan sucks in a breath. "Elana, what're you—"

I cut him off with a raised hand, motioning for him to wait.

I move closer, slowly, unarmed. The shadows pause in front of me. Slowly, they shrink down, down, down, until they melt into a puddle at my feet and absorb into my own shadow. A little relieved laugh escapes me. It's so obvious now. It was never about destroying these things.

I turn back to Aidan, who wears an expression filled with wonder. The others are still fighting hard.

"Stop attacking them!" I shout to everyone. But the sound of splashing water, rushing wind, and smashing rocks overtakes my voice. So I do the most reckless thing I've ever done and step out in front of them, putting my body between the heirs and the shadow creatures.

"No more," I cry and hold my arms out at my sides.

Rian, Rayna, and Calder halt their attacks, staring.

The Gods believe in balance. No force should be stronger than another. Balance must exist in all things. No person can have absolute power. Just like no person is entirely weak, either. We cannot have the brightest lights without the deepest shadows.

This is the final test of the Gods. To show the heirs that even though they are gifted with extraordinary abilities over the elements, there's still balance. The Gods could crush us if needed.

The heirs gawk at me, expressions ranging from shock to disgust. It's a noticeable improvement from when we all first met.

"We need to stop fighting them," I breathe hard. "It's a test from the Gods. We can't win against them."

Calder growls and lifts his hands. "Like Hells we can't. This is a test of strength, and I'm not dying here with you, weakling."

"We can win if we work together," Rian says, wiping his brown hair away from his eyes and putting his hands in front of him, ready to summon the wind.

"No," I say, holding my ground. The monsters behind me writhe, but do not attack. "Don't you see? We're not supposed to fight them. They're meant to show us that balance must exist."

Calder scoffs, but I ignore him, turning towards Rayna and Rian, who seem to be considering my words.

I turn towards Aidan, the only one who saw what I saw. His golden eyes bore into mine, and he opens his mouth to speak, but Calder makes a move, lurching towards me and throwing me to the ground.

Hard rock meets my elbow and bites into my hands. I cry out in surprise more than pain.

"Fight with us or stay out of our way," he snaps, charging towards the creatures with a massive wave in front of his feet. The shadows jerk back to life, racing towards Calder with renewed vigor.

Hands grasp my unhurt arm gently and pull me up. Aidan. "Are you alright?" he nods at my bloody arm. I flex it—it's not broken or sprained, but there's a nasty scrape courtesy of the sharp mountain terrain.

"I'll be fine. But if we don't stop attacking the shadows, none of us will survive," I plead. His grip on my arm is firm, but surprisingly gentle. He brushes several short strands of hair out of my face. Heat rushes through me and my cheeks feel like they're on fire. A smirk tugs one corner of his lips up as his eyes devour my face.

He lifts an arm and another wall of flame erupts between us and the shadows. Heat blasts us from where we stand. Even after he's used so much energy, the power still comes so easily to him.

Calder stops abruptly, shielding his face from the heat, and turns to face us. Aidan looks down to my lips before he lets my arm go and steps in front of me.

"What the Hells are you doing Aidan?" Calder shouts. Utter rage twists his face.

"Asking you nicely to stop attacking them." Aidan shrugs and nonchalantly brushes ash off his shoulder.

"You're listening to her." Calder points past Aidan towards me. My eyes widen, and I'm tempted to take a step back.

"Yes, I am," Aidan says, matter-of-factly.

Rayna and Rian exchange a glance, but make no moves, waiting to see how this shakes out. I, too, hold my breath.

"If you want me to stop fighting them, you'll have to kill me," Calder says, flinging his arms out wide.

Aidan seems to contemplate this for a moment with an exaggerated sound. "That can be arranged."

Steam lifts off Calder's jacket as he barks a laugh. "You think you can beat me in a fight? My element is water. I'll destroy you."

Even I begrudgingly admit that he has a point. Aidan is incredibly powerful, with the most control of all the heirs. But even for him there are checks and balances. He can't change fire's nature.

An explosion sounds. Aidan lets out a burst of fire and Calder barely counters in time with a wave of water. Steam rises from where the two elements clash.

This could get ugly. What ramifications would this have for the continent?

Before I have a chance to second-guess myself, I sprint into the fray. Aidan is readying for another attack but pulls his power back and shouts at me. "What are you doing?"

Calder, however, doesn't pull his punch. A stream of water bursts towards me, and I stare at it, wondering if this is how my story ends. I put my hands up, as if it will do anything to stop the torrent heading right for me.

It's so loud.

Aidan shouts as the wave charges me, the noise like thunder in the apex of a storm. Any moment now I'll be wiped clean from this world.

It all stops. In an instant, the noises cease. I wrench my eyes open, thinking I'll find myself in the afterlife.

Two figures appear before me, in this moment that stands outside of time.

Chapter Twenty-Six

I freeze, staring back and forth between the two figures, my mouth agape.

One shines like a star, golden-bronze skin with pale golden hair glowing like the sun and billowing around her on a phantom breeze. Her high cheekbones, delicately pointed chin, and bright blue eyes remind me of Aislinn. She wears a golden dress woven from glimmering sunlight itself. Golden bracelets adorn her wrists and a golden bow is slung around her back and chest. Two large pairs of stunning, gold-feathered wings grace her back, the feathers ruffling and flexing.

The other figure has creamy white skin and long black hair, like strands of silk flowing around her. She has a soft, confident smile and bright yellow eyes. She's wearing a dress as black as night, adorned with silver stars which shimmer as she hovers closer. Tied to her hip is a sword that matches two gleaming silver bracelets. Two large, black-feathered wings expand behind her. She is the evening sky personified.

"Elana Sable. We are the twin goddesses, Nura and Nisha." The women—no, Goddesses—in front of me speak in unison.

I wrack my brain trying to remember what these goddesses are known for, but I come up empty. They don't represent any of the elements I know of.

As if they can read my thoughts, they say, "we were forgotten centuries ago. We have no temples left and very few still pray to us. We are the sun; we are the shadow. We are the light and the darkness. Neither can exist without the other."

They clasp hands, and the golden goddess holds out her shining free palm. Her voice is harmonious, yet somehow detached as she says, "I am Nura, Goddess of light. Ruler of day and the sun. I grant you my favor and give you my power."

Her sister goddess raises her hand then, and shadows swirl around her like a cape. "I am Nisha, Goddess of darkness. Ruler of night, the stars, and the moon. I grant you my favor and give you my power," she says with a slight smile, sounding unexpectedly kind.

They raise their clasped hands in my direction and a shockwave spears through me. I scream with the overwhelming sensation, the pain and heaviness of their power. Time and space collide and are sucked into me, and I feel something I've never felt before—powerful. My chest aches. I gasp and breathe through it. A few moments later, the uncomfortable pain subsides, and I collapse to my knees, panting.

I feel two wells of power, deep within my core. They feel as opposite as can be, but still a part of each other—and a part of me.

"You were chosen for this burden, Elana. For all things there is balance. Seek the peace of this world, always," they speak in harmony once again.

I'm shaking and still trying to catch my breath, but I bow my head to them. "Goddesses, you honor me."

I spare a glance up, and see the twins exchange a look, sharing a brief smile before looking back at me. "Yes, we do," Nura says. "We have not chosen an heir for nearly a thousand years. Our decision was not made lightly, and may cause some unrest, both in your realm and ours."

Nisha picks up where her other half leaves off. "We chose you to ensure the survival of both our realms."

"Why?" I blurt out, forgetting my place here—as someone being given a great gift who shouldn't question it. I try to soften my words. "Why did you choose me and not Aislinn?"

The Goddesses exchange a look and Nisha speaks. "Everything happened as it was meant to. As it has for generations."

No, that's not right. If it were, then Ash would be standing here receiving her power. I'm about to open my mouth again to deny it, to tell them I'm the younger sister and if they think I'm the eldest there must be some mistake, but Nura cuts me off.

"Do you remember what we spoke to you in that cave?"

I startle, switching gears and digging up the memory of the voices in my dreams. The realization that their voices sound familiar hits me. "I do, Goddesses."

In tandem, Nura and Nisha speak together again, a fragmented piece of what they said to me in the cave.

"Stay true to your heart, for balance will bring peace."

Nisha looks around her. "Once we leave you, time will resume. Evil awaits you upon your return. The trials ahead will not be easy, daughter of Sable. Trust yourself to do what's right, and lead Astrellia out of chaos."

I'm too shocked to say anything. Evil awaits? Does she mean Calder? I open my mouth to ask, but it's already too late. They float backwards and flare their wings. Their forms dissolve in a burst of unimaginable brightness and shadow.

Sunspots dance across my vision as the roaring returns full force. I blink rapidly to orient myself. Water rushes me in all its fury, racing towards me.

I raise my arms, feeling that burning, writhing pressure inside me, two untapped wells of unknown power. With a guttural scream, I reach for the bright one, the safer of the two, and release it all. Searing light explodes out of my body.

Far away, a being older than the land itself opens its eyes and a booming rage echoes across the very sky.

My first conscious thought is the ringing in my ears. There is only warm darkness until I peel my eyelids open. The ground slowly comes into focus. I stand in a circular depression of rock. Water evaporates in front of me. The element was halted in its path of destruction.

Footsteps race towards me and someone slides down the edge of the crater. I put a hand to my chest to quell the energy coursing through me. I blow out a long breath and then there are hands wrapping around me. I can tell by the warmth and the cedar scent that it's Aidan.

"Gods, you're alive." He squeezes me, pressing his lips to the top of my head. "What happened? Calder's water was heading right for you, and then there was a blast of light, and the whole mountain shook."

I draw back slightly, enough to turn around and look at him. He's gazing around at the crater, confusion pinching his brows together.

"Elana, which god granted you power?" he asks quietly, almost reverently, staring around us at the wrecked earth.

The other heirs appear over the top of the crater.

"Hold on!" Rayna shouts, stomping her foot onto the ground. Suddenly Aidan and I are lifted as the rock around us smooths out.

I glance around, looking for the shadow creatures, but they're gone. "Where did the shadows go?"

"They vanished when that light exploded out of you. They dissipated like smoke," Aidan says.

"What was that light?" Rian asks eagerly.

"It...came from me," I say, looking down at my hands. I half expect them to shake, but they remain steady. "It was the power the Goddesses gave me."

Silence as the heirs wait and digest. Rian blurts out. "Goddesses? As in more than one?"

I nod my head and I feel four shocked sets of eyes on me. How much do I tell them? Will they try to kill me if I tell them I carry the power of two Goddesses inside me?

"They are twin goddesses. Nura and Nisha. They are the goddesses of light and darkness."

Blank stares meet me. Aidan, still standing next to me, says. "I've never heard of these goddesses before."

"Neither have I," Rayna says, looking troubled.

"So you mean to say—" Calder's voice is dangerously low "—that you have the power of *two* gods?"

I slowly turn to him, meeting his gaze head on. Inside me, I feel two separate pools of power. One glowing like a beacon, the other dark and endless, churning with rage.

"Yes," I say, watching as his gaze darkens.

I let a kernel of white light shine on my fingertips. The light feels warm, rejuvenating. Like my weariness, weakness, and pain melt away in the face of the sun.

"This is the power of Nura," I explain, then hold up my other hand and try to force the darkness to appear.

The lid on the pool of darkness within me rattles. Inside I feel the volatile power, churning fiercely within. It wants to harm, so I clamp down on it like a vice. I grit my teeth against the exertion.

The heirs watch me expectantly, waiting for me to will the darkness to life. I sigh and shake out my hand.

"I'm sorry, I can't seem to wield the darkness right now," I say.

Rayna and Rian nod. This is new territory for all of us, and I don't want to throw the natural order out of balance. Aidan stares at me, at the fist I clench to stop the shaking. As if he can see right through me, his eyes narrow with suspicion.

"Okay, so back to why we haven't heard of these goddesses before," Rayna says, gesturing at me to continue.

I shrug. "They didn't say much. Only that this is the first time in nearly a thousand years that they've chosen an heir. They claim to be forgotten gods."

"It would make sense," Rian says as he rests his chin on his thumb and forefinger and rocks back and forth.

"What would?" Rayna asks.

"Well, the history of Astrellia goes back around a thousand years, so it would make sense that it's the last time they've chosen someone. They could predate our written history. If all knowledge of them was destroyed, then the timeline matches up. We know that a thousand years ago there was a great war, and the kingdoms of Astrellia united to fight against the evil that was set to destroy the world. These twin Goddesses could have had their temple destroyed and their worshippers nearly wiped from existence."

We all stare at Rian. It's the most serious conversation he's ever had with us.

"What?" he asks, realizing that we're all gawking. "I like to read."

I remember then that Aaranor is home to the largest, most comprehensive collection of books in all of Astrellia.

"I would like to visit the archives of Aaranor someday," I tell Rian with a smile. He flashes one back.

"You'd be welcome, Elana. But keep your flashy sparkler fingers under control. Sunlight damages the books."

I chuckle and nod my head. "Deal."

Calder clears his throat, cutting in with a biting, impatient tone. "Okay, so these long-forgotten goddesses, Nora and Nina—"

"Nura and Nisha," I correct sternly. "Have some respect, Calder, we're still in their land."

"*Nura* and *Nisha*," he says their names with exaggerated slowness. I repress the urge to smack him. "Why did they choose *you* after so long not choosing an heir?"

I shrug my shoulders, choosing to ignore the tone that suggests I'm not a worthy choice. "I don't know why."

Calder glares at me. "Someone as unworthy as you was gifted the power of not one, but two gods. Hotharia won't stand for it."

"What part of you thinks I had any choice in the matter?" I say hotly. "The goddesses chose me like the other gods chose you all. There's no difference."

"She's right, Calder," Rayna says, drawing closer to me. "She didn't choose this. We can't fault her for the choice two goddesses made."

Calder gives her an annoyed look. "Witchcraft. *She* could have coerced the Gods, and that could be how she ended up here anyway. Will the people of Melinor really believe that our tenuous peace can be maintained if one of the heirs has twice the power of the rest of us?"

"My people," Rayna's voice lowers and she steps up to Calder, staring at him in a way that would make most people back up a step. At only a few inches shorter than him, she cuts an imposing figure, "trust that I will protect them against any threats, but most importantly, will strive for peace between kingdoms."

The tension in the air could be sliced with a butter knife. Neither heir backs down.

It's Rian that breaks the silence. "Elana, what are your intentions now that you've been blessed with the power of both Nura and Nisha?"

I blink at him, surprised at the question. A million answers run through my mind, but none seem adequate. For some reason, this feels like more of a test than the trials ever did.

I think back to what the Goddesses told me. Stay true to my heart and seek balance. They also spoke of an evil waiting upon my return. Is this the evil they referred to? Is Calder trying to stir up discontent? Either way, I need to pick the right words to ease their minds.

"My only intentions are to protect my people and provide them with the resources they need to thrive. I will advocate for peace across Astrellia and try to create a better world for future generations," I say, giving life to my lofty, if vague, intentions.

"And do you have any intentions of invading or otherwise harming or hampering other kingdoms to reach these goals?" Rian asks.

I shake my head fervently. That answer, at least, comes quickly. "No, never."

"Good," Rian says, clasping his hands together and turning towards Calder. "She has stated her intentions in front of the Gods, and we were all here to witness it. I have no reason to believe she harbors any ill intentions. Especially considering she can only use one god's power at a time, I don't think we have any cause for concern. Do you?"

A knot twists in my stomach as I wait for his answer. Calder's oily gaze rakes over me, a dissatisfied frown contorting his features.

After what seems like an eternity, he finally looks away and sighs. "No, I'm thoroughly unconcerned by Elana Sable."

His words feel like another jab, but I don't dwell on his venom, especially when Rian says in a cheerful tone, "right, well that's settled then. What do we do now?"

We all look around at each other, unsure. It seems none of the heirs were told what happened when their parents reached the final peak.

A loud piercing cry has us looking up, where two brilliant flaming birds streak across the sky towards us. The two glowing phoenixes light up the sky, a path of golden fire cutting through the blue.

The birds swoop down and in a flash of blinding light, return to their hooded and cloaked human forms.

CHAPTER TWENTY-SEVEN

The Steward stands in front of us, draped in burnt orange robes. His sister, the Maiden, stands next to him in dark green.

"Well met, heirs. The Gods have told us the trials are complete. We were summoned to return you to our home," the Steward says, bowing his head slightly.

"Gather your belongings and we will depart," the Maiden says in her light, musical voice. Her inky dark hair peeks out from beneath her hood.

There's no time for me to revel in the relief of finally receiving my powers. I rush to grab my pack and pick up my daggers where I left them on the ground. They lift easily and are warm to the touch, humming happily. I have no doubt that my ancestor was watching and stayed my blades until I finally used my brain to figure out how to stop the shadows.

As I palm my daggers, I mutter, "Thank you, Hale. You helped me realize the truth I needed to see." I smile and slip them back into their sheaths at my side.

"How are we getting down the mountain?" I hear Rayna ask the two shifters.

Out of the corner of my eye there are two consecutive bright flashes. Two large dragons stand side-by-side, flexing their wings. One is dark, shimmering green, and the other is a dark metallic orange.

"We fly," the orange dragon—the Steward—says in a deep, rumbling voice.

The green one—the Maiden—swishes her tail, agitated.

Aidan, Rian, and I climb onto the green dragon, while Calder and Rayna mount the orange one. Aidan has to help me up, as I'm not tall enough to jump on her back by myself. We settle ourselves between her wings, where her back is flattest. Her scales are smooth but feel like stone beneath us.

The Maiden turns her neck to stare at us.

"Hold on," she says through razor sharp teeth. Her voice is deep and raspy, but somehow still recognizable. I look around frantically for something to hold onto. There's no saddle.

Aidan grabs my hand and places it on one of her tall back spikes, then pauses for a moment, staring at my elbow. "Wasn't your arm injured?" he asks, gently grabbing the arm I landed on when Calder shoved me.

I inspect my skin. I wipe away the trails of dried blood and suck in a breath when I see it's completely blemish free. No scrapes, no angry red gashes remain. It's completely healed.

"It was." I whisper. "How? How did it heal?"

We stare in wonder at my perfect skin. I think back to our other injuries on the journey.

"Our injuries have healed abnormally fast since we first started climbing, but never this quickly. Maybe the Gods did this," I say, my mind churning over rapid healing.

"Would you like to sit there and talk all day, or can you hold on so we can leave?" the Maiden asks, shaking out her neck and staring back at us with eyes like slits. Her whip of a tail smashes the rock behind us.

"Apologies, Maiden," Aidan says with a charming half-smile. "We'll shut up now."

He shifts so he sits behind me, taking hold of the next spike there.

The Maiden flicks her snake-like tongue out at us and flares her wings. With a lurch that has me nearly unseated, she launches herself off the peak and flaps her powerful wings once, twice, three times.

I release a short scream and shut my eyes, hunching over the spike and gripping it with every ounce of strength I possess as the world tilts and plummets, then slowly rights itself.

Ahead of me, Rian lets out a whoop of joy. Aidan laughs behind me. He wraps his arms around my waist and brings his lips to my ear.

"Magpie, open your eyes. You're missing it," he says to me. Feeling slightly reassured with him holding me, I slowly untuck my body and peel my eyes open.

Wind batters my face, and I have to squint to see. Rian lets out another joyful cry, spreading his arms wide to catch the breeze. As the wind breaks, I fully open my eyes and stare in wonder around me.

The mountain range goes by in a blur. The barren rock, the snow-capped peaks, the dried-up rockslide, the chasms, rivers, lakes that look like pinpricks, and finally the lush forest comes back into view. I let out a breathy laugh and lean back into Aidan. He adjusts his grip on me, pulling me closer and resting his chin on top of my head. I relax into him, comfortable and safe in his arms.

"Wow," I whisper, staring at the stretch of the world in view. Sunlight streams through spotty patches of fluffy clouds. It's so peaceful up here; I'd like to stay in this moment forever, wrapped up in Aidan's strong, gentle embrace. I notice my lungs filling with air more easily, my breathing slowly returning to its normal cadence the lower we fly. I hadn't realized how difficult it had gotten the last few days until relief hits me all at once. Gods, I'll never take breathing for granted again.

The Maiden slowly descends, flying smoothly. The towering trees grow closer and closer until we're hovering right above their tips. Her wing beats send them rustling and swaying.

We fly past the scorched earth where Aidan defeated a dragon and was blessed by Enya. I hope the dragon wasn't a relative to these shifters, although I doubt the Gods would allow any shapeshifter to come to harm on their land. It was likely a wild dragon coerced by the Gods, or it could have been an elaborate illusion. Dragons aren't rare in Astrellia. Uncommon, sure, but they still exist in high mountains, remote plains, and forgotten forests.

We near the foot of the mountain, and the Maiden circles her cottage.

What took us twenty days to traverse on the way up takes mere minutes to descend on the back of a flying shapeshifter.

The Maiden circles her home slowly until she's low enough to plant her taloned claws in the dirt. I lurch forward, nearly smacking into Rian, but Aidan's hands hold me back.

"I've got you, Magpie," he whispers in my ear. The sensation makes my toes curl in my boots.

"Off," the Maiden demands the instant we come to a stop. I guess a shifter's benevolence only extends so far.

Rian and Aidan jump down her side, while I slide down her back leg. Aidan grips my waist when I'm within reach and carefully lowers me to the ground.

There's a ground-shaking thump and the Steward lands next to us, spraying dirt with his claws. Rayna hops off his back but Calder, bleached of color, remains. He clutches the back spike and breathes hard. The Steward makes a growling sound which seems to bring Calder's body back to life. He slides down the dragon's side and shakily regains his footing.

Two flashes of light later, the shapeshifters stand in their human forms in front of us once more.

"Welcome back, heirs," the Maiden addresses us. "We bid you congratulations on behalf of the Gods. We have prepared a feast in celebration, and we have plenty of provisions to share for your return journeys."

She leads us inside their small home where a large table has been set with bread, cheeses, nuts, berries, vegetables both cooked and raw, stews, bowls of tiny grains, and a heaping bowl of what looks like mashed potatoes. My stomach makes a loud noise of excitement. None of us move to the table, however, not wanting to offend our hosts.

"Come, sit down. You must be tired," the Steward says, motioning at the chairs. "And hungry, considering I hear no less than three stomachs growling."

To say we fall upon the food like ravenous dogs would be an understatement. We don't even bother with utensils for the first few bites, opting for food that can be shoveled into our mouths with dirty hands.

"Slow down or you'll make yourselves sick," the Maiden chides, shaking her head. "And to think, they call *us* animals."

I swallow my mouthful of buttered bread in a gulp, then take a long drink of water from my goblet. It's only then that I pick up my fork and slowly start to enjoy the meal.

Around the table, I see the others gradually do the same. Once the first uncontrollable hunger pangs cease, we relax back into being more proper royals. Rian even dabs at the corners of his lips with his cloth napkin.

"No meat?" I hear Calder ask as he looks in the various bowls and platters spread across the large table.

Silence falls over the table and secondhand embarrassment for him floods through me. Of course they don't eat meat, considering they can—and probably *have*—transformed into many of the creatures we would usually make into a meal.

"No, young Vernier. We do not eat the flesh of any creature," the Maiden responds.

"At least not while we're in our human forms," her brother teases, with a conspiratorial wink in the Maiden's direction. She responds with a wicked grin, showing off suddenly sharpened canine teeth, her eyes nothing more than reptilian slits. My stomach gives an unsettled lurch, but not from eating too quickly.

"Any news from our kingdoms while we were on the mountain?" Aidan asks our hosts in between bites, probably to steer the conversation away from their predatory forms.

The siblings shake their heads. "No news reaches us here, other than what the Gods tell us."

"How do the Gods speak to you? Is it in your dreams?" I ask before thinking better of it.

The shifters share a wordless look, and it's the Steward who answers. "No, they do not speak to us in our dreams. They speak to us like they spoke to you. In one of their physical forms."

My mouth drops open. I set down the glass of water I was about to drink from. "One of their forms?"

"Yes," the Steward says, nodding his head, a slight smile on his face. "The Gods have infinite forms. They appear differently to everyone, based on each person's expectations. That's where we shapeshifters get our abilities from."

"What do you mean?" Rian asks, eyebrows raised.

"Shifters are descended from the Gods," the Maiden says.

Silence falls over the table as everyone stares between the Steward and Maiden. Rian's mouth opens and closes a few times before he makes coherent words. "You're descendants of the Gods. The Gods that we met. On the mountain."

The siblings share amused smirks. The Maiden speaks, staring at her brother. "Telling them never gets old, does it?"

The Steward laughs, shaking his head in response.

"How *exactly* are you descended from the Gods?" Calder wonders—and honestly, it's a valid question.

"Well, I assume you understand how sex works, right Vernier?" The Maiden's voice is full of humor.

Calder turns a deep shade of scarlet and clears his throat. "Of course I know how sex works."

"Ah, good, then I don't have to explain that bit," she quips, her eyes glimmering emeralds. "You know from history that Gods once walked among humans, before they were confined to this land."

We all nod, and she continues.

"Surely it can't seem that strange for a god to fall in love with a human and make little mixed breed babies. Our ancestors were once incredibly powerful and lived extremely long lives. Over the centuries, that power has dwindled, but it remains in our blood. We have unnaturally long lifespans, and we can change shape, but we aren't as strong and gifted as our predecessors."

Although I'm sure we all have the same question, it's Rian who voices it. "How old are you?"

The shifters don't answer right away, and I'm starting to think they won't until the Steward says, "I am one hundred and sixty-two years old, and my sister is one hundred and forty."

I knew they'd been alive a long time, but I wasn't expecting *that* long. It's incomprehensible one could live for so long and still look so young. All the change they've seen in their lives, the many monarchs coming and going, the people and cultures growing.

"Did shifters only inherit the power to change form?" Rayna asks curiously.

The Steward shakes his head. "Our kind used to have strength far surpassing our own. Physical strength, mostly, and enhanced speed and endurance. We never received any elemental or magical gifts from our godly lineage."

"Seers are also descended from Gods," the Maiden says, almost as an afterthought.

Aidan's head snaps to her, drawing my attention. No one else seems to have noticed, all too busy staringat the Maiden for her to continue.

"Oh yes, they are as much children of the Gods as we are. Unlike us, seers have human lifespans, and because of that, their power is so diluted that sometimes the gift skips generations. That's why there are so few of them left."

I don't miss the brief glance the Maiden flashes in Aidan's direction. She picks up her fork and skewers a stalk of cooked asparagus.

We lapse back into silence and eat our fill. I force myself to stop eating when I feel satisfied. It takes all my willpower not to gorge myself after surviving on next to nothing for weeks. The last time I had a full stomach was at the inn with Aislinn.

Ash, I can't help but miss her. The thought of seeing her again has me looking out to the stables, where Misty awaits.

The Steward catches my gaze and gives me a reassuring smile. "We have plenty of food. Please pack what provisions you'd like for your journey. You must be eager to get on the road."

We understand the dismissal from the shapeshifters, and we thank them profusely for their hospitality.

We pack our bags full of extra food, enough to last for days. I offer to help clean up after the meal, but the siblings wave me away, telling me to get on the road before nightfall.

Before I know it, I'm saying hello to Misty, brushing my hand down her nose as she snorts happily. Aidan helps me saddle her for the long ride home. His hands graze mine a few times, and it sends heat rushing to my face.

"Goodbye, Elana," Rayna says from behind me. I startle and turn around, facing Melinor's heir. "I've got the longest path ahead of me, so I need to get going. I'm sure we'll see each other again soon. Our families will probably plan a summit to celebrate and get to know you more."

I pull her into a hug and she stiffens at first, but then lets out a laugh and hugs me back. I breathe through the tears that sting my eyes. *I will not cry, I will not cry.* Without Rayna, I'm not sure I would have made it through the trials. She gave me the stability and companionship I sorely needed. I'll be forever grateful to her for extending the hand of friendship towards me.

"Thank you, Rayna," I say, giving her one last squeeze before reluctantly letting her go. A pang in my heart has me sniffling again. "I'm so glad I got to meet you."

Rayna smiles brightly. "I hope we will see much more of each other in the future. Give your sister Hells for me, will you?"

I laugh through uneven breaths. "I will."

She says a short but warm goodbye to Aidan before being swooped up in a dramatic hug by Rian. Even Calder gives her a respectful handshake.

I wave as she starts off down the path.

Calder is next to leave, hardly sparing us a glance as he announces his departure. Gods, even his horse looks stuck up, trotting away with its head raised high.

"Share the road with me, Magpie?" Aidan asks, patting Misty's side. His large black warhorse is already packed and saddled. He's been stalling, waiting for me. My heart warms at the thought.

"I'd love to, Prince, as long as you don't hold a dagger to my back and call me bunny," I tease, thinking of the first time we met.

His golden eyes crinkle as he chuckles. Gods, I love the sound of his laughter.

"You better not put a blade to that pretty woman, Aidan, or else I'm telling Aislinn," Rian says as he appears in front of Misty.

Aidan grunts his agreement, giving Rian an affectionately playful smack on the back. "Are you heading out too, Yarrow?"

Rian nods. "I think we'll have a quicker journey with the wind at our back. It'll be good to be home."

I smile sadly at him. Another friend is leaving. It's strange that I think of these heirs as friends now, but after all we've been through together, there's no other word to call them.

I catch him off guard with a quick hug. "I'll miss you," I tell him. He hugs me back, patting the top of my head like I'm a child.

"No tears for me, Elana. We'll see each other soon. Hopefully without any life-or-death trials hanging over our head." He laughs, and the contagious sound brings a soft laugh out of me, too.

"Goodbye, Rian," I say as he mounts his chestnut-colored horse and gallops off, a strong wind at his back.

Aidan reaches a hand out towards me. I turn and he nods his head at Misty, and I realize he's offering to help me onto the saddle. With a smile, I place my hand in his and he gives me a boost.

"It's just you and me, Magpie. Ready to go home?" Aidan asks as he mounts his stallion in one quick motion.

"Let's go," I say, urging Misty forward. She takes off at a gallop. I spare a glance behind, at the small house, where a phoenix perches on the chimney, and a cloaked woman watches from the doorway, hand raised in farewell.

CHAPTER TWENTY-EIGHT

We canter along until our horses tire. By the time we slow to a walk, the sun is starting to set beyond the trees, bathing us in golden light.

Feeling the need to practice my power, I create a ball of light next to me. It shimmers and shines. It doesn't flicker like fire, but it does move slightly, reflecting different colors. I send the ball of light above us and feed it more energy. It hovers over our heads and glows brightly, casting shadows underneath us.

I feel Aidan's gaze on me and turn to see him with a satisfied smirk on his face.

"What?" I ask.

"I knew the Gods had something special in mind for you," he says. "But why did you lie about your power?"

My heart lurches, hammering hard in my chest. "What are you talking about? I didn't lie."

He chuckles, shaking his head. "You're a terrible liar, Magpie. You lied when you said you couldn't use the darkness."

I sigh. The *other* pool of power stirs inside me, waiting, begging to be used. There's no point in continuing the farce with him. I trust him enough to know this part of me.

"I'll show you why I lied."

I let the glowing orb fade away, then slowly draw on the other well of power. Unlike the warm, comforting feeling of light, the darkness feels dangerous. It claws its way out of me, fighting tooth and nail to be let out into the world. I suck in a breath and struggle to let only a fraction of it bleed through my fingers.

"I can't control it," I grit out through my teeth. "It scares me, and I didn't want the others to know. Especially since Calder was already worried that I had two abilities."

"Fuck him," Aidan snarls. "Don't pay any mind to what that bastard says."

His sudden anger sparks my surprise and the shadows lunge, spilling from my hand, coating the path around us, coiling like snakes ready to strike. Misty startles beneath me, making worried noises. Darkness swirls around Aidan's horse, and the beast lets out an unhappy snort. I blow out a breath and reel the shadows back inside me. Inch by terrible inch they retreat, until I shove the lid back on that terrible power and take a few calming breaths to seal it.

I don't realize I'm shaking until a hand pulls Misty's reins from my trembling fingers.

"We'll stop here for the night," Aidan says, leaving no room for argument. Not that I have the mental strength to argue right now.

Aidan dismounts and helps me off Misty. He ties our horses to a nearby tree and sets up our small camp. The whole time I stand in place, clenching my fists to stop shaking, to stop the shadows that try to spill through the cracks in my composure.

Aidan grabs my arm and leads me into the forest, away from our horses and camp. I let him, focusing solely on my breathing and squeezing my fists hard.

"Okay," he says, gesturing around him. "It's safe here. Let the power go."

"What!?" I shriek. My eyes snap to his and darkness takes advantage of my momentary lapse in concentration, leaking from my hands. I snap my fingers closed with renewed vigor.

"I can barely control it as it is, and you want me to release it?" I stare at him, wondering if he's experiencing shock or some other side effect of overeating after near-starvation. He looks fine—more than fine, if I'm being honest—but his words don't make sense.

He shakes his head, a serious look on his face. "Keeping that much power inside you is dangerous. It needs to be released. Our power is tied to our energy. This much energy trapped with no outlet will continue to build until it explodes. You have to let go."

"I can't. I'll hurt you," I say, even as I believe what he says about energy building. When I first felt the power it was strong, but not this overwhelming. It's growing impatient. I already feel like keeping the lid on this darkness is taking its toll. My whole body shakes with stress and a headache hammers away in my skull. At this point, I think I have a matter of minutes before I explode—or the shadows explode out of me.

A fire roars to life between us, starting small, as Aidan says, "you won't hurt me. I can take it."

I sweat with exertion and have no choice but to believe him and hope that this power isn't as deadly as I fear. I'm moments away from disaster, from fracturing, when I give in, releasing a breath and letting my fingers relax.

What uncoils from within me feels like a wave of death. Inky blackness shoots out of my body in all directions. I scream with effort as I try to stem the flow, but it bursts like a dam, raw power with no control.

The wave hits Aidan's fire and for a moment I'm worried I'll see the fire bank and die, but the flames only grow. I let out a tearful, relieved laugh.

All around us, the world becomes encased in dark. Trees sway and bend away from the power, as it sweeps across the forest like a harsh wind. The power explodes out of me in uncontrolled waves, stretching out as far as I can see.

Slowly, so slowly, the well empties. I experiment with control, grabbing wisps of shadow as they pass me. I wield them like whips, slashing them through the air. I send some shadows up trees, coiling like vines. I grab hold of the dissipating darkness and mold it, sending it above our heads to blot out the setting sun. We're cast into shadow and the world turns shades of blue and gray, only illuminated by the light of Aidan's fire. Crickets begin to chirp under the blanket of false night.

Feeling a stronger grip on the power now, I reach my hands out to grasp hold of it. It bends easily to my will and I force it down, peeling away the layers until the dusky sky is visible again. Still, I push the shadows down, down, down, until they hit the ground where I command them to dissipate.

I breathe heavily, staring down at my hands. Once I expelled the first burst of power, it was easier to control than I had thought. Better, even—it felt *good* to wield the darkness, to harness the power that had seemed so volatile and dangerous.

I scan for damage around me. The weeds and underbrush around me appear wilted and pushed down by some force, but they still live.

In front of me, the fiery orange wall dissipates. Aidan walks towards me, a proud smile on his face. And damn if that doesn't feel good, too.

"Gods, that was incredible," he says, close enough now that he reaches out and tips my chin up to meet his gaze. "You are incredible. You'll need to work on controlling and forming it, but that amount of raw power is impressive.

A flush washes over my face, staining my cheeks pink. "I had no idea the power could do any of that. I won't keep it locked away again."

"Good," Aidan brushes his hand softly down the side of my neck. "Having power can be dangerous, for even the strongest of us. I've seen my mother literally melt her shoes during a heated argument when she's gone too long without an outlet for her fire."

My breath hitches at his gentle touch. I close my eyes and lean into him. "It felt so good to release it."

Aidan's smile turns ravenous as he trails his hand softly down the side of my neck. "Did it?"

"Oh yes," I whisper and tilt my lips towards him, tempting him ever so slightly. His hand wraps around the back of my neck.

He leans in close, dragging his mouth along the column of my neck and up my chin. His breath tickles me, and I shiver. Finally, he pauses above my mouth. I don't move, and hardly breathe, wanting him closer, closer.

"I love to see you take control," he whispers against my lips and I snap.

I fist my hands in his hair and claim his mouth with my own. He groans into me. I sweep my tongue out, tasting him. His hands wrap around my waist, tugging me closer.

I break off to catch a breath, and he trails hot kisses down my neck and collarbone.

Gods, I want him so badly. But a thought at the back of my mind reminds me of his engagement, and the woman named Nadia. Before I cross this final barrier with him, I need to know who she is, and what happened between them.

I release his hair and pull back slightly, putting my finger to his lips. He startles, but his gaze lands on mine and he sees something in my expression that gives him pause.

"Aidan, I want to go further, but I—" I pause, trying to find the words. "I keep thinking about Nadia," I say.

This hits exactly like the ice-cold bucket of water I know it is. Aidan's hands stiffen on my waist and his eyes darken. I want to give him the time he needs before he tells me about her, but I also can't get involved with a man who keeps his ex-fiancée a secret.

"If you don't want to tell me about her, that's okay, but I...I don't want my first time to be with someone who's keeping secrets from me about a past lover," I say, speaking quickly.

Surprise and something like guilt crosses his face as he looks down at me. "You've never been with anyone before?"

I clear my throat, feeling shame crawl up my neck. "No, I haven't. Not like this. Not like I want to be with you."

Aidan sighs and visibly relaxes. He lets go of my waist, but takes my hand gently, leading me back to camp.

"I'll tell you about Nadia, but it's not a story for the middle of the woods. She deserves better than that," Aidan says. Something twinges in my heart at those words.

He leads me back to our camp. The horses graze nearby, oblivious to the power I expelled and the solemnity of the conversation we're about to have.

Aidan sits down on his sleeping roll, pulling me down next to him. He starts a fire in front of us and stares at it as he tells me of her. He never lets go of my hand.

"Nadia was the daughter of a powerful family in Ocarin. Her father, a duke, was one of my mother's closest allies. We grew up together, since their massive estate was a short walk away from my castle. We were as close as friends could get. Our betrothal was a political one, suggested by the duke and my mother. Nadia and I were both satisfied with the match, knowing it was our best chance at being happy. My father, however, despised the union. He's always coveted more power than he deserves. He proposed a match to Calder's cousin."

My mouth drops open. Calder's cousin?

Aidan squeezes my hand tighter. "My father would have gained Hotharian favor and a sizable estate in the kingdom. I agreed to meet her to appease him, but she wasn't even sixteen years old, and she was dimwitted. The decision was the easiest to make. I chose to marry my best friend. We were due to wed this summer, after I returned from these trials. But last winter her whole family became sick. It was an illness unlike any our healers had seen. She died, as did most of her family, and it felt like a part of my soul died with her."

I suck in a few breaths, staring at our clasped hands. "I'm so sorry, Aidan."

"I am too. She was a wonderful person, full of life. She didn't deserve to die like that, slowly, painfully," he says, giving me a sad smile. "I couldn't even see her in the end. The healers wouldn't let me close enough to say goodbye."

The healer part of my brain kicks on. There are many illnesses that could cause someone to die painfully over time, but for the illness to take an entire family, young and old, and be contagious enough to keep visitors away...something doesn't sit right with me. For Aidan's sake, I hold back my thoughts.

We sit together next to the fire, enjoying each other's company. Some time later, when the sun is a distant memory in the sky and a yawn breaks free from my control, we lie down next to each other. Aidan rests at my back, his arms holding me and his head buried into my hair.

The next morning, I roll over and a warm hand caresses my cheek.

I peel my eyes open and see Aidan's face in front of me. His hair is the messiest I've ever seen it, but there's a soft smile on his lips.

"Good morning, Magpie," he says.

"Good morning, degenerate," I smile back.

A chuckle, and then Aidan releases my face and sits up, rolling his shoulders.

"As much as I'd like to lie around all day, we need to get moving," Aidan's voice is light, but I sense an undertone of restlessness.

I sigh and stand, stretching my arms over my head.

We eat a small meal and pack up our camp quickly. Aidan once again helps me onto Misty. We ride at a slow pace this morning, neither of us wanting to accept that our paths will soon split. I recognize the trees and the bend of the path and realize how close we are to the fork.

"Aidan," I ask in a voice so small it comes out a whisper as I twist Misty's reins in my hands anxiously.

"Yes?" he asks.

"What do we do when we go back to our homes? What if I want to...continue to see you?"

His lips pull up into a smile that doesn't reach his eyes, as if the thought weighs heavily on him too. "Then we will continue to see each other. Whether or not we have to make up feeble excuses to do it."

My eyebrows pull up. "What excuses would we use?"

Aidan seems to think for a moment. "You want to travel to Ocarin to try our famous lava cakes. Or perhaps you're in need of charcoal for healing poisonings and only the purest kind, crafted by the finest fire-gifted heir will do. Maybe you fancy the taste of our mineral water, and you want to sip it right from the source. I also hear that Ocarin women love bathing in our hot springs, for soothing their monthly body aches. Or maybe I need to find time to get swordsmanship lessons from Aislinn, or to hunt down giant scorpions. Perhaps I merely want to visit the most beautiful princess in all five kingdoms, to improve foreign relations."

A blush works is way across my face. I'm about to respond when a ball of fire races straight towards us. Aidan's response is like lightning, sending his own burst of fire out to meet it. The two collide and explode, sending sparks flying. The force of it nearly sends Misty into a panic, but I keep a steady hand on her reins.

I raise my hand and pure light bursts from my palm, bathing the path ahead of us in a blinding glow.

"Elana, wait," Aidan says, but at the same time I hear another voice.

"What the Hells?" That voice shouts. Oh Gods, that voice. It utterly shocks me.

The light vanishes and I jump from Misty. My feet take the brunt of the landing, and I'm running before I can think twice. Aidan calls my name, but I'm focused on her voice.

In front of me, the path splits off into two directions and I veer to the right, where a person rubs her eyes in the aftermath of the light burst.

"Ash!" I cry, tears falling down my cheeks as I sprint to her.

Aislinn has a fraction of a moment to ground herself before I barrel into her, wrapping her in a fierce hug.

Chapter Twenty-Nine

S uddenly, the weeks without my sister are erased and it's like I'm reunited with the other half of my soul.

"Gods, El! You scared me half to death!" Ash squeezes me as hard as I cling to her. She's the first to pull back, but only to scan every inch of me. I know what she's doing instantly.

"I'm fine, Ash. More than fine," I smile at her through blurry vision. I quickly wipe the tears away with the back of my hand.

Ash nods and lets out a breath of relief. "Good. That's good."

A wide smile brightens up her already golden features. "What was that light? Was that some kind of fire? Is that your power?"

I shake my head, giving a short laugh, before I hold my palm up between us. "No, it's not fire. My powers are...different. Look."

A little tug on the well of light inside me and my hand glows like I'm holding a miniature star in my palm.

Ash stares at it, mouth agape, eyes squinting against the brightness. "What power *is* this, El?"

"It's light," I say. "Gifted by one of the forgotten goddesses, Nura."

I let the light extinguish and stare at her confused face. My joy at seeing her again after weeks is suddenly disrupted by my own confusion as to why she's here.

"Ash, what are you doing here?"

Ash seems to shake herself from her shock and pulls a rolled piece of parchment from her pocket. "I received a letter from Queen Amira of Ocarin a week ago. She informed me that I should meet you at this spot at midday today. And so, here I am."

Queen Amira. I spin around and quickly scan the path I ran from. Misty stands there, waiting with Aidan's horse, but he's nowhere to be seen. I hear his voice, though, on the other path, deep and clear. There's another voice there, too, higher in pitch, but from the distance I cannot make out their words. It was his mother who shot the fireball at us, the only other person alive who can wield fire.

But why would she tell Aislinn to meet us here? And why would Ash listen to her? "She asked you to meet me here, and you actually went along with it?"

"I wasn't going to show up—believe me, I wasn't. I've never spoken to her outside of formalities at summits, but she wrote that you would need my help, so I came. Although it doesn't *seem* like you need my help." She nods at my hands, a twinkle of pride in her eyes.

"I'm so happy to see you, Ash." I smile at her, and look back to where Aidan's and my horses wait.

She notices my glance behind me too, and her eyes narrow. "Elana, whose horse is that? Who controlled the fire that I saw?"

I'm not ready to have this conversation with her, but it seems I don't have much choice given this devious twist of fate.

I grab her hand, squeezing gently, until she turns her gaze back on me. "It's Aidan's horse."

She sucks in a sharp breath and tries to pull her hand from my grip, but I hold on and cut off whatever tirade she's about to launch into.

"Aislinn," I say, dropping my voice in earnest. "Be nice to him. I wouldn't be here without him. I promise I'll tell you how it all happened later. For now, please trust me."

I don't know how else to convey all that he is to me. And all he's done for me these past few weeks.

She takes a deep breath, searching my face, before exhaling slowly. She finally nods her head and I know I've won her over.

"Come, let's go say hi." I smile and tug her along towards the other path.

We approach the two figures as a tall, dark-haired woman releases Aidan from a long hug. She pats his cheek tenderly as she smiles up at him with pride.

I recognize Aidan's features on her immediately. She has the same dark hair, pulled into a sleek knot at the back of her head. Her bronze skin glows in the sunlight, and she wears billowy black pants that bunch together at the ankles, paired with riding boots. Her sleeveless top is maroon with gold embellishments, framed by a long, flowing black short-sleeved coat, also trimmed with gold. It extends past her knees but is thin enough to see through. I haven't seen this style of clothing before, and in it she cuts an imposing figure.

She turns to regard Aislinn and me. Her golden eyes shine with confident intelligence. A soft smile grows on her cheeks as she meets us on the path. Next to me, I feel Aislinn tense and stand up straighter. Aidan stands next to his mother and nods at us with a token half-smile.

Remembering my manners, I dip into a curtsy, but the queen chuckles and waves the gesture off. "There is no need for that, Princess Elana, dear. We are peers."

That startling realization hits me and temporarily knocks me off my axis. Dumb with shock, the words that escape me are something along the lines of, "oh, alright, thanks."

Another warm chuckle and the queen steps forward, reaching out her hand—I assume for an introduction. I place my hand in hers and she brings her left hand over our two clasped ones. The act is odd, but not intrusive or uncomfortable. Her hands are as warm as Aidan's.

"It is wonderful to finally meet you, Elana Sable," she says.

"Likewise," I stammer, and immediately regret not saying something more eloquent.

"I see you received my letter, Aislinn. Thank you for making the journey." She addresses my sister and Ash gives her a charming, practiced smile.

"Of course. I had to come when you mentioned that Elana was in danger." There is a slight edge to Aislinn's voice, one that Queen Amira either ignores or doesn't hear.

She smiles at us. "Ah, yes, please forgive me for bringing you here under false pretenses. There is no immediate threat, but I believe traveling back together will benefit both of you."

I can't deny that I'm overjoyed to see Ash again, and I'm even more excited to be able to travel home with her.

Ash doesn't respond to the queen, instead turning her attention to Aidan, nodding her head at him. "Hello, Aidan."

He gives her a challenging smile. "Hello, Aislinn."

"I understand that I have you to thank for making sure Elana made it off the mountain alive?"

Aidan's gaze lands on me. "We all saved each other, in one way or another."

Before I have a chance to interject and emphasize how much Aidan helped me, Queen Amira turns to her son.

"We need to depart. Go ready your horse." She turns back to me, and squeezes my hands, still clasped in hers. Her grip is warm. "If I may offer you some advice, one ruler to a future one?"

I almost startle, but I nod and turn to Ash. "Can you please grab Misty for me?"

She nods, gives the queen an assessing look that promises violence if anything happens to me, and follows Aidan down the path.

When she's out of earshot, Queen Amira speaks. "I see the way my son looks at you. And I want you to know that you are always welcome in Ocarin."

A blush furiously works its way across my face and down my neck. I wonder what, exactly, she sees. She was only reunited with Aidan moments ago. "Thank you, Your Majesty."

Queen Amira looks down at our hands, her kind smile momentarily dropping. Her voice turns quiet. "I see what you will become, child, and I see what you will sacrifice to get there. My heart aches for you."

I'm stunned, all words and thoughts emptying out of my head with a sharp exhale. A chill snakes its way up my spine, coiling around my chest and squeezing.

"The path you walk will not be easy, but stay true to your heart, and the world will be a better place for it. Be brave, dear one. Be the light. Be the darkness. Be the gray space in between. Fight for your own destiny."

She lets my hand drop to my side and blinks slowly. For a fraction of a second I see a shadow, a glimpse of something on the center of her forehead opening. A third eye.

I gasp and take a half step back. Queen Amira puts a finger to her lips and winks at me. Aidan and Aislinn appear before us, horses in tow.

Ash gives me a questioning glance, which I ignore. I'm still reeling but shove the feeling down deep.

"It's time to go, son," she says, giving Aidan a meaningful look before facing Ash and I once more. "It was an honor to meet you, Elana. I look forward to seeing you more in the future. Aislinn Sable, it was a pleasure seeing you, as always."

Ash and I dip our heads respectfully as she strolls to her horse.

"I'll go grab Hector and bring him around," Ash says, leaving Aidan and I standing there alone. I silently praise Ash for having sense.

His golden eyes search my face. There are a million things I want to say, a million ways to say goodbye, but words catch in my throat. I swallow them down, and they're thick, viscous. I blink rapidly against the stinging that builds in my eyes.

"Magpie," he whispers, reaching out a hand. I want to bat it away. I want to insist he come to Adrithia with me, or insist that I go to Ocarin with him, but we both know that can't happen right now.

"Your mother is watching, and Aislinn could see," I say, unsure of how much he wants everyone to know.

A smirk pulls the corner of his lip up. "Let them. I don't mind if you don't."

He's giving me the choice. Do I want my sister to know? She would keep this a secret for me, I know she would.

So I step into his embrace, and he pulls me tight to him, wrapping his arms around my waist. My arms go around his shoulders and I press my face to his chest.

"I don't want to say goodbye," I whisper, and hate how weak it sounds. Aidan doesn't seem to mind. He squeezes me tighter, pressing a kiss to the top of my head.

"I know. We'll see each other soon. I'll write to you as soon as I get home and we can figure out which ridiculous excuse we want to tell our families for getting away."

I chuckle into his shoulder. "Sounds perfect. I'll be waiting."

He pulls away only enough to press his lips to mine, slowly, like we have all the time in the world. The kiss lingers long after he pulls away and walks back to his mother.

I watch as they expertly mount their horses and trot off down the path. Aidan looks behind, holding his hand up. A small bird made of fire bursts from his palm and flies around my head, leaving a small trail of smoke as it disappears into the clouds.

The heaviness of the past few weeks hits my shoulders, and my knees shake. Suddenly, I'm so glad to have Aislinn here with me, to travel this road together so I won't feel the crushing weight of loneliness.

I'm still glad of her presence even as she says angrily, "you wanna tell me what the fuck happened these last few weeks now?"

Chapter Thirty

"One, how did you become so *close* with Aidan fucking Ashfall? Two, what's the deal with your powers? And three, why is Queen Amira being...nice?" Ash asks, and I see she's met her limit for shocking information. She paces back and forth, still holding Misty's reins with one hand.

I suck in a long breath. Where do I even begin?

"Ash, I'll tell you everything, but can we get back on the path first? I'd like to make it home before autumn," I say. I miss home. I miss Aric and, to my surprise, my parents. I miss the simplicity and the routine of life at home. Although, I'm sure that's all about to change.

Ash ceases her pacing and lets out a deep breath. "Okay, you're right. You can explain on the way. Come on, I left Hector down the other path."

Hours later, I'm still talking as we ride. Aislinn listens intently while I tell her about the trials, in the order they happened, I tell her about Calder trying to kill me, and about the failed alliance he tried to forge with Aidan. I tell her how he nearly died, and how I was only able to save him with the scorpion venom, at which she scoffs and calls it "a waste". I leave out some of the details of Aidan's and my relationship, but I tell her about when he caught me from the rope ladder, and when he stood up for me to Calder.

Finally, I tell her about my trial. About meeting two goddesses. Her head snaps to me, eyes wide with shock.

"You met *two* goddesses?" she asks me.

I nod. "The forgotten twin goddesses of light and darkness, Nura and Nisha. They granted me their powers."

Again, I hold up my hand and allow white light to surround it. Ash stares at it, the light reflecting in her wide green eyes. I let the light burn on, while I raise my other hand. I reach for the second, unpredictable well and grip a tendril of shadow. It wraps around my wrist up to my pointed fingertips. I snuff out the light and banish the shadows.

Ash's mouth is open, her eyes wide and her face pinched. She struggles to speak for a moment. Her jaw moves, but no words come out. She furrows her brows and tries again. "This is unlike anything I ever imagined, El."

Slowly a wide smile lights up her face, reminding me how beautiful she is and how hard she worked to have the future that is now mine. A kernel of concern and sadness lodges in my stomach.

"If I could give this power to you, I would in a heartbeat." I speak before I even think about it.

Ash's smile turns to a stern thin line. "Elana, enough. I am truly happy for you. Even if the Gods had chosen me, I wouldn't have been given this gift. This power was meant for you. I don't know why you think you don't deserve this, but you do."

I turn away from the intensity of her gaze and the determination in it, instead staring at the path straight ahead.

"You need to accept that you deserve this, El," Ash presses.

"I still don't know why I was chosen. The goddesses didn't say anything except *'everything happened as it was meant to,'* which doesn't make any sense. They gave no explanation. It's all so frustrating," I say through a frown.

We ride in silence for a few moments. The only sound is our horses' hoofbeats on the dirt path. Ash breaks it first. "The goddesses know what they're doing. I trust their decision. I trust you."

I flash her a smile, but she's staring straight ahead. Her confidence in me is unshakeable, and for that I'll always be grateful. I shift in my saddle, eager to stop for the night. When I turn to Ash to suggest it, she's already halfway down Hector.

"Might as well stop here," she says, planting her feet on the ground and turning to offer me help.

Tugging on Misty's reins, I make the jump down myself. The landing could have been better, but I don't twist an ankle, so I consider it a win.

We share a meal of provisions from the shapeshifting siblings. Ash asks where I got the food from, and I feel my tongue tying when I try to answer. Strange, I wasn't even about to say shapeshifters. I settle for calling them friends, and though Ash looks like she wants to press for more information I turn away and she relents.

"So, how are things back home? Anything exciting happen while I was away?"

Ash swallows down a bite of bread with a swig of water. "Mother's being her usual self. She tried to convince me to marry Duke Lyon's son in your stead. Of course I refused. You know he's about as dull as a damn rock."

I snort. "That man couldn't say something interesting if his Gods-damned life depended on it."

Ash laughs. "Truly, how does one become that boring?"

I shake my head. "I doubt even the Gods know."

She waves me off with a smile. "You'll be happy to know that I've been thoroughly investigating General Calix."

My eyebrows shoot up and my gaze shoots to her. She's barely repressing a smirk. "And?" I demand. When we left Harold's Hill, I had a knot in my stomach, seeing how the general had been treating people from villages away from the capital city. Hopefully the residents of Harold's Hill have begun to recover after Aislinn slayed the giant scorpion that took up residence nearby.

"And I'm not finished yet, but from what I've uncovered so far, he's as corrupt as we feared."

My eyes narrow, although I'm not shocked by the news. There was always something off about that man. "What can be done about it?"

Ash considers, for a moment before answering. "There's only one way to make sure his corruption is cut out at the source. We need to remove him from office and give someone else command of our armies."

"Would you do it?" I ask. "Command our armies?"

Her sharp gaze slides to me. "I would consider it."

Another question passes through my mind. "I'm surprised Father let you run the investigation on your own."

"I didn't give him a choice. I informed him once I started interviewing townspeople. He was so furious with what's been going on that he didn't even reprimand me for not asking permission," Ash says with a devious grin. "He told me he doesn't wish to hear about it until I gather every last scrap of evidence there is to find."

A short laugh bubbles out of me. "I can't wait to hear what you discover."

She's probably been giving our father a run for his money, with all the extra time on her hands. I wonder what Aric has been doing with all his extra time. "How's Aric?"

"He's been brooding since you've left. Unusually quiet, keeping to himself. There were a few days when he disappeared entirely. I was worried he went after you, until I found him on a days-long bender at Sandral's seediest pub. After that, father reassigned him until you return, and he's been taking his new temporary job as household guard a little too seriously," she says with a tone that I recognize as exasperation. I wonder how many times she's been at odds with him since I left. I always played peacekeeper between them.

A bender has me worried, though. Aric has been known to enjoy a drink or two on his free days, but it's not like him to go on multiple-day binges. It seems my departure may have impacted him more than I thought it would. I sigh. I'll see him soon and can ask him what the Hells he was thinking then. Hopefully he doesn't still harbor the notion that I'll run off with him and start a new life.

"I bet he'll brood even more when you come home with all these stories of what you and Prince Aidan fucking Ashfall have been up to," Ash's eyebrows quirk up, her smirk back in place. She's purposely goading me.

"Sister, if you're wondering about Prince Aidan fucking Ashfall and I, all you have to do is ask." I give her a conspiratorial wink, which has her fake gagging into her water canteen. "Although I understand maybe there are some things sisters shouldn't tell each other? Like, what's going on between you and a certain Melinorian princess named Rayna?"

At that, Ash nearly chokes on her water. "What?" she blurts.

"You heard me. I have the letter that you wrote asking for her help in protecting me. And I heard about how *close* you two are. Care to fill in any details?" I ask in a teasing tone—but the question is anything but a jest.

My sister takes another swallow of her water and clears her throat.

"Rayna and I are...close friends," Ash says, looking back towards the mountain, as if she could see through the Gods' Territory all the way to Melinor.

"If you don't want to tell me anything, that's fine," I say gently. "But know that if you two were more than friends, I'd be happy for you. Happy that you have someone like that."

A small smile creeps up her lips. "Thank you, El." She heaves a dramatic sigh. "We haven't really had time to figure anything out between us. Our duty was always in the way. But maybe now..."

She trails off, but I catch her meaning. Perhaps they will get time to explore what they are to each other now that one of them doesn't have to worry about ruling a kingdom on the opposite side of Astrellia.

That's one of the major downsides to being an heir. Many matches are made for strength and power, not for love. From the stories our mother told us, our parents were lucky in that regard. They were matched together in a power move for Adrithia but ended up falling in love. I don't even want to think about the potential matches my mother will try to force on me.

My mind slips to Aidan. How many more proposals will he receive? Will his father try to make another betrothal for him out of desire for more political strength? Is there a future where we could ever be together?

These thoughts threaten to overwhelm what's supposed to be a joyful reunion. I push them aside and think of something else.

Out of the corner of my eyes I notice Ash staring back up the path, gaze unfocused. She's probably thinking of Rayna, and how close she was to seeing her.

The next morning, we wake at dawn. I want to hit the road early. I'm eager to return home, and Ash is eager to oblige. I notice her casting glances at the path behind us while we pack.

I'm about to open my mouth to suggest a visit to Melinor when the sound of twigs snapping has me drawing my daggers. Our horses neigh and stomp nervously, tugging against the tree we tied them too last night.

Two sets of feline eyes—one yellow, the other blue—appear suddenly on the opposite side of the path. I breathe a sigh of relief and sheathe my daggers. The two cats stalk forward, their piercing eyes trained on me until Ash draws her bow in one smooth, swift motion.

Their backs arch slightly and they bare their teeth at her, growling menacingly.

"Ash, wait!" I shout. She doesn't loose her arrow. "Put your bow away. They're friends."

"You know these cats?" She looks at me like I've lost it. After scanning my face for a moment, she sighs and shakes her head. "Of course you do."

She relaxes the bowstring and puts her arrow back in her quiver. The black feline steps closer to Ash, its nose working as it sniffs her. Its yellow eyes slide back and forth between my sister and I before it bumps its head against Ash's hand, purring loudly. My mouth drops in shock.

Ash breaks out into a grin, stretching the top of its head affectionately. "Oh, what a big sweetheart."

The white feline sits on its haunches in front of me, craning its neck to peer down at me. Its wide blue eyes are nearly identical in hue to the Goddess Nura's. I smile up at the cat.

"Hello, Goddess," I say to the creature, who bends over and licks my cheek with a move more befitting a dog than any cat I've met. I decide to keep that bit to myself.

"Did you just call the cat a Goddess?" Ash asks, suddenly petting the black cat very carefully.

"Yes," I tell her with a smile. "I don't know whether they are the Goddesses themselves or a piece of their being, but they are Nura and Nisha."

I run my fingers through the thick, warm fur of the cat in front of me. "Have you come to make sure I don't get into any more trouble in your territory?"

The white cat lets out a low grumble, which I take as an agreement.

"These cats saved me from Calder's first attempt to kill me on the mountain," I tell Aislinn.

She nods at me, then turns her attention back to the black feline. "Thank you for watching after my sister. She means everything to me."

A deep meow sounds from the black cat as it pushes harder against Aislinn's head scratches. The white cat makes a low noise and the felines exchange a look and turn towards the path to Adrithia. The white cat looks back at me, its blue, jeweled eyes capturing my attention. It lowers its head and nudges me sternly in the direction of home.

I glance over at Aislinn and the black feline is doing the same to her.

"You want us to leave?" I ask, holding up my hands, gathering my pack, and shrugging it onto my shoulder.

A firm nod and a low whine are my reply. I've never felt this nervous energy from the cats before. It feels urgent that we leave. I jump back a step and rush to Misty. Ash is already there, attaching her pack to Hector's saddle. The horses are surprisingly calm now, unaffected by these giant predators in their midst. Perhaps they sense the spirits of the Goddesses.

A few minutes later we're saddled and facing the path. The felines stick close to us as we take off at a canter.

The cats escort us to the gate despite the journey taking most of the morning. When we get there we slow our horses, and I turn in my saddle to bid farewell to our companions. They stand side by side, watching us with sharp eyes.

I lift a hand at them, at a loss for words. The white cat gives a long purposeful nod, and the two turn around, running back towards the mountain.

I look to Ash, who is staring off past the cats at something unseen. She senses my gaze and her attention snaps to me.

"I guess they mean for us to hurry home," I say with a slight shrug of my shoulders.

"I'm not about to question the will of the Gods. Shall we?" Ash asks. In response, I urge Misty forward in a gallop.

Ash lets out a whoop and Hector breaks into a gallop, keeping pace at Misty's side. The promise of home is less than a few days ahead, and I intend to return as someone worthy of the crown that the Gods thrust upon me.

CHAPTER THIRTY-ONE

We ride hard on the path home. We stop at Harold's Hill for the night and are greeted by an overjoyed Agatha. Aislinn pays her in more gold coins, which are snatched up in arthritic fingers before they settle on the bar counter. Again, I'm impressed by her speed. I can only hope I move as quickly as she does when I'm her age. What's even more surprising, though, is the speed with which she tosses the coins back.

"Yer money's no good 'ere, princesses. We 'ave ye to thank fer killin' the beast!" She chuckles, waving off Aislinn's attempts to pay again.

Apparently with the giant scorpion gone, the townsfolk have been able to keep their livestock safe, and no more villagers have gone missing. To our surprise, there is even meat in the stew that night.

Our evening and the next morning pass quickly. Agatha and her daughter see us off once more. Her husband still snoozes on the bar. All seems well in the small village.

Ash and I make our way quickly, passing through the plains and the rolling hills of the northeastern part of our kingdom.

During our brief moments of rest, mostly to give our horses a break, Ash insists that I practice my abilities. First, she has me throwing light balls around, growing and shrinking the size on command. She demands that I bring out the darkness more, getting familiar with it so I don't shy away from the power. She repeats the same thing Aidan said about not keeping it hidden away. Then I practice imbuing weapons with light and darkness. I create blinding bright arrows that explode on contact and encase my daggers in wisps of shadow as I strike out with them.

I've discovered that the darkness behaves like a tangible thing. I can mold it to fit other shapes and wield it like a whip. It's effective at blocking out light in an area, or lurking in naturally dark places, in the shadows of trees, under brush or feet. I feel the strongest connection to it after dusk. In contrast, the light is more powerful during the day. I can produce a blinding flash, burning orbs, and I'm starting to figure out how to focus the light into concentrated, burning beams. I haven't been able to recreate the explosion that I produced on top of the mountain.

Ash pushes my limits, demanding I keep an orb of sun suspended above us while we ride and a tendril of shadow at my fingertips. The toll on my energy levels is taxing, and I'm starving and exhausted every time we take a break.

Before I realize it, we're back in the lands I recognize leading to Sandral and our castle. Sudden anxious nerves overtake me, and I look to Ash.

"What happens when we get home?" I ask.

Her hazel eyes meet mine, assessing my apprehension. "There will be a presentation ceremony. Nothing elaborate. You'll stand in front of the temple and father will present you to the kingdom. You'll show off your fancy new powers, the people will cheer, and everyone will finally believe that you were rightfully chosen."

"Are people still rioting over the fact that that I was chosen?"

Her features harden. "There's a small group Hells-bent on stirring up trouble. Most of the unrest has died down. I think people are waiting to see what happens when you return from the mountain. The people causing problems unfortunately make a surprising amount of noise for a group so small."

I swallow hard. What will the revelation that I carry the powers of two long-forgotten Goddesses do? Will it help or hurt my cause?

Another distressing thought lights a fire in my mind—the other heirs, except Aidan, believe that I can only use the power of one goddess. If they find out I can use both, it could cause political trouble for us.

"Ash," I say, tentatively. "The other heirs might think I can only use the ability granted to me by Nura."

A sharp inhale from my sister has me wincing. I stare down the path, intent on looking anywhere but at her.

"Why would they think that?" Her voice is stern. Gods, she sounds like our mother.

I swallow hard, sensing her barely contained ire. "When I was first gifted the powers, the darkness felt dangerous and I couldn't control it. Instead of telling them that I was afraid to use it, I may have let them believe I couldn't use the power of darkness."

My sister lets out a deep breath. She puts a hand to her temple, rubbing slowly. "Okay, I understand why you did it."

She pauses, and I risk a glance at her to see she's deep in thought. "We'll figure it out. Rayna will understand, and she will convince her parents all is well. I'll write her a letter when we return. You should do the same for Aidan."

I bite my lip. "He already knows. He knew I was keeping the darkness inside, and he helped me wield it for the first time."

Aislinn stares at me for a beat before nodding. "All right, good. We won't have to worry about Ocarin. Which leaves Rian and Calder."

"Rian and I became allies. He owes me a life debt for when I saved him from the whirlpool. He will understand. I'll write to him," I tell her.

She nods. "We need to brainstorm how we inform Hotharia. I'm sure Father will have ideas."

The feeling of unease that had me in a chokehold moments ago loosens. The tops of the white granite peaks of our home come into view. A feeling of relief washes over me until Ash clears her throat.

"Mother is planning a ball in celebration of your triumphant return. She's been talking to her lady's maids about it since you left. I believe she intends to invite all the eligible bachelors and entertain marriage proposals for us. My rejection of Lord Lyons' son will be the first of many—for the both of us, I'm afraid."

She doesn't bother hiding the disgust in her tone. I don't blame her. The idea of marrying someone based solely on what they can provide our family—and in most cases without having met them—is a distressing thought.

Ash and I don't get time to talk about how tedious the ball will be, however, because we're approaching the large gates at the entrance to our home. A guard on top of the watchtower sees us and shouts something to his companions. We watch as several guards scramble, and then the gates creak open.

We urge our horses through them, heading for the stables. A loud horn blows a cheery tune. I resist the urge to cover my ears. People start to funnel out of the castle, reminding me of ants after their mound has been disturbed.

Among the throng I see Gwen and some of the other cooks, Senara, my mother and sister's lady's maids, my father's courtier Rigel, and then Aric, with a wide smile on his face.

"Oh Gods," I say, already embarrassed from the attention. "I guess it's too late to sneak in through the kitchen."

Ash chuckles, finding my plight entertaining. "Come on, try to enjoy the attention. You've gone through Hells to gain your power, now try to enjoy all the respect of your people."

A grunt is my only acknowledgement before our horses are swept up in a crowd. I don't think I've ever seen all our castle staff in one place at one time, but now they all clap and cheer as Ash and I dismount our horses. Thankfully, I don't stumble when I hit the ground.

Not two moments after my feet touch the ground I'm wrapped in a strong embrace.

"Princess, you're home," Aric says into my hair. The hold unnerves me slightly, but I'm so happy to see my friend again that I allow him this. I hug back gently for a beat and then pull away.

I smile up at him. "Hello, Aric. Hope you've been well."

His face crinkles with his own smile, his blond hair glowing in the late afternoon sun. "You travel halfway across Astrellia and face trials by the Gods, only to return and think of others right away. Gods, I've missed you."

"I missed you, too Aric."

We're interrupted from further conversation when a low voice booms my name. I smile despite the dozens of eyes on me.

My father stands a few paces away. He's breathing hard, like he ran from somewhere inside the castle. His arms open in front of him and I rush into them.

"Elana," he whispers, "I'm overjoyed to see you safe and sound."

I smile into his shoulder. We pull away after a moment. Pride shines in his smile, the sight of which has me in tears. The man of stone has a pretty big heart after all.

"Come, we have much to discuss, and your mother will be back from the Temple soon. She's been praying for your safe return since you left us," he says.

He turns and heads towards Ash, who's unbuckling her pack from Hector's saddle. She pauses and lowers her head to him as he approaches. He ignores the gesture and pulls her into a hug.

"You left with nothing more than a note and terrified both your mother and me. I hope in the future you'll do us the courtesy of at least informing us of your plans," he says as he pulls away from the hug.

"Apologies, Father. I was under the impression that Elana was in danger," Ash says.

"And was she?" he asks her. His gaze darts back and forth between us, assessing his daughters for any signs of wounds.

I shift on my feet, wondering what Aislinn wrote in her letter to them, if she mentioned Queen Amira at all. "No. There was no trouble. It was a smooth journey home."

He nods, his shoulders dropping slightly in relief as he leads us towards our home. I look back at Misty and the stable boy already leading her towards a big bale of hay. Some household staff are taking my and Aislinn's packs towards the castle. Aric walks a few paces behind us, and when I briefly glance at his face, he gives me a warm, soft smile.

Father leads us into his study and Aric dutifully stops outside the door to stand watch. He closes the door behind us.

"How did it go?" Father asks the moment it shuts. It's rare that our father outwardly shows emotions. Usually we feel them in how the ground reacts, but now his face betrays his excitement and curiosity.

I take a deep breath and hold up my hands, summoning both elements at the same time. An eerie darkness fills the room, blocking the windows and plunging us into inky shades until the light from my other hand bursts free, illuminating us in stark relief against the shadows.

The breath leaves my father's lungs as he stares at my hands, at the darkness around us, and the orb of light, now hovering in the center of the room.

The door flings open and my mother's voice startles us all. "Elana!" It's nothing more than a shriek.

She, too, pauses, looking around in shock at the elements spilling from my hands. Behind her, I see Aric stumble back a step. We momentarily lock eyes and I see alarm in his gaze before he schools his features into careful neutrality. He quickly mumbles an apology and shuts the door.

"Elana." My father's voice is quiet, grave. "What power is this?"

My mother interrupts him with a sweep of her hand as she puts her hands on my shoulders, taking in every feature of mine. "Not now, Devon. Let me see my daughter."

Even the king must acquiesce to this fearsome woman, going silent as she studies me. I feel like a child again under her intense gaze. I snuff my powers out, allowing the room to return to its normal golden-brown hues, illuminated further with a few candles.

"You're unharmed?" my mother asks.

"Yes, I'm fine, Mother."

"Good." She breathes out and wraps me in a quick hug. I'm so taken aback that I barely put my arms around her before she lets go. "Now, answer your father. What power do you possess?"

I spend the next few hours telling them everything that I told Aislinn, leaving out the details about Aidan and me.

We send for food and Aric brings in platters laden with roasted meats and potatoes. My stomach growls eagerly. As we eat, my parents pepper me with questions, mainly about the twin goddesses and my powers.

Finally, I explain my unintentional lie to the heirs. We all agree that I must inform them of the truth immediately. I pen letters to Rayna and Rian, explaining that I discovered how to use the darkness, and I didn't mean to deceive them. I renew my vow, promising to uphold the peace between kingdoms. For Hotharia's letter, both my father and I write. The message I write to Calder informs him that I've discovered how to use my second power, but I insist on only using it to protect Astrellia's peace. At the suggestion of Aislinn, I cut my palm open with my dagger to sign all of the letters in my own blood. To sign in blood is to swear to the Gods. It's a sacred act that holds the same meaning across the entire continent.

The last letter I write is to Aidan. I inform him that all the heirs know that I'm able to wield both powers, and I hope it doesn't cause Ocarin any trouble with Hotharia. I pen a few sentences about the return journey, and my last line reads, *"I miss you, degenerate, and hope to have a pathetic excuse to see you soon. Yours, Elana"*

Ash takes the letters to the hawkery to be sent immediately to the other kingdoms. I imagine she's adding her own message to Rayna's letter. The thought warms me.

I stifle my fifth yawn in the last few minutes. The sky has darkened, and the exhaustion of the long journey seems to have finally caught up with me.

"Get some rest, Elana," Father says, noticing my sluggish state. "Tomorrow you will be presented to the kingdom."

I think the words are supposed to excite me, but all I feel is dread. The last time I stood in front of my people, it didn't exactly go well. The thought sits in my stomach like a block of lead.

CHAPTER THIRTY-TWO

I t's midday and I stand on the dais next to my father. My mother and Aislinn stand one step behind us, facing the throng of Adrithian citizens. The brutal heat once again scorches my neck, and it's reminiscent of the last time I stood here. I'm dressed in a similar striking blue dress with silver accents, but this time my long auburn hair is swept up in braids and affixed to the back of my head. The weight of the golden crown upon my head is nothing compared to the weight of my anxiety.

I try not to fidget as my father speaks about the history of the heirs, how for generations Sables have been chosen to protect Adrithia and uphold the peace between kingdoms.

Aric stands at the foot of the dais steps, right where he was at the Crowning Ceremony. He and a dozen other guards keep the pressing crowds in check, a measure that wasn't needed previously. My conversation with him last night as he walked me to my rooms pricks at the back of my neck.

"Princess, that power I saw," he started, as if unsure what to say. "It wasn't from any of the five Gods, was it?"

I sighed, prepared to explain this for the fourth, but not the final, time. "Not from any of the known Gods, no. My powers come from the two forgotten Goddesses. Nura, the goddess of light and Nisha, goddess of darkness."

His eyes went wide and he stammered over a response. "But how? How is that possible?"

I shrug my shoulders. "The Goddesses willed it, and so it is. The powers are a part of me now, like my father's is a part of him."

"Yes, but won't this cause upset between the kingdoms? You have twice the gift they were given." He grabbed my arm then, tugging me to a stop in the hall outside my suite. If I

weren't so tired I would have snatched my arm back. I knew he meant well, but his words seemed to imply that I wasn't qualified to deal with the situation.

"We're handling the other kingdoms. I'm confident the heirs will see reason and uphold our peace. Well, most of them, anyway."

He put his arms on my shoulders. "Which heir are you concerned about?"

I tried to duck away from his grip, but he held fast. All I wanted was my own bed. My own pillow. To take a bath and get out of those Gods-damned clothes I'd been wearing for weeks. He was preventing me from doing so. I took a long breath and exhaled, trying to be patient with this man who had been my closest friend for years.

"Does it matter?" I wondered.

He released my shoulders and stood up straighter. "I am your guard, and as such I need to be aware of any potential plots against you. If I know who your enemies are I can protect you from them."

Gods, he took his job seriously. I relented with a sigh. "Fine. Right now, the only kingdom we're worried about is Hotharia."

He stiffened slightly and nodded. "Thank you for telling me. I'll tell the household guard to assign extra men to you until we know how this news plays out."

I was too tired to argue. I nodded at him and wished him a good night as I retired to my rooms.

I snap back to the present as my father's voice rings out clearly over the crowd. "I present my daughter and your future queen, Elana Sable. Gifted with the power of not one, but two Goddesses."

Before the crowd has a chance to react, I lift my chin and raise my arms. A hush falls over the gathered people. This is my moment. My moment to prove to my people that I will protect them and lead Adrithia into a peaceful, prosperous future.

Shadows rise from my feet, swirling around me at my command. With a wave of my hands, I summon the shadows from nearby buildings, from under the platform on which we stand, from every corner that the midday sun does not touch. They rush around me and weave through the crowd harmlessly, but showy. Gasps and shouts break out. I revel in the moment. Here and now, they will finally see me.

A bright light appears in my hand and I toss it up like a ball, suspending it in the air above my head. I feed it, and watch as the light grows larger and larger, until it is the size of a carriage. I bring my hands together and the light explodes in a flash, driving the shadows away and blinding everyone for a moment before both shadow and light vanish, leaving the crowd dazed.

I speak and have to force myself to be articulate as I shout. "The long-forgotten twin Goddesses Nisha and Nura, of darkness and of light, have honored me with their strength."

The crowd goes silent, hanging onto my words— the words that my family and I planned out early this morning. Everything has to be perfect. "I will use this power to protect all citizens of Adrithia and keep the peace that generations of Sables have upheld."

I close my mouth, gritting my teeth together to stop my jaw from quivering while I wait for the crowd's reaction.

Time passes slowly as the people start to look around at each other, as if they need to collectively decide whether or not to accept me. One cheer rises up from a young woman with dark hair no older than me, standing somewhere in the middle of the mass of bodies. A second cheer joins hers, then a third, a fourth. Soon raucous shouts fill Sandral's square.

A relieved laugh bubbles up inside of me. It's almost unbelievable that they would accept me so easily after a few sentences and one display of power. My father raises his hand in a wave. There's a proud smile on his face.

I risk a glance over my shoulder at Aislinn, and her look mirrors my own. In a split-second decision, I reach out for her, offering my hand, to pull her next to me. If anyone deserves this praise, it's her. I wouldn't be alive today if it weren't for my sister. She looks surprised, but accepts my hand. I tug her to my side. The cheers only grow louder.

Father pulls Mother to his side and we stand on the edge of the dais together, united in front of our people.

Days after my presentation to the kingdom, I write my second letter to Aidan. I recount the events of the presentation, and how strange it was to be cheered for. I tell him of my studies with my father, learning all manner of statecraft and politics. I tell him my lessons with Ash have continued, but now include regular appearances from my father, who helps me wield my powers. I also inform him that our top alchemists are studying the glowing fungus from the cave on the mountain. They're making good progress, already getting it to reproduce and multiply. Soon we may even have a new light source, and I joke that I'm going to name it after him.

I ask him how his return journey went and if he has any news from the other heirs. At the end I sign off the same way I did the first letter. *"I miss you, degenerate, and hope to have a pathetic excuse to see you soon. Yours, Elana."*

He hasn't replied to my first letter yet, but I'm not concerned. I've only been home for five days. If everything went well on his travels, he should have gotten home two days ago. He could have taken a detour on his way or run into some bad weather that prevented him from traveling. Or maybe he came home to a new marriage proposal courtesy of his father, and he's been busy telling him and the new woman off. Again, though, I'm not worried.

I deliver the parchment to the dovecote where our messenger birds are well-tended by staff. A particularly speedy hawk is dispatched with my rolled-up letter.

I'm dreading the rest of my afternoon. Mother has requested my assistance in the preparations for the ball in three weeks. We will be hosting the entire Adrithian court and nobles from across the kingdom. The castle must be prepared for an influx of guests. I convinced her that the theme of the ball should be masquerade, which will be my one saving grace. I'll get to hide behind a mask the entire night. Being the center of attention was always Aislinn's thing, not mine.

The royal seamstress has already been to our castle twice to show off fabrics and collect measurements for my mother, Ash, and myself.

Our castle's grand hall is hardly used formally, besides for holding court. We only host balls on special occasions, such as my sister and I coming of age, or my father's fortieth name day. Mother has been beside herself with excitement over planning this one. She's managed to work the entire household staff into a tizzy. There's a frantic energy in the air setting everyone on edge. Even Senara has been zipping around running extra errands for my mother.

I don't understand the big deal. Surely there's only so many ways one can decorate a grand hall, and any meal Gwen comes up with would be sufficient, but Mother has been tasting and refining the menu for days.

At least Sandral's citizens will profit off this. Inns are fully booked, and taverns and shops are hiring more hands in preparation. It seems everyone is too busy preparing for this ball that even the unrest at my crowning has quieted.

In the weeks that pass by leading up to the ball, time flows quickly. Between training and shadowing my father during meetings with his advisors, I soak up all his tactics in statecraft. He doesn't enjoy the small talk or gossip of the court, but he listens to everyone. I try to follow along as he decides which noblemen need funds for farming to keep their territories fed and which seek to fill their own coffers. He occasionally asks for my judgement on matters we've discussed ahead of time, to allow me to practice in a diplomatic setting.

We hold my first court a few days before the ball. It's a small gathering held in the great hall, and several lords and ladies come with grievances and news. I observe while Father provides solutions and an ear to those who need it.

Aric stands behind me a step, my living, breathing shadow again. He's hardly let me out of his sight these past few weeks. As is customary, General Calix stands near the bottom of the steps, representing our army in case any threat needs to be addressed. I narrow my eyes at the back of his head, remembering Harold's Hill, and the fear of the villagers there. I wonder how Ash's inquiry into him is going and make a mental note to ask her after this.

My usual chair on the dais has been discarded, replaced by a throne my father commissioned from Sandral's most highly regarded carpenter. I sit on my father's right side on the beautiful wooden seat. Designed to reflect the Sable family as well as symbolize my powers, it's solid black with a white cushion. It's the same height and shape as my father's, with the family crest adorning the high, peaked back, at least a foot taller than my head. It's horribly uncomfortable, but Father says it's supposed to be. The more relaxed we get in our role as monarchs, the less we strive to be better for our people and our kingdom. I suppose there's some merit to the idea, but right now all I can think is that my ass aches and my lower back is on fire. The crown on my head puts strain on my neck, but Father insists I wear it when acting in any official capacity.

We're about to wrap up for the day, and I'm silently thanking the Gods when Ash stands up from her seat at Father's left and stands in front of us with a stack of parchment in hand. She bows to the thrones where father and I sit, and the sight twists my stomach into uneasy knots.

"Rise, daughter, and tell us what matter you wish to present so formally," Father says calmly, and I see curiosity in his raised eyebrow.

"Thank you, Father," Ash responds, holding out the parchment to Rigel. I realize they are all letters. "I bring substantial evidence that General Calix has committed treason."

Chapter Thirty-Three

It feels like the entire room has flipped upside down. The lords and ladies in the hall cry out in shock and outrage.

General Calix spins around, pointing a meaty finger at my sister aggressively. "Slander! Lies from a bastard bitch!" I see red at the insult. He makes a sudden move towards her, his hand going to his broadsword. With Ash facing Father, she doesn't see this movement. He starts to unsheathe the blade and I snap.

Without my conscious effort, the careful lid I keep on my shadows bursts open, and five tendrils shoot out from the ground around the general. They wrap around his arms, his legs, and one curls around his throat, cutting off any further protests. I command the shadows to hold firm but keep him alive.

The court falls into an uneasy silence. Some people look at me with surprise, some with horror. Ash spins around, sees the general with his hand still wrapped around his sword's hilt, and then spins back to me. Her eyes are wide, but a proud smile curves up her lips.

My skin prickles and I feel another gaze on me. I take one look over my shoulder and Aric quickly glances away, but not before I catch the pinched expression on his face.

"Thank you, Elana, for restraining General Calix." Father finally speaks, giving me an approving nod. I understand it to mean *don't let go of him yet*.

I reinforce the darkness, testing for any weaknesses as Father leans forward in his seat and addresses Aislinn once more. "Treason is a hefty accusation, Aislinn. Explain," he says.

"The general has been profiting off our smaller villages for years now, demanding payment for protection, which is their basic right as citizens of Adrithia. I have compiled signed complaints from over thirty citizens from two dozen villages. Their accounts are there." She nods to the stack of letters the courtier now holds. "And many of those I approached are willing to testify in person against him."

The general makes a noise of protest, struggling against his bonds. I tighten the one around his neck slightly. He sputters and goes white. I watch him squirm for a few more moments, reveling in his helplessness, before I loosen my hold and watch with satisfaction as he sucks in a breath.

"You have met these citizens firsthand?" Father asks, ignoring the general's plight.

Ash nods, her tone low. "I traveled to many of the villages, and from those I was unable to visit I received letters signed in blood, swearing their truths."

Mutters break out amongst the gathered nobles. Father motions for his courtier to step forward and grabs the first letter. He cracks the wax seal, opens it, reads, and sets it aside. He opens the next one and starts to read. His face remains like stone, impassive except for one muscle that ticks in his jaw with more and more vigor as he reads. Everyone in the hall waits with bated breath as he repeats this with the next ten letters. Finally, he puts them back into the arms of his courtier and waves him back as he stands.

It's customary that I stand when he does, so I rise as well. He addresses the room with a booming voice. "I have read enough of these firsthand accounts. The evidence is overwhelming, and because of this I charge General Calix with treason. He will be detained and will stand trial in two days. This is a serious crime and will be treated as such. Guards, take him to the dungeons."

Several household guards converge on Calix, and only when they have him firmly in hand do I drop the shadows. His face is red with rage as they drag him from the hall, as he loudly swears his innocence.

Father's face is set with a frown as he releases the court. They all bow and make haste out of the room. Only father's courtier, Ash, Aric, and I linger. The door closes behind the court members.

"I'm sorry Father, for making such a revelation at court, but I was worried he would try to flee if he got wind of our suspicion."

Father shakes his head. "There's nothing to apologize for. You did well. When you returned from the border of the Gods' Territory and told me I didn't want to believe you. But I'm proud of how you handled the investigation. I'm sorry the findings were correct. Calix served our family for many years. I can't believe I didn't know what was going on in my own kingdom, right under my damn nose."

"Don't blame yourself," Ash says. "Elana and I only discovered the treachery after staying at Harold's Hill and witnessing the consequences of Calix's actions firsthand. The village became a feasting ground for a giant scorpion."

"What will his punishment be?" I ask suddenly.

Father assesses me for a moment before answering. "Treason is punishable by death, but how would you sentence him, Elana?"

Of course he would make this a teaching moment. "I need more information first. Why did he do it? And where did the money go that he was conning from villages?"

"Why does that matter?" Ash says a tad sharply. "You saw the effect he had on Harold's Hill as well as I did."

I try and fail not to look shocked at her outburst.

"I'm not denying that his actions led to horrible consequences, but if he was doing it to support a sick family member, or giving money away to those in need, we should take that into account, right?"

Father and Ash answer at the same.

"No."

"Yes," Father says.

They both look at each other for a moment before Ash looks away. Father turns to me. "You're right, we should look into it more. Aislinn, can you talk to some of the captains and his close friends and try to get an idea of his possible motives?"

She doesn't look particularly happy about the assignment, but she nods and responds, "yes, Father."

It doesn't take long for her to dig up what Calix has been doing with the money. She meets with us the following morning. Calix's friends were all too eager to turn him in for favor in the princess' eyes.

She tells us that he purchased a brothel in Sandral and two more in Tierth. He spent nearly all of his free time at his establishments, abusing the women there, according to some of the men who had seen and heard him. Meanwhile, he would leave his wife at home for days at a time to care for three young children.

Ash already paid a visit to his wife and children. The conditions they live in are barely a step above squalor.

Laden with this information, the three of us come up with a punishment that isn't death, but is severe enough to be suitable for his crimes. It takes some convincing, but Aislinn eventually relents that death isn't the best option.

The morning of the general's trial, I send a fourth letter to Aidan. I don't know why I keep trying. He hasn't sent a single response yet. The disappointment weighs heavy in my chest, and I decide if I hear nothing back, this will be my final letter. Even the thought has my stomach in knots, but I don't want to seem desperate.

At the trial, Father looks resplendent in a dark blue tailored coat and pants. He looks imposing as he takes his seat on the throne. I take the cue to sit once he does, and Mother and Aislinn follow suit. The three of us wear simple dark blue dresses, and due to the formality of the event we're all adorned in our crowns.

The full court is present today. Noble men and women line the sides of the hall, to bear witness to the trial. Many nobles have traveled to Sandral for the ball, which is why we have the full house.

Calix is brought before us in chains. His normally clean-shaven face has several days' worth of stubble and his clothes are rumpled, but he still looks healthy.

The trial starts with a repeat of the accusations. Calix fiercely denies all of it. Letters are presented, and then villagers are brought forward to testify. It's lucky so many made it to Sandral in time, eight in total.

Their tales tell of different hardships, depending on which village they're from, but the one constant is that Calix charged them for protection services. Some villages paid, others didn't. Those that didn't were attacked by bandits or vicious monsters. Those that did lacked the funds to purchase enough food and fuel for the winter, and many villagers starved to death.

The crowd hangs onto every one of the villagers' tales. And how could they not? Their suffering is hard to listen to, but I force myself to hear every word they speak, to acknowledge all the wrong that has been done to them before we can begin to fix it.

Finally, several members of the army step forward and retell everything they've told Aislinn. A woman near the back, by the grand staircase, cries silently, dabbing at her tears with a handkerchief. I recognize her as Calix's wife, and my heart aches as she tries to hold herself together.

At the end of it all, Calix finally confesses with tears in his eyes, saying he owed money to some mercenaries and needed a way to pay it back. His addiction, as he calls it, started after he paid his gambling debts, and only grew as he could afford a more lavish lifestyle. Greed is his sin. He gets down on his knees and begs for his pathetic life.

I realize I pity him. Here is one of the most powerful men in Adrithia, and he's sobbing on his knees in front of the whole court.

"Guilty," someone calls from the back of the room.

"Guilty!" Another, louder voice takes up the cry.

Soon the hall erupts into chants of *"guilty, guilty"* and it's too loud to speak over. Father stands abruptly and holds his hand up to silence them.

"Lords and ladies of Adrithia, thank you for joining us to witness the trial today. Based on the evidence and Calix's own confession, I find him guilty of treason."

Cheers erupt from the gathered nobles. He raises his hand once more and silence falls.

"The traditional punishment for treason is death, but in this case, we believe death is too swift a justice." Father pauses and motions to me. "My daughter, Crown Princess Elana, has decided on a better sentence."

He motions me forward. When we discussed this punishment, we knew we had to spin it to make it sound more severe than death, which is exactly what I do. Father wanted me to be the one to announce the sentence to court. He said it will help them recognize me as the next ruler, and give me valuable speaking practice.

I let out a deep breath as I stand up, brushing down wrinkles in my dress. I try to channel some of Aislinn's effortless confidence, and my mother's grace.

"For this egregious crime, death is too easy," I say, addressing the entire court for the first time. "He betrayed our most vulnerable citizens, and for that he will have to make recompense. But a swift death won't erase the years' worth of suffering he caused. We therefore strip him of his lands and titles, seize his assets, and cut off his access to funds. He will always be known as a traitor. Furthermore, for the rest of his life, he will work to undo the damage he's caused to the impacted villages. He will build a small army outpost in each village and train a small regiment of soldiers there, under supervision of one of our trusted captains. We will use his own assets to cover the cost of the construction and to pay for the extra soldiers. Our least protected citizens will no longer live in fear. I know this will never be enough to repay them for their struggles, but I hope it will be a start. We must band together to protect *all* Adrithians."

The echoes of my voice ring out around me as I take a small step back, my role now complete. I'm not sure what to expect, but it certainly isn't the thunderous applause that follows my words.

I stand uncomfortably there for a moment before Father appears at my side. He waves some guards forward and they drag Calix from the hall.

Slowly, the nobility begins to filter out. I see Calix's wife start to leave too, her handkerchief pressed to her eyes.

"You did well, Elana," Father says, placing a comforting hand on my shoulder.

I don't want to lose sight of the woman in the crowd, so I answer quickly. "Thank you, Father. There's still one more thing left to do."

He follows my gaze, and nods when he sees the woman. "Of course, go speak with her."

I give him a quick smile and run down the hall, slipping between lords and ladies, who are all trying to congratulate me on a fitting punishment. I nod and smile as I weave my way through the crowd. The dark-haired woman is only a few feet in front of me. I lightly tap her shoulder, and she spins around, her eyes still filled with tears.

"Y-Your Highness," she stammers, bowing.

"Please, there's no need for that. I'm hoping you could accompany me to the gardens for a moment?" I ask, pulling her out of the way of the moving people.

She nods.

I smile and lead her to a side hallway, where we escape through a small, unadorned door. Outside in the gardens, I take in her disheveled appearance. I realize I don't even know her name. Aislinn always refers to her as Calix's wife.

"What's your name?" I ask her.

"Mira," she says, looking down at her feet.

"Mira, I'm sorry for the hardship this trial has caused you."

She shifts her gaze to my face. "It's not the trial that caused me hardship."

My eyes narrow out of confusion. "What has?"

"My husband is not a kind man to me, or to his children. I've always done my best to please him, but it has never been good enough," Mira rubs a spot on her shoulder. The action catches my attention and she averts her eyes, dropping her hands to her side.

"Has he been violent towards you?"

She doesn't speak, doesn't meet my gaze, only stares at the wildflowers growing around us. Her non-answer is practically confirmation. Rage boils over in me, but I've already ordered the sentence. I can't change my mind now, after promising he would keep his miserable life in front of the entire court. The only thing I can do for her is this.

"I'm sorry for all you've endured. I can't change the past, but I can make sure your future is more pleasant. Calix managed to hide away much of his gold from the brothels and his private army. Most of it will go back to the villages he harmed, but we would like to give a portion of it back to your family so you and your children can live comfortably. Furthermore, if you ever find yourself in need of work, there will be a position here for you in the castle."

Her gaze slowly raises back to meet mine and tears flow down her cheeks. She sniffles, and quickly presses her handkerchief to her nose. "Your Highness, thank you so much. I don't know what to say."

I give her a smile. "There's nothing to say. Take care of your family, and never worry about where the next meal will come from."

She reaches forward and takes my hand in her shaking one. "I'll never forget this kindness. If you ever find yourself in need of any assistance I can provide, I'll be there."

I squeeze her fingers and then send her to the royal treasury with a signed decree from my father. When I told him of my plans for helping Calix's wife, he immediately worked it out with our courtier. Turns out, Calix had squirreled away enough money to provide for more than a dozen families for several generations. Why he decided to keep that money from his own family is beyond us.

We also couldn't figure out why Mira had chosen to stay with him when he treated her so poorly but meeting her and seeing the phantom injuries he inflicted, I finally see why.

As I head back inside, I resolve to check up on her in a few months, to see what a life free from her husband's abuse will bring her.

CHAPTER THIRTY-FOUR

"Everything must go perfectly tonight." My mother's voice abruptly wakes me the morning of the ball as she charges into my bedroom. "Elana! Wake up! There's so much to do."

My eyes easily adjust to the darkness of my room. Candles are lit but still, darkness lingers. There's no way we're already behind schedule when the ball isn't until dusk.

"Get her up and dressed." My mother addresses someone in my sitting room before turning back to me. "No going back to bed. Today must go perfectly."

I groan and throw my covers back over my head until I hear her heeled shoes stomp out the door.

"Miss, I brought you some tea," Senara says from the foot of my bed.

I reluctantly sit up. "Thank you, Senara."

I grab the delicate cup from the tray she carries and take a sip, sighing with contentment. It's perfect. Ginger, but the bitterness is cut with a bit of honey. "Is it even dawn yet?"

"Afraid not, Your Highness. Your mother is...strict...about her schedule," Senara says, wincing.

A tired laugh bubbles out of me. "My mother's not here, Senara, you can insult her."

She hums innocently. "I would *never* insult the queen...to her face."

I nearly spit my tea out but swallow it through a cough. "You've been hanging around Aislinn too long. She's a bad influence."

She gives me a wink and then throws open the curtains. Sure enough, it's still pitch-black outside.

Senara turns and pulls something out of the bag she carries, wrapped in cheesecloth. It's a small, still-steaming loaf of bread.

"Oh, you are my favorite person." I tell her.

She gives me a dazzling smile. "Technically your mother forbade you and Aislinn from eating anything today until the feast tonight, but I know how cranky you get when you don't eat, so this is really to save everyone. I snuck it out of the kitchen when Gwen had her back turned."

I chuckle and snatch the bread out of her hands.

At that moment the door to my suite swings open and a disheveled Ash stumbles in.

"I don't see why we have to be awake this early. The party isn't until sunset. There's no way it'll take that much time to get ready. It's bad enough we have to wake up this early, but to *fast* all day too? It's absolute torture. Mother thinks it'll make our stomachs flatter, but all it's going to do is make me angry."

She stomps into my bedroom amid her monologue, and her gaze instantly falls onto the bread in my hands. "What is that?"

Not thinking twice, I hide it behind my back. "Nothing."

"Where did you get that bread?"

"Nowhere," I say, doing everything in my power to avoid looking at Senara as Ash prowls closer.

Her gaze whips to my lady's maid anyway. "Did you bribe Gwen?"

Senara is the picture of innocence. "Of course not, Your Highness. I snuck it out while she wasn't looking."

Ash lets out a bark of laughter. "Oh, I always knew I liked you."

Then she turns her attention back to me. "Hand it over."

"No." I throw back the covers, launching myself out of bed. I won't let her pin me into a corner.

"Yes," Ash says, stalking closer. Senara takes one exasperated look between us and hurries from the room. She's been my lady's maid long enough to know it's about to become dangerous.

"Absolutely not. Get your own. Senara stole this for me. Go ask your lady to get one for you." I pivot on my feet, keeping my side to the door, my escape route.

Ash notices at the same time and lunges for the door. My shadows wrap around her arms and legs, holding her in place. Her eyes go wide as I skirt past her and into my sitting area.

"Elana! Release me!" She grows angrier by the second. I chuckle and take a bite out of the bread, savoring it.

An animalistic growl escapes her lips as she thrashes ineffectively against the bonds holding her.

I rip the bread in half, inhaling the delicious steam, and then release Ash from her hold. I toss her half of the loaf. She catches it in one hand as she regains her footing.

Senara, from her spot near the corner, lets out an audible sigh of relief.

"This is for everyone's benefit," I tell Ash with a quick smirk at Senara. "I may get cranky when I'm hungry, but you, sis, get downright violent."

She flashes me a feral grin and tears into the bread.

Mother's idea of preparations includes a morning of following her around while she tells the staff to redo half of their hard work.

She hands Ash and I each a piece of parchment as we walk through the halls. "Here is a list of suitors for each of you who will be in attendance tonight. You will pick three from each list and offer them one dance. One only—we don't want to show favor towards any family until we've had the opportunity to evaluate a proposal."

"Mother, we've already discussed this." Ash tries handing the parchment back to her. "I will not marry anyone due to status or what they can offer the crown. Elana feels the same way. We will not be dancing with anyone this evening for the sake of a marriage proposal."

Mother stops in her tracks. "Aislinn, Elana, you are both princesses of Adrithia and the kingdom must have an heir. Stop pretending like this is some fantasy world where you get to choose what you want to do and who you'd like to wed. You've both known this since the day you were born. Your main duty is to Adrithia, and everything else falls dreadfully far behind."

"I would do anything to protect this kingdom. But marriage, Mother, should not be forced upon a woman no matter the circumstance," Ash says angrily.

"Don't be so dramatic. You act as if marriage is the end of your life. I see I've been far too lax with you two. So here is my command, as your queen. You will go to the ball and dance with three suitors from the options I've presented you with. If you do not, then so help me I will drag you to teas and luncheons where you'll have no choice but to entertain these suitors for the next year." She finishes her speech with a huff and spins on her heels, continuing along like she never paused in the first place.

There's no speaking to her when she gets like this, so Ash and I don't bother. We follow her with sour expressions.

We pass the courtier and I stop him before he scurries away, probably on some important business for Father.

"Any letters for me today?" I ask, trying to sound neutral, but from the look of pity on Ash's face, failing miserably at it.

"No, none today, Your Highness," he bows.

"What about any news from Ocarin?" I ask, trying not to think the worst.

He scratches his short beard and shakes his head. "We've heard no news from Ocarin since before Aislinn returned to escort you home."

I nod, doing my best to mask my disappointment. "Thank you."

He bows once more and takes his leave.

Still nothing from Aidan. I don't know what to think, if something has happened or if he doesn't want to see me. Even if he didn't want to see me, I would have thought he would have the courage to write back and tell me.

I push the unwelcome thoughts out of my mind. Finally, midday approaches and Mother returns us to our rooms with orders to get ready.

Senara helps me bathe and style my hair. She fashions it into braids and coils them onto the top of my head. It's similar to my presentation ceremony style, but this time I loosen them up when she's not looking, leaving a few wispy strands out in front of my ears and by my neck.

We don't worry about makeup, other than painting my lips a dark red and applying kohl around my eyes. The top half of my face will be covered by a mask tonight, anyway.

Mother enters my suite with the seamstress. In the woman's thin hands is my dress, *the* dress. It's the most stunning piece of clothing I've ever seen. She's truly outdone herself this time. Senara helps me put it on behind my dressing screen.

The fabric is soft and so comfortable as it pools on the floor at my feet. The skirts of the dress are light, not the dreadfully heavy fabric I'm used to wearing. Shimmering gold stars are woven into the material starting at my waist and trickling down until they disappear into the black near my feet. The dress is fitted from my bust to my waist, where the stars break through the black. The bodice sits low enough to show off my cleavage and meets at my shoulders, where it comes to points. Long, sheer sleeves are adorned with the same tiny gold stars that grace the skirts and bodice. Delicate gold chains cross my chest. The back is low and has more of the same gold chains between my shoulder blades.

"It's perfect," I tell the seamstress as I step out from behind my changing screen.

She beams and bows her head, then presents me with my mask. It's gold with black embellishments to complement my dress. It sits over my nose and extends past my forehead, where one black feather sticks out on the side.

I top off the look with a gold headdress designed to look like sunrays, extending from the crown of my head and fanning out.

I smile to myself in the mirror. My mother loudly complains about the colors behind me, expressing for the fifteenth time her disappointment that they aren't our family's silver and blues.

"It's amazing," I breathe, twirling around so the thin skirts billow out around me. I turn to the seamstress. "Thank you."

"It is an honor to have you wear my designs," she says with a smile. I'm sure it's also an honor to receive the hefty amount of gold these dresses cost.

But no one could deny that her work is immaculate.

Ash walks in at that moment, her dress catching the light from my windows and reflecting sparkles on the walls and ceiling. Her dress is a shining silver, with glimmering white gems woven into the sleek fabric. Thin straps hold up the low-cut bodice. The shimmering fabric, fitted to her body, falls to the floor and puddles around her. I've never seen her look so radiant.

"Ash, you're so beautiful," I tell her. "You shine like the stars."

She waves me off and gestures to me. "Thanks, but I think everyone will know true beauty tonight when they see you."

The seamstress hands Ash her mask, a dazzling silver piece to match her dress. She turns to my mother. "It's time to get dressed, Your Majesty."

Mother looks outside at the already waning sun.

"So it is. I'll see you both at the ball, on time." She emphasizes the last bit, then leaves my rooms in a hurry, the seamstress following.

"Is there any chance you think they won't notice if we ditch?" I ask Ash.

She turns doubtful eyes to me. "Absolutely not. I'll get blamed if you're not there, so you're going."

I sigh and throw myself onto my settee. My stomach makes loud unhappy noises. The weeks on the mountain taught me how to deal with hunger, but for some reason now it feels more painful. Perhaps because I've been smelling the kitchen since dawn.

Ash and I pass the time guessing who will wear what. We know that Mother's dress will be blue and silver. She never strays from what's expected of her. Ash thinks some other members of the court will try to wear our colors to gain our favor. I anticipate at least one lord and lady will end up looking like a peacock.

A knock sounds at my door. Aric opens it and clears his throat. "Your Highnesses, it's past time. Your mother is in a panic."

I look at the waning light from my window. "Shit. She's going to be furious."

Ash merely rolls her eyes. "When isn't she?"

As if we have all the time in the world, we slowly strut from the suite. I glance at Aric, who's all dressed up for the occasion in a pressed navy tunic. He even combed his blond hair back, something I've rarely seen. He wears his trademark sword at his side. I hope he will find some time to relax tonight.

"You look handsome this evening, Aric. Perhaps you'll find a nice, well-mannered lady to dance with." I keep my tone light, but I hope he catches my meaning. I hope he finds some *other* lady to dance with.

"Perhaps," he says. His stare lingers on me. I pointedly avoid meeting his gaze.

Aric escorts us to the entrance of the great hall where we're to make our grand appearance, and then leaves our side to go stand watch inside the grand hall. Mother and Father stand outside the large ornate double doors, arm in arm. Aislinn and I share a triumphant smile because her elaborate floor-length dress is a dark navy as we predicted. One quick look at Mother's face tells me she's furious.

"You're both late," she nearly snarls. Ash and I exchange glances.

"What's done is done, Maris," Father says, squeezing her arm with his free hand. "Let's get this over with. I'm starving."

Apparently, even the king had to fast today.

Mother gives a curt nod to one of the attendants, who bows stiffly and then rushes around to a side servant's door.

Triumphant music filters out to where we stand, and we hear it crescendo, then fade naturally. The doors in front of us swing open, and our courtier announces our entrance.

"Presenting His and Her Majesty, King Devon Sable and Queen Maris Sable." Thunderous applause rings out as my parents step through the doors, then descend the staircase.

"Don't trip, sis," Ash whispers to me, instantly putting fear into my head.

She squeezes my arm as we step forward.

"Presenting Their Highnesses, Crown Princess Elana Sable and Princess Aislinn Sable."

We walk forward as more applause assaults my ears. We smile through our masks and slowly descend the stairs. By some miracle, or perhaps the Goddess' intervention, I manage not to fall.

Once we reach the foot of the stairs we're immediately swallowed by the crowd. Men and women approach and tell us how radiant we look and how honored they are to have been invited.

Ash nudges me when we pass a lord and lady who are dressed like peacocks, and I choke back my laughter.

We smile, nod, and say polite phrases, casually moving through the lords, ladies, dukes, duchesses, and other distinguished guests. Many of them nudge their eligible sons forward, citing all kinds of accomplishments from being skilled at arms, to being talented artists, to being blessed with large feet or any possible feature that could be considered a benefit.

Ash and I shake hands, nod in thanks, and tell nearly everyone, "it's lovely to meet you," all the while trying to make our way to the buffet. After what feels like forever, we grab plates—unethically small plates—and pile them with as much food as they can take.

We escape to the nearest towering stone column and hide behind it while we devour our food. The music has picked up again and couples begin dancing. Ash and I stay hidden, trying to avoid the eyes of any bold men who have a notion of dancing with a princess.

Ash finishes her plate first, chasing it down with a flute of white wine.

"Your Highnesses," comes a tentative, nervous voice. Ash and I turn to see a young man standing behind us, head bowed.

Ash gives me a look like I'm forgetting something, and I start. "Oh, right." I swallow a mouthful of cheese and clear my throat. "Rise."

He straightens, and plasters on an anxious smile. "Forgive me for the intrusion. I'm Lord Kentswin, and I've come to ask if you'd honor me with a dance, Princess Aislinn."

Ash and I exchange a quick look. I don't recognize his name from my list of eligible bachelors, but I see a slow, saccharine smile spread across my sister's face. Ah, so he must be on hers. "Yes, I would love to dance."

The man, who is barely old enough to be called that, appears shocked. It seems like he hadn't thought Ash would accept. He's at a loss for words, and my sister's smile grows more feral.

"Shall we?" she asks. He nods, holding out his slightly trembling hand for her. She takes it and pulls him onto the dance floor.

I'm struck with a sudden pity for the boy. She's going to eat him alive.

I finish the food on my plate and adjust my mask. On the dance floor, Ash spins literal circles around the poor boy, who struggles to keep up. She tugs his arms and forces him to move with her.

Two of the young men I was introduced to on my way to the buffet are on the bachelor list, but neither one of them dared to even look at me. No one has approached me, but I catch occasional glances from the young men and eager looks from their mothers.

To my dismay, someone does approach me now, bowing low. "Your Highness, it's a pleasure to finally meet you. I'm Lord Percival."

A knot twists in my stomach, but I shove the feeling down and paste on what I hope is a friendly smile, even though internally I'm hoping Aislinn will show up and flash one of the daggers I know she's hiding under her dress to scare him away. "So we finally meet in person, Lord Percival."

He gives me a smirk and trails a salacious look up and down my body. "I know our engagement had to be temporarily put on hold while you were in the Gods' Territory, but now that you're home I look forward to resuming our courtship. A kingdom like Adrithia needs a strong King, and there's no one better suited to the task. Tell me, Princess, how many babies do you want?"

I balk, not sure I can believe the nerve of this man. But I can believe he's on his fourth or fifth drink, based on the smell of his breath. "Excuse me?"

He leans in close, the light of the nearby lanterns reflecting off his elaborate garb and mask. He's dressed in a ridiculously bright doublet, cerulean blue with silver accents. It's a gaudy take on my family colors. His sour alcohol breath threatens to gag me as he puts his face near mine, as if he's saying something scandalous. "It's obvious I'm a cut above the competition. None of your other suitors own a jewel mine. My family is the wealthiest here."

Before I have the chance to say what's on the tip of my tongue, Aric appears at my side, his hand on the hilt of his sword.

"Get lost, Lordling," Aric says.

Lord Percival puffs out his chest, raising a finger to respond, but Aric starts to slide the blade free from its scabbard. The lord deflates and scurries away without another word. I let out a long breath.

"Thank you, Aric," I say.

He doesn't respond, only nods his head and crosses his arms in front of his chest, facing the dance floor where Aislinn makes a fool of the boy who asked her to dance.

"I think she's enjoying herself," Aric says. A passing staff member, all dressed up in blue and silver, holds a tray of drinks out towards us. Aric grabs two glasses of wine and hands me one.

"Yes she is, although I don't think the same could be said of that boy she's torturing," I laugh and take a long sip of the wine.

It's sweet, with a hint of yellow coloring. I'm pretty sure this qualifies as a dessert wine, although I lack the experience to say for sure. Mother has only allowed one glass for Aislinn and I at dinners, and only of the dry reds that she loves. I was never a fan of the chalkiness. The smooth sweetness of this white has me taking another long sip.

"Your dress is so beautiful, Princess," Aric says, moving closer. I'm now trapped between him and the pillar I hide beside.

"Thank you," I say politely, drinking more wine to avoid having to speak. I drain the glass with a final gulp and attempt to turn the conversation towards someone else. "Have any of these noble ladies snagged your attention yet? I've seen a few of them making moon-eyes in your direction."

"No, I only have eyes for you tonight," Aric's voice is hoarse, and he clears his throat. He leans over me, staring down, as if he's about to whisper sweet nothings in my ear. I duck away from him and spot a table with glasses of pink wine. I trade a full glass for my empty one.

I look at the dance floor, trying to make desperate eyes at Aislinn for help, but she's in a battle of her own, as a new song begins and she gets swept up by a dancer who can nearly keep up with her. The boy she had been dancing with bows and walks slowly off the floor, red-faced and breathing hard. Ash dances like she fights, trying to out-maneuver her partner. The man beside her now has the speed and strength to almost match her.

Seeing I'll get no help from her on this, I drain the glass I'm holding in two gulps while I scan the crowd for any other escape route. A pair of golden eyes behind a black horned mask catches my attention. My feet move of their own accord, heading in his direction. Aric steps in front of me, blocking my path and view.

"Will you please do me the incredible honor of dancing with me, Your Highness?" He looks hopeful, pleading almost. It reminds me of when we were children, chasing after Aislinn and her latest maniacal idea that'd get us all into trouble.

I heave and give in. "All right, Sir Aric. One dance," I say, setting my empty glass down on a nearby table and extending my arm. At least this will count towards my three dances this evening.

His answering smile lights up his face as he takes my hand, leading me onto the dance floor as another joyful tune plays. I scan the crowd for the man wearing the horned mask but see nothing except nobles craning their necks to watch the princesses of Adrithia and their partners on the dance floor. No doubt I'm causing some gossip for choosing a guard as my first dancing partner, but I don't care. Let them talk.

I was never a talented dancer, and it seems like Aric isn't either. We're too rigid and mismatched in our steps. A few of my moves could even be called sloppy as we bump into another dancing couple.

"I'm sorry I'm not good at this," Aric says. There's a tint of pink to his cheeks.

"I'm not either, so don't worry. It'll give the court something to talk about."

He tugs me a little too hard into the next steps and I stomp on his foot with my slipper. "Sorry." I wince.

"I guess we'll have to keep practicing until we get better," he says. "We could practice every day if you'd like. I know it's too late to ask you to run away with me again, but we could still be together here."

A lump works its way up my throat and makes it difficult to breathe. I feel warm and uncomfortable, and I don't think it's all because of the wine. Suddenly, everything is too much, the crowd, the noise, Aric's hand on my back and his tight grip. I need to get away.

I drop his hand and step back, shaking my head.

His brows pull together and concern wrinkles his forehead. "Princess?"

"I-I need a moment," I say, backing towards the throng of onlookers.

"Then I'll go with you." He starts, moving in my direction.

"No." I say as firmly as I can. "Do not follow me."

He looks like he's about to protest, but I don't give him a chance. I turn on my heels, flick my fingers, and sparks of light, twinkling like stars, erupt from around the grand hall. People gasp and cheer in wonder, clapping as they enjoy the show I give them to cover my abrupt exit.

I escape out a side hallway and through a door leading to the gardens, where I rush to the section of night-blooming flowers. My first few calming breaths come out ragged as I do my best to center myself. I rip my mask off and wipe at the anxious tears that slowly trail down my face.

Footsteps sound behind me in the grass and I suck in a sharp, angry breath.

"I want to be alone, Aric," I snap without turning.

"If you didn't want me to follow, Magpie, you should have done a better job with the distraction. A few sparkling lights? It may be enough to keep the nobility's attention but I've had you in my sights all evening."

My heart stutters, and I feel my pulse flutter in my throat. He's here.

Thoughts eddy from my brain as I spin and launch myself at him. His golden eyes crinkle in amusement as he catches me. I slam into his muscular torso and he wraps me in his arms, lifting me off my feet. I breathe in deeply, the familiar smell of cedar overwhelming my senses.

"Magpie," he whispers into my hair. His lips touch the crown of my head and I shiver.

"Aidan, you're here," I say into his shoulder, where I've buried my head. The thought sinks in, and I pull back. He's here. Why is he here?

He's hesitant to pull back, but gently unwraps his arms after a few moments. He's wearing dress clothes—a long tailored black coat with gold embellishments, dark pants, and a belt around his waist with his mask tethered to it along with one of his daggers. He's devastatingly handsome, and I'm about to open my mouth to tell him, but a solemness in his eyes gives me pause.

"I've come to warn you. Adrithia is about to be under attack."

CHAPTER THIRTY-FIVE

I stare at Aidan in shocked silence. My kingdom is going to be attacked? By whom? I open my mouth to ask him, but another question blurts out instead, "is that the reason you didn't write me back?"

Aidan sighs, running a hand through his curly mess of black hair. "I didn't even realize you've been writing. I've been on the battlefield since my return to Ocarin. My mother...received word that there was going to be an attack, and we rushed to meet the threat with an advance guard."

He's been on the battlefield for weeks? My eyes rake over him from his dark, unkempt hair to black leather boots, searching for any signs of injury. Seeing none, I bring my gaze back to his face.

"Your mother received word or had a vision?"

Aidan gives me a long look, then lets out a humorless laugh. "It would have been nice of my mother to include me in her scheming. I didn't realize she told you about her visions, but I think you might be focusing on the wrong thing here."

"She didn't tell me as much as she allowed me to see her third eye. But you're right. I'm sorry. You've come from the battlefield, and now Adrithia is about to be attacked? Tell me everything," I say.

"Elana!" Ash's voice cuts Aidan off before he can start his story. "There you are."

The train of her silver dress is in her hands as she runs to meet us. She pauses as she sees who stands in front of me, dark hair reflecting the moonlight. She gives me a look that I know means I'm going to hear about this later.

Aislinn looks at Aidan and gives a wolfish smile. "Hello, Prince Aidan. Welcome to Adrithia."

Aidan, to his eternal credit, bows his head slightly to my sister, a smirk playing on his lips. "Princess Aislinn. It's a joy to see you, as always."

"I'm aware," she croons, then sharpens her tone. "Why are you here?"

"I was explaining to your sister that I've come here from the battlefield to warn you that your kingdom is in danger," Aidan repeats.

Ash drops her dress, instantly turning serious. "Is that why you haven't responded to any of my sister's letters?"

Aidan groans and rubs the bridge of his nose. "Yes, that's why I didn't return her letters. You two really like to focus on the details, don't you?"

"You're dressed for the ball. If you came here from battle, why aren't you clothed for war?" Ash asks, crossing her arms in front of her chest, staring him down. And to be fair, she has a point.

Aidan smirks, but it's me that he turns to when he answers. "I got information from a reliable source that there would be a masquerade event when I arrived. So I purchased some clothes in Sandral, and then borrowed an invite from a nobleman that I met in a local inn."

So, his mother told him about the ball and he stole an invite from some sad sap he happened to encounter on his way here. I smother a chuckle as Aislinn regards him coolly. To my surprise, she lets the issue drop.

"What's this about you warning us?" she asks.

"An invading force from the south landed on our southern beach weeks ago and started laying waste to every village in its path. My mother and I met them in battle with a group of our elite soldiers. With our combined powers we were able to drive most of the force back to the sea. They sailed further down the coast, where they tried breaching our borders again. We beat them back again, and again, and again. We suffered heavy losses. On their retreat, some of their forces split off. A few ships sailed to Hotharia, and a few headed to Adrithia. I rode straight here to warn you." He pauses, waiting for our reaction.

He left his own kingdom to warn us. A warmth fills my chest.

"Who attacked you?" Ash sounds concerned. Her tone makes me uneasy.

"We don't know. This enemy is unlike anything we've faced before. They flew no banners, and they didn't speak. They didn't give demands, or request gold or jewels. Killing my people and destroying the land seemed to be their only goal. We don't know where they came from other than the south. They don't tire and they fight like they don't feel pain or fear. They bleed like humans, but they don't act like us. It's like they're possessed."

Aidan's eyebrows pull together, and I can only imagine how many of his soldiers he watched die. He pulls his coat open to reveal a shoulder bag beneath. He opens it up and pulls out a wrapped bundle. "Their weapons contain some kind of lethal poison. One small scratch is a painful death sentence for our soldiers. Our best healers haven't been able to find a cure."

From the bundle he produces a thin, black dagger. Aislinn and I lean in close to inspect it. The edges appear wickedly sharp, but it's the sleek black metal that catches my attention. The flat sides of the blade seem to be emanating darkness. I hear whispers, something drawing me in. I can't quite make out what the rhythmic tune says. I know I could hear more clearly if only I touch the blade. Shadows rise up around me, responding to whatever is pouring off the blade.

"Do you hear that?" I ask, drawing my hand close to touch the dagger.

Aidan's voice shocks me out of my trance, "Elana, don't touch—"

When I am less than a finger's length away from the blade, purple energy leaps from it and sends a jolt of pain through my hand. I gasp and jump back, light subconsciously bursting from my fingertips. The surface of the blade ripples, and then the darkness within the metal fades as it returns to a normal silver color.

"What the hells just happened?" Aislinn asks, looking from my hand to the dagger.

Aidan's concerned gaze is on me. "Are you hurt?"

I stare at my hand, flipping it over, searching for the source of the momentary pain, but I find no marks. I'm completely unmarred. I hold it up for Aidan and Aislinn to inspect. "No, I'm alright."

"That blade was imbued with the poison that has been slowly killing my army. Whatever you did—" he stares at the blade, now shiny, polished metal "—seems to have expelled the poison from it."

I gape. "I have no idea what happened. It's like the light acted by itself, like it sensed the threat, and attacked it."

Aislinn lets out a sigh, "Elana, maybe we need to have a lesson on not touching strange objects that radiate evil."

A small smile pulls at Aidan's lips. "You're truly a wonderful being, Magpie." I smile back at him. It is such an incredible relief to see him again, even with the terrible news he brings. I stare at the blade again, trying to make sense of what the whispers meant.

"Did anyone else hear the whispering?" I ask, almost afraid to, since I know how crazy it sounds.

"The blade was…speaking to you?" Aidan quirks up an eyebrow.

"It sounded like chanting, or a song," I say, closing my eyes, trying to recall any words. But it all sounded unintelligible.

Aislinn and Aidan exchange wary looks. "No, there was no voice that we could hear," Aislinn says.

I shrug my shoulders. "Never mind, it was probably the wind or something."

"Will you meet with our father, Aidan?" Aislinn asks, saving me from my embarrassment.

"Of course I will. If you will have me, I'll stay until the King decides what to do. My kingdom is safe for now, but should that change, I'll leave to defend it."

Aislinn nods, turning her back. "I need to get back to the ball before our mother comes looking. I'll inform the king of your presence and request that we prepare guest quarters for you. Elana, before you come back inside, why don't you take Aidan on a tour of the gardens? They're nice and *solitary* this time of night." She walks away, swishing her hips like she hasn't embarrassed the daylight out of me.

Aidan chuckles and turns back to me. "Have I ever told you that I like your sister?"

"Try living with her." I fight the urge to roll my eyes and scoff. "But, on this she is correct. The gardens are one of the only places where we won't be disturbed or spied on."

I grab his hand without thinking and tug him through the towering arched trellis where clematis vines grow. The cobalt flowers wrap around the trellis and dangle down, touching the top of Aidan's head as we pass under them.

"Gods, you are radiant in that dress, Magpie," Aidan says as we walk.

I flash him a wide smile, then nod at him. "You clean up pretty nicely too…for a degenerate."

His answering laugh sparks pure joy within me. "I almost ripped that boy off of you on the dance floor when I saw what a fool he was making of you. What did he say for you to abandon him in the middle of the song? Not that I'm complaining."

"It doesn't matter," I say, because it doesn't. Nothing matters right now other than Aidan being here.

The moon is out, and it feels like the Goddess Nisha is watching as I bring Aidan to the fountain in the center of the rose garden. I can't believe he's here. Aidan is here, in my kingdom. It's almost like a kernel of myself has returned to me after these weeks apart. I didn't realize how much I missed him until I saw him again.

"You're here," I say, turning to face him.

"I'm here," he acknowledges, staring down at me with his molten gaze. "When my mother first had her vision, I was worried that all the kingdoms were under attack, but our scouts confirmed that it was only Ocarin. When the group of enemies broke off and headed towards Adrithia, I had to warn you."

"How large is the group?" I ask, trying to think of the questions my father or Aislinn would ask.

"Nearly a thousand. Not an overly large force, but trust me when I say it's more than enough to wreak havoc."

I suck in a breath, nodding my head. Goddesses, I can't believe my kingdom is about to be thrust into battle so soon after my return from the mountain. What if I'm not ready? What if my powers fail and-

Aidan suddenly grabs my hand and kisses my fingers. I shiver, the heat from his kiss lingering. "I can see that brilliant mind working. Do you really want to spend our alone time worrying about something that can wait until the morning?"

I suck in a breath. He's right, of course. I don't know how long I'll have him alone. "No, the only thing I want to think about is you."

He raises an eyebrow but seems to take it as an invitation. "Did you miss me, Magpie?" Aidan asks, grabbing my waist and tugging me to him so my back is against his warm body. One of his arms is across my hips, the other gently caressing my neck.

"No, of course not," I lie, because the truth is much more terrifying.

"No?" Aidan chuckles, his face pressing to the side of mine, his breath tickling my cheek. The air around us heats noticeably.

"You didn't miss these hands?" He moves his hand slowly down my neck, tracing my collarbone, then lower, caressing the metal chains of my dress and then lower still, passing over my breast. The sensation is overwhelming. Warmth pools in my core. Everywhere his hand goes, a trail of scorching heat follows. Not enough to burn, but enough to ignite me. I feel more alive than ever.

"Definitely not," I say through shortened breaths, closing my eyes. His hand slowly moves further south, trailing down my waist and to the tops of my thighs. I suck in a breath, willing him to go further.

"Well, then, maybe I should stop." He pulls back and releases me. I gasp and stumble as my weight returns. A chill takes hold of me. I whip around and grab the collar of his dress coat.

"Don't you dare stop," I say, crashing my lips to his.

Aidan groans against my lips and backs me into one of the many stone statues that adorn the garden. This one is partially covered with climbing hydrangeas, and the vines are all around me. He's careful to brush my skirts back as he leans into me so he doesn't step on the delicate fabric. Curtains of branches catch in my braided hair, but all that matters is Aidan. His mouth. His hands. His everything.

He pulls away from my lips to press steamy kisses down my neck and collarbone. It feels like the air is on fire around us. Shadows writhe around us, pushing against his back, pushing him closer to me.

"You've learned some new tricks," he says against my skin as I let out a breathy laugh.

The sound of a sword unsheathing from a scabbard shocks me. Aidan pauses with his mouth against my collarbone and snarls, readjusting my skirts as he shields my body from view. He turns around to face the threat, pushing me behind him.

"Unhand the princess!" Aric's booming voice sounds around us in the garden. He grips his longsword with two hands, aiming it right at Aidan's heart.

"Who the Hells are you?" Aidan asks, and the temperature around us spikes for an entirely different reason.

I shove myself in front of Aidan, holding my hands out to Aric. "Aric, wait!"

"Your Highness, are you alright?" Aric doesn't look at me, but glares daggers above my head at Aidan. He continues to point his sword.

"Yes, I'm fine, Aric," I say, crossing my arms in front of my body. Shadows play at my feet, mimicking my displeasure at being interrupted. "I'm perfectly safe, so put your sword away."

"Listen to your princess, guard. Your presence is unneeded and unwanted here." Aidan holds up a single hand and bright red flames dance above his fist.

Aric lowers his sword with a start. "P-Prince Aidan," he stammers, finally lowering and sheathing his blade.

Aidan glares at the sword, tracking its movements until it's safely in its scabbard. He extinguishes his fire.

"My apologies, I didn't know..." Aric trails off as if he isn't sure what it is he doesn't know.

"No, you wouldn't know, would you? I suppose I can't fault you for that, this time," Aidan says. Aric stiffens at the threat.

Before he can do anything foolish, like get himself killed, I let a flare of light flash from my hands. Aric startles and backs up, finally looking at me.

"Your Highness, apologies for the...interruption. I thought you were in danger." He looks at me with round eyes.

"Again, Sir Aric, I'm quite alright. I'll be inside with the prince in a moment. I'm sure you have other duties to attend to this evening. I'll look for you in the morning. You're dismissed." I'm rarely ever this formal with Aric, and a twinge of guilt sits in my gut with my words, but I don't want him getting himself in—literal—hot water.

Hurt flashes briefly in his eyes and he opens his mouth at once, but closes it. He looks between us again, and then asks, "how long will the Prince be staying here? So I can ensure that there are adequate guards assigned to the guest wing?"

I glance at Aidan, whose distaste is written all over his shadowed face. His gaze is on Aric's sword, though it's firmly in its scabbard. "Aidan will stay for however long he wishes. Goodnight, Aric."

"Goodnight, Your Highness." He takes the dismissal well, bowing sharply at me while keeping his eyes on Aidan. I wait for a few moments until Aric is out of earshot before I exhale loudly.

Strong arms wrap around my shoulders, pulling me against Aidan's warmth, his lips caressing my ear. He whispers, "I think I've made my first enemy in Adrithia. In almost record time too." His breath against my ear causes me to shiver and goosebumps to raise on my arms.

"You have a habit of causing trouble wherever you go, don't you?" I ask, teasing.

"Hmm," he murmurs against my hair, "I like the sound of trouble. Perhaps you'd like me to cause some more, *Elana*?"

The way he says my name makes my toes curl in my slippers. My breath hitches. I'd give anything to hear him keep saying it.

"I would love that, actually," I say, but pull away from him. "Unfortunately we've got a ball to attend. Since you decided to crash it, I'm assuming you intended to dance?"

A smirk lifts one corner of his lips. "Is this your way of asking me to dance with you?"

"I'm not asking. I'm informing. It's your duty to dance with me since you're a guest here. I want what's owed to me."

I wrap my fingers around his and tug him along. He doesn't resist and follows me with ease. We head back inside, where the noise threatens to overwhelm me, but I'm grounded in Aidan's touch. We put our masks firmly back into place before entering the hall.

"Ready?" I ask, looking at our entwined hands. I wonder if we should drop them.

"Let them see," he whispers, catching my gaze. "Let the court gossip and wonder who has captured their princess' heart. We'll give them a good show."

I laugh and step through the doors, side by side with him. The crowd parts for us as we head towards the dance floor. They crane their necks and stare at Aidan, whispering amongst themselves.

The orchestra maestro sees us approaching and quickly signals the end to the song. He waits for us to get into position in the center of the hall and murmurs something to the musicians, who shuffle the pages of their music quickly.

"Who is that masked man?" I hear over and over.

We stand facing each other, one hand raised toward each other while we wait for the music. Other couples give us a wide, respectful berth.

The instruments start their tune, beginning with the violin, and we start our dance. Aidan grabs my hand, leading me through steps that I normally would have faltered on. He uses the right amount of pressure to guide my body through spins and twirls. I trust him completely, and he doesn't let me misstep. I laugh, because I don't think I've ever been this happy at a party. My dress fans out around me, the black and gold swirling and catching in the light. I raise my hands mid-spin as the music crescendos and send golden sparks of light to the ceiling. They rain down around us in a shimmering arc, and I land back in Aidan's arms effortlessly.

The music starts to fade and Aidan draws me close, putting his forehead to mine. His grin shows off his dimple. We're both breathing hard. The song ends and the roar of cheers around me fades as Aidan and I drink each other in, sharing the moment.

"You are the most stunning dancer I've ever seen, Magpie," he says quietly.

"I only danced so well because I had the most talented partner to lead me," I respond. He lets out a low sound that sounds like an agreement. It makes me laugh.

We step away and he bows to me as I curtsy, and together we walk off the dance floor arm in arm as the next song begins.

My parents watch us, enraptured, from the side of the dance floor.

I turn to Aidan. "Would you like to say hello now, or later?"

"Now. After a show like that, I doubt it would be good form to avoid the king and queen."

I nod and pivot towards my parents. My mother wears a charming smile, probably hopeful that I've fallen for one of her top suitors.

The nobles who were speaking to my parents find somewhere else to be as we stop in front of them.

"Father, Mother," I say with a dip of my head, then gesture to Aidan, who stands noticeably relaxed next to me, as if he meets the monarchs from other kingdoms all the time. "May I present Prince Aidan of Ocarin."

Aidan lowers into a respectful bow. My mother's charming smile drops a fraction, which is as much surprise as she'll ever show. Her gaze slides to mine, in a way that says I'll also be hearing about this later. Father reacts with practiced ease, his smile widening as recognition sets in.

"Prince Aidan, welcome to Adrithia. Aislinn mentioned that we had a royal guest in our midst, but I wasn't expecting the heir of Ocarin," he says in a genuine welcoming tone.

"King Devon, Queen Maris, you must forgive my unannounced and uninvited arrival. I'm afraid I have urgent business with you, but it can wait until after the ball, of course," Aidan's voice is smooth and charming as ever.

My mother clears her throat. "Thank you, Prince Aidan. I'm sure you can understand the importance of events like this in finding suitable matches for our daughters. In fact, I just received a promising proposal from a duke's son for our crown princess."

My face heats with rage, and I glare at her. She stares right back.

Aidan, however, doesn't skip a beat. "I'm sure whoever Princess Elana chooses to wed will be worthy. I have never known her choices to be anything but perfect."

Mother narrows her eyes and her lips tighten the smile across her face. "How lovely."

Shadows creep up around me unbidden at my sudden anger with her. Father looks at the writhing pool at my feet and turns to his wife. "Maris, I believe it's our turn to take to the dance floor. Aidan, we look forward to speaking more with you once the guests leave."

Aidan dips his head in acknowledgement as my father leads my mother onto the dance floor. A new song starts and they begin their dance, one they've perfected over many years attending balls.

Ash finds us through the crowd and confirms that a guest suite has been prepared for Aidan. The three of us make small talk for the rest of the evening, Ash doing her best to be cordial to Aidan, until slowly guests start filtering out. I'm relieved to be next to him again after these weeks apart, his warmth a comforting sensation at my side. It's strange, but I didn't notice how profound of an impact he had on me while we were together until this reunion.

The hours tick by, and eventually all the nobles leave. I guess it's a few hours before dawn, judging by how tired I feel.

Finally, my parents approach us again and my father gestures down the hall, to his study. "Thank you for your patience, Prince. I hope you enjoyed the party. Let's find a place to talk."

CHAPTER THIRTY-SIX

The five of us sit in Father's study in our finery. This room is large, but the heaviness in the air makes it feel cramped.

"Thank you for meeting tonight, Prince Aidan. I'm sure you've traveled a long way and would enjoy some sleep, but I wanted to hear you out tonight rather than wait until the morning," Father begins. "Why have you come to Adrithia?"

"Ocarin was under attack," Aidan says, bluntly. "We beat the enemy back, but they sailed in the direction of Hotharia and Adrithia. I rode here from the battle to warn you."

There's silence, as Mother and Father take in this news. Mother looks at Aidan's clothes and voices the same concern Ash did earlier. "You're wearing formal clothes, yet you say you've come from the front?"

Aidan nods. "Yes, Your Majesty. I had information that Adrithia would be hosting a ball when I arrived, so I came prepared."

"How did that information get to you?" Mother's eagle eyes are sharp on him.

He doesn't shrink away from her intensity. He meets it head-on. "My mother, Queen Amira, is a seer."

Utter shock fills my mind. I never thought he would offer his mother's secret to my family, something I'm sure so few know about. The revelation causes Ash to gasp. My mother even blinks a few times, rapidly. Father leans forward in his seat, folding his hands together and resting his chin on his thumbs.

"Your mother is a seer?" Ash breathes out, as if needing to hear it again.

"Yes," he nods. "That's how she knew about the ball, and that's how she knows where the enemy will attack you in Adrithia."

"You say enemy. Who is attacking us?" Father asks, eyebrows pulling together.

Aidan takes a deep breath. "We don't know. They wore no sigil, carried no banner. They made no demands, and my mother couldn't *see* visions of their goal. All we know is they sailed from the south and started laying waste to our land. They kept no prisoners and stole nothing from the villages."

My father frowns. "Did you take any alive and question them?"

"We took dozens alive and questioned them with every tactic. They did not utter a single word. These humans, if I can even call them that, do not feel pain. They don't cry out when struck, and they don't falter with an incapacitating blow. They bleed like us, but they are not like us," Aidan's voice is grave as he addresses my father.

"This is difficult to believe without proof. Did you bring any?" Father asks.

Aidan shifts in his seat and pulls the wrapped dagger from his satchel. He unwraps the blade, which now looks completely ordinary, and then looks at me. "This was my proof. There was some kind of poison imbued in the blade. The metal was black and one tiny cut was enough to infect and kill anyone it came into contact with. Until your daughter somehow purified it."

Eyes turn to me.

"Is this true, Elana?" Mother asks.

I nod, shifting my gaze to look back and forth between my parents. "Yes, it's true. Aidan showed us the blade earlier, and it was solid black. It seemed to call to me, to my powers. When I reached out towards it, my light reacted and hit the blade. It turned back to regular steel and is now safe to touch."

I demonstrate this by touching the blade. Nothing happens.

My father turns to Ash and asks her, "you saw this happen too?"

She nods. "Yes, Father. It happened exactly as they both describe. The blade was black and there was an ominous energy around it until Elana touched it."

My parents exchange a concerned glance.

"Where does Queen Amira say Adrithia will be attacked?" Father asks.

"The enemy sailed south after they failed to take Ocarin. My mother had a vision that they would attack close to the border, east of your port city, Tierth. She said there is a stretch of land that slopes down to the sea. That is where they will strike."

As far as I know, the entire southern coast, except for the Shallow Bay, is a rocky cliffside, with no easily traversable land. I'm surprised they wouldn't attack Tierth itself, although the city has incredible defenses and is well-protected by our military.

"I know the spot," Father says with a heaving sigh. "I redesigned the landscape years ago to stop farmers' fields from flooding. It's the only accessible location on the south coast. How soon?"

"We don't know exactly. That's not how her visions work. She can see general seasons and can guess based on visual cues and events when things will happen. We know it will happen soon. We saw three ships sail south. My mother saw us arriving there before the battle, so we also know there's enough time for us to ride there."

"Us?" Mother's brow quirks up, her mouth a thin line. "That's a bold assumption."

"Maris, enough," Father says, leaning back in his chair. "It's Adrithia that's under threat. Of course we'll go."

Ash and I breathe a collective sigh of relief. Some of the tension in Aidan's shoulders subsides.

"Devon, what if this is a trap set by the Ocarins? To get us to rush to the coast, while they march their army to Sandral to lay siege to our castle?"

"I left my kingdom after weeks of war to help protect yours, and you think this is a ruse?" Aidan rises to his feet suddenly. The temperature in the room spikes, and there's fire in his eyes as he stares down my mother.

To her credit, she doesn't flinch. My father, however, stands to his full height. "I do not take kindly to my family being threatened in my own home."

The ground rumbles beneath our feet. Aidan doesn't take his eyes off my mother, but the temperature cools slightly. My father turns his attention to my mother. "Maris, I do not believe Queen Amira would scheme against us. Our alliance is strong, and I believe our daughters."

Finally, Mother sighs and looks away. "Very well. I guess we go to war, then."

"Yes, to war," my father repeats.

It takes us until dawn to make our plans. Father summons Aric, Rigel, and several army captains to his study, and gives a brief explanation and orders. We will ride out tomorrow morning. It'll take all day and night to prepare our regiment stationed in Sandral. We dispatch orders for the army in Tierth to ready to meet us. Aric takes the letters to the hawkery while the army commanders head to rally their soldiers.

When asked how many invaders will arrive on our shores, Aidan couldn't give an answer. He said his mother never saw the number of ships. But we know it'll be at least three. His mother didn't see the outcome of the battle but warned that we should double however many soldiers we think we will need.

Father asks Aidan if he will go back to Ocarin now that we've been warned. It's the smart move. He still has his kingdom to protect. If his mother's vision is wrong, or if they get attacked from another front, no doubt he would want to be there to defend his people. But Aidan's eyes flick to me and he declares that he will stay and help us fight.

"Why?" my mother asks, clearly still not convinced.

"Because it's the right thing to do," he says as we exchange a heated look that has me swallowing hard.

Mother tries insisting that I stay at the castle with her, but I refuse. I'm going. I can't let Father, Ash, or even Aidan risk their lives for Adrithia while I sit cozily in my castle. Father says it's my choice as future monarch. If there's a chance that I can heal the poison of their blades, I have to go. I may not be able to fight as well as Father or Aislinn, but my powers have the potential to save lives.

The sun has fully come over the horizon by the time we disperse to get some rest. I walk Aidan to his guest suite.

"Are you really going to fight with us?" I ask him as soon as we're out of earshot from the rest of my family.

"Yes, Magpie, I'll fight with you," he responds with a tired, wry smile. The look reminds me of how he appeared the last few days on the Gods' Peaks.

"You don't have to. I wouldn't blame you for going back to defend your own kingdom."

"I believe we promised to look for ridiculous excuses to spend time with each other," he says with a light tone.

I pause my steps, and he pauses with me. "I'm being serious, Aidan. Why are you really doing this for Adrithia?"

His gaze is penetrating as he meets my stare and finally sighs. "It's still the right thing to do, Elana. If I am selfish now, tuck tail and scurry back to my own kingdom, how am I setting an example my people will follow? If the worst were to happen, and Astrellia gets launched back into another great war, what good is it to be selfish?"

Aidan rarely shows this side of himself to the world. But I've seen it before, when he opened up about Nadia, when he told me about his family, and when he helped me control my darkness in the woods. I believe him.

"I'm also going to protect you." He steps closer, and cups my chin with his fist so I look nowhere but at his face. His thumb lightly caresses my lips. "There's no way I could live with myself if you went into battle against those things alone."

I melt into his touch. "You know I wouldn't be alone, right? My sister will be there. My father, too, and our army."

"Hmm, yes, but they're not me," he says and presses his lips softly to mine.

I can't argue with that.

The kiss is soft, sweet, and over before I get a chance to deepen it. That one kiss erases the lingering sadness of missing him these past few weeks. I smile up at him and motion down the hallway. "Your door's on the left."

He gives me a nod and moves towards it. "Where can I find your room?"

I point down the hallway. "All the way at the end of this hallway, past the grand staircase. First door on the right."

"Then I'll see you in a few hours, Magpie. Get some sleep," he says, opening the door.

"Goodnight, Aidan."

"Goodnight Elana."

CHAPTER THIRTY-SEVEN

I fall asleep quickly but wake after only a few hours. My nerves prevent me from falling back to sleep. Senara helps me brush out my tangles of hair, snarled from sleeping in braids.

A knock sounds at my door, and Senara answers it. She lets Aric inside, who sees me still in my nightgown and blushes, turning away.

"Your Highness, I'm sorry to disturb you. I wanted to apologize for last night."

So much had happened last night that I almost forgot about the uncomfortable dance and even more uncomfortable interruption. "It's alright, Aric."

I stand up and throw a wool coat over my gown so he doesn't feel embarrassed. Senara, helping me get ready for the trip, places a few clean shirts in the same pack I used for my trip to the Gods' Territory.

"I still wanted to say I'm sorry. I can't stand the thought of us being at odds and—" he sees the pack and his forehead crinkles in confusion. "Are you packing?"

I figured he would have caught on, considering he was there for the conversation with the war council. "Yes. I'm leaving with my father and our army."

Aric's eyes go wide. He lunges forward and catches my arm. I look up at him in shock. "Princess, no. You can't go. It's too dangerous."

"Aric, let go of me," I say sharply. He releases me and stares down at his hand like he didn't mean to grab me. "I'll be perfectly safe. My father, sister, and Aidan will all be there. Besides, they won't let me on the battlefield. I'll be back with the healers, treating the wounded."

"But if something happens to you, all will be lost," he insists.

"Look, I know you're concerned, but we're going to be okay. We're well prepared for the attack, thanks to the forewarning from Aidan," I explain, hoping to quell his fears.

"That's what I'm worried about. Do you really trust him? You've known him for less than two months. Why would he claim to help a rival kingdom?"

I shake my head. I'd already heard enough doubts about him from my family. They don't know him like I do. "Aidan has earned my trust over and over again. He is risking his life to help us because it's the right thing to do. Now unless you have anything constructive to say to me, I have to get back to work. I leave in the morning, and I need you to stay here and protect my mother."

Aric looks even more thrown off by this. "Princess, my duty is to protect *you*. Your mother has her own guards. I must go with you."

"No. While we are away, the capital will be even more vulnerable. I need someone I trust to look after this castle, my mother, and this city. We're only taking the army with us, so Sandral's guards will remain, but they need someone to lead them while we're away. I trust you to do this, Aric."

He stares at me for a long moment before he relents and nods his head, defeated. "As you wish, Your Highness."

Aric leaves and I finish packing with Senara. She flashes me a few meaningful looks.

"What is it, Senara?" I ask, trying to avoid her gaze as I pack medicines carefully into my satchel.

She clears her throat delicately. "Something has changed in him, Your Highness. Something that worries me. Ever since you left, he's been different."

I've noticed it too. Like the friendship that existed between us before this has shattered, and in its place is only a man pining after someone he can't have. I keep hoping our relationship will return to the way it was before, but so far it hasn't.

"I've seen it, too. I don't know how to fix it."

She considers this, folding my leather training pants into a small ball so they easily fit inside the pack. "Sometimes, things that are broken cannot be fixed. Sometimes they can only be let go."

I stare at her for a moment and then give a short laugh. "I need to talk to you more often. You're wise beyond your years."

She gives me a delighted smile as we finish packing.

A little while later I find myself knocking on the door of the guest suite. A bed rumpled Aidan opens the door, a smirk pulling at his lips. "I should have known you couldn't stay away from me for long."

I roll my eyes at him. "I came to see if you needed anything before we set off tomorrow?"

"No," he growls, voice low, leaning against the doorframe. "Unless you're on the menu, Magpie."

"Not here, you degenerate. The walls have ears."

He lets out a hum. "Yes, I know. Your guard has been making the rounds outside my door quite often."

"He what?" I ask sharply.

Aidan takes a step back, gesturing to the guest suite. I follow him inside and he shuts the door behind me. "How well do you know him?"

"I've known him since we were children. Why?"

"The great sword he carries, it looks to be of excellent make. Was that a gift from your household?"

I narrow my eyes. "No, he brought that with him to the city when he was a child. He said it was a family heirloom."

He considers this before nodding. "Be careful around him. The people we trust most have the capacity to hurt us the most."

Inwardly I sigh. I've heard more warnings about Aidan and Aric in the last day than I care to in a lifetime. It's making my head spin. I trust both of these men with my life, but they're making it incredibly difficult to want to be around them right now.

Before I have a chance to say so, there's a knock on the door. Aidan raises an eyebrow at me and moves to open the door once more.

"Is my sister in there?" Aislinn's voice slices through the tension with its sharpness.

"Do you two have some sort of sense to find each other, or are there spies I'm not seeing?" He steps back and she brushes past him into the room.

"I don't need spies when you two are so incredibly obvious," she retorts. I see something large and black in her hands.

She walks up to me and holds it out. It's a piece of armor. Specifically, a breastplate. There's a golden design of a sun framed by wisps of dark shadows stitched into the thick leather.

"This was the best the blacksmith could come up with on short notice. When we get back from this battle, we'll have to commission an official set, but for now, this will do. The rest of the set is still being made, but he got this done first so you could try it on."

I stare in awe at the craftsmanship. "Help me put it on. I don't know how."

She smiles and unbuckles the sides, telling me to put my arms out. I do and she slides two pieces over my head until they rest on my shoulders. She fastens the buckles on the sides and walks around me, inspecting it from every angle.

The leather is stiffer and heavier than I thought it would be. I rap my knuckles against the front of it, and it makes a dull clanging noise.

"There's metal underneath the leather, to give extra protection against blades. We hope you won't be anywhere near the fighting, but in case you are, we couldn't have you going to war vulnerable," Ash says.

I look around for a dressing mirror and finally spot one in the corner. The woman staring back at me appears strong and unafraid. I catch Aidan's eyes in the reflection. He gives me a half-smile and a shallow nod.

"A perfect fit," he says, and Ash agrees with him.

I glance at the armor again. The reality of wearing it, of preparing for battle sinks in. I've been trying to repress the feelings, but deep down I'm terrified. I take a deep breath to steady myself. I can't show this fear to anyone. Not to our army, not to my parents, not to Ash or Aidan. I must show strength, because that's what a monarch does.

"I hope you don't see battle to know how effective it is," Ash says, and I give her a wobbly smile.

I secretly hope not either. Unlike my sister and father, I'm not skilled with weapons, and while this power makes me feel strong, I don't know if I could kill with it. And from what Aidan described of his recent battles, killing blows are the only ones that will stop this enemy.

Instead of focusing on the upcoming fighting, I think of the healer's tent and all that I will need. We've already packed dozens of cots and all manner of medicine and clean bandages. We will need clean water when we get there and lots of grain alcohol, both for cleaning tools and for easing the pain of the injured and ill.

I flex my fingers, feeling the well of light power underneath my skin. I remember how I purified the blade, and wish I had more time to explore this gift. If Clarisse were here, she would no doubt help me figure out how the purification works.

"El?" Ash's voice breaks me out of my reverie. "Where did you go?"

"Oh," I say suddenly. "I was thinking about Clarisse. Do you know where we can find her?"

Ash furrows her brows. "I might be able to send a letter to her. Why?"

"I need her. She's the most skilled healer in Adrithia. I don't know how my powers work for purifying poisons. She might be able to help me develop them."

My sister nods. "Okay, write the message to her and tell her where to meet us. Then meet me in the kitchen. I'm going to run your armor back to the blacksmith."

She gestures at me to lift my arms and I do. She unbuckles the breastplate and takes it with her as she rushes out the door.

"Is Clarisse your healing master?" Aidan asks when she's left the room.

"Yes, she used to live in the castle until my mother kicked her out. That was a few years ago. But if anyone can help me figure out how to use this power, it's her."

"Then I hope she gets your message."

I find some parchment and ink in the guest suite and scrawl my message. If she gets this letter in time, I have no doubt she will come.

Aidan and I walk to the kitchen, where Ash meets us. She hands the letter to one of the kitchen staff, a man who's chopping a large pile of carrots. She says a few words to him, hands him a coin, and he nods. She tells us he's a friend of Clarisse's and knows how to find her quickly.

We spend the rest of the day checking on our soldiers and supplies. The afternoon passes in the blink of an eye. The closer we get to nighttime, the more my anxiety grows. But I stomp it down, refusing to allow it to the surface.

After dinner, I'm so exhausted that I nearly stumble down the steps, and only Aidan's strong hand prevents me from taking a tumble. He walks me to my rooms and we say goodnight. We share the briefest kiss before Ash walks down the hallway, mumbling something about doors existing. Thoroughly embarrassed, I retreat into the comfort of my suite.

I toss and turn, but Senara must have been sent by the Gods, because she appears with a cup of calming lavender tea. The mixture of herbs puts me to sleep within moments.

"El, wake up, it's time to go."

I peel my heavy eyelids open to see Ash's face hovering over me, candlestick in hand. Her blonde hair is neatly braided and she's clothed in riding gear.

I sit up and reel slightly, a wave of dizziness knocking me off-kilter.

Ash braids my hair for me while I eat a few bites of egg and bread. My stomach has a sour feeling, so I'm careful not to put much into it.

I dress, attaching my twin daggers to my hips once more and grab my satchel from Senara. There are tears in her eyes as we say goodbye again. She won't be coming with us. War tents are no place for a lady's maid. The preparations bring back memories of when I left for the Gods Peaks, only this time the stakes are higher. Father is confident in our victory, although I can't help but notice Ash's assessing and pinched looks at our plans when she thinks I'm distracted.

We leave my rooms and nearly walk right into Aric. Dark circles sit under his eyes and it looks like he hasn't slept.

"Aric, are you here to see us off?" Ash asks him with a wry smile.

He doesn't look at her or acknowledge her. His pleading stare is trained on me. "Please don't go, Princess."

"We've already had this conversation, Aric. I'm leaving, and you can't change my mind."

"It's not safe, please."

Ash steps in front of me. "Do you doubt my ability to keep my sister safe?"

"Or *my* ability?" Aidan's voice sounds from the opposite end of the hall. He walks with a confident swagger and a dangerous smirk. The passageway warms in his presence.

Aric pales. "No. Of course not. It's been my job to keep Elana safe for over a decade, and that's all I'm trying to do."

"Do you know something we don't about the invaders?" Aidan asks with narrow eyes, stopping next to me.

"I know that it's a battle, and battles are bloody and dangerous. She shouldn't be anywhere near a fight like that."

I take a step forward. "Why shouldn't I? Some soldiers in our army are younger than me, and they're women, too."

"They've had years of training. I'm only trying to look out for you," Aric pleads. His large eyes remind me of Rufus when he begged for table scraps.

"Like I told you before, I'll be in the healer's tent, helping the wounded. There's nothing to worry about." I try to convince him as much as myself. "I hope you guard my mother as closely as you've guarded me. We have to go. I'll see you soon."

He stares at me for a few more moments before bowing his head and stepping to the side of the hallway.

Mother is at the stables with Father. They're locked in a tight embrace when we approach, whispering words to each other. It feels wrong to interrupt this moment, so we hang back until they release each other. My mother hugs Ash and me and kisses our cheeks. She even gives Aidan a brief nod.

Our horses are already saddled. My heart warms to see Misty again after a few weeks without riding her.

We meet up with the army on the south end of Sandral, where they've been gathering supplies. It'll take six days of travel to reach the coast, with us only stopping a few hours each day to give the horses and us riders a rest.

Large carts carrying tents, food, weapons, and medical supplies are pulled by several teams of horses at the back of our procession. Because of our need to arrive as quickly as possible, we could only bring mounted troops. About three quarters of our force are foot soldiers and had to remain behind.

Since we're also pulling warriors from Tierth and have two strong elemental wielders on our side, we believe this will be more than enough to drive the attackers back, whoever they are.

That mystery nags at us all. We feel like we're going in blind, despite the knowledge Aidan has passed onto us. It all boils down to the unknowns. We don't know the enemy, or why they're attacking us. It sets us on edge.

It's early morning when the tall marble towers of the castle finally disappear behind us. I turn to Ash, who gives me a slight smile, and Aidan, whose expression holds a grim determination. Together, I hope we're enough to save the kingdom.

CHAPTER THIRTY-EIGHT

It's been five and a half days since we left Sandral. According to my father, we've been making good time. We should reach the coast early tomorrow morning. We stop early tonight, allowing the horses and soldiers extra rest before the last push.

Ash and I set up our shared tent in between Aidan's and Father's. It's a difficult task when Aislinn redoes everything I touch. First the stakes aren't in the exact spot she told me, then the canvas was crooked, then the ground wasn't flat enough for her. Eventually I sigh and raise my hands, admitting defeat. It's best to let her take charge rather than argue.

We set our last stake in the ground and a large fire breathes to life behind us. Aidan somehow got his tent set up by himself and started cooking in the time it took both of us to do one thing.

Father leaves to make the rounds among our soldiers. It's a nightly ritual for him, one that he says boosts morale and keeps loyalty high. I offer to go with him, but he tells me to stay and relax. I understand what he leaves unsaid. Soon, there won't be any relaxing.

Ash, Aidan, and I sit on the ground and eat. My nerves grow more weary by the hour. All around us is a flurry of activity. Some people eat, some people drink and dance, some people sit by themselves and look like they're about to cry.

"How are you supposed to feel before a battle?" I ask them.

They glance at each other with a shared expression that to me looks akin to shared concern. Though Ash has never seen a war, or even an intense battlefield, she has killed men, and she's had war training. Considering Aidan is the only one among us who has been through an actual battle, he has firsthand knowledge. She gives him a brief nod.

"Nervous. Ill. Some people vomit before battle. Others drink. Some fuck. Some train with their weapons, and some prefer to stare up at the sky wondering when it will be over. There's no right or wrong way to feel about going to fight. Whatever you feel right now is perfectly normal."

I nod and flash him an uneasy smile.

"Aidan's right. It doesn't matter how many battles you've been in or how talented a fighter you are, your mind will react how it chooses to," Ash says. "Only experience can temper that response."

We head to our tents early with the intention of being fully rested for tomorrow. I'm exhausted after the full day of riding, but I roll from side to side on my sleeping mat. Ash snores softly on the other side of the tent.

After what seems like hours of tossing around, I admit defeat and crawl out of the tent and into the cool light of the full moon. The cool night air kisses my skin and I instantly relax, letting out a deep breath.

Aidan sits by the fire, watching the flames. When he notices me, a slow smile spreads across his face.

"Can't sleep, Magpie?"

I smile in response. We've been here before.

"Take a walk with me?" I ask, and he's at my side before I can utter another word.

Our camp rests in the middle of a large open field. On the far side of the field is a tall, grassy hill, and that's where I lead Aidan.

"So why can't you sleep?" I ask him.

Aidan is quiet for a few beats. "I lost friends during the last battle. My powers weren't enough to save them. I can't bear to lose anyone else."

I risk a glance up at him, and his eyes are sad, but his fist clenches on his sword's hilt.

"I'm so sorry about your friends, Aidan. Will you tell me about them?"

He's silent for a moment. I can only imagine what's running through his mind—probably memories he'd rather forget. "It's okay if you don't want to. I understand."

"No, I want to. I just don't know where to start..." He trails off, then takes a deep breath. "There's Zayne, who was one of my coterie, my most trusted advisors and warriors. We've all known each other since birth. Zayne was the youngest of us and was always trying to prove himself, even though he didn't need to. He was one of us, through and through. He was the first to charge into the onslaught on the first day. A few minutes into the fighting he got nicked with a blade. He collapsed a few minutes later. Within an hour, he was dead. I was there when he took his last breath. It was the worst moment of my life."

I grab for his hand and squeeze it.

"Zayne's death was the first. I lost several commanders and more than a few gifted warriors. People who I had trained, or trained alongside me since we were children," Aidan takes a long, slow breath.

"I'm sorry, Aidan," I say again, because I'm not sure what else to say, but I try anyway. "We will make their sacrifice mean something. We'll stop them."

He gives me a sad smile. "I know we will."

We lapse into a brief silence and Aidan seems to collect himself. "Your turn. Why can't you sleep?"

We reach the other side of the hill, and I sit in the grass, staring up at the stars. Aidan sits next to me.

"I'm afraid," I barely whisper.

Aidan hears. "I was scared, too, when I went charging into the fight. War is not easy. But we'll make it. We'll survive."

He grabs my hand and kisses the top of it gently. His breath tickles my skin, and this little act sends sparks of heat to my chest. My breath quickens. I've been so anxious about the upcoming battle that I haven't had time to think about Aidan and me together again.

We're alone on this hill, and now I only want to think about us. If there's a chance we're going to die tomorrow, I'll not die without finishing what we started on the Gods' Peaks weeks ago.

"Aidan," again, my voice is hardly a whisper. "I want to be with you tonight."

"You *are* with me, Magpie," he says in a playful tone.

I groan and roll my eyes. "You know what I mean, degenerate."

He grips my hand tighter, then leans over me in the grass, trailing butterfly kisses from my hand to my neck. He whispers against my skin. "You're sure?"

"Yes," I breathe, which turns into a moan as he captures my mouth with his own.

With barely a thought, I raise a wall of shadows around us, cutting us off from view in case anyone decides to take their own midnight stroll. Aidan creates a few fires around us, glowing dimly above the grass.

I bite down gently on Aidan's lip, and he groans into our kiss. One of his hands grips my thigh, the other gently teasing my breast. His fingers brush my nipple and I gasp. He swallows the sound like he wants to taste it.

He unbuttons my top with one skilled hand, and my fingers fumble for his buttons for a few moments before he chuckles and pulls his shirt off over his head.

I gape at his chest. His long scar is on display, and there are several barely healed bruises across his abdomen. My fingers graze them and his muscles stiffen. He lets out a short, breathy laugh as I hit a particularly sensitive spot. He stares down at me, taking in my form.

"Gods, you're so beautiful, Elana," he says. He kisses back down my neck, to my chest, then gently sucks the peak of my breast into his mouth.

The feeling sends a shockwave of pleasure throughout my body. I grip his hair and let out another moan. His other hand releases my thigh and moves to the waistband of my pants, slipping underneath the fabric.

I release his hair and undo my pant buttons, sliding them down.

"Elana, wait, I'm not taking any tea." Aidan trails off, and I know what he's saying—asking, really.

"I am," I whisper against his lips. I've been taking tea since Clarisse taught me how to make it. It helps regulate my painful cycles, while also preventing pregnancy. "Now don't make me beg, Aidan."

His laugh rumbles against my lips. "Only in my dreams."

My fingers move to grasp him. He growls his approval. When our clothes are off and nothing separates us, he flips us over so I'm on top. His impressive length presses against me.

I lower myself onto his hardness and the world comes apart. I dig my nails into his shoulders at the feeling. There's pain at first, but it's quickly overwhelmed by pleasure I've never known before.

We move against each other in perfect rhythm. A wave builds inside of me, and I make a noise deep in the back of my throat, moving my hips faster. Suddenly Aidan flips us once more, using the leverage to drive himself deeper, deeper.

Finally, the wave crests and stars burst around us. I cry out and he covers my mouth with his. I'm still reeling when the flames explode upwards and he follows me into pure bliss.

We lay in the grass, our limbs tangled together. My eyelids droop slowly, but I trail my fingers over his bruises again.

"What are these from?" I ask.

"The last battle in Ocarin. My armor stopped the piercing blow from a sword, but it still hurt like Hells," he says, still sounding slightly breathless.

That rattles me. He was so close to dying during the battle. I sit up and stare down at him.

"Promise me you'll be careful, Aidan. Don't do any heroic shit and get yourself killed."

Aidan trails his fingers across my back in a soothing motion. "I promise, Magpie."

I wake up at dawn to a warm feeling surrounding me. I take stock of everything in a second. I'm curled up in Aidan's arms on the soft grass. We managed to put our clothes back on before falling asleep, which was a miracle considering that neither one of us could keep our eyes open for longer than a few seconds. My shadow wall dissipated sometime during the night, but luckily there's no one around, because this is a bit of a compromising position for a princess.

My movement causes Aidan to stir. His hand tightens around me slightly and he whispers into my sleep-rumpled hair. "Good morning, Magpie."

A flash of heat washes over me at his low, suggestive voice, and I want nothing more than to repeat last night with him all day locked in pure bliss, but we have a battle to fight.

"We have to get back to camp. The army will be waking soon," I say.

Aidan sits up. "I would burn the entire world down if it meant I could stay right here with you forever."

"We've got a war to win, then afterwards we can talk about spending a whole day together. No burning necessary."

We share a long, passionate kiss, and then force ourselves up to face the day. I tell Aidan to go around the field and walk back into camp from a different direction, as a precaution.

Ash is awake and packing up our tent when I get back. "Where have you been?"

"I went for a walk to calm my nerves," I say as casually as possible, moving to help her roll up the canvas.

"Oh, really? An all-night walk?" Her eyebrows are high, and I blush under her eagle-eyed stare. "Relax, I'm not going to rat you out, El. You deserve to be happy. But also be careful."

I let out a low laugh. "I always am."

Aidan appears a few moments later from the opposite direction I came from, and Ash gives him a stare. "This should be obvious, but if you hurt my sister, I'll flay you alive."

"You're right, it is obvious. I have no intention of ever hurting Elana," Aidan stares right back.

The two stand at an impasse for a moment, until Father approaches with his horse, breaking up the tension. There's a flurry of movement as tents are packed, fires doused, and horses mounted.

Ash helps me don my full set of armor, since no one is sure we'll have time when we get to the coast. To my utter surprise, it's not uncomfortable. It fits like a coat and the shoulder and arm guards don't weigh me down or hinder my movements. The chest piece, while heavier than any clothing I wear, doesn't prevent me from sitting or bending over. Even the leg guards are comfortable. I'll have to petition to raise the blacksmith's wages when we get home, because this craftsmanship is impeccable. My daggers are at my hips again, and I pat them, feeling a comforting warmth through the leather sheaths.

The procession of soldiers is noticeably quiet today, as if the anticipation of the up-coming fight weighs heavily on everyone's shoulders.

It's midday when a shining, sparkling mass appears in the distance. Father halts the procession and orders camp to be set up on the opposite side of a small ridge, and for preparations to begin. He nods to a few of the high-ranking army commanders and us to follow him. We canter down to the coast.

The rocky shoreline becomes visible, and with it a large patch of sloping land that runs down to a sandy beach. The slope is about as wide as our castle, with two large, protruding cliffs on either side of it, making an imposing wall.

The sea is beautiful. A brilliant cerulean color with a wide, golden sand beach that expands out into the shallow waters.

"Sir," one of the military commanders says. "You could raise the cliffs again and cut off their access."

It's something we discussed before. Father could certainly do it.

"If we prevent them from breaching here, they could sail back to Ocarin, or sail a day west and attack Tierth, putting our most populated port city in jeopardy. We will stop them here. Drive them away for good and leave no survivors to take information back to wherever they're from."

The commander that spoke up nods his head. "Yes, Sir."

I stare off into the distance of the great blue expanse. What other continents exist out there? To my knowledge, there are no other lands close to ours, which is why peace on Astrellia is so important to our survival.

As I gaze out, a half dozen black dots appear in the distance. I blink and narrow my eyes, trying to discern if they're a distant sea mirage. The shapes slowly take form.

"Father," I say, pointing at them.

He unhooks a spyglass from his belt and aims it at the dark shapes.

"Ships," he confirms in a tight voice. "Six of them."

Six ships. Not three, which nearly overtook Aidan's advance guard.

"Can you see any sigils? Are we sure they're the enemy?" Aidan asks.

My father looks again. "They're flying plain black colors. Wait, two of them have sigils—"

"Father?" Ash asks, putting her hand to her eyes, trying to block out the sun to see further.

"Two of them fly Hotharian banners."

CHAPTER THIRTY-NINE

We all gape.

Two Hotharian ships sail for our coast, along with four others from lands unknown.

"What?" Aidan demands, anger darkening his expression.

Father hands the spyglass to Aidan, who takes a long look. His snarl of rage is enough to confirm the sight. "Those traitorous bastards."

"They'll pay for this," Ash says viciously. "The fools."

Father turns his horse sharply. "Back to camp, with haste."

We ride back as quickly as our horses can carry us. "Elana, see to the healer's tent. Make sure preparations are complete. Aislinn, follow me, we will organize the lines. Aidan, I do not give you orders, but you might want to send a letter to your mother. Let her know of the betrayal of your neighbors to the north."

Aidan nods and exchanges a wordless look with me before riding to the rear of the camp, where a group of messengers wait. Ash follows Father into the thick of the army. I urge Misty through the rows of tents as well until I come to the rear quarter, where a few large healer tents are raised.

I dismount Misty and a young squire appears to take her to the stables. I nod my thanks at the boy, then head into the main tent. I stop short.

A familiar woman with hair pulled tight to her head stands there, organizing metal medical instruments on a table.

"Clarisse!" I cry and race for her. She turns at the last moment and I crash into her. She's slightly shorter than I am, but with a muscular, thin frame. There are silver streaks in her light brown hair that weren't there the last time I saw her.

"Princess Elana," she says, squeezing me as hard as I hold her. "I got your letter and rode straight here. Nearly rode my poor horse to exhaustion, but she'll be alright."

"I'm so glad you're here. I don't think I could do this without you," I say, pulling away from her.

Somewhere in the camp, several horns sound, then people shout as boots hit the ground outside the tent.

"The battle will begin soon. I wish we had time to catch up, but we don't."

Clarisse takes my hand in hers. "Tell me what you need from me, and quickly."

"Hotharia has betrayed the Astrellian peace, and have sent two ships to reinforce the invaders." I tell her quietly, so the other bustling healers don't overhear. "We don't know who the attackers are, only that they carry with them strange weapons imbued with poison. One small nick with the blade is enough to kill a man. Prince Aidan of Ocarin brought one of the weapons to substantiate his warning. It had some kind of dark aura that called out to me. My powers reacted, and somehow purified the blade. I don't know how or why it happened, but I need your help to learn."

Clarisse takes a deep breath. "You lay the fate of the army on my shoulders after seeing me for the first time in years? You could at least buy me supper first."

I burst out a bark of laughter as my father walks into the tent.

"Lady Clarisse." His voice is shocked, but in a pleasant way.

Clarisse bows low to him. "Your Majesty, it's wonderful to see you again."

"As it is you, old friend," Father says, and there's a genuine smile on his face. He gestures to the tent. "Is there anything you need here?"

She shakes her head at him. "No, we are well-stocked and well-prepared."

"Glad to hear it," he says, and then turns back to me.

"Elana, my daughter," he starts, putting a warm hand on my shoulder. "Our time is short, so I have to say this quickly. I want you to know I'm so proud of you. The twin goddesses could not have picked a better person to bestow their gifts upon."

My brows knit, and my eyes narrow on him. "Don't say things like that. You know it's bad luck before a battle."

"I should have told you weeks ago. Months ago. Even before you were chosen, I've always been proud of you. It was a failure on my part not telling you sooner."

Worry flashes through me. "Father, stop it. Tell me after the battle is won."

He nods his head, the lines around his eyes crinkling with a smile. "Of course I will."

Then he pulls me into a long hug. I'm tempted to pull away and yell at him some more for jinxing our situation, but another part of me clings onto this moment, until he steps back.

He leaves the tent as quickly as he arrived, leaving me staring after him seconds after he's gone.

"Show me your powers, Elana," Clarisse says, placing her hand on my shoulder and returning my attention to her and our one goal. "I understand you've been blessed with two."

I nod and let a burst of light form in one hand, and a tendril of shadows wrap around my other. She looks back and forth between the two powers, her eyes wide.

"Oh my," she says.

She studies the light, waving her hand in front of the glow, then through it. Her brows furrow. From her apron, she pulls a large sewing needle. In one quick movement, she stabs her finger, deep enough to wince and draw blood.

"Clarisse!" I cry, yanking the needle from her finger. A droplet of blood pools there and runs down her finger to her palm.

She pulls her hand back, but nods at my hand. I look at her in confusion.

"The light, Elana. Use the light," she says, presenting her bloody finger to me.

In my shock, my powers dissipates. I stare at my hand, disbelief over what she's asking me to do. I want to call her a fool and deny that I possess the ability she thinks I do. But another part of me screams to do it, do it, do it. I let the light flow from my hand to hers and watch in utter fascination as her wound seals shut.

Tears prick at my eyes as I stare at her unblemished finger. I'm too stunned to move, to say anything.

"Sunlight has healing properties. Congratulations, child. You had the power in you this whole time," Clarisse says, wiping the tears from my cheeks.

"Clarisse!" Another voice shouts out from inside the tent, and then Aislinn is there, wrapping the healer in another hug.

"Oh Aislinn, darling," she says warmly.

The two pull apart, and Ash studies me. "El, are you okay?"

I give her a wide, wobbly smile, then take Clarisse's needle and stab the tip of my own finger.

Ash gasps and rips the needle from my grasp. "You idiot! What the Hells are you doing? Have you lost your damn mind?"

I hold my finger up to her and before the blood has time to drip past my first knuckle, light pools in my hand and the tiny wound closes.

My sister gapes at my finger, then grabs my hand and flips it over, studying every inch of my skin. "How did you do that?"

My smile wobbles again as I think of all the people I can help. "It's my power, Ash. Light can heal. That must be how the purification worked for the poison as well."

Ash continues to stare at me, shaking her head. "Elana, you're incredible."

She opens her mouth to say more, but three sharp horn blasts sound, and she stiffens. "That's the call to leave. Listen, El. Our reinforcements from Tierth never arrived. We sent a few of our fastest riders there to see why, and hopefully meet them along the way. But Tierth is at least a day's ride away. If the worst should come to pass, you must leave us and return home. You are the heir, and you must survive. Do you understand me?"

Ash wants me to leave her? In what world does she think I'll actually agree to that? There's no way I would ever leave her or Father behind.

I'm shaking my head. "No, Ash. I'm not leaving without you or Father. I will not leave our army."

Clarisse puts her hand on my shoulder. "Listen to your sister, Elana."

I shake her hand off. "No! I won't do it."

"I'll make sure she gets home safely, if it should come to that," Aidan's deep voice comes from behind Ash.

"You will do no such thing," I snap at him. "Because I will not abandon my family or my people to die."

"Elana, you must. You are Adrithia's hope. Besides, it's the king's orders." Ash crosses her arms in front of her chest.

"He can come and tell me that himself. I do not recognize that order," I say.

"Elana, if I have to drug you and make Prince Aidan carry you out of here, I will," Clarisse says, nodding at him. He lifts his eyebrows at her, as if surprised she knows who he is. "Don't give me that look, boyo. I'm rather perceptive. And besides, you stink of ash."

Aidan lifts his shirt to his nose, sniffs it, and then gives his shoulders a shrug.

Outside the tent, orders are yelled, and the camp empties.

"I have to go, sis," Ash says, giving me a long hug. "I love you."

I suck in a breath, holding on to her as if I'm afraid she will disappear the moment I let go. And maybe she will. As much as I'm mad at her for suggesting I go on without her, I still love her just as much. "I love you, too. Please be careful out there. If I see you in this tent for healing, I'll kick your ass."

She lets out a chuckle and pats my braided hair. "I'll be safe."

Then she pulls away and I'm facing Aidan. Tears are already pouring down my cheeks. He wraps his arms around me and I inhale his cedar scent, taking in his warmth. "Remember your promise to me, you degenerate."

He kisses the top of my head, then pulls back to bring his forehead to mine. "I remember. I'll come back to you, Magpie."

Then they're both gone, and it will not be the last time I see them. It can't be. I let myself cry and fall apart in Clarisse's arms for a few moments before I piece my heart together and get back to work.

Chapter Forty

There are ten healers split between three tents. Four of us in the main tent, and three each in the smaller tents.

Several older squires, stable boys, and messengers mill about while we wait. Messengers wait for news, and we wait for bodies to heal.

One of the squires, a young red-headed boy named Jakob, who must be around thirteen, keeps us well-informed of what's happening on the battlefield.

"Your Highness, the enemy has landed," he says about an hour after the soldiers left.

I nod my head, thanking him, and he goes rushing off to spread the news.

All is silent for what feels like forever, and then we start to hear thunder crashing, distant cries, and the earth itself groaning under my father's power.

"Your Highness, the battle has begun," Jakob says, bursting into the tent.

"Thank you, Jakob. You're doing a great job," I say, wanting to tell him to be careful, to find somewhere to hide, but his bright blue eyes and beaming smile have me staying my tongue. He rushes back out with renewed fervor. Everyone has a job here today, and this is Jakob's. He probably worked hard to become a squire and bring honor to his household by being here. My stomach cramps sharply as I think of a child near the fighting.

I pace back and forth between cots, stomping the grass flat beneath my feet.

Clarisse tells me that this is the worst part. Waiting with dread, not knowing what is happening close by.

"Help!" A voice suddenly cries, and Jakob and another squire appear in the front of the tent, dragging an unconscious man. Several healers rush forward to help them. They lift the soldier onto a cot. A black dagger protrudes from his side.

"Careful, do not touch the wound or that blade. It's a poisoned dagger," I command, and they step back. I rush to the side of the cot. Black veins protrude from the man's side, moving steadily towards his heart. He moans in pain.

Clarisse appears next to me. "You can do it, Elana. Take a deep breath and focus."

I nod, taking a few slow breaths and reach out with my light. The dark energy hums nearby, and the shadows near my feet writhe in agitation. I extend my hand and the energy within the blade shoots out, but within the healing light it vanishes, nullified. The small section of the blade that I can see is a dull silver color with no ominous aura pulsing from it.

"Okay, it's safe. Hold him steady while I remove the dagger."

Clarisse braces the man's legs. Another healer applies pressure to his shoulders. My hand wraps around the hilt of the dagger and I tug slowly, but firmly. Using my other hand, I send healing energy into his body. Blood pours from the wound for several seconds until it slowly clots and then closes under my touch. At last, the immediate danger is gone. I sigh and drop my arms.

"Well done," Clarisse says, examining the wound. "How do you feel? Any drain on your power?"

I take stock of the wells within me. They're both still full to bursting. I shake my head at her. "No, it barely had an effect."

She nods as a few more soldiers are brought into the tent, trailing blood. "Good. Because we're going to need you to do that all day."

We triage the injuries as they come to us. Those that aren't life-threatening are handled by skilled healers. The wounds that bring soldiers close to death, or the ones that have been poisoned are handled by me.

This system helps conserve my energy, which slowly begins to drain after several straight hours of healing. The injuries that are less severe can hopefully be tended to tomorrow, when my energy refills.

I take no breaks, against the urging of Clarisse. I hardly take the time to drink a few sips of water in between patients. My hands are so caked in blood, both dried and fresh, that I struggle to remove arrows, daggers, and the occasional spear from a patient's body. I have to ask for assistance from one of the other healers.

My powers perform miracles, but they can't bring back the dead. Some soldiers are brought to the tent so close to death that my light doesn't find anything to latch onto to.

Clarisse is the most skilled healer and splits her time between triaging and making sure patients live long enough to be healed by me. We work well as a team, even though she yells at me more than once to drink some water.

It's midafternoon when I get a status report from one of the messengers. It's not Jakob. I haven't seen him in well over an hour. I try not to let that thought linger in my mind. Things are not going well at the front. Our reinforcements from Tierth haven't arrived yet, and our army is tiring. The enemy is slowly wearing down our soldiers. They make push after push, careless of the dead they stomp on in their wake. Worse yet is that there seem to be more ships on the horizon, heading inland.

As if in answer to this news, the sounds seem to grow louder outside. My mind drifts to Aislinn and Aidan. I want nothing more than to leave this tent and help them in whatever way I can. I tap the daggers at my side, humming with the thought of being unleashed.

There's an influx of wounded, and the cots fill up quickly. We lay people on blankets, sleeping rolls, straw, anything we can find to keep them off the blood-slick and muddy ground.

"I don't think things are going well," Clarisse says, giving me a look.

"Not helpful," I say, moving around her to purify a woman who has been pierced by a poisoned arrow. Gods, she looks younger than me. She's one of the lucky ones, she'll live.

There are shouts and screams from outside our tent and I unsheathe the blades at my hip, ready to fight. The tent flaps fly open and a creature made of fire appears. It lights up the whole tent as the healers and conscious soldiers gasp and cringe away from it. The light dims slightly, enough for me to make out the shape of a small wyvern. It lets out a screech and flaps its wings in front of me. Tied around one of its outstretched talons is a rolled-up piece of parchment. I untie the ribbon and the wyvern vanishes with a little *pop*.

I unroll the letter, hands slick with blood. A short message is scrawled there:

Go to the front. Go now. Unleash the light. Help them or all will be lost. - Amira

My hands start shaking. I stuff the parchment into a pocket in my pants. My breath comes in gasps.

"Elana, what is it?" Clarisse asks, placing a hand on my shoulder to steady me.

"I have to go," I whisper, but over the noise of the tent and the battle, she doesn't hear me.

"What?" she asks, brows pulling together.

"I have to go to the front. They need help," I say, louder this time, steadier.

Clarisse's grip on me becomes hard, unyielding. "No, Princess. Your duty is to stay out of the fight."

I shake my head. There's no time to explain everything to her. My resolve hardens to steel within me. "I'm sorry, Clarisse, I'm so sorry. You're going to have to keep working without me. I have to do this."

She moves to block me, but in one swift movement that Ash would be proud of, I spin out of her way and run out of the tent.

I whistle loudly as I race through the camp until I see Misty barreling towards me. She skids to a stop in front of me, and with strength I didn't realize I possess, I jump onto her back. I don't have to urge her on—it's like she knows exactly what I need. She turns around and bolts for the coast.

Goddesses, I think to myself, *please let me make it in time. Nura, Nisha, guide me.*

Chapter Forty-One

Salty sea air whips my face as Misty crests the hill. I don't know what I expect to see, but it's not this writhing mass of bodies. There are no organized lines, no rules of engagement being followed. Everywhere I see bodies crashing against each other. Silver suits of armor clash against black leather-clad enemies. My breath catches as a tide of fear washes over me. There is no balance here. There is only chaos and death.

In a panic, I momentarily forget my mission and frantically scan the battlefield for my sister, for Aidan, for my father. I need to see them, to know they're okay. Halfway down the slope to the shore I spot a brilliant flash of fire. Aidan. Even from this distance I can see that where his attention turns, enemies dissolve to ash. A gleaming sword slices an attacker nearly in half near him, blonde hair poking out from under the wielder's helmet. Aislinn. My gaze continues to rake over the bloody expanse until I spot chunks of rocks flying through the air. I see my father and several commanders near the front lines, holding back the tide of enemies. There's a flash of flame above his head and he reaches up to catch a familiar flaming wyvern.

Black weapons flash in the fray, and I remember why I'm here. I shove the lump in my throat down and urge Misty towards the field of death. Our soldiers can't fight properly if they're terrified that one small cut could kill them. If I can neutralize the poison in all of their weapons, it will give our army hope. I think that's what Queen Amira's letter meant, anyway.

When I'm close to the battle, several Adrithian soldiers take notice and approach. I jump from Misty's back and land on my feet. "Misty, go back to camp." I yell over the noise and smack her hindquarters. She tears back up the hill and out of sight.

"Your Highness, what are you doing here?" One of them, a captain judging by the insignia on his arm, yells over the screams of nearby soldiers.

"I need to get to the center of the fighting," I shout back. "Will you help me?"

I don't say why I need to get there, in case I fail. I don't want to give him false hope. The captain nods. Perhaps he sees my desperation, or perhaps he wants to hope. He says something to the group of men and women around him, about ten in total, and they form a protective circle around me, shields high.

"We'll get you there," he tells me.

I nod and withdraw my twin daggers. They hum in my hands, as if sensing the carnage and preparing to fight.

My head quiets as I focus on my surroundings. Our group pushes into the fray, moving slowly. We carefully step around fallen bodies as we progress, and I try not to notice how many are wearing the shining steel armor of the Adrithian army.

One small, crumpled body gives me pause. Red hair matted with drying blood, bright blue eyes staring up at the sky. I suck in a sharp, ragged breath. Jakob. Gods, he's only a child. The young squire has an arrow protruding from his chest. Sorrow pangs viciously in my chest, but the captain grabs my arm and tugs me further into the fray, away from his broken body.

The enemies move like beasts, attacking viciously with no defense. They slash, stab, and cut wildly, only stopping when they're completely incapacitated.

We barely make it a quarter of the way through when warm blood splatters my face. One of the soldiers on my right takes an arrow through his exposed neck. He falls like a sack of potatoes and doesn't get back up. The others close the gap without looking back. The young man's brown eyes stare after me, unseeing.

A scream rips through the air, and I whip back around to see a soldier from the front of the group collapse, her armor drenched with slick blood as it pours from her stomach. She cries out in pain, which turns to a gurgle as blood fills her mouth.

I bend down to heal her, but the captain grips my arm again, wrenches me up, and pushes me along. "We keep going!"

Do not let their deaths be in vain, I tell myself as we make steady progress towards the center. We lose two more after a spooked, riderless horse barrels through our group. One enemy launches himself over the soldiers around me and swipes at my face with his sword. My daggers react instantly, practically moving by themselves, parrying, and then in one swift motion cutting deep into the attacker's stomach. The ease with which the blades slice is alarming, but I don't have time to stop and think about it as we continue pushing towards the middle.

One by one, the rest of the soldiers guarding me fall until it's the captain and I, dodging blows and trying to push forward slowly.

An attacker charges, and I block, but I don't see the second one who rushes my back. The captain is there, parrying the blow with his shield.

He turns to me with a determined smile. "You alright, Princess?"

My mouth opens, but the words don't come quick enough to warn him, as a spear finds its home in the captain's back.

His eyes go wide and he turns around, hurling his sword at the enemy who threw it. It hits home and the enemy falls. The captain stumbles, then slams to his knees. I hold a ball of healing light in my hand as I reach for him.

"G-go," the captain chokes out as he shoves me away. A flash of a black blade and his head tumbles from his body, landing face-down in the blood-soaked dirt at my feet.

I don't even know his name.

Fear and horror grip my body. Three attackers close in on me as I stare at the ground, gaping at all that's left of the nameless captain.

"Elana!" A cry sounds, and suddenly my world is awash in flame. It wraps around me, incinerating the attackers who were less than an arm's length away from dealing a killing blow.

The fire dissipates and Ash is there, pulling me to her. Aidan stops next to us, using his flames to keep the enemy at bay.

"You idiot, what are you doing here?" she screams. There's so much fear in her voice.

"I'm here to help," I whisper, still staring at the captain's head.

Ash shakes me, and I finally tear my eyes away from the ground. "We have to get you out of here."

She looks to Aidan and then motions back to the camp, to safety. "Can you clear a path?"

Do not let their deaths be in vain, a voice within me whispers.

I suck in a deep breath and remember the note Queen Amira sent. *Unleash the light.* I push off my sister. "No! I have to be here. I can help."

Ash looks at me like I've lost my ever-loving mind. "Elana, we're losing ground. There's nothing you can do. You need to leave, right now."

"No, Ash. Listen to me," I grip her arms tightly through all the blood and grime that cover them. "I think I can purify all of the poison. That's why I came here."

She gives me a hard look, but it's Aidan who speaks first as he keeps the fire going around us. "What do you need from us?"

I look between him and my sister, who finally gives me an encouraging nod. I sheathe my daggers at my hip.

"Are we in the middle of the fighting?" I ask. They're both taller than me and will have a better idea of where we are in the field.

Aislinn looks around, but turns to Aidan, who has more than several inches on her. He gives a glance in all directions, then says, "we're pretty close. Slightly closer to camp."

"It'll have to do," I say, closing my eyes. "Keep the enemy off me while I focus my power."

They work together, moving like two predators unleashed on their prey. Aidan's fire keeps most of them at bay, but several bold ones charge in regardless. Aislinn meets the ones who get through head on, dispatching them with ease.

I close my eyes, putting my trust entirely in the two most important people in my life. The wells of power sit inside me, the bursting source of darkness, and the nearly-emptied well of sunlight. It'll be enough. It has to.

I plunge my hands into the pool of power, dredging up every last drop of light. My body thrums with the power, the energy. *Do not let their deaths be in vain.*

Somewhere outside my body Ash sucks in a sharp gasp. I block it out and focus on healing and purifying. I form that power into a ball in my hands, building it, demanding more and more from it. I shake with the effort of containing it. *This will work*, I tell myself.

"Cover your eyes," my voice trembles. I scrape the dregs of light from the well and when my mortal body can contain it no more, I throw my arms out wide.

An explosion of light rockets from me. Next to me, Ash and Aidan shield their eyes with their arms. I expand the circle of light wider, pushing it out in all directions. The enemies shriek and cower away from the brightness. I watch as the weapons lying on the ground near me turn a normal silver color.

I continue to push the light out in every direction, further, and further, until I see the dome reach the towering cliffs on both sides of the sloped field. My arms shudder as I hold them out and force the purifying light to extend all the way to the beach. A little more, a little more. Something warm trickles from my nose. I grit my teeth and shove all the remaining energy I possess into it. Someone is screaming. I think it's me.

"Magpie, that's enough. Let it go," Aidan's concerned face appears before me. His hands gently cradle the sides of my face. "You're going to burn up your energy. Let go."

I suck in a shaking breath, trying to see around him to the beach. He doesn't release me.

"You did it, El," Ash says, coming to stand next to Aidan. She puts a comforting hand on my outstretched arm. "Now you have to stop."

I'm not sure if my body or my power gives out first, but one moment I'm trying to figure out how to let go of the light, and the next I'm limp in Aidan's warm arms.

Chapter Forty-Two

"Magpie, come back to us. Please," Aidan whispers against my forehead.

"Is she going to be okay?" Aislinn asks as awareness prickles my senses.

My body feels like it tumbled over a waterfall. I ache everywhere. Slowly, I peel my eyelids open. Ash's hazel eyes rake over me, from head to toe.

"Elana!" she cries as we lock gazes. "Thank the Gods, I was so worried."

"Did it work?" I rasp, and raise my hand to wipe away the blood from under my nose.

"As far as we can see, you purified every poisoned weapon from here to the coast. You even healed some of our injured soldiers on the field," Aidan says. "You amaze me, Magpie."

"Always happy to exceed your expectations, Prince Aidan," I groan and sit up.

Aidan keeps a steady hand on my back, providing support if I need it. I do. The simple act of sitting sends my head into a tempest. The world spins around me.

"Easy. There's no need to exert yourself," he says.

I let out a few long breaths. Around us, the battle still rages. A group of Adrithian soldiers have rallied around us, fending off the enemy without the threat of poison.

Cheers start to rise up from near the camp, and the sounds of weapons clashing gets quieter and quieter.

"Are we winning?" I ask, glancing between Aidan and Ash.

A smile grows on my sister's face. "They're retreating."

A wave of relief hits me and I shakily get to my feet, thanks to the help of Aislinn's steadying arm.

The group in front of us begins cheering, too, but abruptly cuts off. The men and women part, revealing the king, blood-soaked and panting.

"Elana, what are you doing here?" he asks sharply, approaching us.

"She purified their weapons, Father, and healed our soldiers," Ash says with a proud smile.

Father points down the beach, and I see a piece of parchment clutched in his hand. "Two more ships have landed, and more are on the horizon."

I cease breathing. Darkness gathers at the corners of my vision, pushing inwards.

"What?" Aislinn demands sharply.

"The enemy is falling back to regroup before they charge at us anew. I'm ordering a retreat. I'm going to split the shore and crush those bastards under the weight of the earth. You need to get out of here immediately."

I hear my own heartbeat in my ears. This doesn't make sense. Queen Amira's message said to use the light. And I did. Everything should be okay now.

Aislinn stands. "Father, let me stay back with you. I can protect you."

Father shakes his head. "No. Go with your sister and Prince Aidan. That is an order. I'll be right behind you."

I shakily get to my feet. "I can help you. I can still use the darkness."

"No, Elana. You shouldn't even be on this battlefield. Your presence here puts all of Adrithia in jeopardy."

A feeling like shame hits me, and I sway on my feet. Ash uses my momentary weakness to grab my arm in an ironlike grip and tug backwards. Aidan takes up a position on my other side.

"Wait!" I shout, reaching out for our father. "Let me help!"

Horns are blowing, several short blasts. The signal for retreat. Our soldiers immediately withdraw, running back up the hill. Within moments, the four of us are the only ones left on the slope. On the beach, a dark force is regrouping.

Father turns his back on us, facing the enemy alone. All of this is wrong, wrong, wrong. He shouldn't have to do this alone.

Ash tugs me along. I try to rip my hands from her grasp, but she holds fast and continues to drag me away. Aidan stands on my other side, arm on my waist, encouraging me to keep moving.

The enemy has fully regrouped, joined by a legion of fresh soldiers. The tide of unending dark-clad warriors races up the hill towards my father. He stomps his foot to the ground, sending rolling waves of earth tumbling down the slope. It slows their onslaught, but one archer manages to loose an arrow. It hits Father in the thigh. I scream, breaking free from Ash's grip, hurtling towards him, trying to coax out any remaining healing power within me, but I'm empty. There's nothing left. My arm waves uselessly in his direction.

"Get her out of here *now*!" Father's voice booms over the bloody battlefield.

I dig in my heels, using all of my remaining strength to stay. Ash hesitates for a moment, looking back at our father with something like indecision. Aidan looks across the field, towards my father, and his face twists in pity, grief.

"Elana, we have to go," Aidan's face appears in front of me. His hands cup my cheeks as he forces me to look at him, only him. "We need to leave this place. We won't survive an assault of that magnitude. Your father knows what he's doing."

I suck in a breath, my tongue nearly tripping over my next words. "We cannot leave him here alone."

Aidan closes his eyes, puts his forehead to mine. "He's buying us time and will join us when he's done."

"*No!*" The word is a hoarse shriek, cut off by a wracking sob.

"I'm sorry, Magpie, I'm so sorry. You can hate me for this later," he says. Before I have the chance to react, he picks me up and hauls me over his shoulder, then starts running up the hill. Aislinn runs behind us. Tears stream down her cheeks but she doesn't look back again.

I do. I see it all. I scream and pound on Aidan's back.

"Let me go, let me go, let me go," I say around shuddering breaths and gasping sobs. He doesn't stop.

Through my blurry vision I see my father lift his hand above his head. The endless tide of death rushes for him. He brings his fist down to the earth with a cry, and the world shudders.

At our heels, the ground splits. The once gradually-sloping field to the sea cleaves and breaks off, then collapses into itself in a wave of rock.

Everything shakes. Aidan loses his balance and falls, cradling me to his chest so he bears the brunt of the impact. Aislinn crashes to her hands and knees next to us.

She looks back at the chaos and sheer power that our father unleashed. Behind us, rock churns and folds, crashing into a chasm as wide as we can see. The sea rushes to meet the crater, turning a once beautiful beach into a nightmare of seething elements.

A flash of silver armor, and I see our father on a solitary column.

"There he is!" I point him out and Aislinn zeroes in on him. He's on one knee, the leg with the arrow in it must have given out. Father's arms are outstretched as he commands the earth itself to wipe away our enemies.

I crawl out of Aidan's arms and kneel next to my sister as we watch our father decimate an army.

Father, seemingly satisfied, looks toward the safety of the coast once more. The entire rock column moves in our direction. Every second brings him closer to us.

He doesn't see the sole survivor of the carnage, climbing up the back of the pillar. He doesn't see the man raise his sword and plunge it into his back.

A scream rips from my throat. Father turns towards the man, with the sword still sticking out of his back. With a savage punch he hurtles the enemy into the churning earth below. He falls to his hands and cranes his neck to look back at Ash and me. His lips are turned up in a slight smile, even as something dark drips from them. He raises his hand. In farewell. To his daughters, his people, his kingdom. Then he slowly falls forward, into the abyss of his own creation.

"No!" Next to me Ash screams, reaching out her hand over the edge, as though she can catch him.

We watch his body disappear into the chaos, all traces vanished. Buried in rock and swept away by the ocean.

I scream again, wrenching myself out of Aidan's grasp so I can lean over the edge, desperately searching. Ash's arms tug me away from the precipice and she hugs me fiercely.

The one remaining ship that escaped the chasm changes course, sailing back to the southern horizon, as if held back by the fracturing of the land itself. No future ships will find safe harbor here.

CHAPTER FORTY-THREE

We win, but there is no cheering. We win, but the price is too high to feel anything other than sorrow. We win, but someone will have to tell my mother that her husband isn't coming home, and we have no body to bury.

I collapse on the muddy slope, my legs refusing to move. Aidan has to carry me back to the camp.

As we pass the throngs of soldiers, they remove their helmets and bow as we pass by. Word must have spread, then, of my father's sacrifice. Ash is silent as a ghost as we move through them, heading for our tents.

A grand blue tent sits near the middle of the camp. Not one of us enters it.

Aidan carries me to the tent I share with Aislinn and lays me down on my cot. He excuses himself to find us some food and water. Ash lays down next to me. We lay there for hours, crying and holding hands. Aidan brings in a canteen of water and two bowls of hot stew, which sit on the small wooden table next to us, untouched.

The next morning, I wake next to Aislinn, our hands still entwined. My eyes are raw and swollen, as if I'd been crying all night. One glance at Ash's face tells me she probably has, too.

Slowly, I unwrap my fingers from hers and crawl off the cot, trying my best not to wake her. She bolts upright as soon as I move.

"Ash, go back to sleep. I'm going to find Aidan," I tell her.

It's no surprise to me, however, when she jumps off the cot with me.

"We'll face this day together," she tells me and I nod, grateful.

The camp is quiet. People mill about, but no one talks loudly, or laughs, or fights. Everyone looks as lost as I feel.

Aidan stands near a fire with a metal cup in his hand. He looks up from the flames and our eyes meet. I almost fall to pieces right there. Aidan drops the cup, spilling water into the grass. He closes the distance between us in two strides. Then I'm in his arms, breathing his cedar scent.

"Elana, I'm so sorry," he says into my hair.

Aislinn walks off, to give us some privacy, or to be alone, I'm not really sure. All I know is Aidan and I cling to each other as a fresh wave of hot tears rolls down my cheeks, soaking his shirt. I'm so angry with him, for taking me away from my father in his final moments, for not allowing me to help him when I could have done something. I should have done something. But right now all I feel is loss, and all I want is to be held.

After what feels like hours, I step away. The duty I abandoned by giving into my sorrow comes rushing back to me.

"I need to help Clarisse with the wounded. Then I need to speak with all the remaining commanders," I say.

Aidan follows me to the healers' tents, where I spend an exhausting hour expending my barely refilled power healing all manner of wounds. Clarisse gives me many pitying glances, which I ignore. Aidan is a steady presence nearby. I don't know whether I want him near, but I don't have the energy to tell him off.

Once I've healed all the injuries possible in the three tents, Aidan and I head back to the center of camp. Aislinn stands there with one commander.

He bows as we approach. "Your Highnesses."

"Hello, Commander..." I trail off, realizing I don't know his name.

"Darren," he says with a dip of his head.

I nod back. "Commander Darren. What's the status of the army?"

"We lost nearly half of our soldiers." The words hit me like lead. Of the thousands we brought with us, thousands will never return to their loved ones. "That number would have been much higher if not for your help healing our wounded and neutralizing the enemy's weapons."

I stare at the ground. It's too much loss, too much sacrifice.

"Commander, why didn't the reinforcements from Tierth come?" Aislinn asks, her voice cold and hard.

Commander Darren shifts on his feet. "Our messenger sent a bird upon his arrival there to investigate. It seems they never got the letters requesting reinforcements. They never knew a battle was being waged so close to their city."

A startled gasp escapes me. "The letters never got there? How did this happen?"

"It seems they were either intercepted, or the messenger never sent them," the Commander says.

The realization hits me like an ice bath. I watched those letters go from my father's hands to someone I trusted. With a sharp inhale, Aislinn comes to the same conclusion as me.

I turn to the commander, letting my rage coat my words in venom. "Commander Darren, I need you to send a message with our quickest bird to apprehend someone in the castle."

Ash and I exchange a look, and she gives me a quick, approving nod.

"Who shall I detain, Your Highness?"

"My guard, Aric."

Acknowledgements

Wow, I don't even know where to start. This dream would not have happened without my friends and family who have supported me along the way.

Andy, thank you for all the love and encouragement. You, who motivated me to keep going when I wasn't sure I could go on, and provided a constant ear to listen when I didn't know where to go with the story, or when I had something exciting to share. Thank you for pushing me to finish the book.

To Katie, I can't thank you enough for being there for literally every step of this. From that first Nyquil-induced dream sequence, to a full-blown plot, to the first chapter, to the last sentence. Thank you for reading the story before anyone else did, for the messages in the Google doc, the text messages with a LOT of capitalized letters, and the chats over discord. You kept me on my toes and pushed me to write so I could get the next chapter to you. Thank you for being my fire-poker best friend for life, love you!

Thank you to my family. My parents, brother, and sister-in-law, even though we may be far in distance, your support reaches across the country. Love you!

To all my friends and family who have encouraged me along the way. Ashley, Karlie, Mackenna, and Marisa, thank you for cheering me on!

Laura, thank you for the absolutely stunning cover art! Laura R. thank you for coaching and encouraging me. Nia, thank you for the beautiful character art.

Finally, to you, dear reader, for taking a chance on this story. I'm so honored to share the first part of Elana's story with you.

About the Author

A dreamer born into a world without dragons, monsters, and magic, Morgan has spent her life daydreaming in the clouds.

From practicing sword fighting with sticks in the backyard, to mixing her own potions in the mud with various wildflowers, she's always kept a little spark of her own magic alive.

With her debut novel, The Awakening of Gods, she hopes to introduce you to one of the many fantasy worlds she regularly dreams about. Morgan lives in Wisconsin with her partner-in-crime and two rescue dogs, Cleo and Piper.

You can follow along with her author journey on Instagram or Threads @authormorgankielisch. Or sign up for the newsletter on her website: www.morgankielischbooks.com

www.ingramcontent.com/pod-product-compliance
Lightning Source LLC
Chambersburg PA
CBHW070617300726
48975CB00006B/1843